Acknowledgements

Thank you to all those who gave me encouragement, their valuable time and a modicum of cajoling. You have helped make this happen for me.

Uncle Mazhar for telling me the story of kite flying.

The Leeds Writer's Club who taught me how to write, rewrite, and then rewrite some more.

My lovely friends – Jane Adams, Samina Sabir and Jean Moss.

My wonderful family – Zehbie (Fats) Yousuf, Rob Bonass, my parents, and my husband (this is where the cajoling comes in).

Finally, to Sufia, Daniyal and Maryam – the little people who inspire me.

About The Author

Zarina Bonass was born in India and brought up in Belfast. She moved to Leeds to take up a post-doctoral position and fell in love with Yorkshire's wild moors and rolling dales. She currently lives there with her husband and three children.

A family holiday in Andalusia provided the inspiration for this book.

Zarina Bonass has a PhD in Molecular Biology (which will be put to good use in her next book).

ISBN – 13 978-1514701829

ISBN – 10 1514701820

Copyright © Zarina Bonass

All rights reserved. No part of this publication may be reproduced, stored in a retrieval system or transmitted, in any form or by any means, without the prior permission of the author, nor be otherwise circulated in any form of binding or cover other than that in which it is published and without a similar condition being imposed on the purchaser.

Cover design: Camilla Fellas (**www.camillafellas.com**)

Zarina Bonass

The Boy With The Patang

Part I

When the Dawn is Still Dark

Chapter One

My father told me that I was marrying a genius. He complimented me on my good luck, placed my husband-to-be on a pedestal and thought my happy future sealed.

I am Sahira, meaning The Moon. In the spring of 1967, I was twenty years old and in my final year at the Sikimpur Royal College for Arts. I was also considering, with all the naïve optimism of youth, my first marriage *rishtaa*.

The *rishtaa* that came for me was a surprise to us all. My sisters had been receiving *rishtey* since they were sixteen, although they had both been in their twenties when they had finally married. I, on the other hand, had attracted no such interest. I was not as accomplished in Sikimpur high society as they were; I did not fit in with parties and fashion and make-up.

Often, I would wander out into the garden, into the fading glare of the sun, away from chattering voices speaking so animatedly about themselves and their high-flung lives. Amongst the greenery and the free-flying birds, I felt that I could breathe more easily. But, all too soon, I would be missed by my mother, who would send out a servant to fetch me away from the ill-favoured sunshine.

'*Dhup bahot tez hai. Under aow. Kaale hojayenge!*' Ammaji would scold.

To be dark was considered unattractive; to have pale skin was considered beautiful. So I would come in grudgingly.

'Is it not enough that I come to these parties?' I would ask. 'Why is it important that I should also join in?' Of course, I knew the answer.

'By joining in, other mothers will get to know you. That way, you will be at the forefront of their minds when it comes to arranging their precious sons' marriages.' Ammaji would explain this many times, with growing impatience.

I was fed up with these words and so, one day, I argued.

'Why is it so important that I marry into the Sikimpur elite?'

'And who will you marry then?' Ammaji replied crossly, 'Some *dhobi-wallah* from Lalmali? You do not understand the importance of a good marriage. You have everything here, but without them you would struggle. I should know! Do not forget, I came out of Lalmali, and I know what village life is truly like. I will not have any of my children living in such a way.'

Still, I argued. 'But Ammaji, what if I do not want to marry just yet?'

'Just yet? What do you mean, Sahira?'

I shrugged. 'There are other things that I might want to do.'

'Such as?' Ammaji looked at me with suspicion. 'What else might you want to do? Mmm? Soon you will receive your BA. That is a good enough education for a girl. At least, before marriage. Men do not like to marry girls who have been exposed to too much education. They think they will have too much to say.'

'Too much independence of thought, you mean.' I muttered. 'Or maybe they are worried that their wives will turn out to be cleverer than them.' It made me angry how Sikimpur society – no, not just Sikimpur, but all the world - could not allow girls to progress, for fear of what that might lead to. 'I do not understand how this can happen?' I continued. 'It is absurd for one part of humankind to treat another this way.'

'Perhaps, but it is no worse to how the rich behave towards the poor, or those with power to those without.' Ammaji, who had been plaiting her hair, broke off to look at me through the mirror. 'It is the experience of life that will teach you these things, Sahira, not all those books that you read. After marriage, well, it is up to a husband what he wishes you to do.'

'But marriage is surely not the only future that a girl has to settle for?'

'Settle for?' Ammaji shook her head at me. 'Marriage is not settling for anything. It is an essential part of a girl's life. It is everything. It can be all of happiness or...' Ammaji lowered her voice and sounded at once sad. 'I have seen it when it has been a prison for a girl.'

Her voice trailed off and she looked the saddest that I had ever seen her, sadder even than when her parents had died. Her face became a faded rose. She was thinking, I knew, of her niece who had been married at fourteen to the youngest brother of five. She was treated badly by her in-laws, more like a servant than a member of the family, and rarely allowed to see her own kin. Even when pregnant, she was expected to do far too many of the household chores: take care of the other brothers' children, stay up until her own husband returned from his night-time duty to make him fresh *chapatti*. Ten years of this unkind treatment had marked my cousin down. My lovely cousin, who had once been robust, was now like a withered leaf of late autumn.

And so, when I saw Ammaji gaze, heartbroken, into the empty space beyond me, I sighed and protested no more.

Instead, I tried hard to sparkle, but I could not be what I was not. I could not even shine a little, and so Sikimpur high society thought of me as odd and unsociable: quite unsuitable for their *ladli* sons. Not even the great Shamshad name could make up for the unknown that was me. Ammaji fretted that I may never get married, and Abbaji tried his best to reassure her that it was just a matter of time.

'You will see,' he said. 'Sahira will surely get many *rishtey*. Only the other day, my sister was telling me that Rahman Sahib was paying her much attention at the Talats' *daawat*. Their son, Rauf, has just passed his Bar exams and is returning next month from *Welayat*. He will surely be ready for marriage then...'

Ammaji nodded with genuine joy at this thought.

Alas, the stars that bring people together were not shining upon me just then. The Rahman's son did, indeed, return to Sikimpur and, three days after that, his parents announced his betrothal to Miss Nighat Sultana, the pretty flower-daughter of the Rahmans' best friends. Ammaji congratulated Mrs Rahman in public and mourned a lost son-in-law in private.

But then a *rishtaa* did come, and the morning that brought it was brilliantly bright. The rain that had fallen during the night had steadily been burnt off, leaving behind the dusty, musty smell of drying land. My sister, Laila, with her belly like a full crescent moon, was visiting us with her two year old son, Isa. He was a lively thing and she was easily tired.

I kept an eye on him as he splashed in the pool, tumbling and diving while Laila took to the shade of the covered veranda. Soon I went to join her and Isa wandered off to find my parents with new demands, 'Cricket *khelo*!' So, my parents had been made to play cricket for a long while, in a garden that was both large and uneven, and lent itself to much fun for a two year old. Whilst my nephew laughed with delight, my parents sweated and puffed with a ragged good humour until they could take no more.

Abbaji persuaded the boy to sit down on my lap, under the spreading branches of a banyan tree, while he slumped in a sturdy chair. Ammaji had ordered ice-cold *nimbu pani* to be brought out, fanning her shattered body with a fallen mango leaf.

So, this is how we were, strewn about, when the telephone rang, clear and shrill. Ammaji, not yet recovered, appeared perplexed, and looked at each of us in turn. Laila had shrugged through near-closed eyes.

'It is bound to be for you, Ammaji. It always is. You will have to get up sometime, so it may as well be now.'

This made Ammaji grumble. 'Why can somebody else not answer the phone? I am in no fit state to talk to anybody. And what a time to call anyway: just before lunch! People can be very inconsiderate.'

Laila had opened her eyes. 'But it will be for you,' she repeated. 'So you will have to get up anyway to talk to them.'

Ammaji glared at Abbaji for support, but he had shrugged also, 'She is right. It will be for you.'

And so, Ammaji had struggled with much noise out of her chair and made her way through the wooden lattice doors inside. We none of us spoke as we listened to a half conversation.

'Hello. Yes, this is she. Oh, *Asalaam-alaikum*. Yes, very well, thank-you. My daughter and grandson are over, so we... Yes, he is a lovely boy, and very energetic too.' Then there was a pause.

Ammaji had looked surprised; smiling yet, with some good news from the other end of the telephone. She turned to us and frantically waved for Abbaji to come in.

She finished the conversation with, 'I will certainly speak to her. She will probably need a few days to think about it, you know how she likes to think. And of course, I will have to talk to her Abbaji. *Khudahafiz.*'

The receiver was clicked back onto its cradle with Ammaji's hand still resting on it. She closed her eyes as Abbaji gathered around her impatiently.

'Well?'

Ammaji opened her eyes and, with excitement in her voice, told us, 'That was Mrs Altair. With a *rishtaa* for Sahira from her son, you know...' Ammaji had stared out to where I sat with incredulity. 'Sami...'

'Sami? Sami Altair?' Laila had struggled from her chair and into the house as Abbaji repeated with a happy astonishment.

'A *rishtaa* from Sami Altair! This is wonderful.' He declared. 'You know he is one of the finest young men in the city. He is building a magnificent business with the inheritance that his father left him. It cannot have been very much, a lecturer's savings, that is all. And he has been sure to look after his poor widowed mother. He is still very young, you know, only twenty-four. Everyone in Sikimpur knows of him.'

Abbaji had clapped his hands and turned to me. 'He must be worth quite a bit now. And such a brain. Why, he is a genius, that boy.'

It was a phrase that I had first heard some two years ago when, during the course of his PhD, Sami Altair, had published a paper in the Journal of the London Mathematical Society. Abbaji had borrowed a copy from Suha's husband, Uthman and, seated in his wicker chair, he had read the title of the paper with slow and pronounced awe.

'Integration of the λ Calculus with Algorithms – the Development of a New Computer Language for the Regulation of Simple Systems'. Abbaji had studied the page for a few seconds before looking up and, with a reverent twinkle in his eye, remarked, 'It is the mark of a true genius to have such an unfathomable title to one's work.'

With this acclaim, Sami Altair became the jewel of Sikimpur, shining brighter when, through the course of developing his beautiful theories and ideas, he became quietly wealthy. It was his potential for greater wealth that made him of profound interest to the mothers and fathers of ambitious Sikimpur: this genius and his ingenuity.

Chapter Two

Sikimpur, the town, was an ancient and bustling place located on the western coast of India. By Indian standards it was a wealthy place, with tree-lined avenues and grand *haveli* that were well maintained. Its wealth had come from it possessing an almost perfectly carved natural harbour, which the East India Company had exploited as a trading port. They paid the then ruler of Sikimpur, Sultan Noor-u-Din, a handsome levy on all their ships laden with timber and silk which left Sikimpur, and all of the steel and weaponry that entered it. When the British Raj took over the authority of the Company, the port's importance grew and so, by default, did its wealth.

Even before the arrival of the *ferenghi*, my family had been part of the merchant class that had used the port to trade with the world outside of India. In those days it had been the cloths of India: cotton, linen, silk. Today, those commodities had been expanded to include exotic fruits: fat ripe mangoes, juicy guavas and milky coconuts. Thus, by Indian standards, my family was considered extremely wealthy. I, being born into this family, the fabled House of Shamshad, knew that my fate hung on a golden thread.

As head of the Shamshad family, my father was fiercely proud of this heritage. As children, while the crickets were rasping out their tunes - and with the rustling leaves to accompany him - Abbaji would gather my two sisters and me together on the veranda and regale us with the account of our ancestor, Idris Mehboob, whose tremendous gallantry had achieved for us our esteemed name, our venerable status.

Abbaji would start the drama with a mock sadness: 'It was in those times when son fought father, brother fought brother, nephew, uncle and, - on one occasion - even father fought daughter. Of course, much of this great land of ours was desert then, a scrubland worn out with all the blood that had been shed and the treachery that had been committed. The country was growing wild and its people becoming unruly.'

Then, suddenly, Abbaji's voice would change to a brighter flow: 'But then Ghulam Iqbal came, a mighty warrior King, so tall that his squires had to stand on their helmets to put his armour on him, and so broad that a new breed of horse was bred that could take his straddle.'

At this point, Abbaji would pause and allow us to picture this mighty King. He would lean back in his chair and draw deeply on his pipe, slowly releasing a thin wisp of smoke that would come to us with the warm smell of tobacco smoulder. In my juvenile mind the King's steed was transformed into a unicorn whose hooves set off sparks as it galloped over the battleground, and Ghulam Iqbal, a mythical figure, whose silver sword struck down the evil enemy with one almighty blow.

Intrigue established, Abbaji would then lean slightly forward and, taking the pipe from out of his mouth, he would continue: 'That is when our ancestor, Idris Mehboob fought with great daring for this mighty warrior King, at the encounter that will forever be known as *The Battle of Dazed Sikimpur*.'

We could almost hear the battle rage; see with our own eyes the bravery of Idris Mehboob, as Abbaji continued: 'Then, at the end of this conflict, the King gathered his loyal servants about him. With the smoke from the cannons still rising and the wounded being tended to, he bestowed upon them titles, gold and land. And, for our valiant Idris Mehboob, he created the House of Shamshad. It was "the best of titles", Ghulam Iqbal had said, "for the best of men!"'

This last sentence would never change. The rest of the story came and went; bits were added, bits were removed, but this last phrase was ever present. In time, we joined in with bold voices and our chests puffed out: 'The best of titles, for the best of men!'

In the spring of each year, Abbaji's audience grew. To celebrate the mango harvest, my parents would throw a party for all of the Shamshad clan. They would gather from all parts of the country - aunties, uncles, cousins - and there would be mayhem all about with shouting, laughing, teasing, music and much gaiety. Our sunken pool would be filled with frolicking brown bodies and the grass would be trampled under the feet of gambolling children.

After lunch, when the adults had eaten too much to move and lolled in repose across the veranda, Abbaji would lead the gaggle of still lively children across the garden and down the stone steps to where the acacia grew. He would settle himself on a trailing branch, while we scattered ourselves around him like cushions. There, he would retell his well-worn tale, while we children scratched the ground with our fingers, stretched our restless limbs and wriggled around.

Ammaji would listen to these enthusiasms with a shake of her head, and tell us a different tale. She told us of 'an ancestor whose heart thumped mightily with cowardice rather than bravado: a proper *darpook*.' In her version Idris Mehboob Sahib did not lead his troops into battle. Instead, he had sat, hidden at the back of them, hoping to quietly go home once the fighting started. Unfortunately for him, his horse had been startled by the noise of cannon fire and leapt forward before the trumpets had sounded, with the poor, desperate knight clinging on for dear life!

Ammaji told us this behind closed doors, making sure that Abbaji and the servants were out of earshot.

'It was after this that Idris Mehboob left the army and became a farmer. He was much happier ploughing fields and tending to his cattle.' Ammaji would look at each of us in turn, her voice stern and serious: 'Now, I am telling you this because it is important that you know the truth. But there is no need to hurt your Abbaji's feelings. Sometimes, people enjoy embellishing their past a little. Besides, your Abbaji means no harm, so why upset his boat, eh?' She made us promise not to tell anyone else about the things she had told us. We promised dutifully and ran off to play, forgetting all the things that she had spoken of.

Those days were fun - all our trappings of wealth were fun - but Ammaji never let us forget her roots either.

To balance our honey-jar existence, Ammaji would take us holidaying in Lalmali, the village where she had grown up. My grandparents still lived there, refusing my mother's pleas to move to Sikimpur. They said they would miss the quiet dignity of Lalmali, that Sikimpur was too modern for their simple ways.

'What will you do when you have to introduce us to your friends?' Nanima would ask. 'You would be ashamed of our roughness and our village ways.'

And although Ammaji protested, they were stubborn in their refusals.

'It is better for us all if we stay here,' Nanajaan told her. 'We have our respect here. As long as you bring our grand-daughters to see us regularly, then we are quite content.'

What I remember of Nanajaan is a much-lined face and snow-white beard. His voice was very soft, as though his lips were traced with silk. He would save up his Indian army pension to buy us biscuits and shiny *gulab jamun*.

In his house was the only time that we were allowed to drink *chai*. In the mornings, when the cockerels were crowing and the sun had not yet warmed the land, we would crouch on low stools around the kitchen and watch as Nanima made a pot of *chai* on her crude hearth. The back door would be flung open to allow the smoke to escape: frail, wood-burn smoke that smelt so sweet.

When the *chai* was ready, Nanima would pour it into small, chipped cups with fading patterns and hand one to each of us. We would clasp them in our hands for warmth, dip our hard, sweet bread rolls into our drinks and watch the liquid rise up the bread and disappear from the cup. We would always ask Nanima for another cup. This time, with Ammaji watching disapprovingly, we would pour out some of the *chai* into the saucer and slurp it slowly, as we had watched Nanajaan do. It amused him to watch us copy him and he would wink at Nanima saying, 'Ah, they are proper village *bachiya* now.' It was his amusement that kept Ammaji quiet, drinking her own cup of *chai* in silence. It was the best tasting *chai* we had ever had: sweet and milky and warming.

At night, we would all sleep on the floor of my grandparents' room, on ageing mattresses and sheets, with blankets to cover us in winter, and the bats circling over our heads, hunting for insects before finding their way out. For a time we were scared of these nightly visits, for a cousin had told us that the bats would bite our ears off as we slept, but Nanima would not stand for this nonsense.

'Do you think the bats have time to stop and bite your ears?' she would ask. 'They fly fast and have no interest in you. Now do not be such *busdil*, and go to sleep.'

The cousin who had told us this was given a sound smacking and made to sit out on the front steps, holding his ears for the badness he had done.

On bath days, Ammaji's widowed aunt would come round and pour coconut oil onto our scalps, massaging it through our hair, working her fingers expertly until our heads were dizzy and we grew too restless for her to continue. Then she would braid our hair into thick plaits and we would be allowed to play about in the narrow lanes that criss-crossed the path outside my grandparents' home. We would gather dust as we played with the other children of the neighbourhood, growing dark and murky from the street dirt until Nanima called us in for our baths. We would be made to crouch, naked, out in the paved courtyard of the garden, as Ammaji scooped water from a large iron cauldron over us, and Nanima scrubbed us with the Palmolive soap that she had bought especially, so that we shone again.

Oblivious and carefree as we were, we did not see the labour of village life; the women washing clothes down by the river, the back-breaking work of grinding spices for our meals; the daily routine of separating the grains of rice and lentil from small stones and chaff. And, of course, there was the inconvenient nature of the electricity and water supplies.

The electricity could go at any time. It was not missed during the day: at night, however, we would be plunged into darkness, and have to resort to lighting the lamps, which smoked and smelled so strongly of kerosene.

Water would only come to the village every two days. My grandparents had a tap at one corner of their little garden and Nanima would line up all of the available pots beside it the night before. In the morning, sometime soon after *Fajr* prayer, taps all over the village would splutter suddenly and spring into life, and shouts would go round, '*Nal! Nal agaya*!' The women and children of each household would leap out of bed and rush to fill their pots before the precious water supply ran out and the taps, which had once been so full of life, would be left dripping - plop, plop, plop - until they were dry once more.

This was all fun for us; we were excited by the sudden darkness and the rush to help fill pots, with the water splashing round our feet and the pots clinking, clanging, all cheerful sounds to us. Those days were good days, made better when Abbaji had a toilet installed at the rear of the garden so we did not have to go out into the fields accompanied by my cousins, a *lota* of water and a bar of soap.

The innocence of our youth lasted until my grandparents died, one following the other. Then the house missed them, and something of their missing spirit left behind a shell that could not be filled without their warmth and simple love.

These, then, were my earliest memories: days of the blithe spirit, together with my sisters, listening to a tall tale of daring, and sitting in my grandparents' home drinking *chai*.

Abbaji was mesmerised by the prospect of having Sami Altair as a son-in-law.

'How magnificent it would be; the pleasure of talking to him about his ideas.' At times he got quite carried away. 'Why, we may even be able to do some work together! I am not sure how, for I do not really understand his field of expertise, but I do know that computers are going to be of great importance in the future.'

Surprisingly, it was Ammaji who became cautious.

'I do not know if you are ready for married life, Sahira. Allah knows you are of marriageable age, but... you still seem so young, so unprepared for things. But then, maybe it will be good for you.' She raised the palms of her soft hands up to heaven. 'I just pray that everything works out for the best.'

My sisters were equally measured in their comments.

'It is a big step, getting married,' Laila told me. 'The demands made on you will be great. You know, being the wife of such a successful man, you will probably have an extensive social diary. And then, there is his mother. She is... well, she is quiet, but that just means that you do not know what is lurking there. Especially now that her son has made all that money, and they have transformed their small bungalow into that huge house with the wonderful name, *Gulabi Ghar*. Oh yes, his mother will be really enjoying herself now. Although, Allah only knows why they need such a big house.' Laila winked at me, knowingly. 'She must be hoping for a large extension to the family. She will expect a lot from you, and she will probably also resent you at the same time.'

'Laila!' this scolding voice was Suha's. My eldest sister was a fan of Mrs Altair because of her association with the late Pundit Nehru. She had protested on rallies alongside him during India's struggle for Independence, and the Father of the Nation was a great hero of Suha's. 'Mrs Altair is not like that. She will not be the jealous type of mother-in-law. But-' she broke off to study me and continued with an air of irony. 'I wonder why she chose you?'

'Chose her?' Laila made a face. 'Suha, what a term. It is so vulgar. Like choosing your favourite *mithai* from the *mithai* shop.'

'Oh, you are such a *buddhoo*,' retorted Suha. 'What I mean, is that the Altairs have never been very sociable and it is at parties that us *mithai* get seen. So where has Begum Altair got her insight into our *pyari*, Sahira?'

There was silence, a lingering pause of thought. I, too, wondered at the thinking behind Mrs Altair's interest.

Suddenly, Suha spoke up with a burst of inspiration. 'Of course! Professor Goldberg! It has to be.'

'Professor Goldberg? But he is my tutor.' I frowned at Suha. 'I do not...'

'Of course!' Laila clapped her hands. 'He is a great friend of the Altairs. At least, he was of Professor Altair when he was alive. They were always together. He must have...'

'Oh, but that is ridiculous, Laila.' I could not see the logic of this claim. 'To think that Professor Goldberg is responsible for this *rishtaa*! I am sure he has many more important things to do. Besides, I rarely see him. So no, it cannot possibly be. Why, you might as well say that Begum Altair went to see a fortune teller as to suggest such a thing.'

'A fortune teller!' Ammaji had come into the room. The door was open and her light *chappals* had not made a sound. 'You should not be discussing this *rishtaa* in such a manner, Sahira. A girl should be shy when she receives a *rishtaa*. Demure about all things to do with marriage.'

'Why?' I asked irritably. 'I do not feel in the least bit shy about it. It is my *rishtaa*, after all. Why should I not discuss it openly?'

'Shh!' Ammaji frowned at me and shut the door. 'There will be many things in life that you do not understand, but that does not mean you have to question everything. Some things must be accepted. They are part of our culture, our traditions. A girl and her reputation are delicate matters. The way a girl behaves reflects her nature, and also,' Ammaji sniffed proudly, 'the way she was brought up.'

'Ha!' I grinned. 'By you and Abbaji. My behaviour reflects on you. If I am shy and demure, then people will say how well you and Abbaji have brought me up.'

'Yes, yes, yes,' Ammaji said impatiently. Then she smiled. 'Besides, it was not Mrs Altair who sent the *rishtaa*, but her son, Sami.'

This was unexpected news and I could not help but whisper in surprise, 'Sami Altair sent the rishtaa!'

The news delighted my sisters, though.

Suha let out a low whistle. 'Sami Altair chose you! *Meyri pyari* Sahira, what *jadoo* have you been working on him?'

'*He* chose *you* for his *mithai*!' followed up Laila. 'My goodness, Sahira, what have you been doing to capture Sami Altair's interest?'

'What do you mean?' Ammaji looked at Laila sharply before turning to me. 'What does she mean, Sahira? Do you and Sami Altair know each other?' Her voice rose an octave. 'How do you know each other?'

I was still dazed with the knowledge I had just gained and so, when I answered her, my tone was edgy. 'Of course I know Sami Altair, Ammaji. Everyone knows Sami Altair. He is the genius of Sikimpur.'

'Do not talk that way, please. You know what I am asking you. Do you and Sami Altair...?'

'Oh Ammaji, what a thing to ask!' Suha cut Ammaji short. 'Laila was only teasing. Sahira is a good girl, just a little *ajeeb*.'

'Teasing, teasing, teasing! You are too fond of teasing, you sisters. You give me a headache trying to decide when you are serious and when you are not.' Ammaji placed her hand over her forehead, rubbed it hard and then pointed at the door. 'Please go, Suha. Laila needs to eat and to rest. I have asked Mina to put out some fruit for her. You have some, too. You have been looking pale. See how I still care for you, in spite of your cruelty to me?'

Suha rose to go and kissed Ammaji on the cheek, sorry for her teasing.

'Do not be annoyed, Ammaji. After all, who else can I tease so and still have love me?'

Ammaji nodded in mock disbelief. 'Yes, yes. That is always your excuse. But go now. I need to talk to Sahira.'

Suha and Laila left, closing the door behind them, their footsteps and easy chatter moving along the stone of the corridor and into the light of the dining room. Soon we would be able to hear music as Laila - who was very musical - would put a record on the old gramophone. She insisted that her unborn baby could hear the sounds that were created by a needle and passed on to the world through an over-sized funnel.

In my room, Ammaji ran a finger under the tight cotton of her blouse.

'It is hot in here. Why have you not got the *punkha* on?' She flicked the *punkha* switch, but nothing happened. The *punkha* remained static, as it was. '*Arré*, the *bijli* has gone again. We must get a generator for such times. How is India to progress when, even in a place such as Sikimpur, the light can go at any time?' She moved along my bed and patted the *rezai* beside her. 'Come, sit by me, *beyti*. I want to talk to you. You have not told me how you feel about this proposal. I had hoped that you might give me some indication, but I cannot tell whether you are happy or not.'

'Happy?' I thought about that word. Happy was such a strong word. 'Well, I am not unhappy about it.' I replied

I was not sure how I felt about the actual *rishtaa* at that moment. So unused was I to proposals that I did not know what to think of this one. And now, of course, all I could think about was that it was Sami Altair who had 'chosen' me.

Ammaji took my chin in the palm of her hand and tilted my face upwards. She looked at me until I felt uncomfortable with her attention and moved my chin clear of her hand.

'Suha knows why Sami Altair wants to marry you,' she said. 'It is obvious. It is why I could not understand your lack of *rishtey*.' Ammaji smiled into my eyes. 'It is because you are beautiful...'

'Oh, Ammaji!' I turned my face away crossly, but she shook her head.

'But it is true, Sahira, and you know it. All of my daughters are lovely: but you, Sahira, you are the most lovely. Do not look at me that way. I am your mother and I love all three of my daughters equally, so I can say this without prejudice. The Shamshads may have the titles, but they lack the delicacy that runs in my family. And you, *meyri beyti*, you have that delicate trait of my family, while your sisters have more of the Shamshad line in them. They have that pale haughtiness while you- true you are a little *sanwli*, but that is probably because you are too fond of the sun so now the darkness has been burnt into you- you are fine featured '

I was embarrassed now and felt the blush rise in my cheeks. Ammaji had never spoken like this to me. I could see the pride in her eyes as she talked of her family, but her words covered me in pale misery.

'I shall not marry Sami Altair if that is why he proposed,' I told her.

Ammaji looked astounded. 'But why? There is nothing wrong with a man falling in love with a woman for her beauty. A man is sought after for his standing and his profession. For a woman, it is her beauty that...'

Although I knew that what Ammaji said was, unfortunately true, I could not completely agree with her design for beauty. For me, it was when Abbaji had taken me up to the roof to watch the sun rise on a cool September dawn; it was Ammaji's face when the first of her roses came into bloom, or the scent of jasmine at the height of summer.

The villages were the real closets for beauty; the girls who lived there were many times more beautiful than I. The peasant girls washing clothes in the river, fetching water from the wells and cooking simple meals. Raven hair, doe eyes and skin the colour of spring saplings. They were endowed with the true nature of beauty, while we society girls were its mere reflections. Oh, how easy it was to be attractive when one's life was pampered to the point of staleness.

While Ammaji was still talking and I was still thinking, the *muezzin* sang out the *azan* for *Maghrib* from the window of his minaret. Ammaji stopped talking, pulled up the *pallo* of her sari over her head, and became concentrated in prayer. When the *muezzin* finished, she rose to go, saying, 'After all, both a woman's beauty and a man's standing are gifts from the Almighty. We should not turn our noses up at these attributes. As long as they do not turn a person's head and we admit that it is to Allah that all things are due.'

Chapter Three

Two days later, Sami Altair left for England on a business trip. He was not due to return for some three months. This event sparked fresh discussions, never-ending discussions that my family revelled in.

'A man who has recently proposed does not go away just like that,' Laila told me. 'And for three months! He should have waited for an answer. It makes me wonder about his feelings for you!'

Abbaji shook his head. 'No, no. He is a genius. He will do things that we do not understand. This is completely normal for a man such as he. He is nervous about waiting around for an answer, so he is keeping himself busy by going away. It is exactly the right thing to do.'

Ammaji thought as Laila. 'But three months? I think it is most peculiar.'

Suha hugged me tight in sympathy. 'I cannot understand why he is going away so soon, but never mind. It is not important. You must try not to care about that.'

'But I do not care,' I told her. 'What difference does it make?'

Suha looked at me approvingly. 'That is good. And, of course, you must carry on as normal. We will go out for lunch on Saturday. Uthman will not mind. I will tell him he can go to the Gymkhana Club with his friends. There is a big polo match on, I believe.' She clicked her fingers. 'Munif Sahib is giving a concert next week at The Taj Hotel. I will get two tickets for it. You like him, do you not?'

I did not; his music was sickly sweet, as if his sitar strings were laced with sherbet, but I nodded anyway. Suha was a great admirer of Munif Sahib and would not want to hear my opinion of her beloved musician.

The child on my bed began to stir, stretching and yawning out of sleep. She began to take little gulps of air that would soon result in a petulant cry of hunger. Suha, recognising this, suddenly became a mother again. She rocked her baby soothingly on the mauve silk *rezai* of my bed whilst unbuttoning her blouse.

'It is Mariam's feeding time,' she said. 'She has become very moody about it. Ammaji tells me it is because she is teething, and her gums are certainly quite red at the moment. It takes her a while to settle into her feeding. You should go. I need to get the both of us properly comfortable in this heat.'

I nodded, knowing what this meant: Suha, still plump from her pregnancy, removing much of her upper clothing, and sitting or lying in strange positions. Poor Mariam did not like the hot weather. She had been born in the winter time, when the skies were more opaque and the coolness of the mornings lasted throughout the day.

So I left Suha to her mothering and took myself out, out into the release of the deep garden and out to the open arms of the old banyan tree. Round to the side of the house, I could see Abbaji taking Uthman, Suha's husband, beyond the boundaries of the garden and into the cotton fields. They were chatting in earnest, their heads low, lost in a discussion about yield, rainfall, machinery - all those things that occupy the farmer every day.

From the fields rose several dust balls, all pluming in a line. These came from the gathering of the painted lorries, waiting to take the farm workers back to their homes. They had worked a long day in the fields, harvesting the traditional rabi crops of this region of India: cotton, wheat and barley, as well as the sugar cane that had come up early that year.

The branches of my banyan tree grew thickly above the grass, gnarled like a washerwoman's hands. I sat on the hard ground beneath it and, gazing up at its entangled mesh, I thought of marrying Sami Altair. Yes or no - those were the two words that were dancing before me. It took less than a second to say either of them, but then to live upon that utterance? That would take a lifetime. I felt like Robert Frost's traveller, standing on a path where two roads diverged. How long would I stand there, standing on a periphery, just on the edge? Yes or no? Like a slow-breaking day when the dawn is still dark.

As I sat there, two cranes flew overhead. They were late, this year, in leaving their winter home by the Langi River and flying north. They were going to live their other life now, up in the cold, rugged land of Afghanistan. Watching their flight, I tried hard to imagine another life for me, a picture of Sami Altair and me. I had trouble seeing it clearly, for what I knew of Sami Altair was not a lot. I remembered him plainly only once, when his father had died and my parents had gone to his house to pay their respects. I had been quite young then, maybe twelve or thirteen, and he about sixteen. It had been quiet in their home, a sombre shadow hanging over everything. Even the dogs in the yard were silent and lay indolently under the old peepal tree.

Inside the hushed drawing room had sat Mrs Altair, with dark rings around her eyes and the plain simple sari of a widow. In the instant that I saw her, I thought of her as kind. She smiled at me and, although I was not sure whether she actually saw me fully, she somehow noticed that I sat timidly between my parents. She turned to the boy by her side and spoke to him.

'Sami, *betey*, why do you not take...,' she looked at me. 'What is your name, *beyti*? Yes, Sahira, of course... Why do you not take her to see the *patang*?'

Then Mrs Altair had noticed the look of uncertainty on Ammaji's face. It was a delicate matter. Young girls were not sent up onto roofs with young boys who were not related to them. It was a matter of a girl's reputation which, as Ammaji was fond of saying, 'is like a fragile vase, and who would want such a vase that had a chip in it?'

'Oh, but of course, my niece will go too.' Mrs Altair called out a name. 'Suraya!' A girl with russet apples for cheeks soon came into the room. She was older than both Sami and me, but resembled him enough to be related. She salaamed to my parents as Mrs Altair asked, 'Suraya, you are not busy, are you?'

The girl shook her head. '*Nahin*, Phupujaan, I was just helping to clear the lunch plates away.'

Mrs Altair smiled bleakly at her niece. 'You are a good girl, Suraya. Such a help. Do you mind going up to the roof with Sahira and Sami? You do not mind, do you, *beyti*?'

Suraya had shaken her head again. 'No, I do not mind. I can take my embroidery with me.'

It was the season of kite flying. The skies of Sikimpur were bright with these *patang*, skipping, flipping, darting suddenly to cut an opponent's string. From the flatness of the Altairs' roof, children could be seen running about in the street, in their gardens, some on their own roofs, their hands fastened tight around long, trailing strings, their eyes skyward at the *patang* flitting in the breeze. Suraya, tall and delicate, sat with her cloth and thread on the low wall that surrounded the roof and was soon lost in concentration.

Sami had brought his *patang* out, green and blue; it was brand new, not yet flown.

'Baba bought it for me before he died.' Sami looked at his *patang* thoughtfully. Suddenly, he looked like his mother had, with darkness around his pale brown eyes. 'I have not thought about flying my *patang* this year, but now I suppose I should.'

I thought, then, that maybe he resented me. But then he had smiled, and, from a corner of the roof where the grand branches of the neem tree spilled over, he brought out a jar filled with a thick, dark liquid - aloe sap - and a tin box, which I guessed contained finely-crushed glass. Like so many other children in this season of kites, Sami Altair would have gone to the park where the aloe plants grew and tapped their leaves for the slow-flowing sap.

I had watched him as he mixed the sap with the crushed glass and then, laying out the length of the *patang* string, some fifty feet, on the ground, he smeared his mixture along it. The crushed glass made it easier to cut an opponent's string cleanly. His pale, slender hands worked deftly, efficient in their work so that he finished without a single cut on any of his ten fingers. Under the hot sun, the mixture soon dried and Sami handed the loose end of the string and the empty spool to me, crying out as he ran away with his *patang*.

'Come. Let us see how good you are!'

I had laughed, delighted because I knew what to do. Carefully, I wound the treated string around the spool and then nodded at Sami Altair, who ran again, releasing his *patang* so that it caught the wind and was thrown high into the air. I skipped after him, letting the spool spin freely in my hands so that the string was let out, fast at first, and then slowly. My *chappals* clipped pertly over the sun-baked stone as Sami and I chased the other *patang* around the roof, laughing with glee as the clinging glass on the string glinted in the bright air of sunshine.

Eventually, Suraya put down her cloth and needle and joined in the merriment. She had long limbs, like Sami, and covered much more of the roof than I ever could, laughing gleefully, becoming ever more ruddy-cheeked. We captured three *patang* that hour; one was torn but the other two were pristine and Sami Altair handed me one of them to take home, a reward for my skills with the spool.

I had forgotten about that day, but now it ran like a reel of film through my mind. In that past moment I had known Sami Altair as a boy, a flyer of *patang*; now that past was turned upside down, made into something else by the passage of time. I had not thought of him in all the time that had passed, but now he was all I could think of. It was not just his face that I could see clearly - an open, honest expression; but I remembered also his voice - soft, reserved in a self-conscious way. I remembered too that he wore glasses, such serious, adult things that made his eyes so solemn, a wise boy-child. Then, I was sure, in that instant, that Sami Altair had not sent his *rishtaa* for my looks, nor yet for the great Shamshad name but for some reason of his own, some reason that could not be a negative to my way of thinking.

That night, I lay in bed and gazed out of an open window into a sky stirring with starlight, and it was then, with all that clarity before me, that the decision was made. Yes or no? It was not so strange that we did not love each other, or barely even knew each other. Falling in love came after marriage, as one became familiar with the other, came to trust and be intimate with the other.

I lay for a long time with this question rolling alongside the sleep that was claiming my mind. And it was my mind that was very much involved; for my heart, there was no real stirring, none of excitement anyway, but maybe the trembling for an unknown future.

But, yes or no? Still the decision had to be made. My heart was of no use really. And so I relied on my mind, and it made itself very clear. There was no reason to say no, it said, none that mattered, anyway. However, there was every reason to say yes. That was what it said, whispered, shouted, in black, white and rainbow colours.

I stayed there a while, my limbs lazy and my mind drifting, but the night air that came into my room from the open window was blowing through now and so, eventually, I rose to close the shutters of my window. I was caught by the sight of the garden that was all dark outlines in the depth of night: the roses that I had helped Abbaji to plant, the trees we had climbed as children, the ripe fruits we had gathered. The smells were fuller, released from the light of day as they were, and the crickets were chirping. I shivered though the night air was not so cold and pulled the shutters down tight.

The garden was shut out. I took a deep breath and began, there and then, the preparation of saying goodbye to it all.

Chapter Four

Laila went into labour in the early hours of the next morning. We woke to the noise of the telephone ringing out through the calm of the sleeping house. My parents left for the hospital, Ammaji flushed with excitement and worry.

'Hurry, hurry, we must get there soon,' she cried. 'We should be there when she gives birth. This is her second time and her first was difficult. She will be worried and I must be there to reassure her.'

Ammaji kissed me absent-mindedly as I rubbed my eyes.

'There is no need for you to come,' she told me. 'We will let you know what is going on. But make sure Maha gets the vegetables that we need for dinner. Tell her to get to the market early and take care to look carefully at what the *sabzi-wallah* offers her. He always tries to put in a few rotten ones with the fresher ones.'

I nodded at all of Ammaji's instructions, listening to her through sleepy ears and pulling my shawl tightly around me, as the chill of the early morning began to seep through my body and into my bones.

Finally, my parents were seated in the car, the doors banged closed, and they were driven away by our yawning driver. I waved to them and turned back to face the house, standing grandly as it did in its wide open land and shining as the sun began to rise, slightly blurred, behind it. It had the peace of an empty house, with the morning light creeping through its spaces and between its walls.

I could have returned to bed, but I was almost awake now and it seemed improper not to stay with the new day. I gathered up a cushion and a book from my bedroom and wandered into Abbaji's drawing room. The carom board was still laid out on the games table with its counters flung around its surface, an unfinished game from the day before.

This room had been built, almost in isolation to the rest of the house, by my great-grandfather. It had its own entrance out into the garden and allowed my great-grandfather to entertain his male friends without their having to go through the main body of the house. At that time, the women of the house were kept in strict purdah, away from the gaze of unrelated men. These days, Abbaji still drank tea and played cards there with his friends, sometimes talking well into the early hours of the morning. But these days, the rest of us used it, too: to listen to the wireless or to read, to do whatever we wanted in an air of quietude.

Outside, the sun was still forming in fullness, and its pale light came in between the latticed slats of the room's bamboo walls. I opened up the doors to the outside so that there was light enough to read my book with its pencilled notes in the margins. I found that I could not concentrate, my head ached slightly with broken sleep and I could not help but stare out into the openness before me, into the strengthening light that was rearranging colour and form.

Soon, I heard the servants up and moving around, one sweeping the stone floors with a crude broom made out of rushes, yet another pulling out clothes into various piles ready for the day's washing. Maha came out to me to ask me about breakfast and I thought today I would have fruit, just some fruit; some slices of guava and melon, perhaps.

When she returned with my meal, I gave her Ammaji's message and she nodded, with her dark, oiled head glistening in the rising sun.

'It is Friday today so there should be fresh vegetables, but that *kamina sabzi-wallah* still tries to sell the old week's produce.'

Ammaji would have scolded Maha for her language but I did not. It meant nothing; simply the phrases that she had grown up hearing and now used as part of her everyday discourse. I could not use this language myself for it sounded alien and coarse on my tongue but on hers it tripped off like an intake of breath.

'Shall I come with you?' I asked.

Maha shook her head. '*Nahin*, Sahira Bibi. If you are there, then that *kamina* will turn on even more of his false smiles and you will not know what he is up to.'

'I do not have to say anything to him. He does not have to know who I am.'

Maha examined my face and hands with her eyes. 'You will not have to say anything, Sahira Bibi. He will know anyhow. Besides,' she looked down at the book that lay, spine up, on the table, 'you must concentrate on your studies.'

I looked down at the table, covered with discarded things: book, plate, cup. Picking up the book, Dickens' *A Tale of Two Cities*, I sighed. 'Yes, my exams are starting soon.'

My parents arrived home late in the afternoon, long after the sun had burnt off the chill of the interrupted morning. They looked tired, their faces drawn, their limbs hanging wearily by their side. Laila had not yet given birth, and they had been told that they would do well to go home and wait.

Ammaji, who held doctors in high esteem, told me of the obstetrician's opinion.

'Dr Shafi says that the labour is progressing very slowly. She may not give birth today, even. I will go back this evening with some *gajar ka halwa*. It is Laila's favourite and it will give her fresh strength. She was very tired when we left. I do not think she even knew we were still there.'

Abbaji, too, was weary; needing sleep, concerned for his daughter and unsure of what to do. They sat down to eat a frugal lunch, the smell of *parathas* and freshly cooked *daal* filling the house. Little was said over the meal, even by Ammaji, who did not usually like silence. Her thoughts were with Laila; they tired her out with their worrying nature and soon afterwards she was persuaded to go to bed.

'But, you must call me as soon as there is any kind of news,' she insisted. 'I really should be there for her. It is not right that I am not there. I shall not be able to sleep until I know she has delivered safely.'

Abbaji steered her firmly upstairs to their room. 'Yes, but Dr Shafi himself told you to go, and you know that Laila is in good hands. You will be the first one they call when the baby arrives.'

Ammaji sniffed. 'Of course I will be!' and then added, a little less assured, 'They will phone me before her *sas*, will they not? I am her mother, after all.'

I nodded to her and smiled reassuringly. 'Of course they will.' To back up my argument I added, 'Laila will want you to be the first to know. She will make sure that Nasir phones you before his own mother.'

And so, Ammaji went reluctantly to bed and slept soundly, betrayed by the snores that penetrated her bedroom walls.

In the meantime, our *bawrchi*, Mina, who had spoilt Laila since she was a child, prepared some *gajar ka halwa* with 'the more expensive almonds and the sweetest of carrots for Laila Bibi.'

When it was ready, Mina lovingly applied delicate silver foil to decorate its surface and cut it into squares. Carefully packed into an ornate mithai box, she sent it, with her love and very solemn duas, to Laila Bibi's bedside. And when Laila gave birth later that night, with Ammaji by her side, our beloved *bawrchi* claimed that it was her *gajar ka halwa* 'made with those special almonds' that had hastened on the birth.

Laila named her daughter Noor, meaning moonlight.

'For indeed, she is like the very light of the moon,' Ammaji told us proudly. 'Such a bright and clear light.'

When I went to visit Laila and her baby in the hospital, I saw that she was right.

'She is beautiful,' I told her as I held the child in my arms and rocked her gently.

'The most beautiful little girl I have ever seen, but do not tell Suha that.' Laila sat up gingerly and smiled. 'She looks like you. Yes, even my *soosral* can see that. It is the reason we named her after the light of the moon.'

We received many phone calls over the next few days as the news of my *rishtaa*, 'Sami Altair, no less!' travelled to the acute ears of our many friends and relatives. The more curious of these came to visit. My aunts by marriage hugged me tightly, too tightly, and smiled at my parents with the wide, but closed, lips of a common regret. What a waste, they were thinking. How much better would their own daughters be suited to being Mrs Sami Altair than this reticent niece of theirs? I watched their double chins wobble under the glare of the electric light, feeling embarrassed and sorry for them. Later, Suha had made much fun of their strangled good wishes.

'Did you see how tightly Lubna Chachi hugged Ammaji? Almost enough to squeeze the life out of her. Oh, you really must marry Sami Altair now, Sahira. It would be wonderful to watch her face at the wedding.'

Ammaji did not approve of this joking.

'Do not talk like that, Suha. It is most unkind. She is only worried about your cousin, Parveen. She is almost twenty-five, you know, and not one single *rishtaa*. Any one of us could be in that position. It is not something to make fun of.'

'Oh Ammaji, you know that she is only jealous because the *gaun-walli's* daughter has caught the eye of Sami Altair and she cannot stand it. She has always looked down on you because you come from Lalmali.'

'Still, you should not talk about her in that way, Suha!' A remonstrating voice spoke out behind us. 'You have a sharp tongue and you are not always careful about how you direct it. It is unkind of you to make fun of a worried mother, and one who is a relative, too. After all, Parveen is also your cousin and you should be concerned for her welfare.'

Uthman had wandered into the dining room where we were sitting. He was the son of Abbaji's youngest brother, and favoured in the family for his mild nature and generosity. He was deeply religious and it showed in his face; the calmness of prayer and meditation was written there. Suha's marriage to Uthman had worked out well for both Abbaji and the Shamshad clan. Uthman was the heir to the Shamshad title, being the eldest of the next generation of Shamshad boys, and now that he had married Suha, Abbaji's grandchildren would inherit Shamshad Bagh and much of its lands.

Uthman put a tray of bitter sweet lemonade on the table and sat down to face me. 'And what will become of this *rishtaa*, my dear sister-in-law? You know that everyone is waiting on the decision.'

I adored Uthman. He had a high forehead and a nose that was sharp, but his smile was effervescent and he spoke words that were wise. He was also the most trustworthy person I knew, and funny, too. Most importantly, he knew how to handle my wilful sister and tame her. And she was not easily tamed.

I saw Abbaji look at me. 'As you know, it is up to you, *beyti*. There is no-one here who will tell you one thing or the other.'

Ammaji put down the apple that she was peeling, and nodded. 'It is your life for you to live. You know what we feel. He is a good boy, and it is a good *rishtaa*...' Then she paused and bit her lip before continuing. 'But you are twenty and this is the first one that you have received-'

She was cut short by Abbaji's sharp voice. 'Razia! What a thing to say! Twenty is still very young.'

'Yes, yes! I do not mean anything by it. Of course, Sahira is sure to get others, but your sister-in-law is very worried about Parveen, and I-'

'-do not want to be in the same position?' Suha finished Ammaji's anxious sentence.

We could not hear Ammaji's protests with all the laughter that ensued.

When the merriment had died down, I wriggled a little uncomfortably in my chair and said, 'Well, I have decided,' I began. 'And what I have decided is that, yes, I will accept this *rishtaa*.'

There was a deep silence; only the ticking of the large grandfather clock could be heard from within the house.

The knife in Ammaji's hand was frozen, as was her face.

'*You* have already decided!' Ammaji dropped the knife and stared at me. 'All by yourself? Without discussing it with us?'

'But Ammaji, you said it was my decision.'

Ammaji nodded her head. 'In the end, yes, of course. But you have reached such an important decision by yourself without asking, without talking about it? We are in a better position to advise you. We are older; we have an experience of life and marriage. These decisions should not be taken lightly.'

'I did not make it lightly. I have thought it over long and hard, and I am sure of my decision.'

'And what of your Abbaji and myself? What about our opinions? Do they not matter to you?'

'Of course they do, but I was quite sure what your opinion of Sami Altair was. Are you unhappy with my decision?'

'The decision is...' Ammaji frowned and shook her head. 'How can you have thought about it by yourself without consulting us? We are your parents, and you are so young. Too young to-'

'Too young to decide to get married?' I interrupted.

'Yes!'

'But if I am old enough to get married then why am I-?'

'That is not the point! Just because you are old enough to be wed, do you feel that you no longer need your parents' advice? Not once did you mention what you were thinking.'

'There was no such opportunity; you were busy with Laila.'

Ammaji waved my defence away with her hand. 'Oh, that is just an easy excuse. It has always been the same with you, Sahira! You have always been so secretive. You never tell me what is in your heart. If you cannot tell your mother, then who will you find to listen to you?'

She shook her head with the disappointment of a parent whose child no longer clings to her. 'You children always think that you are old enough to think for yourselves,' she continued. 'But you do not understand how to make such important decisions for yourselves, what to consider and such.'

Then Abbaji, whose eyes were full of reproach, also, said sadly, 'It is true that you have made a good decision, a sound decision. However, I am sorry that I do not know how you came about it. It would not have hurt you to come to your mother and talk to her about it, and it would have done her much good. Yes, yes, I know...' He put his hand up to stop my protests. 'We were much concerned about Laila, but that did not mean we did not have time for you.'

And so I was made silent, with my head held low. Even Suha had nothing to say, which was unusual for her. Ammaji pushed her chair roughly back and slid the apple peelings into her open palm. 'I must go and see to dinner.'

She left the room with her shoulders slumped. Abbaji too, left us, gathering up his recently delivered paper with downcast eyes. 'I have not yet read today's paper. I have some time before dinner.'

As he trudged away shaking his head, Suha turned to me.

'You really are a *pugli*, you know. More than I thought you could be. I don't suppose you even thought of talking to anybody about this *rishtaa*, did you? Even Laila and I would not think of doing such a thing, making such a decision all alone.'

For a moment, she looked quite fierce; her cheeks reddened and her mouth became rigid.

'How can you understand so little of propriety?' Suha sat back in her chair and gave me a dry look. 'Maybe marriage will make you understand; it will certainly need to.' She sat forward suddenly and launched her eyes into mine, and I was struck by the concern in them. 'I pray that you learn to do so before you absolutely have to!' She folded her arms and continued. 'The trouble with you, Sahira, is that you think about yourself too much.'

'Do you think that I am selfish, then?' I was taken aback by her accusation. 'That is not fair, Suha! I am no more selfish than you or Laila.'

Suha held up her hands. '*Arre*. I did not mean anything so simple. You are more complicated than to be described as just selfish.' She made a face. 'No, you think too much *into* yourself. You forget about those others around you, about letting them in.

It was growing dark when Suha and Uthman left us for their own home. Suha was exhausted; motherhood seemed to have pulled on all the natural energy she possessed and drawn away from her the summer of her days. Ammaji was concerned about her pallid complexion and shortage of breath.

'You have been out too long. Make sure you go straight to bed. I will get the tonic from the hakim sahib tomorrow. It is very effective and will help you gain back your *taqat*.'

'Oh, do not fuss Ammaji.' Suha's own concern over her health made her impatient with Ammaji's. 'Uthman's mother fusses enough.'

'She is your *sas*,' Ammaji replied indignantly, 'while I am your mother. I have a right to fuss.'

Uthman pulled his wife away. 'Come on, Suha. You are tired and it is making you unnecessarily irritable. You need to get some sleep.'

'Yes, maybe you're right,' muttered Suha, rubbing her head.

As she moved to kiss Ammaji goodnight, Uthman spoke quietly to me.

'I went to school with Sami Altair, you know. He was some years below me, so I didn't know him all that well. But I do *remember* him well, for he always won the prize for mathematics, and he always seemed so embarrassed when he did so. All the other boys would show off their prizes, while he would put his quietly away. After he left, the college named the mathematics prize after him. They invite him back each year to present it.'

Uthman paused and looked away from me, out into the moonlit path where the bougainvillea bloomed. He drew in a deep breath as though smelling its fragrance. 'What I am trying to tell you, Sahira, is that you must take care of the decision you have made. Make sure that you stand by it always, for I do not think he is someone who would know what to do if he were hurt.'

'I do not plan to marry him in order to hurt him,' I said crossly. 'Why would you think such a thing?'

'It is not what I think.' Uthman leant his head in close and spoke softly. 'But there is something deep within you that is...' He hesitated, searching for a word that was me. 'I do not know. Suha said it well when she described you as complicated. Sami Altair is simple in his thinking. You must take care of his simplicity.'

Suha came over to join us. '*Khudahafiz*, Sahira. Take care and remember to talk to our parents once in a while.' She whispered the words carefully in my ear as she hugged me tightly.

The noise of their car faded into the deep of the night and left us to the quiet again. My parents walked back into the house together and left me alone on the steps. I could hear the crickets singing to their mates and see the distant stars that illuminated the garden as a hundred paled shades.

To the senses these were all beautiful things, but I felt them as the harmony of nature passing judgement on me; I felt myself chastised.

Chapter Five

The wedding invitations were sent out, delicately perfumed notes of powdered blue: by the mail train to guests who lived far from us or delivered personally by Abbaji to as many guests as lived close by. For this occasion, he brought out his most precious Rolls-Royce Phantom. It was paid even more attention than usual; polished so its maroon and cream trim shone, and tuned so fine that it purred. It was driven with much care through the streets of Sikimpur on its highly important errand.

My grandfather had won the Phantom as a fifteen year old boy, in a tennis tournament organised by the last Nizam of Hyderabad, Mir Osman Ali Khan Siddiqui. The Nizam, at that time, was caught up in the celebrations of his third marriage and, when my grandfather came forward to receive his winner's prize, the Nizam suddenly realised that there was no prize to hand out. Disconcerted, he had announced that, because my grandfather had played so well, he could name his prize, any prize that he desired.

Heady with delight, my grandfather, not yet old enough to drive, named every schoolboy's dream: the specially commissioned Phantom that sat gleaming in the courtyard, as his prize. The Nizam, though he must have been shaken, remained true to his royal word and obliged.

The date on the invitations was towards the end of October. It was Ammaji's favourite month for weddings, well away from the customary flourish of weddings in December.

'It is a good time, cooler and quieter, but not too cold.' She looked at me critically. 'By then, *Inshallah*, you will have lost some of that *sanwli rung* from your face. Of course, you will never be as fair-skinned as your sisters but at least you can be a little less dark. Also, the *haldi* should help with your complexion.'

During the day, Shamshad Bagh rang loud with the discordant *hangama* of wedding preparations, with the shrill, indignant voice of Ammaji rising more times than it was calm. In the evening, however, all this red mist seemed to melt away and Ammaji was serene once again. Gone was the irritation, the manic fever that had prevailed over her tone and her body.

Maybe it was the setting of the still fierce sun, or the quietening of the streets beyond our walls. Maybe it was just that Ammaji had always preferred the moon to the sun, the night to the day.

Although summer was coming to an end, the evenings were still balmy and light. Ammaji had the roof laid out with many *shatrangi* - heavy woven rugs that soon became scattered with flower petals, shiny sequins and the earthy smells of green *mehndi* and yellow *haldi*.

In the evenings, the *shatrangi* roof would ring out with the joyful sound of women - friends, family, servants, all joking, teasing and gossiping as they prepared items for the wedding. They were busy weaving garlands of marigolds, moti and jasmine, grinding sandalwood with water, blending the thick, pasted *mehndi* and decorating the silver trays that would carry some of my wedding garments. Candles and kerosene lanterns would burn there from the time after *Maghrib* prayer, until the *muezzin* called the women away for *Isha* prayer.

The house, the garden and the streets beyond our walls were filled with the fragrances of celebration and slowly, Shamshad Bagh was transformed; lights to adorn the house, *shatrangi* for the lawns and marquees for the guests. There was great noise and frenzied activity until the wedding day itself. Then, all came floating back down to earth again and that day took place in a tranquil sea.

I stood immobile, as in a trance, while Ammaji and my aunt wound my sari round and round me until my still body shone like the silken shell of a luminescent pearl. While they were dressing me, I gazed at myself in the mirror, a being I could not recognise for I was brilliantly transformed in diamonds and gold, my eyes were dark with *kajal* and my lips and cheeks were bright cherries.

And, like the newness of my appearance, I realised that this was my moment for stepping bodily into a new land. Now I was set on a new course, a boat which *Kismet* had repositioned with a single breath.

Ammaji, with her hands trembling, threaded a large gold tikka through the parting of my hair so that it hung in the middle of my forehead, and placed the golden embroidery of my sari *pallo* over my head. Then, she stood back to look at me and her eyes began to redden with the emotion that had built up. She cried at what she saw; tears of joy and happiness, and pride for a daughter now grown up. She held me away from her by my shoulders.

'You are a true bride! How grown up you seem all of a sudden. You were such a child and now... it is as if the years have been suddenly taken from me. My last daughter is leaving me. May Allah grant you both a long life of happiness and prosperity.'

She clasped me tightly and broke down again. Khalajaan, Ammaji's younger sister, prised her away and, holding her firmly, turned to Suha.

'You take Sahira down. I will bring your mother soon.' Then she turned back to Ammaji proclaiming, '*Aye, hai*, we women are always crying; when our daughters are sitting at home waiting for *paygham* and then when they get married also. It is a happy day for you. You are the mother of the bride and you must smile.'

My sisters and cousins led me away, out of my bedroom, down the grand staircase and into the front room, where my future awaited me. It was crowded with women: relatives, close and distant, friends whom I had known as a child and ones that I did not recognise. For a moment, they fell silent as I entered, appraising me, the brilliance of my diamonds and the finery that swathed my body. Then, they began to murmur, drowning each other out with their low whisperings. With my head lowered slightly with the weight of the sari *pallo*, they became a blended blur of colour and jewels and whisperings.

All the furniture had been pushed up against the walls and a deep red satin carpet had been laid out along the width and breadth of the floor. I was led to a corner of it and, with much rearrangement of my sari, I sat down, my back resting on a large purple velvet cushion. The Imam, Sheik-al-Hamdi was already there, standing to one side. Apart from Abbaji, he was the only man in the room.

There was a hush as the Imam came to kneel by me. As he read the *Nikkah* in a loud and steady voice, I could smell the slight odour of sweat that came off his stiff jacket. When he asked me for my consent, I did not hesitate, but concentrated on his henna-dyed beard and answered 'Yes' with the clarity of a bell.

Out of the corner of my kohl-lined eyes, I saw Abbaji sitting solemnly beside me, his hands clasped tight and his eyes on the ground. And I noticed that he breathed out a sigh of relief, for he had not been truly sure of his impulsive daughter's reply, that she would not suddenly re-think her decision and refuse to go ahead with this propitious union.

Ammaji, who had come in soon after I had, smiled with dry eyes now. She, too, looked relieved, for she had asked me many times if I was absolutely sure of what I was doing and I had always replied with a dismissive, 'Of course. I have thought about it carefully.'

But my unconcerned answer always failed to remove the concern in her eyes. She, like Abbaji, would not feel settled until she had heard my positive reply and finally, they could relax. Finally, they could rejoice. There were three daughters well brought up, three daughters well married.

How different Ammaji looked now, compared to those months before the wedding, when she had exhausted herself with preparations: haggling with jewellers, dressmakers and florists. She had studied the guest list endlessly, pared it down, expanded it and worried over old rivals that would meet.

'*Arre*, it will never do to have Junaid Begum anywhere near her ex-husband and his new wife.' and 'How can we can keep the Qureshis and the Aamirs apart? They have not spoken since their great-grandfathers duelled over the Nawab's eldest daughter. What a waste of time that was. She had already eloped with her elderly tutor.'

Ammaji had talked constantly throughout the whole of the preparations, driven everyone crazy, while we had done the same to her by being too slow, too argumentative, too obtuse to appreciate her. The best of her explosions were during the disputes she had with Suha. So alike, they both had mulish natures and high pitched voices when excited.

Ammaji would accuse Suha with: 'You girls always think you know best when, actually, you have no real experience of these matters. You are married, yes, but who arranged your weddings? I did, of course! But you... just wait until your own daughter thinks she is very much grown up, then you will understand.'

And, of course, Suha, being Suha, would reply: 'Really Ammaji, what is the point of using that argument? The wedding is in three months' time and you are still being so emotional.'

'Emotional! How dare you talk to me like that? Did I bring you up for this? Forty hours of labour for this? Just because I allow you to help, you think you have the right to, to…'

By now, Ammaji would be overwhelmed by bitter sobbing and Suha would roll her eyes to the heavens. Abbaji, meanwhile, would groan at this too familiar scene, leave his own work and go to Ammaji's side, comforting her with his gentle voice.

'You must not upset yourself, Razia. It is her condition that makes her so snappy.'

He would wave at me to take Suha away, into another room, somewhere away from Ammaji, where I would scold Suha, and also take her side. Later, Suha would apologise to Ammaji in a muttering, forced way and Ammaji would accept in a grudging, martyred way.

During the *Nikkah*, Sami and I had sat in different rooms, for he was not considered *Mahram* until we were formally married. Once the *Nikkah* had been completed, and all the women around me had given their congratulations and best wishes, I was led out into the garden, near to where the fountain was, and where a pair of ornate chairs waited, plush in red velvet and gold trim.

There was a seriousness to this small procession - I, with my eyes lowered, my cousin, Parveen, guiding me, while Suha held the *pallo* of my sari in place. I longed to lift up my head, to relieve some of the tension in the tired muscles of my neck, but I dare not, for I knew that Ammaji would be swift in berating me.

Sami was already there, in the garden, watching as I came to sit down beside him and our eyes met briefly. I took him in - a tall man, wearing a white *sherwani*, its long jacket embroidered with gold thread around the high collar and the cuffs. His pale face was shining under the labour of the occasion and his cheeks were flushed. He smiled at me and became a grown version of the boy that I remembered - the boy with the *patang*, and I was relieved.

I looked away, my gaze falling upon the lawn that was as transformed as the house: its arches entwined with white and purple orchids, lanterns resting on pedestals and tiny lights threaded delicately through the branches of our many trees. I could smell the jasmine and moti garlands, the food that was being served, and the *mehndi* that had come out bright orange on my hands and feet. It was a strange mix that made my head ache slightly and I was glad that I was sitting down.

Beyond the tables that had been laid out for dinner, a stage had been erected where the famous Janoon and his company of musicians played their finely-tuned instruments and sang *qawwali*, their voices lilting deep into the celebratory air. Many of the guests clapped in time to the music and soon the air became thick with these melodies. Amongst them, I spotted Ammaji's sister, her hair tied tightly in a bun, and her youngest daughter, Yasmin. They were shepherding the guests towards their places for dinner.

As they did this, two voices suddenly rose above the other guests, one loud and indignant, the other sharp and shrill.

What are you doing here? How can you have the nerve to sit next to me?' the indignant voice spoke first.

'I have every right! I have been invited by the family, so who are you to talk to me in this way?' the shrill voice answered back.

'I cannot believe that I have to put up with this indignity. It is not enough that you steal my husband, you also have the audacity to...'

The two voices became indistinguishable, as each woman tried to gain the upper hand. I recognised them as the love rivals, Junaid Begum and Romana Begum. Somehow, in spite of Ammaji's efforts to keep them apart, they had found themselves together. There was a great stirring of bodies to the right of us as people craned their necks over each other and moved about to get a better glimpse of them.

And, despite Ammaji's strict orders, I found myself giggling and looking beyond my embroidered *pallo* to where the fracas was unfolding. Beside me, I heard Sami speaking.

'I wonder what's going on over there. It sounds very exciting, does it not?'

I turned to answer him but, as I did so Ammaji came by, muttering to herself.

'Oh, no, no, this will never do. How on earth did those two manage to be together? After all my instructions...' She broke off to glare at me with her lips tight. 'Bow your head, Sahira!' she hissed. 'And stop laughing. It is most inappropriate!'

She looked up and groaned. 'Now, I must try to pacify Junaid Begum. It will not be easy; she is a most proud woman.'

Ammaji hurried away and I glanced at Sami. I thought that he winked at me, but the light was dimming so I could not be certain.

'She is proud, Junaid Begum,' he said, 'and with that comes much entertainment.'

I smiled back, not daring to answer him and lowered my head once again, thankful for a moment of Junaid Begum's involuntary entertainment.

Ammaji soon calmed the warring women and, with profuse apologies, had them settled at opposite ends of the garden for dinner. She scolded Yasmin for not paying enough attention to the guests, and then was sorry for being so abrasive with my gentle cousin and took her arm.

'Yasmin, *beyti*, you must go and eat your dinner. You have been most good today and it is not fair that I should be so harsh. Suha shall help your mother with the seating. Go, go, Hyderabadi biryani is your favourite, I know. And this is the best that I have ever tasted. Go, *beyti*, while it is still warm.'

It was Abbaji who had planned and organised the wedding feast; a simple affair for Abbaji frowned upon the false opulence that was popular then. His only profligacy were the two whole lambs that turned slowly on a spit and were stuffed with figs and almonds, and the biryani that had been prepared by his favourite chef, whom he had brought in from the city of Hyderabad.

This last extravagance was justified by Abbaji as, 'It is in the *Purana Sher* of Hyderabad that the best biryani is made, and surely the guests who come to celebrate the wedding of my youngest daughter should taste this phenomenon!'

With dinner over and the lanterns lit, the musicians turned their voices to the art of the *ghazal*: poems sung in classical Urdu. Later still, a *shahir* recited pieces of his poetry, wondrous tales of two hearts finding each other amidst life's storms and tribulations. I, sitting on my velvet throne, listened enthralled at his weaving of a magical scene. From around the garden, through the darkness of the night, voices could be heard in response to the recitations.

'*Wha, wha, wha*,' came the approving chorus.

I could hear Sami's voice, low but clear, as he talked to the many people who came to shake his hand and congratulate him.

I could not hear his exact words, but his voice sounded familiar, a man's voice that had something of the boy in it. Instinctively, I turned my head slightly, just enough to see him, a flicker against the light really; but still the boy that I had known all those years ago, and I smiled to myself. The guests that came to speak to him left him happy and smiling too.

A few of the women came to speak to me, or rather they left a message of the celebration.

'It has been such a beautiful wedding.' 'Allah bless you in your future life, my *beyti*.' 'May Allah grant you with many strong sons.'

And so it went on. I only listened and talked to the voices of those close to me: my sisters, Ammaji and a few cousins and aunts. Thankfully, I was not expected to speak, but to remain quiet in an ocean of babble and laughter. Instead, I let myself watch the people who had come to celebrate my wedding day. The colours of the women were many; they formed a collective rainbow of silks and satin, while the men's Nehru jackets and sherwani were more sober, the uniform shades of grey.

I saw Ammaji wander deliberately through the guests, her head high in the damson clouds, the proud mother. Every now and then she would bend low to chat to someone, smile and thank them for coming. I did not see much of Abbaji, for he was with the men folk, on the other side of the bougainvillea divide.

With the evening upon us and the wedding day coming to an end, our guests began departing to the high, reedy sound of the shenai. It resonated intermittently into the arms of the ink-blot sky, while the music that prevailed was gentle sitar strings and the languorous rhythm of the tabla.

Suha was talking to my new *sas*. The day had been a tiring mix of joy and sadness for Altair Begum: her son was getting married, but she had no husband with whom to share the pride of the occasion. She had talked and laughed, but there had been moments when I had seen her look across the lantern-lit garden at some distant point and her eyes had faded, looking far out, I thought, into the memories of the past. And then, remembering the guests, she would pull herself back to the present and her duties. She would steer guests to the dinner, help them find their seats, admire a Kashmiri shawl.

But now, with the occasion ending and the garden emptying, she had not the energy to sustain her façade and had rested herself in a quiet corner. Ammaji had come across her there and they had whispered together for a while under the blanket of the midnight sky.

Suha had found them in this closeness and intruded; the last of the guests were leaving and they must thank them and wave them off. Ammaji had taken one look at the sad face in front of her and decided.

'You must stay here, Amina Begum. I will explain that you are unwell. And that is true. It has been a difficult day for you, as well as a happy one.'

Suha had taken Ammaji's place. 'I will sit with her. You must go, Abbaji is looking everywhere for you.'

A little while later, my parents stood at the top of the veranda steps and mumbled countless good-byes. They looked exhausted; the light of excitement had finally left their eyes, replaced by the droop of fatigued eyelids.

As the last of the guests left, their splendid cars gliding towards the gate, Abbaji turned to Ammaji. Putting his large, protective arm around her slight shoulders, he kissed her on her forehead, that part where the hairline meets skin - a soft and tender kiss that said so much about their twenty-eight years together. It was a rare moment for them, at least in my eyes. To me, they were my parents who laughed, who talked at cross purposes, and very rarely agreed upon anything. But with that gesture they suddenly became man and wife, life partners, beings in their own right.

Was this the appropriateness of the world, then? What some called 'coming full circle'? Here were two people who had started on their own, now being on their own once more. For once, I felt shut out of my parents' lives and I could not look upon them, for I felt that they had put themselves discretely away.

Chapter Six

We drove to the outskirts of Sikimpur and the Kohi Noor hotel.

A bellboy led the way to the bridal suite. The suite took up almost a quarter of the floor space on the top floor of the hotel, which had spread itself on the shores of Ishar Sagar. The bellboy, a spritely thing with a deep plum birth mark splashed across his left cheek, carried our luggage with great skill. He refused Sami's offer of help, though the luggage would have weighed as much as he did, and Sami rewarded him with a handsome tip.

I stood out on the balcony, allowing the lake air to bombard me with fresh droplets that penetrated through my make-up and stung the skin beneath. I gripped the rail tightly as Sami came alongside me. Taking a deep breath, I waited. *This is it*, I thought, *my time has come*. I did not really know what to do; actions and reactions, they would come together now and my body felt so unready, such a novice to that moment.

Ammaji had tried to talk to me, prepare me for what lay ahead, the ending of maidenhood. However, the mumbled lesson had stumbled with embarrassment when she had strayed briefly onto her own experience with Abbaji. Trying not to listen, I had sat firmly on my hands, wincing, with my eyes fixed on the ground. Finally, thankfully, Ammaji had let it go, exasperated and flustered.

'Your sisters were not so hard to talk to!'

Instead, she had left it to Laila to talk with me. My sister, with all her perspicacity, knew that I knew for, in my last year of school, Laila had borrowed a well-thumbed copy of a tease of a novel from a friend at college. She had waved it in front of my nose, talking loudly about it to show off her maturity, and then hidden it in her desk drawer, where I had found it and done some thumbing of my own.

When she came to see me, however, Laila had shaken her shiny head and muttered, 'I do not know how it is going to be with you. You sound so sure about marrying him, but you will not talk about it and, as usual, nobody really knows what you are thinking. You really are a *pugli*.'

For a moment, she had looked so dreadfully worried that I tried to reassure her.

'Everything will be all right. It is the way I am made; it is what I have done all my life.'

To this clumsy assurance, Laila had frowned.

'Your life until now has been a shelter for you. The world out there will not accept your foibles as we do.' She had shaken her head again. 'And you will be such an innocent in it.'

So, it was as an innocent in the world that I waited for my groom to take me as his wife. Sami placed his hands alongside mine on the balcony rail. His skin was taut and I could see the veins that were running through from fingertips to heart.

'What a lovely night,' he said. 'It does seem so perfect.' He turned to me, smiling and examining. 'I heard somebody tell Ammi that they had not seen such a beautiful bride for a very long time. I believe that they really meant it.' Then he whispered softly, his voice almost drowned out by the breeze with its lake spray and the waves from which it came. 'I certainly believe it.'

I held my breath again and waited for my life as a woman to begin, but my groom of almost six hours did not pull me to him, did not seal my lips with a passion but instead kissed me lightly on the cheek.

'You must be tired. It has been a long day and you must be ready for bed.'

In the surprise of his bland words I yawned, quite uncontrollably, and felt rude with it.

'It has been a long day,' I said, 'and a tiring one, but I think that I am still caught up in the splendour of it all.'

I gazed out across the amorphous bay and thought of Ammaji who had brought my day together so beautifully: the invitations, the flowers, the clothes, the jewellery, the linen; it had all been in pieces once and I had not realised how perfect they would be in their completion. Thinking this, I felt a sudden affection for her and I remembered a moment right at the end of my wedding.

It was as I had gathered the long swathes of my sari together and settled myself into the wedding car that I had heard Ammaji's voice call out to Sami, a plaintive plea in that then still night.

'Please take care of my daughter!'

Those words had rung loudly in my ears and I had turned quickly to look out of the back window at the fading figure, looking frail with hope and fear. I saw Abbaji put his arms about her so that her face was hidden from me, but I could see the gentle heaving of her shoulders and knew that Ammaji, whom I did not think could falter so, was crying uncontrollably into Abbaji's pristine new sherwani.

Sami and I stayed out on the balcony a while longer, talking of the day and the guests, the music and the poet, until the night air turned chilly. Then, I left him to his cigarette and went to disrobe, carefully removing layer upon layer of sari, blouse and underskirt. It was while I was attempting to fold my sari that Sami entered our vast dressing room.

'Why do you not leave that for now? Surely it can keep until the morning.' As he spoke, his eyes looked about the room, avoiding the spot where I stood.

Instinctively, I dropped the sari and folded my arms across my nightshift, a slight piece of material meant to be alluring. My reflection in the mirror, though, spoke of a child, so slight and small, hardly old enough to be given up to her wedding night.

Sami bent down, picked up my fallen sari and handed me one end of it. I unfolded my arms and took the end that was offered to me, holding it high across my chest.

'I had no idea how heavy wedding saris are. There is so much to it, and just for one day.' Sami shook his head with incredulity as we started folding the brocade, the gold thread, so lovingly designed, so delicately stitched. The sari fabric was a red that was not the traditional crimson red of weddings, a colour that I did not suit, for it made my complexion appear florid.

Even Ammaji had agreed with me.

'No, you will never be able to wear the bridal red,' she had observed. 'It would just appear gaudy on you. In fact, you would look like a blood clot. Well, I will have to ask your Abbaji's aunt in Rajasthan to deal with it. She knows the seamstress, Hazoor Begum, well and I am sure that she will be able to design just the right sari for you. I will send her a photograph of you so she can make a start. That way, we will not have to go to Jaipur until later. Yes, she designed the Rani of Kanshu's sari. It was the most wondrous piece of work, *bohot pyara cam*; I have

47

seen the pictures in *Shama* magazine. They say that it was so heavy with jewels and embroidery that the Rani almost collapsed with the weight of it. And she is a big-boned girl, very capable. Can you imagine having such a garment made for wearing in May? With all the heat of a Rajasthan summer?'

'I do not want a sari that will make me feel ill,' I had said with a determined look.

In response, Ammaji had nodded impatiently.

'Yes, yes. For you, it will have to be more simple. Nothing so dazzling. I will explain when I talk to Phupuamma. She will understand, she knows you well.'

And so it was. The sari that Hazoor Begum designed for me glided through my hands like a skater on ice, but it was still heavy.

As I held it, I said to Sami, 'I think it is why brides spend most of their wedding day sitting down. Wandering around with this on would really have tired me out. I cannot understand why women have to be so... so, ornamental, just for one day'.

'No, Ammi would agree with you on that.' Sami drew the gold-spun *pallo* of my sari up in front of him. 'She says that it is just something else that a woman has to put up with for the pomp and pride of the society that we live in. It is just as well that I do not have a sister. Ammi would probably have had her marry in Gandhiji's home-spun cotton.'

I laughed at this while Sami concentrated on disentangling a pearl from a piece of stitching. Slowly, the sari became a folded rectangle of lavish red and gold, silk and embroidery. It shone as the light danced from one of its threads to the next.

'Your mother is very political, is she not?' I began to remove my bracelets, drawing them over my right wrist and easing them over my hand.

'Oh yes, and a great feminist, also.' Sami sat down on a nearby armchair. 'Or at least, she likes to give that impression. For all her fierce independence and belief that women should not be made to rely on men, she misses Baba very much. She lost a lot of herself when he died. It is as if she could not bear to be parted completely from him, and so she buried some of herself with him in the ground.'

Yes, I thought to myself, *that is a good way of putting it*. It was the widowed presence I remembered, sitting almost still that afternoon when my parents had gone to pay their respects.

Sami rose from his chair to help me with my expensive trinkets. The bones of my left hand were not as supple as they should have been, so unused were they to being forced into bracelets a size too small for them. I struggled to remove them; three solid gold rings with seven clinking glass bangles in between each pair.

'Have you some cream?' Sami asked me. 'Face cream, hand cream, you know…'

'I think so, maybe.' I nodded to a shiny patterned bag that sat on a chair, fat with its array of toiletries that had been bought for me. 'In there. There should be something of that sort in there.'

Sami rummaged through the bag, pulling out fancy, colourful bottles of perfume, rosewater tonic and, finally, a pot of Pond's face cream.

'This will do.'

He rubbed a dot of it, the size of a pea, into the solid knuckles of my hand. Deftly, with his lithe and gentle hands, he teased the bracelets off, four at a time.

I rubbed my hand when he had finished, rubbing fast the areas were the bangles had left their mark. Then I smiled awkwardly at Sami and thanked him. The smile stayed there a while after the words had gone, as though I did not know how to have it gone.

Sami looked at me thoughtfully. 'What a funny smile you have. I am not quite sure what to make of it.' He handed back my pot of Pond's cream to me and walked quietly away.

That night, I fell asleep in a bed so large that Sami and I could have made snow angels side by side without touching each other. I climbed into the bed alone, the coolness of Sea Island cotton lightening my tired limbs, and my head resting on the goose down pillow that smelled of a flower freshness. My eyes began to close, drooping with the scent of jasmine. Sami was out on the balcony, having his second cigarette of married life. I wondered if he was inhaling some courage out of the tar and tobacco mix.

Suddenly, I felt very brave. And then, just as suddenly, I did not. Millions of women had given themselves to this same moment and, in that way, I was not unique. But my heart pounded still, for those women were not here, were not me, and whatever was to follow would happen to me alone. My body was to be touched, gripped and used in a way that it had not known before. Images flooded through my racing mind; my body responded by tightening, moving and ultimately wearing itself out. Slowly, slowly, slowly, I fell fast asleep; a sleep that did not bring me dreams on that, my wedding night, only a deep, unflinching slumber.

I awoke with the dawn peering in on me, and Sami crumpled up on the other side of the bed. His snores came through the air as gentle ripples of sound. His face was serene and his hair wet with the heat of the night. He was wearing a pristine white pyjama kurta and his sherwani was flung over a chair sitting quietly in a corner. I looked upon him with a steady stare and instinctively touched my body in the spaces below, where I was still intact.

Quietly, I rose and washed, feeling a strangeness in my surroundings and within myself. I did not want to wake Sami, to face my new husband. I did not understand why he had left me to sleep alone on our wedding night.

I moved about the room, getting dressed, tidying my clothes away, preparing to leave our bridal suite. In time, Sami woke. He looked slightly dishevelled, his hair standing upright and he was yawning.

'Ah, I see you are already awake. I must have been very tired, for it is unusual for me to sleep this late.'

He turned away, stretching and slipped into the bathroom, where I heard him whistling softly as he shaved.

The rest of our honeymoon was spent in the coastal town of Gesmir, a two hour aeroplane journey from Sikimpur. Beautiful Gesmir was hidden away behind a curve of land which, itself, stretched away from the main body of the country. As a thriving fishing town, its harbour was untidy with the wooden and battered boats of Gesmir's fishing fleet, and its bazaars filled with the smells and flesh of the sea.

The sun-baked fishermen, dressed only in tattered lunghis, crouched low on their hunkers amongst the shingle and watched the wealthy visitors that passed by them, neglecting their nets for a moment's curiosity.

Often, Sami would stop to watch them, and then to talk with them. I could see in his eyes how he longed to jump into one of their rickety boats and sail away into that expanse of blue sea, free from this land on which his two feet were so firmly planted. For some reason, he did not ask them; instead, he would look at me with a hunger about him, so that I wished he could say those simple words to the men whom he so envied.

Our hotel, the magnificent Amber Palace, had been built on the shores of the Indian Ocean. It lay in a sort of swoon; not extravagant, nor yet flashy, it glowed like an understated gem; a pearl rather than a sapphire. Occasionally, a lonely fishing boat would bob out the day there, but mostly the view from our balcony remained unchecked. There were moments when, standing with the white sand gleaming and the sea shimmering below, I had to grip the rail hard to stop myself from leaping out into that indefinite expanse. The fault lay with the hypnotic lapping of the waves and the moon hanging resplendent in the night sky; who, then, could blame me for wanting to reach out for them?

Gesmir town offered itself without restraint to honeymooners; there were intimate restaurants, picturesque boulevards and lantern-lit parks. In the grounds of the Hawa Mahal, once a British Residency and now owned by the Maharajah of Gesmir, there had been planted a maze. Known as the Garland, it was a twisting and turning of green-hedged paths through which jasmine and moti flowers protruded like white polka dots.

At night, the Garland was lit with fires that flickered on lecterns and threw up shadows along the fragrant, white petals. Candles floated on the dark pool at its centre and the air was muted with the ending of the day.

At night, the Garland - like the rest of Gesmir - buzzed with romance. And during the day? Well, what honeymooners rose before noon, anyway?

Actually, we did, for we were not natural honeymooners. Sami and I rarely held hands strolling through the park, did not gaze into each other's eyes over candle-lit dinners, and we visited the Garland during the bright sunshine of the day as well as under the hush of night. The city of Gesmir surely frowned upon us, for we were failing to appreciate all that it had laid out for its Love's Apprentices.

And then, one balmy evening, when all was doused in silence, we finally did become lovers. We found each other under the sheets, our limbs surprised by the contact of unfamiliar skin and flesh. Suddenly, the patience and tenderness of Sami turned to fervour and an open desire. I closed my eyes tightly as pain and pleasure took their turn with my body, which became taut with an untried urgency and my breath that hastened with this yearning.

Afterwards, we let each other slide away, embarrassed by the obvious passion and the assuaging flood that followed, and waited till the heat had subsided, the heat that took me by surprise. I lay on my side, slowing my breathing down deliberately, quietening it back to normal and forcing my body to relax. In my mind, there hung a blurred confusion. Whenever I had imagined this moment in my marriage, since I had known with whom it would be, I had not allowed it to be anything but civilised. A very upright thing. Like Sami, my husband, very proper.

The next morning I woke to find myself alone. It was a good time to be awake; nine o'clock, neither too early nor yet too late. I heard Sami whistling before I saw him, coming out of the dressing room dressed very casually and smiling. I thought of the night before and was embarrassed by the pleasure sensation I had felt. Sami, in contrast, appeared nonchalant.

'I have done it!' he announced and sat down on the edge of the bed. 'I have asked one of the fishermen if I can go out fishing with him this morning.' Then his face fell. 'Is that all right with you? I am sorry, I did not think. I had wanted to ask for so long, and then this morning, when you were asleep, I went for a walk and found myself with the courage to approach them. But I should have asked you first.' He looked forlorn, as though a gift had been snatched away from him.

I shook my head. 'Of course you must go. I will be glad if you do, for it will allow me to visit the Hawa Mahal and look around it properly.'

This was better, I thought. Time spent apart, so I could slowly become used to being a woman, on my own, in my own time. I wondered whether the events of last night had changed Sami, whether the release of wild energy had in some way loaned him courage.

So, we honeymooners went our separate ways. After breakfast, Sami walked me to the gates of the Hawa Mahal and we said good-bye, not with a kiss or even a hug, but a congenial wave of the hand. As I went through the gates, Sami walked away jauntily, light-footed and humming, without looking back.

I wandered into the quiet grounds of the Hawa Mahal. The doors of the old Residency were flung open for morning tea and cakes that were being served out on the lawns. I ambled to the back of it, past the sleeping Garland, whose mystic charm had become almost lost with the daylight and to a far corner where lay a wide patch of land, lush green with red roses along its border.

A broken wall ran around the garden, crumbling as the creepers took it over, leaving it forlornly picturesque. A path ran through the middle of this large garden, at the end of which stood the Bibighar, a modest stone home built for someone a very long time ago. New paint had been applied to its walls and a gardener was kneeling by its path, digging up a few rough weeds from the soil. He looked up, surprised, and stood up a little unsteadily.

'*Namaste* Memsahib, have you come to look at the Bibighar?'

I nodded, with my eyes on the unprepossessing building.

'It was built for Governor Pinkerton's Indian wife, was it not?'

'Oh yes, indeed.' The old gardener cocked his head to one side and grinned. 'That is the rumour, and most probably the truth. She was the daughter of the Rajah of Gesmir, a minor ruler of little consequence, but still it is a dangerous story. An Indian princess running away to live with a *ferenghi*! They could not marry, of course, for what holy man would carry out such a forbidden ceremony? Besides, they would both have been killed if they had been discovered, so it is lucky for them that the Rajah did not pursue those rumours.'

The gardener lowered his voice, as if to share a secret with a fellow conspirator. 'Although, they do say that much money was given to the Rajah by the Raj to let the matter drop. Of course, all this was a long time ago, so who knows what the truth really is. But one thing is certain, the Governor and his Indian bride lived together until she died, and had a number of children, too, although I do not think any of them survived childhood. Some people said it was the curse of the Rajah for their thoughtlessness.'

It was a sad story that had lost none of its romance with age. I thanked the gardener and gave him a few *paisa* for entertaining me with a story that I already knew. He seemed happy, pocketed the money and took to his task again, kneeling on a folded piece of towel, grubby with the soil that he dug into.

I hung around a little longer, gazing about at the young trees that were growing upright to the blue sky and the bright colours of the bougainvillea that was climbing over the walls, and imagining what the Bibighar looked like on the inside.

As I hesitated, the gardener spoke up again. 'I am afraid Memsahib, that you cannot go any further, for the Bibighar now belongs to the Maharajah's daughters.' He looked over his shoulder with a disapproving stare at the Residency. 'They have very noisy parties there with their friends, and they are digging up the lovely garden at the back for a swimming pool. They will be walking around almost *nanga* with their friends.' He turned back to me with a look of disgust that slowly changed to pride. 'And I cannot let you in even for a few extra *paisa*, for I am charged with being the guard of the Bibighar as well as its gardener.'

With that the conscientious man began to dig again, moving the soil around and prising roots from their places. He was concentrating hard on his work now and I was a disturbance, no longer wanted, and so I turned back towards the Hawa Mahal. It was lunchtime, so my stomach told me.

The Mahal was a large sandstone building, not as imposing now that it had lost the authority of the British Raj, but more friendly with its carved, wooden shutters and earthenware flower pots that lined the steps. The pictures on the walls inside were mostly of the past: Maharajahs on tiger hunts, sitting proudly in their Rolls-Royces, or riding high on elaborately decorated elephants; there were very few of the Raj occupancy.

Lunch was being laid out in the proud old ballroom that had been transformed into a restaurant. Tables with neat, white tablecloths lined up in rows, and waiters standing ready to serve. I was made more hungry by the sight of them and by the rich smells that were hanging in the air. The waiter, who showed me to my seat, smiled reverently, as though he had waited all that morning to serve me.

I ate my lunch with a fine appreciation: plain rice, fried *behndi* and a chick pea *daal*. I filled my greed soon enough and stayed there a while, exchanging pleasantries with the other guests who looked at me with an ill-disguised curiosity: a lone woman dining out was a most rare occurrence. The waiter, too, had been surprised when I had ordered dishes for only one.

Having done nothing to explain my solitude, I soon tired of their overt interest and took my tea out on the lawns of Hawa Mahal. It was here that Sami found me, striding cheerfully up the long driveway, smiling with his whole body and moving with an unalloyed spirit.

'I have had a most wonderful afternoon,' he said brightly. 'I am very glad that I finally made it onto the sea. I caught five milkfish, which is a very good catch the fishermen say, because they are strong and fast and, therefore, difficult to catch. I have asked the rickshaw wallah to take them to the hotel. I hope he does; I gave him a good enough tip for doing so.' Sami looked anxious and then shrugged. 'He looked like an honest man.' He paused to order a cup of milky *chai* from the smartly dressed waiter before turning back to me with an apology. 'I am sorry, I have been talking too much. How has your morning been?'

'Yes, you *have* been talking a lot but it was good to hear you. I am glad that you finally went. You look very happy, as though you had a lot of fun.'

Sami leant back in his chair and placed his arms behind his head.

'I did. The waters of the ocean are so vast, a seemingly endless entity. I felt eternal, as though, by being there, I was at the very essence of life. And to be there with the men who do it every day was wonderful. They have such a simple outlook on their life, you know, they love the sea as much as they fear and respect it.'

Sami talked on as though he had been out with the old man of Hemingway's story. Eventually, he stopped and looked abashed once again.

'Now, it really is your turn. I will be quiet. I promise.'

I laughed at him, not the least put out, for he had taken on the persona of the young boy while he talked. I told him about my morning and he listened intently, nodding and sipping his drink. I told him of the gardener and the Maharajah's daughters, and also the story of the Bibighar.

'It must have been a very lonely existence for the princess.' I ended my tale with sadness. 'I don't suppose she ever came out of her grounds.'

Sami shook his head.

'No, she could not; it was not safe for her to do so. Not until she died and her body was taken away for burial. The Governor had her buried just behind the walls of the old ballroom, for it was said that she loved to listen to the music of the Residency band when there was a grand State ball. When she was alive, he had a little window put into the Bibighar and a peephole chiselled out of the garden wall so that she could catch a glimpse of the ladies in their ball gowns.'

'How different the Hawa Mahal is from Sikimpur's British Residency,' I said. 'That is very staid in comparison to all this pink and marble.'

'Well, that one has been converted into a college; your old college, in fact, the Royal College of Arts. It was also my father's. He taught there, you know, and later became its Dean, two – no, three - years before his death.'

I had not known that about his father.

Sami carried on. 'Oh yes, he used to take me there often after school and allowed me to wander around the place while he finished his work. I did a lot of my homework in the grounds. Well, round at the Executioner's Spot anyway. It was very peaceful there.'

I shivered and frowned.

'Peaceful? Amongst the ghosts of the executed? I cannot imagine spending any length of time there. I only visited it once in all the time that I was there, and I thought it the most horrid place I had ever known.'

The Executioner's Spot was a patch of bare earth, some five metres square. The high wall that ran alongside this rough ground was splashed with the brown stains of dried blood and dotted with small circular holes. It was the spot where prisoners were shot at the time of the Second Mutiny; later, it was the petty criminals who met their end there. In a corner of the patch there was also a ragged stone plinth. Once, a hangman's wooden pole had stood upright there; now it was broken and its splinters strewn about the ground.

'No, you are right,' replied Sami, 'it is not a nice place, not when you think about these things for long. But I suppose, I was too serious about my own work then to consider the souls of those wretched men. When Baba was made Dean, he tried to have all the bullet holes covered over, but there were too many. Even if they had done so, they could not remove the stains. He would say that it was the memories of the dead refusing to be erased.

Sami fell back into a kind of reverie, and I wondered whether he was thinking about his father, so said nothing for a while, but then a half smile appeared briefly on his lips. I looked at him keenly. What thoughts had put such a smile upon his face? Surely not just those of his father? He noticed my deliberate gaze and blushed a ruby red.

'Well, as you say it was a quiet place. Nobody ever went there.' His manner became suddenly guarded.

'I did not say that.' I raised my eyebrows with inquiry. 'But you are saying it now.' I leant forward and looked directly into his eyes. 'Now, why was it a good thing that nobody ever went there? Surely, that cannot have anything to do with your studies?' I was teasing him for his blushing, but his reaction surprised me with its unexpected starkness.

'No, I mean...' He coughed suddenly, two, three times and then fell into a flustered silence, looking only at the ground and frowning.

'Well?' I persisted.

Sami jumped up out of his chair, which tilted awkwardly. He steadied it with his hand.

'Come, it is time to go back,' he said. 'I will go and pay for your dinner and my *chai*. I want to see if my milkfish have been delivered safely. I shall ask the chef to cook them for our dinner tonight.' Then he added brightly, 'I thoroughly enjoyed my time fishing. Thank you for giving it to me.'

Sami strode away from me in a most deliberate manner, and I was left with an unsatiated curiosity. It appeared that Sami's breast held a secret: one that he was not yet ready to give up. It made me uncertain, all at once, of a man who I thought could hold no surprises. Surely, he was straight and transparent, with no lingering guile? But I seemed to have been wrong. It was a surprise, this realisation, but I could not raise a voice to question it. Instead, I let it go.

In my head, I heard Abbaji's words 'Each one of us has a hold of something that cannot be seen, may not be known. And the more that others pry into it, the more our convoluted souls hold on. It is best, sometimes, to let these things be.'

That night we ate grilled milkfish with plain rice and a ginger-spiced *daal*. Later still, we made love again; a flustering, urgent affair.

Just before noon the next day we left Gesmir, flying above the Amber Palace, with the fishermen in their boats and the Hawa Mahal specks now – toys, almost - when once they had been so real.

Chapter Seven

We arrived back at Sikimpur International Airport some two hours later and made our way through its small, cramped building. There were few travellers about, most people still preferring to journey by train - the lazy winding through Hindustan's rugged countryside, and the interminable stops at its lively stations. It was only the business and tourist classes who took to the skies over India's sprawling landscape.

Outside, in the pale sunshine of October, the Altairs' chauffeur, Malik, was waiting for us, solemn in his freshly-pressed uniform. His moustache had been carefully oiled and the rim of his cap polished. He did not smile when he saw us, but salaamed politely and opened the car door, his eyes fixed on the tarmac beneath his shining, black shoes. It was an important occasion for him, bringing the Sahib and his bride back from their honeymoon, and he was overly serious with it. Satisfied that he had settled us into his beautifully valeted car, Malik busied himself with loading our luggage away.

Sami talked to him briefly in the car, asking after his mother who was in hospital. Malik replied that she was well in a voice that was flat and dull; an aeroplane droning above the clouds. I told him that I would visit her and his narrow face broke into a sunny smile.

'*Apki mehrbani*, Sahira Bibi.'

Ammi, Sami's mother, was awaiting our arrival with an eager smile. She came running down the steps of the house as the car crunched slowly along the drive. With her arms flung open, she hugged Sami many times before she turned to me. At first she hesitated, seeming not to know what to do with me. Her smile, so wide for her son, was reduced to a faint new moon.

'*Meri beyti*,' she said at last. She hugged me lightly. 'How good it is to see you both. You must be hungry.'

'Yes,' I answered untruthfully. We had eaten a hearty breakfast that morning, but Ammi had welcomed us with such a great energy and joy that it was obvious she had missed her son dreadfully and been looking forward to his return with much anticipation.

From the house came the aroma of roasted *zeera*, fresh *dhania* and newly ground *mehti*. In the garden, the flowers that Sami had planted had been watered every day, and the lawns newly trimmed. The bougainvillea had come into flower and the mangoes awaiting their new buds.

Sami led his mother in, his arm guiding her gently up the steps. I followed behind, tracing the scents of spices into the house, which had been swept and finely polished. There were new blooms all around, pots and vases of white lilies, pink camellias and red poppies.

'The house is looking very lovely.' I spoke with a voice that trembled as it intruded. What was I in this place, where these two people knew each other so well? My parents' home had been my cocoon, and now that I had shed it I was not sure how to be a butterfly. I had landed on a new flower but was unsure how to settle there.

Sami sniffed the air appreciatively.

'I am certainly hungry now.'

He squeezed his mother's shoulder and kissed her on the cheek, smiling down at her upturned face. There was a love there that lay deep within each of them, unspoken, but not so shy as to be undemonstrated.

As we took our places, lunch was laid on the white linen tablecloth. Ceramic serving bowls and plates, not so grand a table as that set by Ammaji, but then my mother dealt with the Shamshad household.

We talked of Gesmir over lunch: Sami still full of the sea air and his morning amongst the fishermen, and I regaling the tale of the Bibighar. Ammi listened with great interest and smiles, and told us of her honeymoon spent with Sami's father, sailing in a houseboat on Lake Wular and walking the snow-laden mountains of Srinagar.

'It was very beautiful there. The Mughals were right when they called it Paradise on Earth. Everyone should visit it once in their lives. Just before they die, I think, would be best.'

I nodded for I remembered well my holiday there.

'It is the best place to forget about one's troubles, Ammaji says.'

'Then, it is where Indira Gandhi should be.'

The *Times of India* had been brought in and put, neatly folded, just beside Sami's left hand. He was reading the headlines telling of the internal unrest that was engulfing the National Congress Party.

Ammi looked across at him. 'Yes, indeed,' she said. 'It is a difficult time for Mrs Gandhi, and one that will set up the rest of her Presidency. It is important for her, and for this great nation of ours, that she makes the correct decision. She has just come to power, so who can tell whether she will allow the party to be split?'

Sami shook his head. 'No, surely even she is not so stubborn as to allow that. The National Congress Party is her father's legacy, after all.'

'Yes, but it went through a great many changes under his leadership,' replied Ammi, 'and she was witness to its many faces. It is something that we learnt from our battles and negotiations with the British, how to evolve to gain the upper hand. It was the British who taught us how to turn words to our favour.'

'The days of the British are in the past, Ammi. We cannot be forever blaming them for our own problems, especially now that Mrs Gandhi seems set on making enemies of the Americans.'

'Oh, but that is not entirely of her doing. After all, it was not she who called their national leader a witch!' Ammi's voice began to rise in her defence of Indira Gandhi.

'That is a rumour that has been denied by the Americans. Besides, what can we gain by making an ally of Russia? They are not our natural friends. Historically speaking, the Russians can never be true friends of the Indians. Have you forgotten the part they played in the Great Game? They too-'

'That world is also gone,' Ammi broke in. 'It is further back in time than our disputes with the British. No, no, Mrs Gandhi is right to form an alliance with the Russians. After all, she has more socialist leanings and the Russians will need friends.'

'Ah, you have been talking to your socialist friends again.' Sami rolled his eyes.

'Not just my socialist friends,' Ammi smiled mischievously. 'But my feminist friends, too.'

Sami groaned.

'Mrs Dirwani?'

'Yes, Mrs Dirwani. She believes that Mr Desai, with all his conservatism, cannot stand to be dictated to by a woman and is forcing a split in the Party.'

Their conversation greatly interested me. I came from a mildly political family, mild like coconut milk. Politics was discussed in a precise way: Abbaji spoke of it in terms of finance, while Ammaji of its effect on village life and the price rises, the personalities of politics were rarely analysed.

Suha had been delighted when Indira Gandhi had come to power, not for any great respect of her leadership, but because she was a woman and the daughter of Nehru, the historical Pundit Nehru, whose image Suha had cut out of the newspaper when she was fifteen years old and kept ever since. For Suha, it was more the romance of conflict and revolution than the detail of reason and counter-reason that intrigued her.

Laila, on the other hand, did not care for politics at all. She was more musical; she had more of an aesthetic brain. When she was still unmarried, the persistent crackling of vinyl records turning mesmerically on Abbaji's old gramophone would flood out from her room. She took lessons in mastering the sitar and was elegant seated on a rug, her legs crossed with one knee held high, her light fingers plucking gracefully at one taut string after the other.

The only thing that would take Laila away from her music was the sound of the bangle woman at the door. Then she and Suha would run excitedly out into the sunlight to see the glass bangles jangling on their pieces of string, shining in a myriad of colours. The bangle woman would lay them out on a white square of muslin cloth, delighted with my sisters' enthusiasm, knowing that she would sell well at this house. She would let Laila and Suha choose, encouraging them ever so slightly towards the more expensive ones.

'How pretty they will look on your slender arms,' she would say. 'All your friends will be so jealous.'

Then, she would catch sight of me, my wrist held tightly by Ammaji in a determined persuasion towards her.

'Come, Sahira Bibi,' she would smile enticingly, 'I have just the bangles for you. Not so very shiny but just as pretty as you are.'

'*Dekko kesay hey.*' Ammaji would thrust me down by my shoulders and I would have to sit cross-legged beside the bangle woman, bored and sulky as she brought out five, ten, fifteen bangles and prised them with great effort over the big bone of my hand so that they rattled wildly on my small wrists. Then, having satisfied Ammaji, I would run off to climb the mango trees where the fruit was ripening into plump pods of yellow and red, or lie in the grass reading, and somehow breaking every single bangle, quite by accident, before nightfall.

That evening my parents came to dinner. Abbaji hugged me tightly as he used to when I was a child. He looked at me with a sentimental gaze for I was now something he had lost.

'Are you happy?' he asked.

I assured him that I was and he hugged me again, whispering into my ear. '*Achi baachi*, you have made me very happy too.'

His breath was sweet and his closely-trimmed beard brushed softly against my cheek. He suddenly became new to me, much more than grey flecks of hair upon an ageing face. I squeezed his arm affectionately.

Ammaji, having talked awhile with Sami, came over and untangled us. She kissed my cheek and held onto me.

'You are a grown woman now,' she said quietly into my ear. She let go and searched my face. 'And you are glowing.' That was all that she could say, for her voice became unsteady with that emotion that comes with finding that your child has moved away from you.

She gathered herself together quickly and I was glad that there were no tears. Instead, she looked at me critically.

'Now that you are married you must pay more attention to yourself. A little make-up and some jewellery would be more appropriate. I am not asking that you drip with gold and diamonds or that you paint yourself like a courtesan but you need to present yourself as a *naya dhulhan*. Your in-laws, and indeed your Abbaji and I, have given you some nice sets of jewellery, and they are not for hiding away. You will be getting quite a few invitations now as newlyweds and people will be most inquisitive as to your *jehez*. Do not forget the households that you are now representing.'

Ammi came to join us. She hugged Ammaji.

'Come now, you two,' she said. 'I know you have much to talk about, but dinner is ready and we must not let it go cold.' Ammi took Ammaji's arm and guided her to the dining room. 'Sit beside me,' she said to her. 'We, too, have matters to discuss.'

Ammaji nodded. 'Oh yes,' she replied, 'I am most interested in what you are doing.'

I watched them take their seats, curious at this exchange. Ammaji and Ammi had been distant friends before; now, of course, they shared a closer relationship. But what else did they have to be so intimate about? Ammi was very political; she was outspoken and an extrovert, while Ammaji was more an introvert, more domestic, and yet more anxious over her family. It was true that, in their different ways, they stood outside the core of Sikimpur society: Ammi for her views and Ammaji for her background.

It was the reason why Ammaji was always so concerned about me; it was why she saw the need for the rich jewels and fine clothing.

'It is all very well having the Shamshad name,' she had told me on many occasions, 'but you must also try to fit in. You do not understand how hurtful people can be about even the smallest failings of others. They will make them big and important, and speak ill of you behind your back, while all the time smiling at your face. It is not a kind society, the Sikimpur one. It is full of tongues that are sharpened by petty jealousies.'

Ammaji knew all about the malicious nature of Indian high society because she had not been born into it, and so had tried that bit harder to make sure all that she did was very correct. When she and Abbaji had married, there had been much talk and much hurt for her, the idle tongues of women wagging:

'Shamshad's eldest son has married a village girl. How can that have happened?' 'Obviously she has done some sort of jadoo on him. He would never do such a thing of his own free will.'

It was only because Ammaji had been accepted by Abbaji's family into the House of Shamshad that she was not completely ostracised by the other society women. But she knew that, behind their silly platitudes and loud welcomes, the tittle-tattle was one of cruel displeasure.

Over dinner, Ammaji and Ammi talked, their voices low but not conspiratorial, an earnest conversation. Occasionally they laughed, and it was good to see Ammaji looking comfortable and at ease with another woman who was not her kin. Her face was relaxed, the tiny lines that were beginning to emerge no longer ageing her but instead enhancing her beauty. Her irises became polished orbs again and her cheeks were flushed with a graphic excitement. She looked much as she had done when I was a child, a gentle beauty. Opposite me sat Abbaji and Sami. They too, talked freely, Abbaji asking about Sami's famous invention.

'I am not so familiar with all this computer technology, I am more comfortable with agricultural machinery and that, of course, is more mechanical. I would like to learn more but I do not think I have the energy, or indeed the brainpower. Computer technology seems quite abstract to me, requiring more imagination than I have.'

'I do not think my work requires any more intelligence than what is needed to farm the land,' replied Sami. 'It is a different way of thinking, that is all. After all, I do not understand the seasons or crop rotation in the way you do. Now, my invention requires only that you understand the first rule of thermodynamics. It is a way of keeping metals cool under conditions that require very high temperatures. It dissipates the energy away from the precious metal core. This has been done before, of course, but my method uses a self-regulating device moulded onto the outside of the metal and, because it is inert, it will not interfere with the fundamental properties of the metal. The computer language that I have developed serves to regulate this whole system.'

Abbaji rubbed his beard, grasping carefully at the information that was coming his way.

'That is where the particular genius of it lies,' he said, slowly. 'Of course, we would also have a use for it in our farm machinery. At the moment, we must rest our tractors many times during the day to avoid their overheating in the high temperatures of the summer. This affects both our efficiency and also our productivity. Now, do you think that is something you can help with?'

Sami put his head to one side.

'There is no reason why we should not be able to do that, eventually. Currently, we are only able to prevent malfunctioning in very simple systems. It will take some time, and much thought, to adapt it for larger systems.'

'Yes, of course. A tractor that is having a great number of components is a different matter altogether, for there are many cogs and pistons and such, that interact one with another.'

'It is, indeed, a more complex matter, but not one that is impossible.' Sami smiled at Abbaji. 'It is, as I have said, a question of adaptation.'

Abbaji blushed and could not hide the intense pleasure that this discussion gave him. He sat up a little straighter.

'I will tell Uthman about this. He will be most interested. He is part of your generation and always interested in new innovations.'

Ammi rose from her chair to switch on the light. The light bulb flickered briefly, wavering before coming on fully. I broke off a piece of roti and dipped it into the *bagaray begun*, a dish of aubergine and ground roasted peanuts. As I was chewing, Abbaji looked round at me and winked. His face was lit up by a brilliant light; the soul aglow through his eyes. He was enjoying himself immensely; he felt on a par with Sami, his genius son-in-law. I smiled back at him, glad for him.

Chapter Eight

A few days later, I was in my bedroom laying out clothes for a dinner engagement at Professor Goldberg's house. There was a knock on the door. It was Ammi.

'I have just come to make sure that you are all right.'

Her pale, leather *chappals* clipped lightly over the stone floor, and her feet were pretty in them. Her feet were pretty because they were well-looked after, for Ammi, who had no great regard for finery and cosmetics, could not stand to have ugly feet. Once a week, a pedicurist would come to Gulabi Ghar and take charge of Ammi's well-worn feet. She would pumice them, keep them supple with sweet orange oil and apply orangewood sticks to the cuticles. Then, Ammi would have her nails painted, simple colours with tinted rose oils.

This ritual was Ammi's one vanity: '*The earth of India is very harsh on the feet,*' she once told me. '*Sami's father, being a shy man, had kept his eyes down when we were married, and later told me that he had fallen in love with my feet before he had even seen my face., And so, I like to keep them looking nice.*'

She came into my room that day with freshly-polished feet and wandered over to where I had neatly laid out my sari, touching it gently.

'This is the one you have decided to wear tonight?'

I nodded, wondering whether she was annoyed that I had not asked her opinion, but she looked quietly happy with my choice.

'I am pleased; it is one that I bought especially for you. I thought its sea-green colour would suit you.' She placed her hand under it and, lifting it up, looked over at me. 'Yes, I believe it will suit you very well.'

Her hands then passed to my jewellery set, the *nauratang*: gems of topaz, diamond, ruby, emerald, coral, pearl, sapphire and garnet set in gold.

'I am not so sure about this set, though. It is very pretty, of course; *nauratang*, by its nature, will go with most outfits, but it is a little fussy for this sari.' I saw at once that she was right. The *nauratang* was too playful; its many colours would clash with the simplicity of the sari.

'The pearls, on the other hand,' she continued. 'I think perhaps that the beauty of your sari will be heightened by them.'

I pulled open a drawer in the walnut dresser and brought out the red velvet box which held my pearls. I placed them on the sea-green silk sari and looked up at Ammi, laughing softly. 'Yes, I do believe you are right. You have more of an eye for this than I do.'

Ammi waved her finger at me. 'You are teasing me now. But that is good. I am pleased that you feel you can do so.' Then she became serious, moving away from the bed so that she had her back to me. 'There is no point in having such brilliance and hiding it away. It is not an indulgence or vanity but perhaps it is gratitude we should feel. And, when is a better time to wear these than when you are young and free? I wish that I had taken advantage of my youth, and then...' She cocked her head to one side. 'If I had had a daughter, I think I would have celebrated her wedding with great extravagance.'

I remembered Sami's words about Ammi's preference for a rough cotton wedding dress. He was wrong about that, then. Maybe he had forgotten that his mother was yet a woman after all.

Ammi came back to me, saying, 'For a long time I did not miss not having a daughter of my own. Sami's father had hoped to have a daughter after Sami, but it was not to be, and we were happy enough without this second gift, but then, when he died...'

Her voice trailed off as she stood still for a moment, frozen it appeared, with thoughts that were passing through her. 'I, too, wished for a daughter, selfishly you see, for someone to stay close to me. Sami, of course, was a dutiful son, caring and always wanting to do his best for me; but he was a boy, nonetheless, and therefore not so used to being at home. He had his friends and his hobbies, and I did not want to restrain him.'

I went to her and put my arm around her shoulder, for her voice had become low. She was smaller than I was and could easily have laid her head on my shoulder, but I suppose the newness of our relationship stopped her from doing so. She looked up at me with her wet eyes.

'Still, maybe now I can have a daughter. I know that you have your mother, but Allah has been generous and granted her three girls, so maybe she can afford to be generous in her turn and allow me one of them.'

'I am sure Ammaji can do that,' I replied. 'Besides, I am sure that I am easily shared.'

'You are a good girl, Sahira. I was very happy when Sami said that he wanted to marry you. He has made a good choice.' She bent my head down low and kissed my forehead. 'Now, we must be getting ready. We cannot be late for Professor Goldberg, although it is more than likely that we shall find ourselves waiting for him. No doubt Sami will come up soon, wandering what is taking us such a long time.'

She left the room and I slowly got ready. I should have hurried but all my energy had been removed and replaced by an overwhelming sadness, and also a great deal of gladness, and the two emotions played with my heart for a very long time.

I liked Professor Goldberg, my one-time lecturer at Sikimpur College. An American by birth, he had left the uncertainty of post-war Chicago and travelled to the Middle East, where he spent almost two years witnessing the drama of human conflict and, some said, even participating in it. It was rumoured that the good professor had joined the Fedayeen in Palestine, memorised the whole of the Quran, learnt to speak fluent Hebrew and spent three months in an Israeli jail. After prison, he had decided to move on, trekking through the countries that lay between, until he arrived in Sikimpur.

These stories were the wheels of a well-churned rumour mill, as I have said, but they suited the wild-haired scholar well, for he presented quite a sight: energetic and grey-eyed, dressed as he always was in a cotton pyjama kurta. Two things were certain, though. The first was that he had been deeply affected by the death of Sami's father, Professor Altair, and the second, that he was a master pianist.

The Professor played in much the same way as he looked, with wild abandon. His hair twisted and curled, and he rarely played mellow tunes, preferring instead those pieces that were lively and dramatic. As a host, however, he was more relaxed: guests had been known to be left alone for up to an hour while he saw to a particular correspondence or finished a game of solitaire.

This particular evening, we found Professor Goldberg sitting outside on the grass, his legs dangling into a small sunken pool.

The night was lit up by small lanterns hanging from nails along the wall of his bungalow. Fallen leaves from the overhanging branches of a peepal tree floated upon the water's still surface. In the Professor's hand was a book, a translation of Tagore's *The Gardener*. He was engrossed, looking up startled when his servant coughed loudly.

'Your guests are here, Professor Sahib.' The man spoke with reproach. He clicked his tongue as Professor Goldberg rose hastily, closing his book. 'What is the point of inviting people if you wish to be only reading your books? And look, you have creased your pyjama bottoms! What is the point of my having pressed them if–?'

'*Bas*!' said Professor Goldberg, querulously. 'You are hurting my ears with your nonsense. Go and do something of use.'

The servant sniffed. 'I have many things to do.' He turned to us and bowed, so serious of himself that he appeared comical. Ammi and Sami nodded to him, while I, unsure of him, smiled hesitantly.

Professor Goldberg watched the man disappear inside.

'I am sorry for that. Abdul has been with me far too long and has been allowed too much familiarity.' His accent still possessed some small reminder of his Chicago roots.

Ammi laughed and shook her head. 'There is no need for apologies. Sami and I are quite used to seeing your servants scolding their Professor Sahib.'

'Ah, but Sahira is not.' Professor Goldberg stroked his bushy eyebrows back into shape. 'She is used to seeing me as a man of some authority. Has this shocked you, my dear?'

'Em, I…' I became uneasy. 'I am more amused, I suppose.' I looked at the book that he was waving at me. I remembered that tatty, well-thumbed copy. I was used to seeing it sitting on the corner of Professor Goldberg's desk in his office.

'You know not the limits of your kingdom, still you are its queen.' The grey eyes were fixed on me and I felt my cheeks warming. 'I do not know why, but I always think of Tagore's words when I see you, Sahira.' Professor Goldberg seemed impervious to my discomfort. I remembered that about him also: his frankness and ability to disconcert without setting out to.

He bent down suddenly, and rubbed his ankles. 'I was quite lost to Tagore and did not realise how cold the water had become.' Standing upright again, he waved his hand. 'Come, let us go in. Otherwise, Abdul will be along shortly to scold me for allowing dinner to go cold.'

He led us through the flimsy wooden doors into his bungalow. On the walls inside hung a series of painted silks. They were displays of Mughal splendour and Rajput strength, an India long driven away by colonial rule and progress.

Dinner in Professor Goldberg's tiny dining room was a pleasant, rustic affair. We ate off plates that were slightly chipped and faded, on a table that was a little unsteady. The Professor and Ammi were comfortable in each other's company and I noticed that he spoke to Sami in a familiar, almost paternal way.

'So Sami, now that you have finally married, what is it you plan to do? Have you thought about the matter that we discussed?'

I saw a flash of something in Sami's eyes. Annoyance? Dismay? I was not sure because it was gone in an instant. What lingered, though, was the tautness of his skin across his cheekbones, as if his jaw was held tight.

Ammi raised her eyebrows, the folds of her sari *pallo* rustling with her movement. 'Is this a secret discussion? Or may Sahira and I know something of its content?'

Professor Goldberg shook his finger at her. 'Now, do not look at me in that manner, Begum Altair. Sami and I talk of many things, disparate things, and you cannot possibly know each one of them.'

'It is to do with my work, Ammi.' Sami turned to his mother with an open face. He spoke quickly, rushing to convince. 'I have reached a point where I cannot proceed alone. I need to collaborate with people who have greater experience than me in matters of business, as well as contacts. I am a very small fish, at the moment, and I am finding it difficult to swim alone.'

I looked at Sami with interest. There was a way about his demeanour that made me think there was something else, something he did not yet wish to share. But I said nothing, only listened on with attention. He rarely spoke of his work to me, or indeed to Ammi, but now, seated around Professor Goldberg's dining table, it seemed a subject to be broached.

'Have you some people in mind, then?' I asked.

Sami put the tips of his fingers together and leant forward in his chair. 'There are several options - the University, a communications company that is based in Bombay, and... some others.'

There was a moment's silence before Ammi spoke up, addressing Professor Goldberg. 'So you have been discussing these options together, then?'

Professor Goldberg nodded. 'Yes, that is so. In the absence of a father...'

'Mmm.' Ammi looked at Professor Goldberg with a fixed stare, the corners of her mouth turned slightly upwards in a bemused smile.

We played five rounds of paplu after dinner: laughing each time the Professor declared his hand, only to find that his sequence was incomplete.

'Now, I was sure this time that I had the four of clubs in my set. Where can it have gone?'

He accused Ammi of distracting him by humming tunelessly. She, in turn, rolled her eyes, telling him, 'Oh, nonsense, you are better with your head in a book.'

'But, still you are much improved since the time you used to play with Baba,' observed Sami. 'In a few years' time, you shall master the game completely.'

There was music in the room, Professor Goldberg being a fan of jazz.

'It is the purest form of music,' he told me. 'There is too much high-pitched noise in Indian music. The singing, the sitar - they assault my ears.' He put his hand on his heart. 'I have a sensitive soul, as you know, Sahira.'

Ammi packed the cards away. 'How strange that, having embraced so many aspects of the Indian culture, you still evade our beautiful music.'

Sami rose from his chair, unfolding the sleeves of his shirt and doing the buttons up on the cuffs. 'Please excuse me,' he muttered. 'I am going outside for a few minutes.'

He began to walk towards the door, his hand rummaging in his pocket.

'Wait, Sami. I will join you. My head needs the fresh air, also. It is drowning in numbers, and I am not good with them. I prefer words...' Professor Goldberg broke off when he saw what Sami had drawn from his pocket and shook his head. 'Oh, you're back on those. At the very least you should change to a decent brand. I know, I know, it is because they were your father's brand of choice. But if you must have a filthy habit, then at least do it properly.'

After they had left, I looked across at Ammi. She picked up the box of cards and walked over to the table that sat in the corner, lit up by lamplight. Stopping by the gramophone, she shook her head and clicked her tongue impatiently.

'Oh, this is just noise.' She pulled the needle away from the record. 'I cannot understand how he can prefer this to the strings of the sitar.' The deep, sonorous music suddenly stopped and the room was at once quiet.

I felt uncertain, a little nervous. Ammi was troubled and I did not know how to approach her. She saw me gazing upon her silently and shrugged.

'I do not like his smoking.' She spoke softly, almost to herself, her eyes narrowed as though looking inwards. 'It claimed my husband's life. However, there are occasions when sense is of little use, when a person cannot look to themselves for an answer and therefore turns to...'

She was speaking of Sami. Like me, she must have sensed there was more to the Professor's words than simply the rough progress of Sami's work.

She straightened herself, standing fully upright, and moved slowly away from me, across to the doorway, where she paused and put one hand on the wooden frame. With the other, she pulled the *pallo* of her sari over her head, tucking it under her chin before going out into the dimly-lit corridor. Left alone, I looked around me, at the shelves that were crammed with books. Underneath, tied up tight with rough string, were piles of newspapers.

I walked over to them, just to examine them, walking close to the window with its open shutters, and noticing, as grey silhouettes in the dark night, Ammi and the Professor. They looked for all the world like two rotund lovers meeting at midnight. She was standing close to him, a resolute look upon her face, talking in earnest. Through the spaces of the wooden slats, I heard her mention Sami's name and then, 'I can see there is something else. No, no, I do not want you to break his confidence.' but that was all. She lowered her voice suddenly and the rest of the conversation became like the rustling of leaves in the breeze.

Sami was not there. Instead, on the stone ground, there was an orange light, glowing ever more dim, the remnants of the cigarette butt he had smoked and left behind.

I saw little of Sami in the following days. He left home early when the dew was still slick on the blades of grass, and came home when the crickets were chattering to each other, their love calls hovering amongst the roses. Ammi insisted that we eat our evening meal together, and afterwards, Sami would once again take to his work, shut away in the office.

'The project has reached a point that is very exciting and critical,' he told us. 'I shall not bore you with details but it requires much of my attention.'

'Well, you have been busy with it for some time now,' Ammi said. 'We are lucky that you managed to take enough time off to get married. And not just married, but also go on honeymoon!' She smiled at her son indulgently.

Sami, with equal indulgence, rolled his eyes and teased. 'And now, you will tell Sahira how lucky she is that I could spare that time for her, because I have not been able to do so for you.' Then he leant over and prodded his mother affectionately. 'But was this not for you as well? You, who have been wanting to see me married for some time now?'

Such a free and easy relationship they appeared to have, this mother and her only son. Was it the loss of a husband and father that had brought them to this, this closeness in the wake of tragedy?

The relationship between Sami and I was similarly agreeable, but not entirely free. We were not yet a natural husband and wife. Why this was I did not know, but I felt it deep within me that I was the cause. I possessed a quality akin to frigidity, an inability to stand closer than on the edge of what was happening.

This was especially so when we made love; while Sami unwound with unclarified passion, I, even at the height of my pleasure, became something unreal, something outside of myself. I became an observer of my own ecstasy. And afterwards, I would cover myself up hurriedly, feeling my nakedness like a shame. I could not help it, even when I saw the brief hurt in my husband's eyes.

Unlike her son, Ammi spent most of her time at home: *What use have I for the outside world when I have enough here to do?*

It was a reaction, I felt, to the loss of her husband that she felt uncomfortable outside of her familiar walls. Occasionally, she would arrange to meet a friend at the Country Club, and there she would spend the afternoon playing bridge, while I met with my sisters or cousins to talk, play badminton or just to sip fruit sherbet out on the shaded lawns.

Mostly, Ammi's mornings were taken up with organising her household: the sweeping, the laundry, the food. She saw each of the servants in turn, engaging them in conversation, paying attention to what they told her of their families, of their worries and their joys. She made sure that I was present during these times.

'For all of this will naturally pass to you one day, and you must learn that there are ways of talking to those who work for you so that you gain their trust, and not their resentment. You must be sure that they do not feel bitter about who they are and who you are. It is a subtle thing, but most of the begums around here do not care for such subtleties and only wish to flaunt their power over others.'

After breakfast, Ammi would sit out in the garden under the shade of a leafy lean-to and teach the children of the gardener, the cook, and the *dhobiwalla* the basics of reading, writing and arithmetic.

'All children have an intrinsic ambition to learn,' she told me. 'What they lack in India is the opportunity. Especially the girls.' She looked down at the long plaits and eager heads that were bent over their slates, writing with white chalk the lessons of that day. 'We may have gained our independence from the British but what good is that when so many of our girls are still treated as possessions?' Ammi nodded to the back wall of the garden. 'Your father has helped me to buy a piece of land beyond that wall. I am planning to build a proper school there, for the education of girls at first. Then, *Inshallah*, we will allow the boys in. They will be able to have meals there also, for hunger is a great distraction to learning.'

'That is true,' I said. 'I always found it difficult to study when I was waiting for Ammaji to call me for lunch.'

'It shall be named after my late husband,' continued Ammi. 'Your own father has agreed to be a trustee. He knows much more of financial matters than either Sami or me.'

'Oh, so that is what you were talking to Ammaji about, then?' I wondered why Ammaji had not mentioned it to me in all the times we had seen each other.

Ammi, who must have read my mind, looked at me in keen amusement.

'Your Ammaji seems to think that you do not always let people know what is in your heart. It seems that she can hold onto her own secrets, too!'

December and January were cold months in Sikimpur. Cardigans were required throughout most of the day, while at night fires would be lit in the main rooms. The sun lost its glow of bright yellow and became a sphere of foggy paleness. The guava turned yellow on the branch then, and the mornings would be scattered with a light mist. The streets of the city were filled with rickshaw wallahs, who had their faces covered with thin cloth scarves and their bodies with hole-ridden sweaters. On the broken pavements, there were wooden stalls selling roasted peanuts and clay cups of *chai*. A string of students and young men would hang around these rickety stalls, cupping their hands around the warming cups before dashing off to cold colleges and offices.

February would start much the same way; then, about three-quarters of the way through, the sun would begin to strengthen and the land would warm with its rising heat.

At Shamshad Bagh, the work would focus on preparing the machinery and the fields ready for ploughing and sowing. At some point in March, the sun would claim back its full heat, the cranes and the crows would return from the warmer south and all life would begin again.

It was one afternoon, in mid-November, that Sami found me sitting on the lawn, observing the beehives. The bees had flown back to their queen and the mosquitoes had not yet taken their place.

From inside the house came the sound of the piano tuner tinkering on the ivory keys, while in the kitchen the cook was listening to Ms Lata Mangeshkar on the radio. The two became one strangely-blended melody; not unpleasant though.

'Ah, here you are.' Sami handed me a milky cup of *chai*. 'Ammi sent this out for you.'

I thanked him and sipped at the warm liquid. I had not realised how long I had been sitting out.

'I have been watching the bees with their funny dances,' I told him. 'Did you know they use their elaborate waggle dance to describe the location of flowers to their fellow bees? Faris has been telling me about them. He is worried about them being out of their hives this late in the year. He thinks they may have become infected and lost their sense of the seasons. I had not heard of such a thing before, had you?'

Sami shook his head.

'No, but Faris has taken care of bees for many years now, and learnt much from their behaviour. If he is worried, then I am afraid we may have a problem with them. I wonder if he has told Ammi about it. She will be upset if they must be destroyed. She has grown very fond of them, and enjoyed the honey they produced very much.'

Throughout the winter, Ammi would have the whole household, servants included, drink warm milk with a spoon full of home-made honey mixed into it. If the bees did need replacing, then at least last year's honey store had lasted the winter months.

I said this to Sami.

'Yes,' he replied, 'but in the summer Ammi loves to have fresh bread spread thick with the newly-made honeycomb.'

'Well, perhaps Faris will be able to buy in some new bees and have them producing honey by then.'

Sami shrugged. 'Perhaps.'

'Did you know that his brother has won a scholarship to study in Italy?' I asked. 'I do not think Faris knows very much about Italy, except that Indira Gandhi's daughter-in-law comes from there. He is very proud that his brother is going to be studying there.'

'Yes, he is going to Milan, I believe. It has a fine university.' Sami sat down beside me, stretched out his legs, slipped his sandals off and wriggled his toes. 'Faris must be very proud indeed. He has been saving as much as he can to allow Iqbal the chance to have a better life. Faris was worried that he would end up as a street sweeper if he did not have a good education. Iqbal is a very bright boy; it would have been a great pity for him to remain in Sikimpur.'

I knew, although Sami did not say, that it was Sami and not Faris who was going to be financing much of Iqbal's studies. Even if Faris had not sung Sami Sahib's praises, I knew that a gardener's wages, even if he saved for a decade, would not be enough for four years of travel and study abroad. I stared out at the green bloom of garden, thinking of this generous and noble act.

Sami spoke up again. 'I'm glad that you have brought up Faris and his brother, actually. I've been wondering if you wanted to do something similar? Not go to Italy, I mean, but...'

'Study architecture?'

'No.' Sami began to laugh, and then stopped suddenly. Rather awkwardly, he placed his middle finger under my chin and lifted it slightly. The light in his eyes intensified, just as the light of the sun was beginning to wane. I moved my head to one side and my chin slipped away from his fingertip. His brow was smooth and he looked very much as though he were about to let go of a bit of his heart.

'Last year, April, I think it was. Yes, it was April, because I remember that the workmen had finally finished installing Ammi's new kitchen. She was very particular about it and they were very lazy. Ammi had to watch over them diligently, making sure they did not buy poor quality materials when she had paid for superior wood.' Sami checked himself. 'But that is not important, except to remind me that it was the same month that Husna Begum threw a *burra dawat* for her son, who had been promoted.'

I remembered that party, the proud parents and their shy son, who looked uncomfortable with his most dreadful of parties and wore a cardboard smile throughout the night.

'I saw you there,' Sami continued 'and I do not think I would have recognised you as the girl that I met such a long time ago, when Baba had died and we flew *patang* on the roof, except that you stood in the same way and you smiled with the same look in your eyes. And I could see that, in the middle of all the chatter and noise, you were hidden away. Even from a distance, I could sense the concentration of your mind that was elsewhere. You were so far away from the rest of us. I do not suppose you even realised someone was watching you.'

I nodded with the memory of slipping away from the high-pitched gossip that was around me. I could not remember where it was that I had retreated to, but I could well imagine that I would not have noticed the watching intruder at the margin of my absorbed thoughts.

'Ammi saw me watching you,' Sami remembered. 'She did not tut and joke that I should not be looking at the girls, which she would normally do. Instead, she smiled and nodded at me. Then later, when she spoke to me about it, I felt embarrassed, as though she had seen something that she should not have. Do you know, I think that she was pleased with my reaction because of the way she left me with it. She did not speak of it again, but when I mentioned a proposal, she did not look surprised but said that she would see to it.' Sami shifted in his place. 'You were so different, you see, from the other girls of Sikimpur. You had been different even when we had run around the roof that day. You were quiet. You... you seemed left behind by the things around you.'

'Like the tortoise,' I said impulsively.

'The tortoise?'

'Yes. You must know of Aesop's Fables? The Hare and the Tortoise?'

Sami looked at me thoughtfully and I could not gauge the thoughts that were filling his mind.

'The tortoise,' he said softly, 'with its hard shell. Yes, maybe that is what it is. It is what makes you interesting. And also...'

Suddenly, he sighed and rose up from his cane chair. He walked away from me with his hands in his pocket, and then turned and walked slowly back again.

'There is something that I came out to talk to you about and I do not how I came to be diverted from it.' His face became flushed as though he was cross with himself. 'It is about my work. The amount of technology available in Sikimpur is limited. There is no real expertise for what I want to do, which is to develop my basic idea. As with all such things, it needs to be challenged if I am going to extract from it its full potential. I do not know if there is anywhere in India that is technically astute enough to achieve this yet.'

He sat back down in his chair. It creaked loudly with the man's weight of him.

'I have been thinking of the conversation that I had with your father. He had an idea that I would very much like to progress with, but I cannot do so here. It is impossible. Impossible to do many things here really. But abroad,' his eyes, which had been staring at the grass beneath him turned to stare at me, 'I attended a conference on my last visit to England and met someone there, a professor in computing, who was very interested in the idea of my regulatory system. He introduced me to a colleague of his, a Spaniard, Dr Elias Santos-Hernandez, who had just given a most fascinating lecture. I have had many interesting conversations with this professor since I returned to Sikimpur; conversations regarding collaboration. You see, he has contacts within the industry,' Sami's face became animated, 'and he wants to work with me on my project.' Sami suddenly stopped and frowned. 'Do you understand what I am saying to you?'

I breathed in deeply. His news was a surprise; I was not expecting to leave India. Eventually, I replied. 'Of course I understand. You are not speaking in riddles. But where is this place abroad?'

'Why, England, of course.'

'Ah, England. Of course! Where else...?' I echoed his words slowly. They sounded unreal. All my life I had lived in Sikimpur and had not thought of moving away from its city walls. Now there was a place called England, the country that had once ruled over us, whose Queen we still spoke of with some reverence, and that country could be my new home. *Welayat*! I wondered if this was what Professor Goldberg and Sami had been discussing.

'I should have talked to you about this before, of course,' said Sami, 'but I was not sure about taking you away from your parents and your family. I have tried very hard to think of an alternative but there does not seem to be one. Unless, of course...,' Sami drew in a deep breath, 'you do not wish to go. I mean, you could remain here and I would go alone. Live there alone.'

'Yes, you should have talked to me.' I said with some emotion. 'I am not a little child, who will burst into tears at the thought of leaving my family and going away.'

'No, of course you are not. I did not think that way... but you are right. It seems I am not very good at knowing what is the right thing to do. I have not that amount of wisdom in me yet.'

I could forgive him, his oversight when he said this; I too had very little wisdom in me yet.

'But what of your mother?' I asked. 'Will she come too?'

Sami looked out into the fading light with a mysterious smile.

'Oh, I do not think we need worry about Ammi. She will be much better off without us taking up all her life. She has enough friends here who will make sure of that.'

The crickets were starting to sing and the leaves were chattering in the wind, and I, looking out into the calm of the air, felt infused with this optimism.

Chapter Nine

In late December, a week before we were due to leave for England, Ammi gave a small, informal party to wish us a safe journey and a prosperous life abroad.

Going overseas was still something big back then, and going to live in *Welayat* was considered the very best of fortunes. The rains had stayed with us with an unusual unpredictability that year. As more and more guests arrived, the house became suffused with the smell of garlands, silver string threaded through roses and moti, lilies and marigolds. These garlands were the symbol of celebration and good luck. Fresh at that moment, in a few hours they would be wilted and brown, lying in a heap, their scent dissolved with their good looks.

I had invited a friend from my college days, Dr Firdaus Syed, to the party. Now married and a mother, she lived in bustling Bombay these days but had returned to Sikimpur to visit her parents, both doctors, who led busy lives between their private work and a charitable eye clinic that they had set up.

'They get much more satisfaction out of the eye clinic, Sahira, and I think they have come to despise the private consultancy that they do. But of course, they make no money from the eye clinic; indeed, they need the money from their private work to fund it. So, far from retiring, they must carry on as they are.' Firdaus told me this over a plate full of *pakoras* and *chappli kebabs*.

'At least they are doing something to relieve the problems of the poor,' I said. 'Most of their profession do not wish to use their skills for the betterment of the less well off.'

'Oh, Sahira,' Firdaus put her hand over her mouth as she laughed. 'I see that you still have your lofty principles and high ideas.' She lowered her voice and put her mouth close to my ear, 'But tell me how do they fit in with the affluence of the Shamshad family and all this wealth that you have married into? I am sure you have many sleepless nights worrying about it!'

I blushed and she nudged me. 'I am only teasing you. After all, I do not get to see you much these days and soon you will be so far away that we shall have to write to stay in touch. But still, your father must be relieved that you are not his sole heir: you would give away all the family fortune within a few days!'

I nudged her back.

'And I hope that you will follow in your parents' footsteps instead of simply allowing your wealth to pile up into a big mountain of money!'

'Oh no!' grinned Firdaus. 'Why would I do that? I work very hard for it, as does Ibrahim. We will spend it frivolously, and use it to send our numerous children to the very best, and most expensive, schools in the world. They will have everything they need and much more besides. They will be *utterly* spoilt!' Firdaus's eyes were twinkling as she spoke. It was good to see her again. I would miss her terribly when we went away, for she was the only real friend that I had.

But Firdaus was flushed with enjoyment and not melancholy, and so I stayed quiet as she continued to speak. She was looking over at Sami at the other end of the room. He was pouring a drink for Professor Goldberg.

'Allah has been very good to you, you know.' Firdaus nodded when I looked quizzically at her. 'Oh yes. And I do not mean all this money, this fabulous house with its vast rooms and glorious staircase. I mean your husband, Sami Altair. He is not what he should be. Not as I imagined him. He is more real, more affable in a way that matters.' She lowered her voice. 'In fact, he is close to perfect.'

'*Close* to perfect? And what are his failings?' I asked amused.

'Well now...' Firdaus lifted a stray hair out of her eyes. 'I do not know him well enough to tell you that, but just as the tapestry weavers leave a blemish in their rugs to show that it is only Allah who is perfect, so Sami must have a flaw. Besides, you must remember your Wilde: there should always be some room for development!' She suddenly kissed my cheek lightly and whispered, 'I hope you always stay happy.'

I smelled the sweet coconut that she used to shine her hair. Ammaji liked her very much, her openness and her conviviality; Ammaji was very much like her. I, who also liked her very much, had always felt slightly intimidated by her.

'Ah, Firdaus *beyti*, how lovely to see you!' Ammaji had spotted Firdaus from across the room and come over. She kissed her ardently on the cheeks. 'How lovely you are looking. Being a new mother suits you. I wish it were the same with Suha. She has not taken to motherhood well, always tired and so short-tempered now. I am having such a battle persuading her to employ a decent *aya*. The one she has is so lazy and knows nothing of how to soothe an irritable and screaming child, but because she is a daughter of their cook, Suha will not let her go. I think she is worried that the cook will leave also, and good cooks are hard to find these days.'

Ammaji shook her head and tutted to herself. 'Oh, but you do not want to hear about all of that. Let us talk of something else.' She gently touched the necklace that Firdaus was wearing; a large piece all gold and set with the brashest of emeralds. They lent glamour to Firdaus's pale complexion and high forehead. 'What a beautiful set. You were always so well dressed. All that time you spent together, I wish you could have taught Sahira-'

'But Sahira's mind is always on higher things!' Firdaus exclaimed in my defence. 'Besides, she does not need sparkling stones to light up her face. Like you, she is naturally beautiful.' Firdaus spoke with a natural lack of guile, and so Ammaji did not protest and I did not blush.

'Yes, but I still wish that my daughters had a complexion such as yours.' Ammaji gazed upon the flawless skin before her. 'And what about your husband? You have not brought him with you? We have not seen him since your wedding. He was quiet, if I remember, not like you. I hope you allow him a chance to talk.'

'Oh, he talks enough, especially when it comes to medical matters. Then, I do not get a chance to voice my opinion.' Firdaus's face lit up with talk of her husband. 'Unfortunately, he could not come tonight. The baby is not yet used to his parents so he has had to stay at home to look after her. I will bring him to Shamshad Bagh to meet you before we leave. He has heard enough of the days that I spent there with you all.'

They talked for a while longer, Ammaji asking after Firdaus's parents and reminiscing on our college days, when Firdaus had been a frequent visitor to the house. Ammaji, a traditional Indian mother, believed in feeding our guests well, and Firdaus, who loved her food, readily accepted Ammaji's hospitality.

I stood with them, reflecting on the way Firdaus talked about her husband; there was an undeniable love there, as though it had a hold of her. I knew that I did not think about Sami in that way and I had not minded before. Now, watching and listening to Firdaus, I felt my nerves were clogged, they were dull and thick.

'Something is troubling you.' Firdaus was watching me closely; Ammaji had left us. 'There is something in your eyes, like a signal. They are deeper than usual. They really are the windows to your soul, you know.'

'No.' I spoke too quickly. I knew it and looked away from her forthright face.

'You do not love Sami.' Firdaus was so candid. I had forgotten that about her. I was taken aback, by her frankness, and also by what she had said.

'Why do you say that?'

'There is no need to be so shocked, Sahira. I know you too well, and while others may feel shy about saying anything, I have no such problem. And, because I know you so well, it does not surprise me. I love my husband, he is easy to love. I would not have married him otherwise. But you...'

'No,' I said glumly. 'You would not have. But... surely Sami is also easy to love?'

'You are a *pugli*.' Firdaus tapped the side of her head with a forefinger. 'Most women marry believing that they will fall in love, and they do because they have set their minds upon it. But you, you should have known better. You, with all the romance of your soul. How could you do it?'

'I do not know.' My voice was small with my foolishness. 'But I *do* like him. He is wonderful in many ways, but I do not yearn to be with him. The stars do not shine brighter and the earth does not spin faster. And, I do not think he feels that way about me, either.'

Firdaus looked to where Sami stood, tall beside the gentleman he was talking to.

'Then why did you marry him?'

I thought of that afternoon on the Altairs' roof and the laughter that rang out from the boy with the *patang*. But I did not tell Firdaus that story: it belonged to another place. Instead, I shrugged.

'I could not think of a reason not to.'

Firdaus laughed and held up her hand in apology.

'I am sorry, Sahira, but for all the passion that you possess, you hide it away so sinfully.'

'Maybe I can still be happy without loving him. Or maybe I can learn to love him, one day?' It was a remote question.

'Let us hope so, Sahira. Let us hope that the stars do indeed shine a little brighter one day.'

That night, as most of Sikimpur slept, I lay awake, full of troubles. Sami was snoring gently beside me; facing away, sleeping an innocent sleep. Outside, I could hear the last of the monsoon rains that had come visiting; beating down on the window pane like a pronouncement, a calling.

All else was peaceful, in a state of unknowing, it seemed. I edged myself out of bed and pulled a shawl from the chair around my shoulders. My feet were soft in their tread along the hall and down the staircase.

When I reached the wooden doors to the outside, I flung them open, and the patter of the rain became louder and ever-welcoming. I stepped into the beckoning downpour and stood under the unloading sky, my feet dark orange with the wet clay and my body soaking up the wetness. I kneeled on the ground and dug my fingers deep into the sodden soil. I felt it enclosing my fingers, my hands, my wrists, closing in tightly as I clenched my fists. In the darkness, the living senses were those of touch and hearing.

Beyond the garden walls, the heavy sound of car horns penetrated into my space, echoing each other: questioning and answering. But that clamour was unimportant to me, for it was the rain that I had come to feel: it re-kindled my hope. Its unrelenting drama seeped into my unflinching heart and melted it slowly; sinew by sinew, fibre by fibre, chamber by chamber. Melting it into optimism once again. Melting it so that I could believe I may yet find something in Sami to fall in love with. I could not believe that I would live out my married life without that. Whatever I thought of marriage before, I knew now that, without love, it would be a melancholy yellow; a failing liver instead of brightening rays of the sun.

Part II

A Strangely Pronounced Language

Chapter Ten

England loomed up grey, so indistinguishable from the clouds around us that I failed to recognise it. It was only when Sami leant across me and, crooking his index finger at the window, said, 'Look there is your first sight of England!' far too loudly, that I realised there was land beneath us.

I looked down through the clouds at the unfolding of a flat, dull landscape and sighed with disappointment. Sunny Sikimpur was far to the east of us now, a gathering of family and friends who had waved goodbye to us at its bustling international airport. They had congregated like a clinging swarm and I had let myself be hugged, kissed and missed by everyone. But, in the end the faces that I remembered were those of my parents: tear-stained and flushed. I felt a pang like my heart popping.

Ammaji had cried when I told her we were moving to England. In my rush to tell her, I had not considered what her reaction would be. She had taken a sharp intake of breath and turned away from me, suddenly pulling the *pallo* of her sari to her face. She stood apart from me, motionless, leaving me to curse my thoughtlessness. But what had I been expecting from her? Surprise? Dismay? Certainly something more vocal than these noiseless tears. I was not used to a silent Ammaji and so I had waited until she was ready to face me.

'England?' she said, finally. 'Leaving Sikimpur? I did not think of my daughters doing that. I was prepared for them leaving home but to go so far away. I had not thought of that.' She had examined my face. 'You are excited about it. I can tell that, even though you are trying to hide it. And, of course you will be excited. Of course, you are bound to be. We were happy to remain here but you youngsters... your generation; well, the world is opening up for you. Sikimpur is too small for Sami, and certainly it is not enough for you.'

'But you are not happy,' I had said sadly. 'I have upset you. I am sorry.'

Ammaji took my chin in her hand and gazed lovingly into my eyes.

'There is no need for you to be. Just remember there is something here,' she had placed the palm of her hand over her heart, 'that shall always remain with you, as it does with your sisters, no matter how far you go from me.' Then she smiled softly. 'No matter how much some of you quarrel with me.' She had lifted a corner of her sari and dabbed a couple of wayward tears that had rolled down her cheek. 'When do you go?'

'I am not really sure but it will not be for some time. So,' I had added brightly, 'you will have plenty of time to get used to the idea.'

'Get used to the idea?' Ammaji had shaken her head. 'Even when you have been there for some years and are a mother yourself, I do not think I shall ever get used to your being so far from me.'

'But you can come to see us,' I said. 'You can visit Buckingham Palace, where the Queen lives, and go to Harrods.'

'Ah, that is better as a dream, I think.' Ammaji had lowered her eyes and began to fiddle with the bunch of keys that she kept tucked into the waistband of her sari. All sorts of keys: for the solid front door, for the latticed back door, for the hidden safe, for the high-roofed storeroom. Ammaji's footsteps were always accompanied by her jangling keys.

'Now, go and tell your Abbaji. He is in the garden. He will be interested in your plans. Will you stay for lunch? Good, then I must go and let the *bawrchi* know. She will want to cook something special.'

As she reached the steps she had turned to me and said sternly, 'You must watch out for all the pig that the English eat. I have heard they are very fond of that particular meat.'

And with that she had left me. I watched her walk determinedly up the newly-fashioned stone steps and into the house, before I wandered into the garden in search of Abbaji. I had found him tending to Ammaji's roses. Their petals were slowly deserting them, dropping one by one so that the soil below was littered with their fading beauty. Abbaji had looked up as my footsteps intruded upon his labour and smiled his beautiful smile.

'Ah, Sahira. I did not know that you were coming today, but I am glad you are here.' He gazed down at the fallen petals. 'The dying of your Ammaji's roses always makes me a little sad.'

When I told him my news he had looked surprised, smiled and then hugged me closely, saying only, 'England! Goodness, how you have grown up.'

He made me sit on his old, tattered deck chair, while he sat down cross-legged on a trailing root.

'Of course, you have told your Ammaji?' he asked. 'She will miss you dreadfully. As indeed will I, but it is the natural course to take, for Sami and for you. Sikimpur is limited in what it has to offer, and I am sure that you will find much to interest you and keep you busy in England. It has some of the finest galleries in the world. Now, whereabouts are you going? England is a small country compared to India, but still it is large enough to get lost in.'

I could not correctly remember the name of the city that Sami had told me and had shaken my head.

'You will have to ask Sami, I am afraid. It begins with "L" and is somewhere in the north, in a place called Yorkshire.'

'Ah, that must be the town of Leeds.'

'Yes,' I said. 'That sounds very much like the name that Sami said.'

Abbaji had looked disappointed. 'Not London then?'

Again, I shook my head. 'No, not London.'

I understood Abbaji's disappointment. To him, London was the hub of the world. London was fine in the rain and the snow, the fog and the sunshine. Everything fine came out of London: the Queen, Parliament, Lord's cricket ground. The north - even in a country as small as England - was a world away from such fineness.

Abbaji had leant over on his root to tug at an obdurate twig that lay across his path.

'Well, at least you shall be able to watch the cricket at Headingley,' he said, absent-mindedly. 'It is a fine ground. Although not quite Lord's, it still has its own history.'

The root came loose in Abbaji's hand and he had thrown it onto a heap with other discarded garden bits.

'We must make sure you have enough jumpers and cardigans.' He sniffed. 'The cold of the north is quite legendary.'

As I stepped out into the Heathrow air, a chill wind blew full in my face, taking my breath with it. I stepped back into the aeroplane with the shock of cold, but Sami, who was behind me, gently pushed me on.

'Go on,' he said. 'We are here now. Let us be quick and get out of this wind.'

The air stewardess, in her bright blouse and red uniform smiled politely. 'It's always a shock when the wind first catches you.'

I pulled my light coat tightly around me, took a deep breath of English air and stepped out into it.

Inside the terminal, we joined the tide of fellow passengers passing through customs, clutching our navy passports with their embossed Sarnath Lions. Mostly, the faces that we saw were those of men, students who came for a British education and married men who came alone to find work in order to send money home. There were some families too, husbands and wives with their small children all wrapped up warm against the unfamiliar cold. The children stayed close to their mothers, their large eyes peering anxiously around them, some of them chattering, some crying, some munching on biscuits. We waited with them to collect our baggage, watching patiently as the conveyor belt crawled around and around, carrying suitcases that were not ours. Large suitcases, small suitcases, faux leather and sturdy plastic, until I caught sight of two dark grey ones, two of a familiar set.

I looked about me.

'Where are the porters?' I asked Sami.

He laughed as he made his way to the carousel.

'You are no longer in India, Sahira, with porters vying with each other for your attention. In England, my dear, you have to do things yourself.'

I understood now the trolley that Sami had taken charge of. *It* was to be our bearer: a cranky metal thing that creaked and wobbled as we made our way back to the windy outdoors. Sami hailed a taxi - a black Austin - driven, I noticed, by a young Indian man, south Indian, with his dark colour and small bones. Sami opened the door for me before loading our bags into the luggage compartment. The taxi driver looked at me from his mirror and smiled.

'First time in England?' he asked in English. 'I am here for many years: since '65. Now I know London very well.'

He nodded energetically when Sami told him the name of our hotel, The Metropole.

'Oh, yes, of course. That is surely a good style of hotel. Very big; very best one.'

We passed through London, stopping and starting with the run and stutter of the traffic, the driver and Sami chatting while I peered at the city through the window. It was immense: its steel and concrete buildings looming up large around us and all brightly lit in the approaching dusk. It was an intimidating sight, made more so by the strange silence that accompanied it.

Despite the depth of the traffic and the bustle of its peoples, the streets of London were much quieter than the streets of Sikimpur. Where were the car horns, where the verbal discord between pedestrians and drivers? Surely, there could not be so much activity and so little noise! I felt let down suddenly, irrationally, with the people carrying on their whispering conversations; with the drivers and their polite, patient manners.

Thus, I arrived at our hotel in a state of quiet myself, hardly noticing the grandeur of The Metropole's façade. I stood apart from Sami as he checked our reservation and the number of our room, and barely answered when the concierge wished me a happy stay. I vaguely heard Sami send a telegram to his mother, telling her that we had arrived safely. I wondered what it was that we had arrived to.

It was the rain that saved England for me. The porter brought us to our room and, as he began to pull the heavy beaded curtains closed, little drops of it started patterning the windows that stretched from floor to ceiling. I walked over to him.

'Please, leave them open. I want to look outside.'

The porter nodded, looking at me with curiosity before making his way towards the door where Sami stood.

December in London was unfriendly. The coldness of its wind had made fragile my flesh and bones, and left me shivering, even in the lobby of The Metropole. But the rain was soft upon the glass and it came down from the same sky that hung over Sikimpur. It was as though it had come to save me from being lost and lonely, to keep faith with me.

'It is always raining in Britain,' Sami told me. 'They say it is the reason that the land is so green. Unfortunately, it also plays havoc with the cricket calendar. I suppose, that is why England is so poor at the game. When I first came here, I would get really fed up with it, but I soon learnt that it forms a great part of this country's culture. The people dress in anticipation of it, always carrying umbrellas and raincoats. We will have to get used to it, too.'

'The rain will not be a hardship for me,' I replied. 'I like it. I have always liked it.'

'Yes, I remember now,' said Sami. 'Perhaps though, it would not be wise for you to run out into it here in England. You will not find it so warm or so easy to dry off as in Sikimpur.'

We were to stay one week in London before travelling to the north of England - to Yorkshire, and Leeds. The days and nights grew colder and the skies ever more gloomy.

'Ready for snowing,' our concierge at The Metropole told us cheerfully. He stood behind his desk in a gold trim black suit with a pale, moon-faced splendour. I liked him, for he always made sure to wave to me as we were coming in or going out, and he always said something pleasant to me.

For our first breakfast in London, I was introduced to the morning cereal: cornflakes soaked in a pool of milk. It had a water-like consistency compared to the rich, thick milk that came from the buffaloes of Shamshad Bagh. The cooked breakfast was not allowed to us, with its bacon and sausages, and its black pudding. *Congealed blood*! I had been appalled when Sami told me. *What a thing to eat*, I thought, forgetting conveniently the fried goat's brains that Nanima used to feed us during exam time.

I watched a waiter carrying two plates of fried pork, mushrooms and tomatoes to a far-off table.

'Have you never been tempted by this cooked breakfast?' I asked of Sami.

He shook his head.

'You know, I have not. Bacon and the like have not interested me. I seem to have a natural element of repulsion for pig meat. I don't know why, but I found that many of my friends had the same sense of disgust.'

'Yes, I'm finding that too. There is something about its smell that is unappealing. But tell me Sami...' I sat back in my chair and smiled with mischief. 'Have you been tempted by anything else that you should not have? England is so far from Sikimpur, and the strings of what was forbidden must surely have been loosened somewhat.'

Sami smiled back.

'You are right, distance can blur many things. However, my friends looked after my interests, and I theirs. So, no. I was a good boy. A good Muslim boy... on the whole.'

'Ah, so then...'

But Sami interrupted me.

'I did nothing that I would be ashamed of, and nothing that I could not relate to Ammi. But let us talk of now, and your ill-suited clothes.'

The clothes that I had brought with me were ideal for the cool breezes of Sikimpur winters, but failed me against the bitterness of this chilling air. I had with me a finely woven, woollen Kashmiri coat, dark blue in colour with white embroidery around the collar and cuffs, and several woollen shalwars. Sami, on the other hand, had a thick woollen knee-length coat and jumpers with full sleeves. On his hands he wore fur-lined brown leather gloves. When he saw my dressed self, he shook his head.

'Oh dear, we had better go shopping for you. You will not be able to survive in your Sikimpur clothes.'

At first I could not understand this, for standing in our thickly carpeted and wonderfully heated hotel room I felt fine. But Sami shook his head again.

'Don't you remember how cold you were yesterday? It will not be any better today. Do not be fooled by this lovely warmth inside. The street outside does not have electric heaters.'

And he was right; even as we stepped out of the lift into the vast hotel lobby hall, the temperature dropped and I began to shiver. I had not known this kind of cold before, I knew only of light cardigans and cotton socks. This was a cold that required heavy fur and thick boots.

We took a taxi from outside The Metropole; a black cab, as Sami called it. They were famous, he told me; their drivers known around the world for their superb knowledge of London roads. As we drove through the streets, I began to appreciate this. It was a wonderful knowledge, I thought, for the roads of London were woven around its buildings as a complex labyrinth.

Our driver understood that we were new and happily talked to us, pointing his finger out of the window occasionally, to show us.

'St Paul's Cathedral, built by Sir Christopher Wren,' and 'Going over London Bridge now, the new one. The old one was sold to the Americans. God only knows why they wanted it. Reckon they thought they was getting *Tower* Bridge. Now, *that* is a bridge and a half. Beautiful, it is!'

I could not understand most of this man's peculiar accent, but I nodded and smiled at him anyway. I recognised some of the words and he would have been disappointed, I thought, if I appeared confused by his voluble conversation.

Eventually, we came to a final stop outside a building so large that I could not imagine what it held inside. My eyes drifted along its height and width, up and down, side to side, taking in the ornate, white pillars and sky-high windows. I fell in love with it at once.

Sami took my hand.

'This is Selfridges, a wonderful place to shop. Not quite Harrods, but I am sure that you will have fun looking around, and it is the best place to find some suitable clothes for you.'

He led me inside, through copper-coloured revolving doors and into a world that shone with the lights and tinsel of Christmas just past, and I forgot my numb knees and frozen hands. My eyes took in the people who wandered, casually, very confidently, through the aisles. They seemed so elegant to me, with their pale skin and blue eyes that peered from under blonde hair. Most of the women were taller than I was, with big bones and broad, open features. They wore knee-high boots and coats so short that their bare thighs were exposed. How short must be the dresses that they wore underneath, I wondered. For the first time in my life I understood the draw of Ammaji to fair skin and I felt an indelicacy in my own dark colour. I stared at them too long and Sami pulled me away from my fixed place, asking, 'Is something wrong?'

'No, no,' I said quickly. 'I am just interested in my surroundings, the people. It is all so different from what I am used to. The women are very attractive, do you not think? They have such a way with them.'

Sami looked at me with curiosity and I became conscious of what I had said. I do not think that I had ever remarked on another person's beauty, or lack of it, until now. Faced with the English rose...

'I suppose there is something in their poise...' Sami did not sound sure. There was a gruff impatience in his voice. 'Come on.' He pulled me back towards the main body of the shop. 'We have not come here to look at the beautiful women. We must find you some proper clothing.'

We spent the morning enjoying all that Selfridges had to offer. The many coats, hats, gloves and shoes almost made my eyes hurt and my head ache, they certainly made my mind whirl.

Sami clothed me in a long coat of dark grey wool, and I had gloves now and a hat that I could barely see from under, and several pairs of trousers that were far thicker than my loose-fitting shalwars. My feet were warm in their new, thick socks and sturdy boots. I was wrapped up like a parcel and ready now to be outside. I stretched my fingers around in their woollen grey gloves. I was fascinated by their oddness, this knitted wool that hugged my slender fingers and took away their awkward, stiff coldness.

Finally, when we had exhausted our curiosity, Sami asked for the rest of the items we had bought to be sent to our hotel.

'Now, how do you feel?' he asked as we stood outside again. There were more people now walking along the pavements, all busy against the bleak afternoon sun.

'Warm, beautifully warm,' I said, drawing myself in, nestling into my fine woollen coat. 'And also hungry.'

'Good,' Sami said. 'And do you feel adventurous now that you are warm?'

I nodded enthusiastically.

'Come on, then.' He took hold of my hand. 'Let us explore London on foot. It is more fun this way. Do not worry, we shall eat, but something different from what you were used to in Sikimpur.'

We took the underground to Westminster. It was the first time that I had seen the dark skin of African people. I stared at them in the same way that I had stared at the white-skinned women in Selfridges, embarrassing Sami once again.

He took us back into the open air, saying, 'You will get us into a lot of trouble if you continue to stare at every new colour of skin that we come across!'

We headed towards the River Thames, flowing slowly under its bridges. It was beginning to get dark -, a slow lingering dusk - and the lantern lamps had been turned on along Westminster Bridge. The wind, the lights, the people with their winter fur and the darkening London landscape made things very exciting for me.

Soon we were back in the south of the city again and in a restaurant that was small, with white wooden seats and tables covered with brightly-coloured tablecloths. From the interior, deep inside where the kitchen was, there came unfamiliar accents and smells. A big man, rotund and jolly, came out and, seeing Sami, he threw up his hands in an exaggerated gesture. He was not English; I realised this from his exuberance and also his thick accent.

'Welcome back, Signore Sami.' The man shook Sami's hand with great vigour. 'You have not eaten with us for a long time. It is good to see you once again. And this time I see you have the company. Your wife?' He bent down and, taking my hand, he kissed it. 'Ah, finally we see you with a Senora. Such a handsome man and such a beautiful wife.'

'Ciao, Salvotore.' Sami put his arm on my shoulder. 'This is Sahira. She is visiting England for the first time. Actually, we are moving to live here.'

'Ah, to London. That is magnificent!'

'No, not in London. In the north: Leeds.'

Salvotore made a face.

'*Leeds*? But there is nothing there! You should stay in London: it is beautiful, I swear. True, the coldness makes it ugly, but the sunshine makes it beautiful. In the summer, only my Napoli is more perfect.'

Sami smiled.

'Yes, I know. You have told me much about Napoli, and you have made it sound very lovely. So much so that I hope to visit it some time.'

'Ah, you will love it. Salvatore beamed. 'And *la bella Napoli* will love you too! The ruins of Herculaneum, Amalfi where the boats lie... ah, but I will talk about my Napoli for too long and you have the hunger. I will make sure you have a truly beautiful meal today.'

He drew us round to the back of the restaurant, took the rose that was in his lapel and placed it in the empty vase on the table.

'Come, sit.' He pulled out a chair for me. 'I will bring you the best of Napoli cuisine so that you will wish to eat it always.'

The food that we ate was indeed wonderful: fried aubergines, suppli di riso and zeppole. There were flavours that I did not recognise; only the garlic was familiar to me. But it was the spaghetti that was the real challenge, spiralling it around a four-pronged fork and into my mouth before it unravelled. Sami teased me gently.

'You will need to practice this much more if we are to go to *la bella Napoli*. Still, you will have lots of opportunity to do so. Neither of us can cook traditional Indian *salana*, but I know how to cook some pasta dishes, although I am limited in their flavours. Certainly, I do not make them as tasty as this but at least they can be eaten. They kept me from going hungry when I was at Brunel. And now, Italian food is quite one of my favourite cuisines.'

It seemed that way, for Sami had no trouble with our tangled meal, and could twirl and eat with enviable ease. Soon his bowl was empty and he pointed to the shelves about the restaurant.

'Do you see there are many different types of pasta? Over three hundred, Salvatore has informed me. There is the tube-shaped penne, spiralling fusilli, and of course, long spaghetti, the one that we have been eating, and having so much fun with. There is quite an art to it, is there not?'

All around there was chatter, a language that spoke of the sun rising over undulating hills and vineyards that lay heavy with the grape. Then suddenly, from behind the counter where they served the wine, a lone voice rose, loud and expansive, singing an aria that rang through the entire restaurant.

'What is that noise?' I looked around, startled.

Sami laughed, putting his hand up to his mouth, for it was full of spaghetti. 'It is Salvatore. He is singing a piece from an opera, The Barber of Seville, it is called. It is his most favourite pastime, apart from eating pasta and speaking about *la bella Napoli*, of course!'

We lived softly in London, kept in comfort by bellboys, concierges, taxis and waiters. This life was not much different from the one I had led in Sikimpur, I thought. There was the cold, of course, and I walked the streets of London more, whereas I was chauffeured everywhere in Sikimpur.

'Wait until we have our own house and then you must learn how to cook and clean, and maybe even how to drive,' Sami told me. 'Then, you will find many differences, I suspect.'

'Oh, that is all right,' I said. 'It will be interesting, a challenge. A brave new world that I shall have to manage.'

Sami took me to the museums, and I was embarrassed by the sight of the nudes. Instinctively, I would avert my gaze until I came across Rodin's *The Kiss*. It fascinated me with its superior beauty and I fell completely under its spell. He took me to Carnaby Street too, because I was so taken with the young, trendy people of London and their garish, outlandish clothes, which I could never imagine being brave enough to wear. Afterwards, we went to watch them dance at one of the fashionable clubs in the West End. I would not join them on the dance floor, though Sami tried so very hard to convince me. I was too shy to move as they did, in such a carefree and unthinking manner.

At Buckingham Palace we saw the Changing of the Guards, and I wrote to Ammaji about it, knowing that it would please her, and also make her cry a little. I cried a little myself, as I wrote.

Chapter Eleven

It was the New Year, 1968, when we journeyed up to Leeds on the train, travelling on a lovely day when the clouds had dispersed and the sun allowed to shine through.

The trains that ran along the length and breadth of India were virtually unknown to me. When the Shamshad clan travelled, they did so by car, clean and exclusive. Even our visits to Lalmali had been chauffeured. Only once had we been taken on a train, when Abbaji had hired an entire carriage for the family's visit to Rajasthan to see his elderly aunt. It had been splendid, with wide aisles and plump, cushioned seats. We were served breakfast and lunch on mock marble dining tables, and arrived in Jodhpur lively and fresh.

I was very young then, only ten years old and I had enjoyed myself tremendously, leaning out of the window to stare at the Thar desert that stretched out well into the horizon and the men that sat on the roofs of the first and second class carriages, clinging to their cloth bundles and the smooth maroon steel of the train roof.

'Why were they up there?' I had asked, 'when there is so much room in our carriage?'

Abbaji had answered me with mutterings that I could not hear, while Ammaji had drawn away a stray hair from her forehead and smiled weakly.

'It is one of those things that happen,' she had told me.

'Because they are poor and we are rich,' Laila had explained, pleased with her insight.

'Nana and Nanima are poor,' I reflected. 'Do they also ride on the roofs of trains?'

'Of course not!' Ammaji had replied abruptly, frowning at the thought of her parents riding high on a rushing carriage.

Her sharp tone had not deterred me. 'Why are they poor?' I had asked. 'And why are we rich?'

'It is the way of the world,' Abbaji had said by way of explanation. He came to sit beside me on the soft cushion and pointed out into the desert. 'Just as some plants have many leaves and some are covered in thorns.'

His explanation had confused me and I pressed him. 'It is nature, then, that decides such things? Surely, it is Allah who...'

'Look! Look at the gazelles!' Ammaji had pulled me up to the open window and pointed at the skipping deer. 'Are they not beautiful?'

Her trick worked and I forgot my line of questioning, my attention grabbed by the grace of the creatures outside.

Back then, that was all that was required to stop my awkward questioning.

The English countryside that lay outside was bright like spotless silver under the low winter sun. A morning frost lay over the bare soil and naked trees. It was starkly beautiful, as though a piece of Earth's soul was on show. It was very different from the grey gloom that I had seen from the window of the aeroplane, and for this I was glad. We passed a more residential area, where the green grass and hedges faded to make way for red brick and wooden fences. They were such strange houses, square and colourless; they each had their own space and did not invade into another's. There seemed to be many of these homes along the length of the railway line that we had so far travelled.

'Is this what our house will look like?' I asked.

Sami folded his newspaper away and looked out. He shook his head.

'I hope not. They are most unappealing. Anyway, for the time being we will be staying in another hotel, I am afraid.'

Sami had not yet found a house for us to live; for all his organisation, he could not decide upon a place that would be suitable for us. I did not mind so much, but when Sami spoke of estate agents and going to look at houses, I felt quite unsure of things.

'You will enjoy it,' Sami said. 'I am quite sure of that. Can you imagine how exciting it will be to choose your own home? Yorkshire has a particular style of house: not made of bricks, but of a solid stone that makes them look very grand.'

I leant my head against the pane of the window and tried to imagine, in that open bit of countryside, a house made of solid stone that was all space inside for me to furnish and decorate as I chose. As part of my *jehez*, my parents had bought us some furniture: a finely ornate walnut wardrobe, a chest of drawers, a dressing table and three small tables. At the moment, they lay lonely in our bedroom in Gulabi Ghar, but I could send for them later, for they would fit well in a grand solid stone house. The furniture that went with the odd square houses would not be in keeping with the grand houses that Sami had spoken of. They would need grand things in them.

Sami looked at his watch. 'Shall we have some lunch? My head is aching from having risen so early, and I really would like a cup of coffee.'

The dining car was not so full when we arrived. People watched us briefly as we took our seats. We sat across the aisle from an elderly couple who seemed to have finished with lunch and had settled down to tea. They smiled politely and the woman put her delicate china teacup to her lips.

The waiter did not smile as he handed out a menu. He appeared bored, writing our selection with a dull, 'Mmm, yes, lamb did you say? Mmm. Yes, we have fresh coffee.'

When he had gone, the elderly gentleman with greying hair turned to us, speaking in a refined voice.

'You are from India, are you not? I thought so. India, not Pakistan. Yes, you look Indian. I was posted to India before the war, you see. In the Punjab mostly, in Lahore; such a marvellous city, so full of history. Then the regiment was sent to Maharashtra: to Poona. There was a rebellion threatening in one of the villages nearby, and it was necessary that we put it down.'

'I see,' said Sami. He was uncomfortable, I could tell, suddenly restless in his chair. The old man's talk of imperial might against a band of villagers was not pleasant to him.

The old man must have seen this too. He reddened a little and said quickly, a little contritely, 'Oh, we were there for such a short time; nothing much came of it really.' And then he looked downhearted. 'It was the times, you know. War was on the horizon and we were very fearful of losing India... whatever history may say of British rule, we were very fond of India.'

'Fond? Like a master of his pet?' Sami's face - usually so calm and passive - became hard with belligerence. He was brought up by parents who had struggled hard for Indian Independence, and although in Sikimpur, Sami might be tolerant and non-committal about the British in India, in England he was less charitable. It was unusual to see this passion in Sami, interesting for all its rarity.

The man sat up and cleared his throat.

'Yes, I understand your attitude. We did not always play fair with India and her people but I am not sorry that we were there. I had the best days of my life there. All my six children were born there; two of them are still there, in fact.' He paused, reflecting. 'My eldest is buried there. She was a baby when she caught dysentery and did not recover, whilst my youngest has joined one of those long-haired hippie communes.' The old man frowned, shaking his head. 'Frankly, I do not know which is worse.'

Even Sami smiled at this, and his face softened.

'I think it was the right time for the British to leave India,' I entered the conversation cautiously. 'The war made it difficult for you to stay. The war allowed the Independence movement to grow up, don't you think?'

'Well, certainly the war helped it along.' The old man nodded thoughtfully. 'India grew up, and grew too far away from us. Yes, independence was inevitable. But I was sorry to leave. We both were.'

His wife nodded, her eyes lighting up at her thoughts of that enigmatic country.

'It is a wonderful place, she said. 'The diversity of its peoples and cultures are so very remarkable. It is very easy to fall in love with.'

And also to hate. I thought of the little baby who was lost to India and the many others like her. Our food came and, when the waiter had gone, the old man and his gentle-faced wife rose from their table. They both smiled and the old man placed his hunter's hat on his head.

'Well, we shall leave you to your lunch. It was very pleasant to have met you. Goodbye.'

Sami rose to shake the old man's hand. When they had gone, he leant in to me and whispered, 'You have been speaking to Ammi too long. She has turned you into a budding politician.'

'I shall miss my talks with Ammi. She holds some spirited opinions.'

Sami made a face. 'Maybe it is as well that we left before you became too militant.'

I grinned. 'Or indeed, too much of a feminist.'

Soon, the view from the train changed from sleeping fields to the towering instruments of industry. Other train carriages lay by the wayside, sitting idly on parallel rails and waiting for attention. The old steam locomotives were housed in a large building, open at the front, showing their black, neglected engines.

Leeds station was certainly busy, many bodies weaving in between each other, moving towards their platforms or away to catch buses. It was as nothing, however, compared to the stations that I had been upon in Sikimpur and Jodhpur. They had been a seething medley of travellers, traders and men, women and children who had made the platforms their home.

People here strode, fast or slow, chatting, laughing with one another, ushering their children with their buttoned-up winter coats; all orderly and very structured. They sat on clean seats that had been painted blue, read crisp new newspapers and occasionally checked their watches. Indian train travellers rushed or sauntered, and it was always frustrating for them when the train was late or had just left, and the children needed to be scolded or comforted. And there were few seats on the platforms, but that did not matter, for the hard stone of the station floor could be used to sit upon; it was more spacious, if a bit shabby.

In contrast, Leeds station was wonderfully tidy; there was a small tea room in one corner and a man selling newspapers standing near its entrance. A large brown clock hung from the ceiling, the hands on its Roman face showing the time.

Sami left the luggage by my feet and muttered that I should stay inside while he went to get a taxi. I paid little attention to him as I stood and observed the people around me, and also struggled to understand them. Their accents were so peculiar, like heavy weights that could not rattle. I had heard some of these sounds on the train, but been far too involved in the country that we were passing, to pay much notice. Now, though, I was surrounded by it and felt overwhelmed.

'I have a taxi waiting outside. Hurry! Are you staring at people again?' Suddenly, Sami appeared, flustered and frowning.

I picked up the smaller suitcase and followed him outside. The wind was blowing colder than ever and the sun was growing pale behind the gathering of the clouds. We had arrived in Leeds, a city more open than London. It had a neglected elegance to it, its grand buildings coated in the black soot of industry.

The taxi took us away from the centre of the brightly-lit city and out into the dark, winding lanes of the country. We drove for almost half an hour, and arrived tired and hungry at a set of gates that led to a wide, tree-lined driveway. The sky now was a murky grey and the moon shining with a crescent bloom. At the end of the path was a hotel, the kind that I had not seen before.

Aberford Hall was a large country house, with tall, stone pillars and statues that stood poised in old glory. Inside, there was much oak panelling and a sweeping staircase. The grounds seemed to wander out in a vast openness, somewhere where the deer could roam, and beyond that was a wood filled with pheasants, which would become prey to the hunters and their guns at the end of this January month. It was something that Sami looked forward to: *shikar*. Back in Sikimpur, he had spent many weekends out in the jungles of Gujarat, hunting the small monkeys that ran wild there.

'It will be interesting to track down a different kind of prey,' he remarked. 'I have only hunted monkeys and they are cunning, but to try and outsmart the birds that can take to the air... although, of course, monkeys can take to the trees when they are frightened. Also, I am intrigued as to how *shikar* in a wood compares with the jungle.'

At night, I could hear the foxes scrambling and their cries calling through the chilled still air. This northern coldness was something quite different from the London cold. It instilled itself in everything that lived and breathed. The plants were lined with it, the white frost upon the grass. Looking on all of this, I instinctively clasped myself close, pulling my muscles in tight to stop the heat from escaping. The fire that was lit in the great hall of Aberford Hall drew me in, throwing red and yellow warmth at my shivering body. The land outside lay in a fine covering of chill that rose into the air and filled our lungs.

Often, I would sit and stare out of our hotel window, admiring the beauty of the landscape, torn between the warmth and my longing to walk out into it. The snow was coming down in large, white flakes, tumbling through the air and landing softly on the ground below. When I did venture out, my cheeks bore the brunt of the wind that blew and my breath spiralled up into the greying sky. The grass crunched under my feet and, in the distance, the deer were silhouetted against the bare-branched trees, and the lonely birds that circled above me seemed bereft of their nests.

We were told that we had been lucky to have missed the first days of December, when the snow had fallen so thickly and so quickly that cars and lorries had been abandoned along the roadside, and the people of the neighbouring villages had been stranded without power and food for two weeks.

'The Headleys' boy was sick, at death's door, practically. Their farm was cut off so there were no getting word out for a doctor to get to him, and how would they, anyhows? With the snow thigh high in some places. Oh, but they did a clever thing, they did. They only telephoned the BBC to get a doctor out that way quick, and the BBC broadcast it, urgent-like, over the wireless. Only one doctor could get through that there snow, and that were old Dr Bennett, on his horse. Aye, he used to visit all his patients on horseback. He saved the boy's life, he did.'

The girl who served our breakfast told us this tale with a broad local accent and an animated voice. She had a pale, oval face that was wide, and weak blue eyes. This was the Nordic influence, Sami told me, the Vikings with their fair colouring had raided England and brought with them their Aryan genes.

One day, I sat at the window, reading. It was not so compelling a book and so, occasionally, I would look out to see Sami pacing up and down the long drive of Aberford Hall. Every few seconds he would glance at his watch, frown, gaze into the distance and then continue his impatient walk. He did not seem to notice the snow that was beginning to fall or the black pen-stroke birds that were flitting in and out of the trees. His hair was flecking white with the snow that was settling on it. I smiled as I watched, feeling strangely fond of this boy who waited so impatiently for his new toy. Soon, I left him to his vigil and began to put away our freshly laundered clothes. I was lost in starched shirts and newly-ironed trousers, when I heard footsteps running on the gravel path outside and Sami's voice calling out, excited and shrill.

I hurried back to the window and tapped on it to attract his attention. Sami looked up and waved to me from behind the wheel of his new car. Red and shining, it had arrived; finally, the wait and anticipation was over. The dark-suited man, who was standing by the driver's door, handed Sami the keys and he took them with a boyish glee. The car was now his.

Mr Harris, the manager of Aberford Hall, came out with many congratulations, walking around the car, nodding with approval. As I came out to join them, I heard him speak to Sami in his clipped English accent.

'Oh, Mr Altair, a Morgan! What a beauty she is. Such a pity it's so cold and there's snow everywhere. The side roads won't be clear enough, I fear, for you to give her a decent run out, but come the glorious spring I'm sure you'll find it such a joy driving along the country lanes with the top down.'

'It is beautiful, is it not?' Sami called out to me. 'Let's go for a drive.'

I looked upon it in admiration. The car was lovely indeed, the snow alighting upon it, speckling it fast.

'You must drive carefully, now,' Mr Harris said.

Sami nodded. 'Yes, I shall do so. Thank you.'

Mr Harris opened the passenger door for me and I climbed in, my hand touching fine, cool leather. I was amused by the boy sitting beside me, running his hand over the smooth walnut dashboard and then tightly clasping the steering wheel. I waved goodbye to Mr Harris, standing waving with one hand, while the other pulled his jacket collar up around his short neck.

'Better keep to the main roads!' Mr Harris called out a final piece of advice.

Sami gently rolled his new car down the drive and out onto the open road. He drove slowly at first, too taken with the feel of it. The fields that we passed, the trees, the fences, roofs and paths all lay under a white blanket. I looked out onto it while Sami stayed hooked on his motor. Each gear change, acceleration and deceleration engaged his whole body; the curve of his arms, the bend of his knees and the way his face was set in concentration.

This Morgan was some distance away from the ageing Toyota that had once belonged to his father, and which Sami had not thought to get rid of; not just because of his sentimental nature. What was the joy of a new car that would soon be lost in the dust and smut of Sikimpur traffic? What would be the joy of a new car when inching through the noisy, car-ridden roads of Sikimpur, where horns hooted endlessly over each other like an ill-tuned orchestra? It was an odd sight, so many drivers sitting impassive in their unmoving cars, chatting, listening to music and, once in a while, pressing down on their horns, pumping out a hard *beep, beep, beep*. There was no anger, however,, no frustration; just something to help pass the time, a tradition learnt and adhered to.

The incessant, swirling grime of Sikimpur violated and clogged engines, and so Sami had stayed with his loyal, tattered Toyota.

In this, he was not alone. Abbaji drove an old Mercedes that had once been black and had once shone brightly. It was for everyday use, a bit like the work clothes of a labourer. But, in one corner of the Shamshad estate, hidden in the garage under thick canvas dust sheets, was his Sunday best, the Rolls-Royce Phantom I. Every Sunday morning, an hour before breakfast, Abbaji would drive it out into the pale glare of the young sun and walk around it, examining carefully its fenders, its undercarriage, its tyres, and polishing it with the softest of chamois leather. And then, when he was satisfied with his handiwork, he would stand back to admire it, just briefly, before leaning in to start the engine; listening with great attention to the hum of it, before proudly driving down the smooth path that led to the boundary where the garden ended and the fields of sugar cane and corn began.

Chapter Twelve

Now that we had a car, Sami and I set about finding a house for us. We drove out to leafy suburbs, tiny villages and even isolated farmhouses. Many of the houses that we viewed did not suit us, they felt alien inside and we could not find our place within them.

We passed through mining villages, with terraced houses built for purpose, and children playing football and skipping out in the streets. The countryside that we travelled through was glorious in the dim light of early January, the sun low in the pale blue sky. The muddied fields were ridged with ploughed earth, and the barns half full of autumn hay and farm animals. Each time we stepped into this quiet chill, I would pull my coat tightly around myself and hurriedly feel for my gloves.

The people we met stared at us with polite curiosity, always saying a friendly 'Hello' in their broad Yorkshire accents. The smaller children would point at us and whisper to their parents, who would ignore them with an embarrassed smile.

One house we viewed had a swimming pool inside, smooth with small green tiles and water so clear and blue that it could have come from a South Sea lagoon. I thought of our pool at Shamshad, a tank deeply dug in comparison; its mottled green water shimmering in the sun and leaves floating around its surface, dancing as if touched by a breeze. It was only ever filled with water in the morning if we wanted to swim later in the day. Otherwise, it would sit empty, a large sunken pit with rough walls and bits of fruit peelings that the monkeys had discarded.

Abbaji cleaned it himself, sweeping out the leaves, picking up the chewed fruit, scrubbing off the bird droppings. Sometimes, I would help him, climbing down into it and looking up at the trees that surrounded us, like giants gazing in. At the end of the day, the pool water would be drained away to irrigate the orchards through tubing that was lowered in. It was a lovelier pool than this deep blue one, although not so bright and not so polished.

At first, the house hunt was fun. Driving out with freedom and exploring tree-lined avenues, winding lanes and places where there was nothing but a few charming cottages and the essential country pub, with a fire burning brightly in its hearth. There were some strange-sounding names that twisted and turned our tongues and brains: Mytholmroyd, Holmfirth and Keighley. The last of these, pronounced *Keethley*, made me shake my head.

'What a silly language English is,' I remarked to Sami. 'The *gh* already causes so much trouble: sounding sometimes like *ff* and at other times as *ow*. Now there is a new one: *th*! It is a very confusing thing. Maybe this is how the British made the natives believe in their superiority, by using this strangely pronounced language. They were able to rule over so much of the world by confusing all us natives!'

Sometimes, we would stop in these places, eating warm winter soup and drinking hot tea. But all too soon, the novelty of invading other people's houses wore off.

'I do not believe we shall ever move out of here,' I grumbled one evening when we arrived back in our room in Aberford Hall, cold and worn out. 'There cannot be any more houses for us to look at!'

But Sami shook his head, a keen glint in his eye.

'It is there, a house that is to be ours. It is just waiting for us to find it. We cannot give up our search.'

On day seventeen, we drove along the A1. It was very straight and seemingly endless, an old Roman road. I gazed out of the car window at the incessant rows of trees, leaning like old men with their pipes. Now that we were into the last days of January, the weather had eased off into snowless days and nights. We took the turning that led to Tadcaster and drove through this town of breweries and kept on, coming presently to a grand old house, Newton Hall, to the right of us. It was a mansion really, set some way back from the road. It would have been a manor of some grandeur in the past, but now it was unkempt, and the tree-lined avenue that led from the large iron-wrought gates was grassed over, with sheep maintaining the lawns.

We turned right after this sight, away from the main road and onto a narrower, less smooth road heading, as a sign told us, towards Newton Kyme.

'We are almost there.' Sami read the name of the road, 'Croft Lane. Only a few minutes now. Five, no more.'

He was happy. The sun had come out from behind the thin winter clouds and was now sitting low and bright on the horizon.

It was as Sami said. We continued our drive for a few minutes longer, passing by houses with high garden walls and thick privet hedges, until we slowed down and eventually stopped. The house was set back from the road, with a stone wall rather than a hedge, and a single iron gate opening up to a well-paved path. Further along the stone wall there was another, larger opening that led to a wide and loosely-gravelled drive. A car was parked there, big and bold and square.

I became nervous and excited walking up the path to the solid oak door. The house had a charm about it, an old sort of understanding with its large windows and pretty green lawn. I liked this house very much.

The door opened before Sami rang the bell and a man stood, his smile wide and welcoming, a big toe protruding out from the felt of a worn-out left slipper. He shook our hands.

'Hello, you must be Mr and Mrs Altair. I'm Frederick Burton. Do come in out of the cold. I hope we were not difficult to find.'

The inside of his home was a soft yellow in the light of the winter noon. He took us from room to room, telling us the history of each; each coat of paint, each piece of furniture, each lampshade and each picture. There were many items from the Far East: Chinese prints, jade figures from Singapore, prayer mats from Malaysia. Dr Frederick Burton was well-travelled around the Southern Hemisphere for he had been in the British diplomatic service.

He took great pride in what there was - photos of his family, their adventures, his children's graduations, and then pictures of grandchildren, smiling, happy faces, brown with the holiday sun. There had been love in this house, and much life. I could hear the parties, the laughter, the arguments, despair and peace, human emotions that were crammed into corners, and memories residing within the walls.

In the living room we were joined by Mrs Burton. We heard her before we saw her, her wheelchair making its way along the loose floorboards in the hall. She was the reason they had to leave. The house had become too big to manage, with the stairs impossible to climb and the garden too demanding. There was much sadness in her eyes. She had probably hoped to die here one day, in her familiar home.

Mr Burton went quickly to his wife.

'Lottie, my love, there you are. This is the...'

Mrs Burton waved him away with her hand.

'I know who they are. The Indian couple.'

She peered at us through delicate glasses, leaning forward in her chair for a better look, soft wisps of hair falling across her rouged cheek.

'They seem all right. I suppose they will look after the place. And, at least they're young.' She began to wheel herself away from us and, before she reached the threshold, she turned and looked at me with disdain. 'You will need a daily help, someone to come and do the cleaning for you. I don't suppose you've done much scrubbing in your time. And a gardener, also. The garden takes some sound knowledge of horticulture to tend to it properly.'

Taken aback by her assumption, I told Mrs Burton of the pool that I cleaned out at Shamshad Bagh, working away at all the leaves that fell in and the insects floating around it.

'And I am not too bad at pulling out weeds and planting many rows of roses, either,' I added. 'I do not know all there is about gardening, but I am sure that I can learn.'

Mrs Burton's face softened from its hard stare.

'That will be useful, but you have the look of one who has been waited on.'

I conceded her point, intrigued as I was about the 'look' that I had.

'Yes, we had servants, and so, yes, I suppose I am a little spoilt.'

'Well, I hope you have some of the frivolity that goes with that. Throw lots of parties and make sure that the house is always full. It needs laughter, this place.' Mrs Burton looked at me in earnest. 'Thrives on it. That is why we have to go. There's not much laughter in us these days.'

She slowly made her way out of the room, pausing only to say, 'I must go and see to myself. It's my bridge night and I need to get ready. Good-bye, and I do hope you make the right decision for the house.'

Mr Burton gazed after the disappearing form of his wife. His manner became distracted. 'Eh, would you like to see the garden, Lottie's garden? It's quite large, and backs onto the vicarage. I shall miss hearing the church bells ringing out for evensong.'

He was standing in front of the French doors, a slight, angular man who must once have been quite large. Now, however, his skin and clothes slumped on his body and his bones protruded from under his loose shirt collar so he looked like an old, wire clothes hanger.

Most of the garden lay in a crescent repose. It slept right now, with shrubs cut back and the soil lying still under the silver frost. Mr Burton walked with us, pointing out the places where the blue lavender and the pink hyssop and the laurel grew. At the side of the garden, just behind the kitchen, there was a herb garden and beyond all of this was a small orchard comprising two apple trees, two plum and one pear. All were bare now.

'In the spring you'll find them flush with blossom, and the daffodils and snowdrops will be out come February. They're dotted all around the place.' Mr Burton swept the garden with his arm. 'Lottie always planted for the colour of nature: cornflowers, violets and poppies. It used to be so lively when she was in charge. I wish she could enjoy it again but the wheelchair makes it hard for her, especially now that she has arthritis in her arms.'

Sami nodded awkwardly.

'Yes, she must love this place very much. One can see it from her eyes and her words. I am truly sorry that you must give it up.'

Mr Burton leant heavily on his walking stick and looked back at the house.

'It will be all the sadder for Lottie. She grew up in this house, and then we came back to it when her parents passed away and I retired from my diplomatic posting. Now...'

'Where are you planning to go to now?' Sami asked, then reddened. 'Sorry, it is not my business to know your plans.'

Mr Burton waved the apology aside. Indeed his face, his whole manner, seemed relieved by this divulgence, by this sharing,

'No, no. What can the old lose by confiding such things? We shall move to Cornwall, where I come from. Yorkshire is Lottie's county. Her family were true Yorkshire folk, but the family has moved around and we have lost touch with many of them. There's only a cousin of hers left: Rose, in nearby

Tadcaster. They'll miss each other terribly, but my eldest son, Jonathon, lives in Portcurno, on the Cornish coast. He's been trying to persuade us to live nearer to him, so that he can look after us.'

Chapter Thirteen

We settled slowly into our new home. There was something of the Burtons that lingered and we could not undo it with haste. Still, it was fine to be able to walk along corridors without running into other guests and hurrying staff. Our room in Aberford Hall, though accommodating and spacious, was also limited in its appeal. There was a restricted privacy, whereby the door would be shut on the outside world but the maid could knock for the laundry, where meals were chosen from a menu and the receptionist knew of our movements.

The house, void of the Burtons' possessions was a vast, vacant shell but soon furniture began filling in the empty spaces, curtains framed the wide windows and pictures hung on blank canvas walls. Bookcases sat against the walls and the floors became covered with carpets and rugs. We spent our days searching for these items and then waiting with impatient excitement for the delivery vans to bring them to us.

During this time, Sami worked in a room that he had laid out as his study. It had a large mahogany table, upon which was a Parker ink pen that his father had given him and whole sheaths of paper, some written on and some blank. It was here that Sami held meetings and, as I passed by the closed doors, I would hear voices, low and serious, papers rustling and china clinking.

Occasionally, we would drive into Leeds and, while Sami met with his colleagues at the university, I wandered through the shops along the Headrow and Briggate, sitting in tea rooms to enjoy Earl Grey tea and scones with cream and raspberry jam. I visited the City Library, drifting through its rather dull art gallery, and staring at paintings full of a worn countryside and peasants in the midst of their toil. Those people seemed grey, ageing and tired in the face of Father Time's course.

We bought a new telephone for the drawing room. It was cream and large and curved, so unlike the black, sharp-edged telephones that we were used to. We phoned first Ammi, and then Ammaji and Abbaji, speaking to them down lines that crackled and they sounded as though they were at the other end of the world.

With her vivid imagination and anxious nature, Ammaji worried at our isolation. Being so far as we were from friends and family, she was deeply concerned for our wellbeing and my ability to keep a home. Her worries were not unreasonable. She ran the Shamshad household with an impressive hand. She organised the servants, dealt with their belligerence and settled their differences in an almost fluid manner, all without distancing herself from them. This, I think, was because she came from a similarly modest background and so she did not have it in her to demean those beneath her.

At the time, my sisters and I were oblivious to all of this; we rode over it in our sun-filled chariots. Running a household was for married women and I had not been married long. Besides, who could have prepared for this move to England, a move that landed me under the light of an alien sky?

So, when I spoke to Ammaji on our new telephone she was full of questions and advice. '*What are you eating? Oh there will be no halal meat, but at least make sure that it is not pig. Best to stay with vegetarian food, after all, the south Indians seem to manage on it. And the housework? You have one of those modern gas cookers? And also a machine for washing your clothes? Good, but you cannot know how to use them. Yes, yes, you can learn but to look after a whole house will take yet more learning, and it will not be easy. No, it is better if you can get some servants.*'

Sami told Ammaji that we would not need servants; the concept of the middle classes having servants was, in the late 60's, something quite unfamiliar in England. In the background, I could hear Abbaji shouting something and then Sami nodded his head.

'Yes, indeed that is right,' he said. 'We are not in a position to hire someone local. No respectable English woman would come to cook and clean for an Indian, even for the professional class of Indian. It is unimaginable. To do so would be belittling to them.'

I looked about my new home, at the kitchen with its clean surfaces and cupboards, the hall with its shining floor, the windows so well polished. I wondered how it would be to cook food and to clean floors and wash clothes and I believed, in that moment, that we would both starve and fall prey to the diseases of poor hygiene.

Fortunately, Sami knew something of cooking and he taught me how to use a toaster and open tin cans. Coffee was his speciality and, very soon, I became adept at boiling eggs so that the yolk remained runny and the white solid. We discovered the fun of eating hot, buttered scones in the evenings by the fire and scoffing on Cheddar cheese melted on crumpets; all the while sitting by the French doors and looking out on the snow that was still spread across the lawn.

One day, Sami came home in delight.

'I have found something new. It is called a delicatessen! I found it quite by accident when I was looking for the post office in Tadcaster. I was hoping to post those aerograms today so they would be on their way to India before the weekend. Mr Burton had told me it was on the High Street, just past the children's playground, but before I got there I found an amazing place. You know, they hang up meat for drying, like they do in Lalmali, but here it is mostly pork.'

'Well, that's no good for us,' I said, disappointed. 'It does not sound so exciting with foods we cannot touch.'

'No, but there are other foods besides the *haram* things. Lots of cheeses and breads. They let me taste some of them.'

'So that is why you are so late home.'

'It was all very delicious,' he continued. 'They make the bread themselves. Oh, the smell of it is truly wonderful! That bread we have is so tasteless by comparison. You must come and see it for yourself. I told them I will be bringing you.'

And so we went that very minute. I laughed at Sami's enthusiasm over bread and cheese but he was right. The shop smelled so warm and inviting, and we were extravagant in our purchases. Two loaves of bread, one brown, one white, and four different types of cheeses with foreign names that Sami knew from his time spent in Salvatore's place, Mozzarella, Camembert and a florid one that was stained with blue, called Stilton. We also bought some biscuits - water biscuits, the shopkeeper called them - and some butter, too. Then, we spent the rest of the afternoon in greed. Ammaji would not have approved. Where was the meal in some bread and cheese?

But we had fun. In those early days, everything was new and we were alone, and together we discovered them. We would sit in the cold dark evenings, huddled in our armchairs, watching the fire, which I had lit for Sami coming home, as it spluttered and spat at us. We would laugh at my attempts and then Sami would rearrange the logs, showing me, again, how to lay them so that the fire blazed rather than sparked. Our chat was of the day, he with his plans of business and I with my hopes for the garden.

We would take walks around the village, meeting some of our neighbours, who greeted us with a cautious, and then friendly, curiosity. We met Mrs Beresford, the doctor's wife, on her way to meet her two children off the school bus, and the Reverend Bramley, who lived in the vicarage behind our house and who, in finer weather, would rehearse his sermons whilst walking around his garden, and we learnt that Mr Landen, with greying hair, was the headmaster at the nearby grammar school.

Then, it would be bedtime. I would be sorry then, for our affection was not the love that included a yearning passion for each other's bodies, and when we made love, it was with a faltering familiarity that ended in stark satisfaction. Like a task fulfilled or a hurdle overcome. Until the next time.

The housework, however, was not a task that I could engage in. I could not engage with the Hoover and would knock against tables and chairs, cursing them under my livid breath. The surfaces that were gathering dust were too many, and the spray that erupted from the aerosol cans made me sneeze and gave me a headache, while the stone flags of the kitchen floor seemed perpetually littered with crumbs. Soon, I began to avoid looking down for the thick mist of paranoia that took over me.

It was all my grumbling and pessimism that made Sami's mind up.

Aida and Hana arrived in Leeds in the most forbidding of weathers. The skies were thick with impending snowfall and the air was iced over. When Sami showed them out of the car, they shivered with the cold and would surely have raced back to the sunshine of Shamshad Bagh if they could.

They were shy and stayed close to one another at first, until I took them into the warmth of the kitchen and then Aida, so prim and dark, with her lovely teeth shining like torchlight, clapped her little hands and gave a giggle of joy. She let her fingers touch the smooth worktops, opened and closed cupboards, turned gleaming pots about in her hands and stood still in front of an open fridge. It was her paradise on earth, she said, her Kashmir.

Hana, standing in the doorway, joined in her friend's delight so that her long plait of hair, that went down to below her waist, swung about her hips as she moved. In Sikimpur, after she had washed it, she would let it loose to dry in the sunshine and it hung like an ebony curtain that shimmered. On these days, Ammaji would not allow Hana out beyond the garden walls, for she said that the sight of Hana's hair would enchant all the foolish men and cause many accidents.

'*Jadoo*!' Ammaji would say and make her sit out in the garden with her hair spread out over the back of a wicker chair, taking in the heat of the day. In the brilliant sunshine, Hana's thick and luscious locks would dry within the hour and then she would skilfully plait a thick braid and carry on with her chores.

Alas, in Yorkshire's cold air, Hana found that her hair dried slowly, even when she stayed for an age by the fire. She would emerge after a while with her face red and her forehead shining, but her hair still damp. In the end, she developed a severe cold that laid her up for almost two weeks and, thereafter, she suffered badly from headaches and sore throats.

It was then that she decided, tearfully, to have her hair cut. She asked me to do it and I was reluctant. I knew how upset she would be and I did not want to be responsible for it. But she pushed the scissors into my hands and urged me.

'You must. Otherwise, I will have to do it myself, and I cannot face that. Aida cannot do it, she has no idea how to.' Hana spoke with a full heart and I found that I could not say no.

With every snip, Hana took a deep intake of breath and I winced. At first, I cut off a few inches but Hana looked down at it and said firmly, 'That is not enough. I will still suffer from the slowness of its drying. Please cut off some more.'

She closed her eyes and I looked at her lovely trail of hair. It was thick and healthy, and had taken her much of her adult life to grow. I took a deep breath, brushed a few more loose strands out and, choosing a place somewhere beneath her shoulder blades, I cut across as straight as I could. When it was done I gathered the fallen hair together into a piece of newspaper and removed it before Hana could see. I came back to find Hana gazing, with shining tears, at her image in the mirror, turning her head gently from side to side and watching the movement of her shortened hair.

'I do not look like myself,' she said. 'I feel different, too. My head feels lighter. I did not realise how heavy my hair was.'

I nodded. The weight of hair that had fallen into the paper had, indeed, been heavy.

'You will get used to it,' I told her. 'It is very different but I think it is nice.'

Aida came in just then and sniffed.

'Good, you have finally done it. It is far more sensible now. You do not need so much hair anyway. It is not hygienic. That is why I keep mine short.'

Hana looked at her. 'Your hair does not grow, Aida, everyone knows that. That is why it is short.'

'Well, I am glad about that. What would I do with long hair, anyway?'

Poor Aida had no thoughts of her looks. She thought herself gauche and unattractive. As such, she acted that way, never worrying about doing herself up or dressing nicely.

So, our life of bread and cheese came to an end, and we returned our palates to spiced *aloo gobi, daal* and *plau* rice. But, while Aida was happy indoors surrounded by her pots and spoons and ingredients, Hana longed to breathe in the outdoor air.

I had known Hana since we were children, had swam in the pool together and climbed trees in our younger years. Then, we had grown up; I had gone to college and she, our gardener's daughter, had found herself spending more time with her father, her recently widowed father, whom she wanted to stay close to. She would spend her days digging in the soil, listening to his quiet, wise words and, in time, being allowed to organise the new seeds that Ammaji wanted for planting.

She was always outside, until Ammaji had asked her to go to England and keep house for Sahira Bibi. Her father had encouraged her to do this, indeed cajoled her into leaving his side, going to the other side of the world; to be herself and not just his helper in the garden.

Reluctantly, she had agreed, and learnt much quicker than I how to handle the cleaning of the house and the importance of separating the laundry in terms of colour and fabric. However, she grew restless when the work was done and the day was not yet over, but the darkness was drawing in and she was not yet used to the cold. Her ready smile faded and she became quiet, talking in monosyllabic utterances.

Then one day, some three weeks after she had arrived in England, I found her staring out of the large French windows as the rain was falling lightly down. 'I must go out.' Even as she finished her sentence, she shivered slightly. 'I cannot bear to stay inside, even though I fear the cold outside.'

I rose from my chair. 'I will fetch your coat. But are you sure?'

Hana, delicate as she was, had a resolute nature.

'At least into the garden. For a minute, just one minute. It is hard to see it from behind glass windows. I must touch the air outside.'

And so, I handed Hana her thick winter coat and boots, and helped her with the gloves and hat. I opened the door so that she could step out. I watched her flinch briefly against the cold, wet air. Then, once again she smiled, a full smile and her face was alive, bright and fresh. She was beautiful once more.

As the weather became less inclement, Hana began to talk about the garden and especially the vegetable patch that grew in front of the kitchen. Listening to her, I thought how like her father she was. She loved the land, loved the feel of the soil.

Hana and I tended the garden together at first. While I was happy with what we had, Hana had more ambitions. Her education at her father's side meant that her imagination was greater than mine and so she wanted to know more about the English garden - soil composition, sowing seasons, planting out, cutting back, and such.

I took her to the library so that she could find what it was she needed to know, but Hana's English was limited, rudimentary really. We brought the books home and, sitting at the kitchen table, Hana would ask her questions and I would look up the answers, pointing them out to her. She would read each passage carefully in her slow and halting style, becoming familiar with repeating words and, in turn, more fluent. She studied with great concentration and wrote a list of the tools that she needed: hoes and trowels, secateurs and loppers. Soon, the shed was filled with all these goods and Hana felt herself prepared.

We would find her so often, kneeling amongst the flower beds, her hands rooted deep into the earth and her face so attentive that we dare not disturb her. She became fascinated with the theory of cultivation: trailing azaleas, pocket-size primroses and climbing honeysuckle. With time, I left her to her tireless rapture and contented myself with a little rough corner that caught the sun as it rose and was radiant. In it, I planted those flowers that Hana had left behind, those that were wild and free: bright sunflowers, blood red tulips, golden rod and clematis, a tuft of blue bells and tiny pink flowers that Hana ripped from her soil as weeds.

The soil that we clutched with our hands was so very different from the soil of Sikimpur. Here, the earth was dark and a conglomerate of itself; it clung to our clothes and instruments and held the roots firm. In Sikimpur, the earth was more like thickened dust; it would trickle through your fingers as though sieved and fall away with the breeze, and you had to labour and toil hard in order for it to sustain life.

It was springtime and the days were longer now, with not such a vast curtain of darkness at their end. The sunlight that came in through the windows lit up all the surfaces and brightened the rooms. The clump of trees in the orchard came back to life, and what life there was in those soft pink blossoms! In time, these would bear plums, apples and pears, our own to fill our wicker baskets with and take in to Aida.

Sami, whom Aida adored, had a taste for fruit tarts, apple being his favourite, and Aida, with determination, had learnt to cook the British way, asking me to bring her home cookery books from the library and cutting out recipes from *Woman's Own* magazines. All those days then, the kitchen was hidden in a cloud of flour and warm air from the oven, and the smell of bubbling and baking would drift from it, flooding the rest of the house.

Until she came to us, Aida was used to the aroma of hot spices: cumin, coriander, chilli, turmeric. They seemed to belong to the heat of the East; they would draw the sweat from you and help you melt a little. Here, Aida had taken to using herbs like oregano, basil, rosemary, and the more aromatic spices such as cinnamon, nutmeg and cloves. When the weather was still cool and the wind was picking up, these smells kept you warm; they were welcoming, like an open fire.

Sami would sniff the air about him, saying, 'Ah pear tart!', 'Oh, plum pie!' or 'My favourite, apple crumble! Wonderful.'

The last of these was a Friday night treat and, having demolished his sizeable slice, Sami would throw up his hands, rub his expanding stomach and declare that Aida was a genius, that she must never leave him for he would die without her apple crumble. This would make sturdy Aida blush as red as a plum, so deep that the colour surfaced from under her dark skin and she would have to leave the room.

Simple Aida, bold in her features and wide in her smile, had lived most of her life in a small village that was a popular target for the embroidered promises of politicians when election time was approaching. There, Aida should have lived, married, had a handful of children and died, but she had tired of her bullying father and numerous siblings who fought and ran wild, and had run away to the streets of Sikimpur. Here, bewildered by the wailing, churning noise of car horns and closeness of bodies, she had dived out into the midday traffic, causing an uproar:

'Get out of the way, you stupid girl!' 'What do you think you are doing, you crazy cow?' 'Can't you see? Are you blind?' 'How dare you put your filthy hands on my car? It is not for you to touch. It is a Honda, samjey? Not one of your horse carts full of shit. If there is any mark on the paintwork, then I will have you arrested, samjey meri baht?'

This had been all too much for Aida, who was tired and hungry and afraid, and she had coped with it in the only way she could; she had screamed with all the might within her. The sound that came from her had made the car horns stop and the engines fall silent. It stopped the tongues and shocked the people. And then, at the end of her exertion, Aida had fainted.

Abbaji, seeing all this from the silence of his own car, had instructed the driver to bring a glass of water for her from a nearby peanut stall. He had brought Aida to Shamshad Bagh and there she had stayed, refusing to return to her family. That had been almost five years ago, when Aida had decided that to be our cook would be the thing she liked best.

Chapter Fourteen

At first, there was an awkwardness in our being together, for Hana and Aida were not so used to living at such close quarters with their master and mistress. They took the rooms in the large attic space that had once been the nursery, and bathed when Sami was out. In time, Sami arranged for a plumber to install a bathroom between their bedrooms and they were much happier then, and our tight-knit home came together, like the settling of pebbles along the shore.

Hana and Aida soon became part of our household; not servants really, but members of an extended family. We would discuss the night's dinner, argue over what programmes to watch on the new television, and when Hana thought she might want a greenhouse, even Aida cast her eye over the gardening catalogues.

It was out in the garden that Hana fell in love. Beautiful Hana, far more beautiful than I. The influences of her Scottish ancestry were strong. Her nose stood very erect and fine, giving her an air of unforced disdain and with her pale eyes and dark lashes... ah, in another time she would have been worshipped as a goddess. Like Emperor Jahangir's Anarkali, she would have commanded the throne from a pedestal. And, the fact that she hated all this made her all the more alluring, for Hana's shyness over her beauty came from her deep religiosity. She was the one who would rise before dawn to say her prayers and, every morning, after these *Fajr* prayers, we would hear her quietly reading from the Quran. All of this, however, did not stop her falling in love with a *ferenghi*.

It happened one blue spring morning, when Hana was planting the new seeds that would later flare up as summer blooms. The house was empty, with Sami in Leeds, and Aida and I having gone to the monthly market that the farmers held in the field opposite the railway station. It was a rare outing for Aida, for she was still very much a home person, uncomfortable with those things that were unfamiliar to her.

The air had been quiet and Hana lost to her digging, when a shadow had blocked the sun from her. Looking up, Hana had been startled to see a uniformed man, hovering and uncertain, holding out a package to her that was neatly wrapped in brown paper. It was the postman. He had smiled politely at her and explained that he had rang the doorbell several times, with an increasing length of trill each time, but there had been no reply.

Indeed, he had also shouted '*Hello*' but again there had been no reply. When he had been on the point of leaving, he fancied that he could hear a noise coming from the back garden and when he went there he had found Hana tending to the earth. His sudden presence had unnerved her and she almost struck him with a garden fork, but there was something about him that had made her stop.

'I did not need to be afraid of him.' Hana seemed embarrassed as she told me this; her face became delicate with her cheeks enflaming and her eyes turned downward. She began to play with the collar of her shirt, twisting it with her fingers and her hand moved to her forehead, running away the crease of a frown.

'I am sure it is turning quite warm now,' she said.

I could not place it, but her look, her words, which seemed so innocent, made me quite envious. I thought her state of mind utterly wonderful, the confusion and the certainty of it.

Hana looked at me, aware that I was still there, and murmured, 'It is hard to explain, but I have felt a little strange since that moment.'

The next week, Hana came to me and asked whether I would help her with her English, which was limited and basic. With difficulty, she could make herself understood. She could not, however, hold a conversation, at least not one that flowed. Ammaji had tried to persuade her to stay at school, but Hana had refused; she wanted to protect her father from his grieving.

Her chats with the postman were short and endearingly halting, but she wanted to explain to him how it was that she came here, what made her laugh, why she loved the smell of the freshly turned soil.

To help her, Sami and I took to talking to her in English. It was difficult at first - not her understanding us, but waiting for her reply. It was hard at times not to finish sentences for her, especially when the struggling made her squint and grit her teeth. At night, she would always complain of a headache. She would rub her temples with the tips of her fingers and wince with the pleasure of released pain.

The sight of this made Aida sniff. 'What is the point of all of this?' she would say. 'All for a man, huh! There are better things to pursue than a man. And,' she added mockingly, 'after all, you are so religious.'

'I am not pursuing him!' Hana replied indignantly. 'I am not a common harlot. But it is good to better yourself. What is wrong with that?'

Here, Aida shook her head and muttered. 'Bettering yourself is all very well, but only if you do it for yourself.'

'It is for myself!' retorted Hana. 'We have come here, to England, and we should learn to live here. And part of that is to be able to talk with the people here.'

'I know how to talk to the people here,' Aida sneered. 'I can ask for the price of tomatoes, peppers and cauliflower. I can tell them it is too expensive and that the quality is poor. What more do I need to say to anybody?'

We were at the dining table, sipping our hot chocolates. The weather had turned cold that week and there had been a sprinkling of late spring frost on the grass that morning. Outside, with the evening pressing upon the daylight, the fog hung like a chilled drape.

Having spoken her mind, Aida got up from the table and avoiding all of us, she carried her mug out into her kitchen. I watched her broad back as it exited from the room. What she said was true for her. She had no need of anything else, really. She had her kitchen and her stove and her people to serve, and her world seemed filled to overflowing with these. But I wondered if she was happy.

I asked Sami that night and he thought about it for a long while before replying.

'I have not thought of Aida as being happy or unhappy. I do not think she has the need for it. She takes what is there for her and gets on with it. Maybe it is to do with her past life. I do not know.'

'Still,' I said, 'I cannot understand her hostility towards Hana. Why should she take such offence at Hana's efforts to speak better English?'

'I don't think that it is a genuine offence. It is more that Aida is simple. She has no personal ambitions and probably believes that to do so would lead to no good. She thinks of herself as one of the serving class. I think she is content with her life, so yes, maybe there is a sort of happiness there.'

Still I persisted. 'Perhaps she is feeling betrayed? She and Hana came out to us together, they have shared in the novelty of this experience but now Hana has her postman. Maybe that has made Aida feel left behind.'

This made Sami laugh, a loud guffaw that filled the air like the shot of a rifle. I had taken him by surprise and he shook his head.

'You think too much. Let it be. There is no great mystery, only people getting used to each other's ideas.'

So that night, I let it rest, but the next day, Aida asked a question out of nowhere which surprised us all and caused Hana a great deal of discomfort.

'Do you plan to marry him, then?' and though Aida asked in semi-seriousness, Hana replied with a great deal of thought and effort.

'No... Actually, I do not know.'

'Then what are your efforts for?'

And Hana answered, 'Well, for other things, then.' She pointed to the books that were lined in rows along the bookcase and added in English, 'For those. Like the Sahira Bibi, maybe I would enjoy to read.'

This made Aida bristle. 'So, already you think you are too clever for me. You talk *angrezi* to me so as to make me look ignorant, stupid?' She waved her cloth at her friend and said with force, 'But let me tell you it is you who will look stupid to be thinking about this *ferenghi*, it is you who is shameless!'

She left the room with her lips pressing tightly against her teeth and her eyes bright with burning.

Hana looked after her, forlorn and ashamed at her outburst.

'Maybe Aida is right. I shall end up being the fool.'

She spoke in Urdu again, gathering her threads and cloth together as she spoke. She had been embroidering a cushion for her bedroom.

The evening meal was a chilled affair. Hana and Aida did not speak to one another and spoke very little at all. Sami, who had been at work since early that morning, was tired and quiet also.

The dishes were cleared away, and while I helped Aida wash up, Hana went up to her room to work on her cushion; at least that was what she told us.

Soon Aida, complaining of a sore head, went to her bed, and I took Sami a cup of tea. I found him in the living room, without his usual newspaper, but standing looking out at the dark, moonless night.

I gave him his tea, for which he was thankful.

'My head is aching badly. I have had a difficult day today.' He sat down on the settee, crossing his legs.

'It has been a hard day at home today, as well,' I said.

'Yes, I saw at dinner that something had happened to take away the harmony of the household. It was obvious that Hana had been crying and Aida did not look happy. Her *paratha* were hard and the rice too salty. She did not even seem to care about it, and that is most unusual for her.'

'No, it has not been good.' I told him what had happened, ending, 'I don't think Hana meant to be haughty, and I cannot imagine that she was being deliberately cruel to Aida. But I think, from things she has said, that there is something not quite right in her world. I think, perhaps, that thoughts of her postman are causing her trouble.'

Sami nodded. 'Well, it is an entirely new situation for her, new and unfamiliar. Although, of course, they do not really have anything at all. They have only met a few times and that is when he delivers the letters to her.' He picked up his teacup and sighed. 'It is all the more complicated because he is an *Angrezi*. We must try to help her.'

'But how? I am not an expert in relationships, or indeed love. Are you?' I asked jokingly.

'No, no, of course not.'

There was something about the way he held his head when he said this, the tilt of his chin, the despondency in his eyes. It made me think, suddenly from nowhere, of our conversation way back when we had been on our honeymoon, sitting having a polite cup of tea on the lawns of the Gesmir Residency.

'But you do know, I think,' I said carefully.

Sami blushed and frowned.

'I cannot think what makes you say that. After all, you have read more books than I on the subject and will actually be in a better position-'

'The Executioner's Spot,' I interrupted him. 'When you spoke of it being your favourite place in the College, and how quiet it was.'

'It was a quiet place. Very quiet, and also isolated. It was, as you said, not a place that many people visited.' Sami held his breath for a moment, and then let it out slowly. 'You are my wife, and I should not hide anything from you. I believe that is the modern way of thinking. Very well, I shall tell you a thing that I have not told anyone else, not even Ammi. After that, well, we shall see, I suppose.'

Sami unfolded his legs and placed his empty cup on the table by his side. He began his story slowly and appeared to be looking somewhere far beyond me.

'It was a long time ago, when I was young - sixteen years old. It was the day that Baba died. I went to the College in the evening, when there was less chance of meeting anyone. But I did meet someone, a girl, older than me, who had been a student of Baba's. She recognised me and stopped to speak about him. She was probably the only girl - apart from my cousins, that is - who had spoken to me, and I suppose that was enough for me to... to be interested in her.'

'Was she pretty?'

Why did I ask that? I had no interest in such a thing. It was just something to say, I think, for my mind was a huge blank, like a dark cavernous cave from whence there came nothing except that one inconsequential question.

Sami looked mystified. 'Pretty? I suppose so. I mean, she must have been to me, at the time. Back then. It seems so very long ago. I was a boy and she was studying at college. She appeared so... polished. Golden, like the sweat of the sun.' Sami sighed, his breath a tiny whisper of himself.

In the silence that followed, I examined Sami. He was changed with this memory, a bulb of mercury that was rising, a musical note that had changed its chord.

'You look different now,' I said. 'Just now, almost as if you have grown a new skin, almost as if it is a different you.'

'But, of course. I am a different person, not the boy led away from innocence. It does something to the inside, that knowledge, that sensation at such a young age.'

'The inside?' I wondered at that. What was on the inside? Thoughts, dreams, impulses. Desires, hopes, wishes. Is that what the inside amounted to? And the age? Was that then significant, too? But significant to what?

'What was the knowledge that you gained?' I asked. 'Was it of love? Or...' I became quiet, but Sami remained silent, too, and so I said in the end, 'Or lust? Or both, maybe?'

Sami stared at me without answering. Then, slowly, he replied in a quite deliberate tone, in a voice that was distended. 'The Executioner's Spot was a very strange place. And also Baba's death had left me in a very strange way. It brought me into a different world, quite solitary, quite remote. It was hard to resist it.'

I was shocked by this revelation, by the fact of Sami having had a lover. An *Indian lover*! Would it have been different if he had had an affair here, in England, while he had been a student? Yes, for he would have been away from his home and his family, and the things that kept him strictly on the straight path. Besides, English girls, the English way of life was notoriously loose; their morals were lower than the upright Indian, weren't they? Was he still in love with his golden beauty? Was that why he did not love me? I could not be jealous because there was no room for such sentiment in me, but it made me think. He could not resent me, surely? It was he who had proposed, but did he wish that things had turned out differently?

There was a different look in his eye, a distant kind of unknown that I could not delve into. It was a prohibitive look that made me feel sorry for him, that made my heart suddenly leap out for him.

As I watched, Sami moved. He was fumbling in his trouser pocket and eventually drew out, from its interior, a cigarette. He smiled weakly at me and rose from his seat. Just before he walked out through the large French doors, he turned and whispered, 'I think I just wanted to forget that my father had died.'

A chilled thrust of air settled on me and then the door was shut, and all was warm again. He was lost from my sight until a small, orange glow moved slowly across the garden and I could make out the outline of Sami walking quietly through the darkness.

That night, I lay on the very edge of our bed waiting to hear Sami's soft tread upon the stairs, but I fell asleep before he came. In the morning when I awoke, Sami was leaving for work, leaving early, saying *Khudahafiz* in a way that spoke of strain and tension.

I wanted to shrink away from that day, not have to face Hana and Aida dealing with their own hostility. It seemed that those two felt the same, coursing along the halls and the rooms warily, and altogether we made the house feel hollow.

Thank goodness, then, for the rain. April had brought with it light bursts of rain, showers that wet the ground quickly and then abated, so that brilliant sunshine and rainbows could fill the skies. This rain, though it dripped from the trees and roofs, was so very different from the thick monsoon rains we were used to.

As a child, I would be scolded for racing out into that deluge, jumping from the veranda steps as fat, healthy drops came down, and running around with my face turned up and my clothes sticking to me. The noise of that wetness was sometimes quite spectacular, like thunder in a liquid form. The velocity of it would make me laugh while, from under the shelter of the veranda, Ammaji and my sisters would be shouting and waving their arms about. Eventually, Ammaji would brave the monsoon rain and, holding the thin *pallo* of her sari tight around her head, she would rush out, take hold of my arm, drag me inside. She would strip me of my wet clothes, and all the while, as she was scolding me, she would be laughing too.

That April afternoon, the rain came down much heavier than normal. It flowed out of the sky, and was so full that I heard it on the bedroom window, big plops of wetness. When I looked out, I could see raindrops falling to the earth with some considerable force. It was not quite a monsoon, but it was thrilling.

By the layer of trees where the orchard grew, stood Hana, watching and looking skyward. She made no effort to come in. She saw me and waved, smiling through the rain, beckoning to me. I joined her, of course; there was nothing better to do. Together we ran like senseless children around the garden until Aida rattled the kitchen window and rebuked our idiocy.

'What are you doing? You will get ill. Come in, Sahira Bibi. Does neither of you have any sense? This is *Welayat*, not Sikimpur! The sun shall not come to warm you through.'

Eventually, we acquiesced and ran inside. Aida thrust a towel at each of us.

'What would your Ammaji say if she knew about you doing this, Sahira Bibi? And you, Hana - has coming to *Welayat* made you lose all your senses?'

But we were laughing too hard and Aida's sternness came to nothing, except that it came to a lot for it broke the ice and made Hana say, 'But Aida, you should have joined us. It is such fun to let yourself loose sometimes.'

Aida ushered us to the large pine kitchen table.

'Sit down,' she said. 'It is time for lunch and I have tried something new. This is *my* fun. It is called soup. I have made it with carrots and mushrooms and onions. It is like a curry but there are no spices in it, only something called the herb of rosemary. There, Hana, I have learnt some *angrezi* as well.'

Hana hung her head low and dropped her spoon back into her bowl.

'I am sorry Aida for what I said to you. I did not mean to hurt you.'

Aida, who was ladling her own soup out, said, 'Of course you did not. And you are right; it is always good to learn new things. After all, I am learning to do different kinds of food. I am learning how to do *angrezi* cooking, and that is for the Sahib and Sahira Bibi but also, I think, a little for myself. I have enjoyed it and felt some pride in being able to learn.'

After lunch, we stayed in the kitchen as Aida made a start on dinner. Hana and I concentrated on the vegetables, she peeling the potatoes and I slicing onions. Meanwhile, Aida washed small orange lentils in the pan before putting them on the gas stove to cook. I opened the window over the sink so that the breeze took away the steam from the boiling water, which smelled of cooking lentils.

Aida was adding the spices to them, talking at the same time when she let out a sharp cry.

'*Aeiii*. What have I done!' Holding up the edge of her pale blue shalwar top, she showed us the mustard yellow stain that lay there. 'I have spilled some *haldi* powder on myself.'

I slipped off my chair and took her by the arm towards the sink.

'You must get that off soon, before the stain sets fast.' *Haldi* stains were obdurate, I knew, from Ammaji's battles with them. I wet the stain and rubbed the cotton vigorously but it remained there. I shook my head as Aida continued to rub.

'It is no good,' I told her. 'You must take your top off and soak it now. Come, I will soak it in cold water while you get changed.'

'Yes, you are right. I would like to get it out. I am very fond of this shalwar. My niece made it for me before I came to England. Oh, how stupid I have been. To wear it when I am cooking, and that with *haldi* as well.'

I led the bemoaning Aida away, reassuring her as we went.

When I returned, Hana had finished with the potatoes and was concentrating her gaze upon the pages of a thick book. She held it aloft as I came into the kitchen.

'I am reading quite fast now, and understanding most of the words.' On the table beside her was Sami's Oxford English dictionary.

Hana looked back at her book and began to read in a deliberate and precise tone, '...instead of endeavouring to reach me he snatched a dinner knife from the table, and flung it at my head.'

She put the book down and smiled at me triumphantly. 'See, I have been practising. And this is a hard book, I think, to read, so I am being quite slow and careful. It is about the moors of Yorkshire, where it is very windy and lonely. It sounds like a place where the sun does not shine. James has talked to me about them but he uses words that I do not understand - ISO-LATION and BLEA-K-NESS - so he gave me this book to help me.'

I was amused that Hana's postman had now become James.

'You like him, do you not?' I asked.

'Yes, he is very nice, and kind.' She hesitated. 'He has asked something of me and I do not know what to reply.'

'What has he asked of you?

'He has asked me to go out on a *date* with him.'

I looked at Hana, puzzled. 'What does that mean? Which date?'

'I do not know.'

'Did you not ask him?'

Hana shook her head. 'No, I did not want to look as though I could not understand. I told him I would have to ask you first, for you are my family here.'

We wondered what this 'date' could be. A time of the week or month to do something specific? Was it something to do with the garden? Or his postal work?

'I will ask Ava Beresford this afternoon,' I decided. 'She will know.'

Hana looked down at the cover of her book with its portrait of a girl's face, a fresh face of pale beauty and dark hair.

'EM-IL-EE BRON-TEE,' She said the name very slowly, sounding the syllables with a great deal of care, her lips mimicking their roundness and their lengths. 'What is the meaning of *Wuthering Heights*?'

I thought for a moment, trying to remember back to my own studies of the book. 'I think it stands for the wildness of the moors... the wind and the storminess. Maybe the nature of Heathcliff himself.'

'He is not a nice person, Heathcliff.' Hana's mouth was set hard when she said this, but then it softened as she recalled. 'But that is maybe due to his hurting. His life was not so easy, so maybe I should not blame him so much.'

'We are not far from the place where the Brontës lived,' I said. 'Haworth, it's called.'

I had heard of this from one of our neighbours, Professor Hariman, a very serious man in his late forties, who did not seem to worry about the cold and dressed in lightweight suits even when the snow had lain thick on the ground. He spoke in a proper manner, in a way that made everything he said matter, and the pale strands of his fine hair curled like satin ribbon.

His love was the arts, and when Sami and I first met him and he found that I had 'been a student of literature', he shook my hand with great vigour and said, 'Wonderful, wonderful. You must know of the wonderful literary history of Yorkshire. Of Mytholmroyd, where Ted Hughes was born, Bradford where Priestley lived, and Haworth where the wonderful Brontë sisters wrote with such an exquisite pen. You must see them all. You simply must visit them, but especially the moors around the Brontë homestead. If you have any interest in literature at all, then it really is a must. You will find it truly inspirational.'

Later that afternoon, mindful of Hana's dilemma, I asked Mrs Beresford about 'going out on a date' and returned to Hana with an explanation.

'Ava has told me what a "date" is. It is quite all right. She herself went on many dates with Dr Beresford before they were married, and with a few men before that, although it seems that he does not like to hear about them. It means to go somewhere with someone that you like. It is something that people here do before starting to court properly; it is to get to know one another. You can go to the cinema to watch a film, or out to a restaurant, or walk in the park. Dr Beresford took Ava to many dances.'

'Dancing? I cannot do dancing with anyone!' Hana was horrified.

'No, no, of course not. We shall tell him that you must not go dancing. But first, you must decide if you would like to go on a date.'

'Yes,' said Hana glumly. 'I must decide that. I must decide if it is proper.'

She pulled out a crumpled, blue aerogramme from her pocket and opened it up.

'I received a letter from my father yesterday. I am missing him a lot and he is missing me. He does not say so but it is there, in how he writes. How will he be if he learns that I am talking so freely with a man that I do not know? He will be very disappointed and worried that I am going down the wrong path with an *Angrezi*. Also, I do not know myself about it.' Hana sighed. 'I feel so easy with him, with James, but then, when I am praying or reading passages from the Quran, I feel so, so unsure, to the point of badness.'

'Like a hypocrite?' I tried to be helpful.

Hana did not understand the word and I explained it as well as I could without hurting her sensibilities.

'That is the word,' she said. 'It is written about in the Quran, there is a surah about it. To be a hypocrite is to be the worst kind of person.'

'But Hana, you cannot consider yourself amongst them. The hypocrites written about in the Quran are truly wicked people, setting out to deceive others. You are a good person.' I pressed her hand. 'All you are doing is talking. As long as you do not...' I broke off and thought of Sami. Was he wrong in what he had done? The shock I had felt had been of Sami making love to another woman, of being so young, a different Sami in a different time. The morality of his deed did not have such a bearing on me.

'But, am I not deceiving my father?' Hana looked tremendously sad.

There was silence between us, each of us thinking our own thoughts. Then Hana broke it with a slow, quiet voice. 'I shall tell him. I shall write to him this very day.'

'Yes, maybe that will help. But you must stress to him that you talk to James only when he delivers the letters, that it is not a clandestine friendship. Perhaps I should write to Ammaji also. She will be able to talk to him then, or Abbaji at least.'

Hana seemed happy with this decision. Her father was a gentle, softly-spoken man, and proud of his daughter. He had let her come to England when his relatives around him shook their heads and grumbled words of discouragement.

'You are sending an unmarried girl away!' 'That is something very brave, and very foolish. You know what these feringhi are like.' 'She will end up marrying an Angrezi, a kafir.'

Hana's father had withstood their criticism and spoken to Abbaji about it.

'She is motherless, and Sikimpur is no place for her. She does not consider the proposals that she receives, saying that she must look after me instead. But, I will be gone one day and then she will be alone, with no family. Yes I know, Sahib, that you and the Memsahib will watch over her, but what about after that? No, she needs something for herself and so I will send her to England. And, if she marries an *Angrezi*, then that will be Allah's will.'

Maybe writing to her father was the very best thing that Hana could do.

Chapter Fifteen

We visited the Brontë homestead soon enough. It became a family outing, for even Aida and Sami came, a rare occurrence indeed.

Aida shunned the attention paid by the people of Leeds to our darker skins, and only occasionally ventured out with one of us to buy food for the week.

Sami knew that if he was to succeed here in England, then he must work harder than at any other time in his life. His working week often extended beyond the nine to five, five days of the week.

We had not spoken much since he had told me of his secret and, though my curiosity raged with questions, I could not bring myself to ask them.

Professor Hariman leant me his guide to the Brontë Parsonage when he heard we were going and made me promise to tell him what I thought of it. He was excited for me, a little envious also, because I was to see it for the first time.

'You are in luck,' he told me. 'The Worth Valley steam trains are running again from Keighley to Haworth, beginning this month. Tell your husband to park up at the station at Keighley. It is a wonderful experience, completely different from anything you will have seen. Although, I suppose you may have been on the steam trains in India. Still,' he continued cheerfully, 'the Worth Valley locomotives have been restored wonderfully. By volunteers of the Preservation Society, I understand. Oh, and make sure that you wear sensible walking shoes.'

We took a picnic with us and drove through a countryside that was fast awakening with hedgerows green, and fields that were yellow with rapeseed, and red with poppies.

'How pretty it is in the bright sunshine,' said Hana.

'But not as lovely as the highlands and forests around Sikimpur,' sniffed Aida patriotically. 'You will not find the same variety of flowers and trees in this country, where the weather is so cold.'

We laughed, and I asked, 'Oh, Aida, how did Ammaji manage to persuade you away from your beloved India?'

The outdoor air and the camaraderie seemed to play well with Aida's humour, for she laughed back at me.

'I may have moved away from India, but I have not taken my heart away from it.'

The steam train, Bellerophon, rolled into Keighley station, delighting us all with the majesty of its bright engine and carriages. We climbed in like little children on a day out and settled ourselves on its dark leather seats. It took us slowly through the countryside, winding past small cottages and gardens in which hens pecked at the ground and clumps of wild flowers grew.

When we alighted at Haworth, Sami stopped to look around the locomotive yard.

'I shall catch you up in the village, by the Parish church. I will not be too long.' And with that, he waved the three of us farewell to make our way up the steep cobbled hill that led to the village.

It was a sunny day and the climb brought us out in sweat. I removed my jacket, throwing it over the crook of my arm, while Aida stopped often to wipe her brow with the *pallo* of her pale green, cotton sari. People around us were walking up in the same way, struggling to talk as they hiked.

The village began near the top of the climb, its narrow street lined with cafés and shops - sweet shops, bakeries and apothecaries with strange, herbal remedies. Off this main street, tiny tributary paths made their way to other places; gates to private houses, walks around the church and other shops. It was something to see, this village, so self-contained and sure of itself.

Occasionally, a car passed us, sounding its horn to scatter the ambling crowd. We visited some of the shops and bought a few items before stopping at The Black Bull, the public house that stood in a corner of the square and that had been so popular with Branwell Brontë. We took it in turns to sit on his favourite chair, and drank coffee that had cream swirled into it.

Soon, Aida began to shift uneasily in her chair. 'I think, Sahira Bibi that we should go soon. People are staring and it does not feel nice. It is the reason that I do not like to go out in these places. I do not think they have seen many of our kind here.'

I was studying Professor Hariman's guide book, leafing through its tatty pages, and reading bits of interest aloud.

'Well, if we take the path by the side of Haworth Parish church we can go through the cemetery and onto the Parsonage.'

'We should go to the moors. It is important to see them, now that we are here.' Hana's face wore an earnest expression

Looking at her, I realised that she did not understand what the moors actually were. They were a wild and abstract image and, until she stood upon them, they would not be real.

'Yes, of course, the moors. We can take one of the recommended walks.' I listed the routes: Brontë waterfalls, Withens Top, Ponden Kirk.

'And what about lunch?' Aida wanted to know.

'We shall have lunch on the walk. Professor Hariman has told me that that is how to do things. We walk for a while and then we stop to eat.' I closed the book and put it back into my handbag. 'Let's go to Brontë waterfalls. It is not such a long walk, and maybe then we can go on to Withens Top, if we are able.'

As we waited outside The Black Bull for Sami, we ate the fudge that Hana had bought from a shop whose front window was filled with jars of coloured sweets. It was sweet and soft and tasty. Sami joined us in a good humour, pleased with his detour, and we walked past the Parish church and through the cemetery, reading as we went the names and ages engraved on the headstones. Hana prayed softly to herself for the souls of the dead.

The Parsonage lay beyond the cemetery, black-stoned and solemn in the May sunshine. Even with the number of people that wandered through its rooms, there was a hush, like the dim light of the candles that would have been lit there. It was the ghosts of the sisters, one felt, writing at their desks, inspired by the uncasual nature that surrounded them.

We left the Parsonage, each quiet in our own mood, passing by the old stone font and the iron kissing gate with Tom Mix watching us go on our way onto the open moorland. It was the isolation that struck us the most. We stood for some time in silence, gazing at the glory of the heather and fern, each of us mesmerised by this fierce beauty. The intermittent breeze that blew here was cool, and I was glad that I had my scarf tied tightly around my head.

Finally, Aida turned to me.

'It is a very beautiful place to see here. I am understanding why people find an interest in it, and also why Hana reads the book of it in English.'

'Let's walk on.' Sami began to move on up the hill, 'There is a great expanse for us to explore.'

Aida joined him, her fingertips touching the tops of the heather sprigs as she passed them. The dwellings that we found lay mostly in ruins now, with sheep grazing amongst their foundations. The ground beneath us was mostly well laid for pedestrians, with a few muddy areas where the rain of the last few days soaked deeply into the soil and had not yet drained away. As we trudged through these places, I understood Professor Hariman's advice of wearing sensible walking shoes.

We ate our lunch on the near side of the Brontë Bridge, before crossing over and making our way downhill towards the waterfall that was full with gushing water, brown and frothy on its way down to the river. It was quite a sight and also a din, so we had to shout to make ourselves heard.

'Shall we go on to Withens Top?' I yelled.

Hana looked hopeful, but Aida shook her head, pulling her coat tightly about her.

'I cannot go on. The sun no longer shines in this place and I am sure that it is going to rain.'

We looked up at the clouds above us that were moving fast with the wind.

'It is true,' said Sami. 'The clouds are thick now, and grey, and it is not so warm. We do not want to be here when it is raining. It will be very cold then and I don't think Aida is yet ready for that.'

He was right: the day was in a capricious mood.

'Maybe we can come back some other day?' I said to Hana.

She nodded, not quite masking her disappointment.

'I do not want to be responsible for Aida getting wet, especially after she has made us such a lovely lunch.'

We made our way back quickly, each of us now feeling the cold that had come down and the wind that had picked up. As we walked, Sami decided that he alone would go back to Keighley and drive back to us.

'There is a car park behind the Parsonage. I shall come there.' He looked down at our muddied shoes. 'Please make sure that they are clean before you get into the car.'

He gave us a time and left us in a coffee shop, in time for afternoon tea, eating scones with clotted cream and jam, and drinking warming cups of tea. We held them tightly for they gave warmth to our cold hands.

Chapter Sixteen

Haworth continued to have a profound effect on Aida for some time after we returned. Not being able to read herself, she asked Hana to read aloud to her from a book that Hana had picked up in Haworth containing the sisters' letters. This distraction also helped Hana enormously, for she spent much of that week waiting for a letter from her father; even though she had only written recently and knew that the airmail service between Britain and India was haphazard, still she hoped for a prompt reply. She went out twice a day to greet James and came back mostly empty-handed, until one day when she returned with a letter addressed to me.

It was from Ammaji. Instinctively, I knew that it was regarding a serious matter. I knew this from the neatness of her writing. A telephone conversation could not deliver the same gravitas, the same ceremony as that involved in sitting down at one's desk, dipping the nib of one's pen into the ink well, thinking, choosing the correct words to convey a correct meaning, words that could be read over again and then, finally, signing one's name.

I opened the letter with care, sliding the paper knife straight across for a neat, silent cut all the way from one end to the other. At the top right-hand corner was written the date of writing and directly below that the date in the Islamic calendar. The letter was written in Urdu, an Arabic script and so read from right to left.

It began with the greeting,

'Meri pyari Sahira, Asalaam-alaikum.

I pray this letter finds you all well. By the Grace of Allah, we are all doing quite well here in Sikimpur. Your Abbaji sends his love to you and is hoping, Inshallah, to speak to you soon.'

Ammaji carried on in this manner, conveying her best wishes to Sami, Aida and Hana. Then, she wrote that Hana's father had spoken to her of James - she had written his name in English, in an awkward script - and that they were still wondering what to do about the situation.

'Although her father has taken the news very well - for how can he not when his own grandfather was a feringhi - obviously he is anxious about his daughter. I think he will prefer to talk to her rather than write, more for a reassurance, but he does not know what to say. It is hard for men to discuss such matters with their children. It is at such a time when a father misses the mother of his daughter. A mother knows, by instinct, what her child requires. Besides, the emotions and the needs of a girl are very sensitive. Please speak to Sami about this; he is the man of the house. Although he is young, and therefore inexperienced in these matters, still he holds the authority and the welfare of Hana.'

Ammaji wrote some more on this topic, before coming to the crux of her letter.

'Your Abbaji and I are so happy that you have become settled into your new way of life, and also, your new home. Now that you have been married for almost a year, and also have the help of Aida and Hana - you must surely have thought of this yourself - and that is thoughts of having a baby.'

It was not unexpected, this question of Ammaji's, but it was unwelcome, especially coming as it did now. It brought back to me my conversation with Sami and my feelings towards him. What he told me had left me feeling foolish. I remembered, on the night of our honeymoon, I had felt a comfort in the knowledge that we were embarking on this experience together, that it was new to both, that we were virgins. But now? What happened to that assurance, that place of safety? It had fallen away and I felt betrayed, not in my body but in my mind.

Now Ammaji had brought up the question of children, a natural state in a marriage. However, from very early on, I had learnt how to calculate the rhythm and rhyme of my cycle, and that had become the natural state of our marriage. I put the letter away, this ill-timed letter, at the bottom of my drawer and tried to think of other matters.

I called out to Hana, but she was not about.

'She is once again in her garden,' Aida called to me from her bedroom.

I found Hana tying back the stems of the drooping daffodils with pieces of twine. I told her about Ammaji's letter, the part concerning her. She stopped what she was doing and looked up, nodding. Her face was in shadow.

'At least I know that he has received my letter. I hope that it did not make him worry. I was frightened that it would. It will be good to hear his voice again, but also I am a little scared.'

'There is no reason for you to be scared,' I told her. 'I shall be with you. We can think of what it is you would like to say. Maybe, you should telephone this weekend?'

Hana nodded eagerly. 'Yes, then Sami Sahib will be at home and he will help me talk to Abbajaan.'

'Yes,' I said quietly. 'Then Sami will be at home.'

Aida called out to us from the house. 'Hana. It is your Jaymes. He is here for you. Have you forgotten about him? Come quickly. He is talking to me and I do not understand what he is saying. I am ready to go out.'

Hana jumped up, gathering together the scissors and twine that she had been working with. She was flustered and her hair fell across her face from her sudden movement.

'Oh, but I have forgotten that I am going out with James today because of your news to me. I had so much time to get ready, but now I have not.'

I took the scissors and twine from Hana. 'You must go in quickly. You do not look so bad. It will not take long for you to be ready. Your time in the garden has made your cheeks glow. I will go and talk to James.'

Today, it was to be Hana's date with James. They were to walk around the village with Aida acting as their chaperone. Although it was not to a dance or the cinema, and indeed they were not even to be alone, it was a big day and Hana was understandably nervous. James was waiting in the living room with Aida standing in the doorway, smiling timidly.

'Hana coming,' I heard her say in bright English.

James smiled awkwardly, his teeth showing and his dimples growing deep. He was dressed in casual clothes: a smart, white shirt with a pale green pattern running through it and dark blue flares. His top button was undone and he wore a belt around his slender waist. He was newly-shaved and, as I came close to him, I could smell aftershave on him. It was the first time that I had seen him out of his postman's uniform and he seemed not so smart but more real, and more handsome. In the lamplight, his hair seemed darker than normal and his eyes more green.

'Hello, James,' I said. 'How are you?'

James held out his hand to shake mine.

'I am well, thank you, Mrs Altair. And you?'

He spoke well, with only a hint of a Tadcaster accent.

'I am fine. It is a nice evening for you to take Hana out. And Aida, too.'

'Yes.' James looked nervously across at Aida. 'And Aida, too. It is very kind of you to join us, Aida; to give up your precious time.'

I translated for Aida, who blushed deeply. She shook her head vigorously and replied, haltingly, in English. 'Is all right. It is... good.'

James shifted from one foot to the other and as he did so, I noticed the scar above the lobe of his right ear, just below his hairline. He saw me and touched it in a self-conscious way.

'It is a childhood wound. My brother and I were sword fighting with wooden swords, when he jabbed the point a touch too hard at me. It was sore, I remember. I gave my mother quite a scare running in as I did, with a sword stuck in my head and the blood pouring from me!'

I winced with the thought of it, but felt a thrill at the pain that must have been there. It added a certain bravery to the young James, like a hero with a war wound. I told the story to Aida, who forgot herself and began to chatter in thick Urdu.

She stopped suddenly when Hana came in, stepping across the threshold like a mid-summer breeze. She had changed out of her soil-smudged clothes into a crisp, silk, green shalwar. I almost gasped to see something such as she; ethereal, untouchable. James, mesmerised, went quickly to her side and it was at once obvious what a beautiful couple they made.

I saw them off at the door, wishing them a fine time, and went back to the kitchen, alone and melancholy with it, with the happiness that had walked out of the house. I had been due to visit Professor Hariman, I had thought of returning his guide and also, fulfilling my promise of telling him of our trip to Haworth. But, what I did instead was to sit down at the kitchen table and cry, not with tears but with my heart that was swollen with them.

And what caused this was the thought of James' scar. Sami had no such mark; his body was unblemished. Sami, who I did not love. Sami, who I still felt the complication of being let down by, though I did not love him. How, I prayed to Heaven, was I to have child with him?

We ate our dinner out in the garden that night on the raised patio by the kitchen. It had been a warm day, but in the evening there lingered something of May's low temperatures. It was Aida, still taken with her chaperoning walk, who persuaded us. So, clinging to our shawls and jumpers, we found ourselves helping to take out plates and cutlery, food and drink.

Sami brought out the transistor radio and sat it on a three-legged stool. He was about to switch it on but stopped his hand when, from over the back wall along which the Virginia creeper grew, we heard the Reverend Bramley talking. At first, we thought it was to himself for there was no reply, but soon we realised he was reading his Sunday sermon. He spoke it quietly enough so we could not hear all the text, but caught pieces of it when he wandered nearer to the wall.

He finished rehearsing and then we heard a sharp, crackling sound. I recognised it as a stylus needle running along the first few grooves of a record, and then came music, a hymn rising from the funnel of an old gramophone, 'Dear Lord and Father of Mankind, Forgive Our Foolish Ways'. We sat in quiet stillness, overpowered by the beauty of the words and music.

When it was finished, Aida breathed deeply and said softly, 'It is nice to be sitting here, with the garden around us.' She enjoyed the garden, its colours and its smells. 'You have done good things with your lovely flowers, Hana.'

The garden was beginning to flourish; the orchard was hyphenated with clumps of marigold, petunias and violas, while the lawn was filling with the opening blooms of lobelia, fuchsia, azaleas and black-hearted poppies. My own patch was blossoming also, dotted as it was with tiny forget-me-nots and mimulus, bluebells, buttercups and foxgloves. Later, I hoped that the yellow sunflowers would join them, rising above them all to look over the low wall that separated them from the rest of the garden.

As we sat out there, I felt the quietness of our English garden. There was no chirping of the crickets from within, and no cacophony of horns and loud laughter from the streets beyond the house. The only music we heard was the music of '68 coming from our radio that sat on the three-legged stool.

'Yes,' Hana leant back in her chair and looked about her, 'we have a very pretty garden, one that is pleasing to the eye. Soon, I will have something for you, also, for I have been busy with the vegetables. We will have carrots and beans, and also some herbs and coriander, *Inshallah*, to remind us of Sikimpur. We shall have some fruit, too.' she paused to concentrate on the foreign words. 'Straw-be-rrees, and then app-les and p-lums, so that you can make some of your special deserts, Aida. That shall please you, Sami Sahib.'

'It shall indeed, Hana.' Sami nodded. 'I'm already looking forward to it.' He poured some lemonade into his glass and, taking a drink of it, asked Hana about James.

Hana answered in an awkward way. Her afternoon walk with James had not turned out so well.

'I had not spoken to him of being a Muslim before,' she began. 'I was shy to say anything about it, but I could not stay that way forever. And now that I have talked to him I do not understand what he has told me, that he does not have any religion.'

For a while, there was no answer from any of us. In India, there were many ways to worship, be it as a Muslim, Hindu, Christian, Jain or Buddhist. To have no religion was to be considered morally lax.

'Do you mean that he does not believe in God?' I asked. 'That he is an atheist?'

'No, I do not think so,' Hana replied. 'He has told me that he has not thought about God for a long time, since he was a child. He cannot remember why he became this way, but now he does not think about Him at all.'

'Ah, this is why you became very quiet when we were out,' said Aida. 'At the beginning, there was much talking, but then there was much silence. You also did not look very happy, but I did not want to say anything. You looked very sad, Hana, but I thought it would be better to wait. Then I knew it was something important because you did not say goodbye to him in a very friendly way, and you were not so willing to speak to me when we came home.'

I had not seen Hana or Aida on their return. I had gone to bed soon after they had left, caught up as I was in my own misfortune.

'Well, he will surely be thinking of God now, Hana.' I looked across at Hana's unhappy face and felt sorry for her innocent disillusion. 'It is not so bad, maybe. It does not mean an end to things.'

'No, but how can I feel the same way about him?'

Sami shook his head somewhat impatiently. 'Oh, Hana, you are being too hard. He has just met you and you have only just talked of this matter. All that you have discovered is that he thinks in a different way to you. That is all. You have been so long in Sikimpur, living in a certain way and believing only one thing, that you find it difficult to consider other ways of looking at something.'

'But he has not been thinking a different way, you see, for he has not been thinking of God at all.' Hana reminded us.

'No, he has not, but then, maybe you have been thinking too much of God.' Sami sounded unnecessarily irritated. He flicked a fallen dandelion seed from the table and pressed his lips together.

Hana was shocked by this. She took a sharp intake of breath and whispered, 'Too much? Do you think, then, that he is right?'

'No! I am sorry. It is just... I did not mean anything of that sort. But sometimes our beliefs make us inflexible when there is no need to be.'

Sami was caught in his awkward place. He was not a devout Muslim; he went to the Mosque for *Jumma*, the afternoon Friday prayer, and he fasted during the holy month of Ramadan, but he was not a conscientious believer. And, while Aida and I were more mindful of our devotions, we none of us were like Hana, who rarely missed a prayer and was often found contemplating the Quran in the morning. She enjoyed the solace of that time, she said, and the changing of colour and light as the sun came slowly up and the dawn chorus began.

'Tomorrow is Saturday,' I said to Hana. 'You can speak to your father then. Perhaps after speaking to him you will feel better.'

'Maybe.' Hana did not sound convinced. She looked glum. She pushed her plate away and got up. She walked away without another word, heading for the curtain of trees in the orchard.

Aida looked at Sami and me, and then rose also. 'I will talk to her.' She hurried away after the despondent figure.

Sami and I were left alone. In the shifting light of dusk, Sami's face seemed tired. He seemed vulnerable suddenly.

'I must answer to Hana's father for her unhappiness,' he said quietly. 'I shall speak with him also. After all, I am responsible for all things here.' He switched off the transistor radio. The air become starkly quiet; all joviality was gone from it. 'I have been concentrating so much on my work and missed a lot of what has been going on at home. Why, I have not even spoken to this postman properly. That is remiss of me. I have been negligent in my duties.'

'Oh, you can easily change that,' I told him. 'Speak to him tomorrow, when he comes around for his morning duty. At least, then, you shall be able to tell Hana's father that you have spoken to James.'

'Yes, that is the thing to do.' Sami reached across the table and touched my hand. 'Thank you. You are right.' He gathered his cigarette packet from the wooden slats of the table and pulled one out. 'I must think carefully about what to say to James, how to speak to him as a guardian of Hana's. Do you know his full name?'

I tried to remember the name that Hana had told me. 'It is James Hep... Hep... Hepworth. That is it, James Hepworth.'

Sami raised his eyebrows. 'Hepworth? Are you sure?'

I thought back to Hana, when she had told me. 'Yes, I am quite sure.'

Sami nodded and muttered to himself. 'That is most interesting. I wonder...'

I watched him leave me, going indoors now, smoking with long draws on his cigarette, his free hand going through his hair; a greying silhouette. He was so young, with so many important things to do, and to do well.

I let my hand lie where Sami had left it, feeling his touch still, feeling it differently now, almost like a stone. I looked down at it and I knew that I could not allow my shocked reactions to last. They would have to pass before Sami noticed or else I would have to bury them deep. But I knew that, however deep I drove them, they would make themselves unhidden. Besides, it was not Sami's fault that his revelation had shocked me so.

Yet I knew, when we made love from now on, I would always wonder whether his thoughts were filled with another time, another body.

Sami spoke to James the next morning, liking him immensely. I saw them from the landing window, friendly and informal, shaking hands and nodding. Later that day, he spoke to Hana's father. I did not sit in during this conversation; it was a silent request of his, but I passed his study regularly. Sami's voice was even and confident, and with this I was satisfied. Hana sat nervously in the kitchen waiting, with a cup of tea in her hands, for her turn.

'Please, you must come with me.' She took my hand when Sami called out to her. And so I did.

Sami directed Hana to the chair behind his large table. There were papers strewn about, near the front of the table with a pen resting in their centre. Other papers were arranged in neat piles close to the lamp. Each of these piles had a note, written in Sami's neat hand, on top, with a glass paperweight keeping them in place.

I wandered to the shelves that Sami had put up and read through the titles of the books placed there. Engineering books, books on mathematics, statistics, containing formulas that I would not understand, but whose spines looked beautiful with their gold ink against dark grey backgrounds. Over this browsing I heard Hana's voice, cautious at first, talking to her beloved parent. She spoke carefully, using words that she must have rehearsed throughout the night, reassuring words. At the end, she looked relieved and thoughtful. She handed the receiver to me.

'Suha Bibi wishes to speak with you.'

I had spoken to my sisters only twice since we had come to England and it was good to hear the familiar sharpness of Suha's voice.

'Sahira, *Asalaam-alaikum*. How are you?'

I replied that we were well and asked after her and her family.

'Yes, yes we are fine here. The baby has become so big now. Did you receive the photos that I sent you? Those of Laila's baby also?'

'Yes, I have received them.'

'Good, good. Do you remember how tiny Noor was when you left? She is looking more and more like you every day. I think Laila's husband is praying that she does not take after you in character. Of course, I am just teasing you. I have missed teasing you... and also remonstrating with you. It is good to know that you have not changed too much since you have married and moved away. You still have the ability to make Ammaji cross, even from thousands of miles away. You know what I am talking about?'

I did, of course. I had not replied to Ammaji's letter. It was still in the drawer underneath layers of cotton and silk. I had not read it again, although I did think of its contents regularly.

'Well, I have been busy, Suha. Hana, as you know...'

'Oh, you do not need to make excuses!' Suha, who had been speaking quite loudly, lowered her voice suddenly. 'I understand, you know. I have even tried to explain to Ammaji; still she wants me to talk with you. But, I understand her also. A child seals the relationship between a husband and wife, and she is worried that all may not be all right with you, now that you are in England, and that you are not telling her. After all, you are not very good at telling things to her.'

And, even though I was alone in the room, I lowered my voice also. 'There is nothing that is wrong here. There is nothing to worry about. But Sami is very busy in setting himself up at the moment and I am still busy setting up a home of my own. It is very different from Sikimpur, you know.'

'Of course, and also, you would not be a natural mother. You will certainly need an aya for the baby. Still, it is a big thing in one's life, and you...'

'I have married and moved away to a different country,' I reminded my sister. 'These are big things also!'

'Yes, but a child enters the world from you, and you must answer for the consequences of its life here. It is not the same as the fascination of a new country, you know. You cannot return from it if it wearies you.'

I did not answer her for, in essence, I agreed with her.

Suha continued slowly and carefully. 'At least, you do not sound unhappy.'

'I am not unhappy at all,' I retorted sharply. 'In fact, I am enjoying myself very much.'

In the background, I heard Ammaji's voice and my heart beat faster from a sentiment of love and affection.

'Ammaji has come into the room now, so I will say *Khudahafiz*,' Suha said. 'But please remember what we have spoken of. Give my salaams to the others. I will let Laila know that I have spoken to you and that you are well. *Khudahafiz*.'

Ammaji's voice came on the line in a flood of emotion. She enquired after my health several times before asking whether I had received her letter. I answered that I had.

'Well, that is good,' she said. 'I was worried when I did not receive a reply, but your Abbaji kept telling me that you were well and that you had been busy with other things, and that I worry too much. Of course, he is right. But, you must find some time to think of us as well. Yes, I know you do think of us, but it is good to read your words, and to re-read them, and to know that you are truly well. We are not able to see for ourselves and so I must rely on other means to be with you.'

'I promise that I will be more fastidious with my correspondence, Ammaji.' I felt guilty at my filial negligence.

'Please do... well, I will not talk for too long, for it is not cheap to telephone. You must talk to Sami if you find things hard. He is your husband, after all, and he is sensible also. I am happy that you have such a good husband to look after you.'

Chapter Seventeen

The house and garden were filling with laughter and music. The clouds had scattered now and the sky was a topaz blue. The yellow sun was bright and the garden brilliant with colour.

The moisture from the overnight drizzle had evaporated back into the atmosphere, leaving the lawn nicely dry. Guests were chatting to one another, greeting each other while floating up and down tables laden with food and drink.

Hana, Aida and I had spent much of the week preparing the house for this party. While Hana and I had cleaned the house and arranged the tables and chairs outside, Aida had taken care of the food, and Sami the music. Although the guests did not number very many, and we could easily have seated everyone inside, we all of us prayed for good weather for we were missing the garden parties of Sikimpur.

The party was for Hana and James really, and also for our neighbours, who had been so kind towards us when we had arrived in Newton Kyme.

There was a new sort of excitement about. By tea-time on Saturday, we had welcomed our first guests and served them drinks. For the occasion, Aida had made a fruit punch, filling the large bowl with summer berries and orange cordial. She had crushed rose petals and mint leaves into a paste with honeycomb from Reverend Bramley's beehives and sieved it through a muslin cloth into the punch. It was a fabulous concoction.

Sami had bought several bottles of alcohol for our English friends: whiskey, sparkling white wine and a blue-tinted gin called Bombay Sapphire. I was unsure of these purchases: alcohol was an unknown substance in my parents' home. As pious Muslims, they did not drink and would not have countenanced its presence at Shamshad Bagh. It became my principle also, and I brought it with me when I left India, but Sami explained that he had bought it for our guests and they were unused to having a party without it.

'It is a normal part of socialising for them and they will feel awkward without it. I do not think that fruit punch and tea have the same effect, for they cannot be drunk in the same quantities.

Although,' he added hastily, 'I have not bought very much but just enough to make them feel welcome. To help them to relax.'

There was a strong hint in his words and in their tone that made me ask. 'Have you drank alcohol before, then?'

Sami, who had been kneeling on the carpet and looking through a small pile of vinyl records, sat back on his heels. He had been very happy when he had been choosing the music; now, he looked serious and frowned.

'Yes, I have. I must admit to it.' He put down the record that he was holding. 'When I was a student and some of my friends, Indian friends, were drinking, they would try to persuade me to join them. I refused for a long time. But I was curious, for they did seem to enjoy themselves very much. So one day, I went by myself to a pub and I tried some lager, Harp lager, that I had seen them drinking. It was most unpleasant. But then I tried some red wine and it was much nicer. Also, I found I became less anxious when I had some. And so, occasionally, when I needed to relax, when I had many assignments or during exam time, I would have some. Not very much, just a glass, so I did not think of it as wrong.' He looked straight into my eyes. 'Are you disappointed with this news? I am sorry if you feel somehow let down. I have not had any since I finished my time at university here in England.'

'No.' I said this without any hesitation. I did not feel disappointed. What I felt was something strange, like an awakening. I thought of the proverb, *the deepest rivers flow with least sound*. That was Sami, I thought, but he was also open and honest. He did not shy away from telling me the truth when I asked for it. There was much to respect him for other than his genius mind.

I was beginning to understand something of this world; that nothing was so simple as I had once thought it to be, and that was my failure. Or rather, it was due to the shelter of my upbringing. It was a lesson I needed to learn, for in the world was where I was to live, not closeted away under the roof of a sun-blushed sky and a protecting roof.

Professor Hariman was the first of our guests to arrive. He brought with him his sister, Martha, who had come from Scotland to visit. She was very different from him, not so narrow in her build and less solemn. She floated in on an air of summer gossamer, wearing a vibrant, full-length dress with wide, trailing sleeves, making me feel a little dull in pale yellow.

As I led her through the hall, she stopped by the walnut chest that stood high and grand.

'How magnificent!' she exclaimed in delight and ran a slim hand over the carved, dark wood. 'Such intricacy. Did you bring it over from India? Of course you did! You would never get such workmanship in England. Our souls are too plain. Heaven knows we pay enough for our simplicity.' She turned to her brother. 'Earnest, can you imagine how much it would cost to buy such a piece of furniture over here?'

I smiled nervously. 'Yes, we have been very fortunate. We have been able to have several pieces of furniture sent over to us from Sikimpur. It meant that we did not have to buy so much when we came here.'

'Fortunate? Yes, indeed, you are fortunate.' Her grey eyes scanned the entirety of my face. 'I mean, you have such lovely brown eyes and beautiful skin. We endanger ourselves for skin like yours. So much so, that I believe the doctors are now telling us to stay out of the sun. It's no longer a healthy obsession. Too much sun can cause cancer, they say. Isn't that so, Earnest?'

Professor Hariman nodded and took his sister's arm. 'Yes, my dear, it is so. But I don't think you need to worry about that living up in Edinburgh. The sun rarely shines there.'

'Well, you must enjoy the sun while you are down here.' Sami smiled affably. 'We are lucky with the weather today for the sun is shining so brilliantly. Allow me to get you a drink. We have set everything up in the garden.'

Sami showed them out into the open air, to where the marigolds with their golden heads grew, and the bluebells and violets also. Martha Hariman was still talking as they walked out.

'At last, she is gone. She is very chatty, that one.' Aida came warily out of the kitchen. 'I have been needing to take these sandwiches and *pakoras* outside, but I have been afraid to come out of the kitchen. I was scared that she would speak to me and I am sure that I would not be able to understand her.'

Aida had been feeling nervous about this party. Although her English was improving greatly, she was not confident about it, and she hoped to stay in the background as much as possible. I admired her for her bravery. I joined her in the kitchen, taking out the plates from the cupboard, the ones with a deep red rim. They had matching tea cups and Aida thought them striking when the sun shone on them.

As we made our way outside, we found that the garden was filling up. James had arrived and was talking in an informal manner to a distinguished-looking gentleman with a closely-cut beard, who I did not know. I thought that maybe he was a neighbour to whom James delivered the post. I saw Ava Beresford and her husband, Richard, looking around the garden. Ava was amused and pointing at the poppies that grew in a corner. Their children were playing quite freely. The boy, Theo, had brought a red, wooden aeroplane with him while his sister, Tilly, skipped around her parents.

I set the plates down at the head of the table, beside a larger plate of savoury pastries that Aida had arranged around a central decoration of green-rimmed cucumber strips and sliced tomatoes. My gaze wandered round and then lingered too long on the bottles that were lined up with their different coloured liquids. I wondered if Hana had seen them. She had not said anything and I was quite certain that she would not approve if she knew what they were.

'You know, nobody would know if you had some.'

There came a voice behind me, a hushed and conspiratorial male voice that made me turn quickly round, turn guiltily round, for it was as though my mind was being read. It was Mr Landen who had caught me out, and caused me to blush.

'What about it?' he smiled with wicked mischief. 'You look as though you might enjoy a small gin and tonic. I can pour it and pretend it's for me, if you like.'

And, although the very thought of it was foolish, I found myself nodding slowly.

'Don't worry,' he winked at me and grinned, 'I won't tell a soul. And,' he leant forward so that the tip of his fine nose touched mine, 'we can take our drinks somewhere where nobody will see.' From his lips came an unfamiliar smell, sweet and strong.

And then a woman's high-pitched voice interrupted my blushing reply.

'Arthur, what was the name of the villa that we stayed in last summer? Do you remember, the one with the painting of

Leonardo's Vitruvian Man hanging over the bath?' Elizabeth Landen stopped in front of us and looked surprised. 'Oh, I didn't know you were busy, dear.'

She smiled at me through closed teeth and piercing eyes. 'Mrs Altair...' she emphasised my title and took her husband's hand firmly. 'What a lovely party you have thrown. I must talk to your cook about these fabulous titbits. They are simply delicious. I absolutely love what you've done with the garden. Oh, but it's your maid, isn't it, who is the one with the green fingers. Still, you are looking after some of your guests very well, I see. But if you don't mind, I would like Arthur to meet Mr Hepworth. I didn't know that you knew him.'

'Mr Hepworth? James? But, of course we know him.' I was unsure whether there was another acerbic meaning to Elizabeth Landen's words. From the start she had not taken a liking to me, although her husband had always been most polite and friendly. He had even offered to drive me to the doctor's surgery one day, when I had twisted my wrist very badly and Sami was still at work. 'He is our postman, after all,' I continued, 'and also-'

'Oh, don't be silly, my dear!' Elizabeth derided me and pulled at her husband's shirt sleeve. 'Come, Arthur. I think Mr Hepworth would be most interested in your ideas for reforming the school curriculum.'

Arthur looked apologetically at me as he was tugged away. I smiled weakly back, thankful in a sense for his wife's intervention. I could still hear her berating voice. 'Really, Arthur, what is this fascination that you men seem to have with them? You are extraordinarily stupid about her! And there's James Hepworth behaving in a most unseemly manner, too...'

Her voice drifted off, taken away in the direction of the stone steps that led to the greenhouse. I was sure that it would soften much by the time it reached James Hepworth. I wondered what she had meant by her words to me about him. I sighed, for it was not pleasant to be talked about in such a rude manner. But then I caught sight of a bumble bee sipping the nectar from the irises and a butterfly flitting amongst the petunias; the music was lively and my other guests were full of chat and laughter. So, I asked myself, why should I worry that a person such as Elizabeth Landen disliked me so violently?

I saw Reverend Bramley standing close to the open French doors, talking to Ava Beresford. I had not yet said hello to them and they were animated in their conversation. Both had empty glasses in their hands. I ignored the bottles of alcohol, dismayed by my too easy response to Arthur Landen's offer. At least Sami had resisted, for a while, his friends' persuasions.

I filled two fresh glasses with Aida's fruit punch and made my way towards Reverend Bramley and Ava. I passed Aida playing catch with the children, chasing them and giggling as they swerved their lithe bodies out of reach of her clutches. Out of the corner of my eye, I saw the Landens with Hana, James and the distinguished-looking gentleman. Elizabeth was standing to one side of Sami, close to him, their elbows touching.

He looked up and waved to me. I smiled back and raised one of the glasses to him in return. Elizabeth looked up also and, upon seeing me, turned her attention back to her favoured others. I walked quickly on.

'Oh thank you, my dear. I've been too lazy to get a refill, and now you've brought it to me instead. It is most refreshing.' Reverend Bramley took a long sip from the glass that I offered him. 'I've been telling Ava about the bell ringing sessions that I'm organising. Now that the bell tower has been rebuilt and the new bells installed, I'm hoping that St Andrew's will once again ring the changes. Some of my choristers have been trying them out this last week.'

'Yes, we hear them in the evenings,' I said. 'They sound lovely. Aida, especially, finds them most enjoyable. She has her evening cup of tea seated out in the garden so she can listen to their harmony.'

'Well, there's a notice on the Newton Kyme Hall noticeboard about the sessions if she's interested. They are due to start this week. She would be most welcome should she wish to join us.' Reverend Bramley leant in close and said quietly, 'If you don't mind me saying, my dear, she seems quite a sturdy young woman. I'm sure that she would have no trouble pulling on the ropes.'

Ava and I laughed.

'I will tell her that,' I said.

'Oh do, but perhaps if you leave out the sturdy part, it may be better,' winked the Reverend.

'I saw Elizabeth having a little chat with you, Sahira. She looked quite exasperated.' Ava smiled at me in a knowing manner. 'Now, tell me what that was about?'

'Oh, maybe I shouldn't be here,' Reverend Bramley said quickly. 'I suspect this is one of those women's talks that Mrs Bramley tells me men should not be party to.'

'Oh, please don't go, Reverend,' pleaded Ava. 'Sahira and I are not those types of women. We don't have those sorts of talks. Sahira is far too sincere, so any such conversation would be all one-sided. Besides, you always have such an insight into human behaviour. You're a very wise man, Reverend. Maybe you can help Sahira instead.'

Reverend Bramley locked his fingers together and rocked back on his heels. 'Is there a problem between Elizabeth and yourself, my dear?'

'I do not know. I cannot see a reason, but she does not seem to like me,' I told him. 'I do not know why. I have always tried to be nice to her.'

'Of course you have, Sahira. You are, as I've said, a very sincere person.' Ava grinned. 'But, you know, that must make it all the worse for her because you actually have nothing to do with it, other than being here of course.'

'I do not understand, what is wrong if I am here? Unless she does not agree with our coming over to England? No, I cannot believe that for she is always very courteous to Sami.'

Ava laughed aloud and clapped her hands. 'Do you see, Reverend? Sahira really does need help. She's truly guileless.' She linked her arm with mine. 'Lizzy has no thoughts about the Indian invasion of our country, darling. No, she considers herself a liberal. Especially when the invaders possess such wealth and their fathers own Rolls-Royce Phantoms. No, it's when you invade her husband's thoughts that she becomes concerned.'

'Really, Ava! You have a most unfortunate way of saying things. You are far too direct.' The scolding tone of Reverend Bramley reminded me of Ammaji.

'But, why should Arthur think about me?' I asked. 'I have done nothing for him to think about. I do not really know him at all.'

Ava bit her lip. 'Oh, you really are a goose, Sahira. Don't you see? He would really like to get to *know* you!'

I suddenly understood and was embarrassed. 'Oh, I see.'

Reverend Bramley looked uneasy. 'Now you must not upset yourself, my dear. It's not your fault. Arthur Landen, he means no harm, but he can be... well, overtly friendly shall we say, with members of the opposite sex.'

'Oh.' I felt a sudden discharge of energy and I sighed with the notion of Elizabeth disliking me for such a reason. 'That is it then? The reason behind her animosity? I do not suppose she shall ever like me.'

'I'm afraid not, darling,' Ava said gently. 'It's one of those strange things that women hold against one another without having to put any effort into.'

'Now, now, we must allow some charity, Ava,' said the Reverend. 'Elizabeth may be somewhat hard but she has not had an easy life. They were very happy once, as you know. Unfortunately... well, her miscarriages have changed her attitude to life, and caused her to be more aloof than she might otherwise be. It is, I believe, a form of self-defence. We do what we can to survive when the harsh realities of life visit us. And you,' he nodded across at the Beresford children, 'have been very lucky in that respect.'

'You're right, as always.' Ava looked fondly at Reverend Bramley. 'Didn't I say he had a great insight into human nature? As you say, I have been lucky. But you must admit that Lizzy has a rather acute way of reacting to misfortune. She does seem to blame others for their having a less than miserable existence.'

The music had stopped, leaving the air filled with voices and a light summer breeze only. Ava went to look through our record collection and struck up a conversation with Hana by the steps of the patio. Soon there was music again; Frank Sinatra had won them over and now the air was flooded with his casual story songs.

I asked the Reverend Bramley after his wife, Julia, for she had been unwell and unable to come.

'She's on the mend,' he told me with a smile. 'It's just a cold, and a minor one at that. She went out far too early yesterday morning without a cardigan.' The Reverend checked his watch. 'I really should go, my dear. I have to prepare the morning's sermon and make sure that Julia has not been up and about. She promised to stay in bed but, well... with the weather being so nice she will find it hard to be confined. Also, I must catch Martha Hariman before I go. She's asked to do the flowers for the church service tomorrow and I would like to talk over arrangements with her. Ah, here's your dear husband. How are things, Sami? I haven't seen you about for a while now. Are you very busy?'

Sami came alongside me, a glass of Aida's punch in his hand. 'Yes, I am finding that business and innovation are two very different skills for me. Business is quite an art, and a particularly complex one once money and patents are introduced.'

'They're causing you a bit of a headache, are they?'

'Indeed, but I'm told that it is a necessity. If you produce something, you must also protect your right to operate it exclusively if you are to make any money out of it. I was of the opinion that one's creations should benefit everyone, quite freely. But apparently, that is a very naïve way of thinking.'

'Ah, that's the old way of thinking.' The Reverend interlocked the tips of his fingers together and placed them under his chin. 'Of Watson and Crick, and J.G. Ballard, and of finding things out by way of doing wrong as well as right.'

'I fear that time is almost gone, Reverend Bramley. Oh, I understand the need to bring in the money for further research, but I'm only really interested in the research, and the financing of it...' Sami clicked his tongue. 'I should not complain. I am lucky to be in the position that I find myself, whereby I have a chance to make something of my ideas.'

'I see that you've also made good friends of Alexander Hepworth.' Reverend Bramley broke off to gaze at a point behind me.

Sami's eyes followed the line of his gaze. 'Actually, that acquaintance has come about for a very different reason. Hana lives with us, after all, and so it is natural that we meet. But yes, you are right; it is useful to know people who know people. I believe that is the saying?'

'Who is Alexander Hepworth?' I asked.

Sami looked at me in bewilderment and then remembered. 'Of course, you have not met him. In fact, I have come to get you, to introduce you to him. I waved to you to come over but I don't think you understood.' Sami took my hand, so simple a gesture, and said, 'Come, he is planning to catch the evening train to London and so must leave soon. He is due to speak in the House tomorrow.'

'The house? Who's house? What is going on? Who is Alexander Hepworth? Is he the same Mr Hepworth that

Elizabeth was talking about? Is he related to James? In fact, is he the gentleman whom James was talking to? I am sure that-'

Sami put up his free hand and laughed. 'So many questions! I can answer them quite easily by showing you. Come on!'

Reverend Bramley took his leave of us and went to find Martha. I told him that I would be round to visit his wife tomorrow after lunch, and also that I would mention the bell ringing to Aida, although I did not think she would be persuaded to have a go at it herself.

'Please do come and visit, my dear.' Reverend Bramley beamed. 'Julia will be very glad to see you, I'm sure. It will give her a chance to try out the new batch of honey.' Reverend Bramley left us, the sun still shining down on his lovely, polished head.

Mr Alexander Hepworth was, of course, the distinguished-looking gentleman. He was James' uncle and also a member of the British Parliament. I realised then, that it was the House of Commons he was bound to address.

He was a most fascinating person, very well-spoken with a voice that undulated with a slow rhythm. He shook my hand firmly and I noticed a slight patch of red irritation on his throat where he had shaved too closely. Even under the hot May sun, he wore a pristine dark suit and a sombre tie. He had taken his jacket off and his shirt underneath was sky blue. James looked very like him - though less grey, and with his youth, less of an authority. Sami had met The Honourable Mr Hepworth at a lunch given by the Leeds Chamber of Commerce.

'Your husband is a very talented young man, Mrs Altair.' Mr Hepworth addressed me genially.

I was mesmerised by his manner; so charming, so easy. He was also very English, a Conservative. Facially so taciturn and arrogant, different in this way to James, his postman nephew. What, I wondered, did he think of that?

There was a gleam in his eye when he spoke to James, a critical edge to his voice as though he was not speaking his true mind to him. Or perhaps, that was my imagination? But still, I enjoyed watching his exchanges with his nephew, and also with Sami. Unlike James, Sami was treated as an equal; benevolence was bestowed upon him. He did not stand so square to Sami but more together, shoulder to shoulder.

'I shall speak to Louis Grayling about your work,' Alexander Hepworth said. 'I am a man of politics and the people, while Louis has an engineer's brain. He will be able to do more for you than I could.'

Sami looked a little uneasy. He folded his arms and cleared his throat.

'I am grateful to you for your assistance, of course. However, I do hope that Mr Grayling will see the merit of our work and promote it on that basis.'

Mr Hepworth held up his hand and stopped Sami from continuing.

'I've known Louis for many years now. If he doesn't like your proposal, he won't have anything to do with it. It is his reputation on the line, you know, and he will not have it meddled with.'

Alexander Hepworth looked at Sami keenly.

'So you don't hold to nepotism, eh? How on earth did you get on in India with that attitude? Oh, no need to be offended. Nepotism is the unyielding foundation of the British establishment as well. Although, that doesn't always hold true, I suppose.' He looked across at James, an indulgent look of familial grievance.

James seemed bemused by his uncle's mild scorn.

'Sometimes it's better to make your own way in the world, Uncle Alex. Even if you have to post letters to do it.'

'That may be well said, James, but not many young men would turn down a commission at Sandhurst in order to do it.'

'I didn't deserve the commission. You know that. If I'd passed my entrance exams then it would have been different, but I didn't, and it wouldn't have been fair to take the place of someone more deserving.'

'Ha! Don't you believe it! More like some young man with more sense.' Alexander Hepworth raised his eyebrows. There was a thin indulgent smile flickering about his lips, 'And less honour.'

From across the garden, I saw Aida waving to me. She was quite red in the face, flushed from racing about under the swollen sun. There were no children with her now; they were seated at the far end of the table, munching on sandwiches and swinging their legs. Their mother was standing over them, smiling and running her fingers through their tousled, blonde hair. They chatted between mouthfuls, shaking their hands when Ava tried to persuade some tomatoes onto their already full plates and nodding when lemonade was offered. I could not see Richard Beresford or the Harimans, but I could hear Martha's voice coming from between the trees of the orchard.

Aida walked halfway to meet me. She had recovered her breath and wanted to know whether to put out some more food. I looked about me at the guests scattered about. Some were eating, some were not. The table was mottled with varying amounts of food but the flies were busy, and the freshness of the bread and the salad were gone now, turning a little sorry under the day's unblinking gaze. I shook my head.

'We will leave it as it is for now. I do not want to attract more flies to new food. Let us remove these used plates and cups, instead.'

It had been fun, this small party of ours; the music that had been played, the food that was laid out and the easy mingling of conversations. Aida had enjoyed herself immensely.

'The people are very friendly. Everyone has said hello to me, and it is good to be able to come out with the guests and not have to listen to all the talking from inside a hot kitchen.'

'You were certainly having a good time with the children.'

Aida nodded. 'I remember my own brothers and sisters. It is how we used to play together. It would make them very tired, and so they would sleep soundly afterwards, and I would be able to sleep in peace, also.'

She looked across to where the Beresford children were now sitting, on the steps hugging their knees. Tilly's rag doll sat limply on her lap and her beautiful cotton dress was crumpled from the afternoon's fun. Her little brother, Theo, was singing quietly to himself, a lullaby that his mother sang to him.

'They are nice children,' said Aida. 'They do not kick or yell when they want something. They are very tired now. I will take them inside to rest.'

It was still light when our guests began to leave, filtering out into the wider village and their homes. Each of them thanked us and said how much they had enjoyed themselves.

'You have put us to shame,' Martha Hariman told us. 'We should be the ones throwing parties for you, welcoming you with open arms. Of course, I am rarely in Newton Kyme, but next time I visit we will be sure to return your hospitality.

Earnest's house is rather staid, a bachelor's domain really, but I'm sure that I can endow it with a bit of party spirit.'

The Landens left in a much quieter mood, shaking hands and uttering pleasantries. It was Elizabeth who spoke mostly.

'Thank you for a lovely day. The food was absolutely delicious. I wish that I could find such a talented cook. Maybe then, I could invite you all for dinner. Still, Arthur's very busy with work at the moment. He has so many commitments and even more ideas, and I do think that Mr Hepworth was enthusiastic about many of them. That's bound to keep him even more occupied. Probably at the weekends, too. And then, of course, we fly to France once the summer holidays start. Isn't that so, Arthur? Have you been to France at all, Mrs Altair? No, of course not, how silly of me. It's probably just as well; it helps if you can speak French. Both Arthur and I speak it like the natives...'

Arthur Landen was allowed only a brief goodbye. His breath smelled strongly of intoxication and his eyes looked most uneven, and when he shook hands with Sami he let his hand stay there for quite some time.

'It has been marvellous. Thank you for inviting us.'

He found himself being pulled away by his wife.

'Come along, Arthur. Goodbye, Aida. Goodbye, Hana.' She spoke loudly to them as though they were deaf.

The Beresfords were the last to leave, the children gathered up in their parents' arms, their sleepy heads dozing on their shoulders. The door shut behind them and then the house was silent once more, just the stifling of yawns and tinkling of party ware as we cleared everything away. We could hear, from over the hedge, Reverend Bramley rehearsing his sermon for the morning service, speaking eloquently about neighbourly love.

Hana and I brought in the table and chairs, while Aida and Sami washed up. I could hear Sami whistling softly some tune from an old Indian film, and I missed at once the silver screen where there was dancing and singing and much drama of tragedy and joy.

'That is a tune from Mother India.' Hana put down the table cloth that she had been folding and cocked her head toward the kitchen. She began to sing the words to the tune as she continued her work. '*Nagari nagari dware dware dhundu re sawaria...* Yes, I am right. It is very sad, that part of the film. When Nargis

165

finds that her husband has left her and she must find her way in the world with her two small children. And now I am sad thinking about it.'

The night air was still. Our bodies and minds were tired with the heat and the activity of the day, and so our souls were prone to a little nostalgia and homesickness. I took Hana's hand and we held on tightly.

'I wish we had a radio that would play Indian music also,' Hana said wistfully.

'But I have records,' I remembered. 'They are still in my trunk. I do not know why I have not played them.'

'Maybe, you are too afraid to,' Hana said. 'For they will bring back to you thoughts of Sikimpur and what you have left behind. I am missing it terribly, and my father. I think of him often when I am awake at night. I wonder what it is that he is doing, and how he is tending to the garden on his own. Even though I am happy here, I cannot stop missing it.'

I nodded. Yes, I missed the smell of the ripe mangoes, the sounds of Sikimpur nightlife, its language and its noise. I missed the feel of the earth beneath my *chappals* and the smell of the dry earth when a breeze got up. I missed the acerbic nature of Laila's tongue and Ammaji's bewildering concerns. I missed Abbaji's latticed room, playing carrom board and listening to the Test matches on his ancient wireless, and the chatter that went on around them.

'Arre, Boycott has scored his double century.' 'Finally, maybe now he will be satisfied and get out. Then we can get the match moving along. He is a true bore!' 'Yes, but still it is a lot of runs and a very significant score. Let us hope that the Nawab finds his form once again.' 'The English weather really does belong to the Angrezis. It has been raining throughout this summer and now there is only glorious sunshine.' 'But at least we are able to listen to Brian Johnston. Arre yaar, he is a most amusing fellow.'

Yet, I did not miss all of this as a continuous stream; I did not miss it as Hana missed her father. I forgot them at times and would be engulfed by the life I lived here.

It was dark when we were finished clearing the party away, each of us with our own mild headache and drooping eyelids. A slight breeze blew into the house through the French doors that were still open. I brought down a recording that I had of the music from the film Guide, and we listened to Lata and Mohammed Rafi singing, and chatted deep into the night about a land that lay half a world away and its people that we knew, who were waking up to a new day.

We spoke of memories, and became melancholic and merry in turn. And eventually, the record fell silent and we took ourselves to bed.

Part III

A Thousand Shapes

Chapter Eighteen

Just as July was fading, Sami and I flew over the English Channel, across France and over the majestic snow-clad Alps, then down into Spain, the deep south of Spain, that part where Pablo Picasso grew up: Malaga.

It was Sami's vision to go to Andalusia, where the Moors had reigned and the Alhambra and the Mezquite still stood. Also, less romantic and more practical, Sami wished to discuss some aspects of his project with his Spanish colleague, Dr Santos Hernandez. It was he who had suggested we visit him in Andalusia.

'Ah, come out to here, then. I am at my farm; you may come and join me. It will be a holiday for your wife and we shall talk the business.'

Hana and Aida did not come with us to Spain, returning instead to Sikimpur, Aida, with some reluctance, to help arrange a family wedding, and Hana, to visit her father, whom she missed dreadfully.

I bought James Michener's guide to Iberia and also a Spanish phrase book from the bookshop in Tadcaster, and spent the golden evenings of early July sitting amongst the wild bluebells and goldenrod, muttering, '*¿Cuánto valen las naranjas, por favor?*' and '*Mi llama* Sahira.' The sunflowers and marigolds would hear me asking for directions: '*¿Dónde está la panadería, la biblioteca, el mar, por favor?*'

Professor Hariman got to hear of our plans and brought me round his copy of Washington Irving's *Tales of the Alhambra*. He told me that 'At the time of the Ummayids, the majesty of the Alhambra was something to behold. The stories will give you some idea of how it all was, even though Irving wrote his book some four hundred years after its heyday. It is a delightful book, beautifully written. I am sure that you will enjoy it. The stories inspired Pushkin to write his own wonderful poem, *The Tale of the Golden Cockerel*. It is a favourite fairy tale of mine. I used to tell my students to read it when I felt they were becoming too cynical about literature.'

As he handed the book to me he closed his eyes and recited. 'Tale of sense, if not of truth! Food for thought to honest youth.'

In Malaga, near an old decaying pension, we hired a car - a small box with its steering wheel on the left-hand side. Sami studied his map carefully, muttering to himself and tracing the tiny roads with his finger. He spoke at length to the gregarious man from whom we had hired the car, who nodded enthusiastically and pointed at the map where the river flowed across it. Finally satisfied, Sami climbed into the driver's side and handed the map to me.

'We must follow this road. It is the main road that will take us some of the way to Alhama. It is quite long and will be easy to stay on.'

I held the map with a great attention, determined that we go along this road only and not waver. Sami muttered a prayer to himself, the traveller's prayer, before setting off. He drove with a great caution, keeping close to the right-hand verge, while I watched him and the road and the map all with great anxiety.

The hills of Andalusia surrounded us and took our breath away. We had never seen anything like them, undulating green and brown slopes flush with harvest-ready olive trees. Above us, the sky rolled on and on, so blue that our eyes hurt. Soon, we stopped at a service station to buy something to drink. The heat was on the rise, laying the countryside out in sultry waves.

Back on the road again, the hills slipped past us in a continuous stream, broken in places only by narrow side roads that snaked between them. I fell into a reverie with them, while Sami concentrated on the road ahead and the verges that we hugged. A few cars passed us; most were fast, or at least they seemed that way to us who were wary and unhurried. We passed over a river that flowed along the bottom of a ravine, on its way to the sea.

I turned on the radio and tinny tunes played on the Spanish guitar came out at us, lilting melodies of the Iberian Peninsula. I hummed along to them, tilting my head this way and that, until Sami asked, 'Are we close to our turning? I don't want to miss it, and we have been driving for quite some time.'

I suddenly became flustered, aware that I had not been paying attention to the map, aware that I was blushing with embarrassment. I stared down at the map lying limply on my lap, scanning the lines of blue and red and pink, the names of towns and mountain ranges and the green layers of forested land.

'I am sorry, but I don't know where we are now.'

'It is all right.' Sami laughed. 'I know exactly where we are. See?' He pointed at a sign that was approaching to our right. 'We are almost at Salar. Only ten kilometres to go. That is where we come off this road and then follow the one that will lead us straight to Alhama.'

Once our ten kilometres were done, the roads of Granada became narrow. Their sides fell away so steeply that I could only stare steadfastly at the vicious drop on my side. The hillside was littered with stones, big and small, all sharp, waiting to cut through a tumbling body. I was glad that Sami was driving, more in control than I would be, more steady.

A car came towards us in the opposite direction and I watched Sami closely. We passed each other, the other driver nonchalant and carefree, while I held my breath.

'Please don't do that,' Sami said quietly. It was then that I realised that he too had been nervous. Yet his hand was sound, his brow was clear and his voice unshaking.

We entered Salar from the north, a quiet, little whitewash of a town, pristine against the glare of the sun. It was a Saturday, midday, but there was barely a soul in sight. The shops were shuttered up, the playgrounds empty and the boule squares bare. A few mongrel dogs lazed under the trees that lined the main street.

'Siesta time,' Sami said quietly so as not to awaken the sleepers.

Siesta time. How that brought back memories of the hot summer months in Sikimpur, when Ammaji would gather us all in her bed to sleep through the barely bearable afternoons. The sun would be fierce, king of its sky. Bit by bit our lively chatter would dull as we, one by one, were overtaken by sleep.

Leaving Salar, we continued along the narrow, winding road to Alhama. We met very few motorists on the road; mainly they were young couples heading for the beach, or farmers who drove their trucks with one hand and glared at us as they roared past. We continued in this way, careful and cautious along the twenty kilometres to our destination, the sunny town of Alhama de Granada. We passed a number of small settlements, farmhouses and small cottages, all painted in obligatory white. They were pretty scenes, scenes that artists put onto canvas.

It was Sami who saw Alhama first. We turned a sharp corner and he looked far to the right of him, briefly, for it was sensible that he keep his eyes on the road.

'That must be Alhama over there. In the distance. It must be. It is larger than I had thought it would be, much bigger than Salar.'

I looked out and saw what he saw, the town of Alhama de Granada sitting on the edge of a gorge; rows of brilliant white houses perched there, overlooking a great cavernous drop. We were still five minutes away from it, driving along the same narrow road until, finally, we went over a stone humpback bridge of single lane width, and it was there in front of us. Gleaming white houses, thrown here and there along a hillside, upon which grew trees with clumps of fruit weighing them down. And, rising high above all this like a guardian, stood the bell tower, the campanile of the church that had buttresses along one side and arched windows.

Like Salar, Alhama was asleep. Doors were closed, shops and houses alike, and the human population gone from the streets. It was eerie, that silence of the sun, like a ghost town. Brightly-coloured bunting hung across the narrow streets, stuck onto the outside of window frames.

The main road opened up onto a pretty square, with flowers dotted around its edge. In one corner of this square, a playground lay, empty and still, the children out of the heat, sleeping, dreaming. A few elderly men sat on wooden benches, languid under the canopy of a carob tree. They talked quietly, as the elderly do, leaning forward on their walking sticks and chewing on tobacco. This whole scene was dominated by a large, red stone wall that had small windows overlooking the square. This was Alhama's Moorish castle, inhabited still, but looking gloomy and foreboding.

Sami stopped the car to study his map again. Looking up, he pointed to a cobbled street that lay beyond the square and to the right.

'That is where we have to go. Our cottage is just down that road. We should be able to find it with ease. It is near to the church and we cannot miss that. It is very large, as we have seen, with its own bell tower. We will be able to hear the bells ringing.'

'It will be like being back in Newton Kyme then, listening to the bells of St Andrew's.'

Casa Azul, our home in Alhama, stood at the end of a narrow lane. We left the car at the bottom of the lane and walked up the cobbles, past a row of terraced houses with their doors firmly closed and their balconies filled with bright red begonias. The door and window frames of Casa Azul were painted blue, a brilliant blue in that brilliant sunshine, the sunshine that flooded into the rooms and illuminated its white walls.

A woman let us in; she was friendly, with a face as round as a shining coin. Speaking mostly in Spanish, with a smattering of English, she made herself understood with a great deal of added gesticulation. She was Anna, our Andalusian maid, who would also cook for us and help us with her local knowledge.

The garden outside was not large, but it was a pretty sight. A rough and uneven wall, built of a grey-white stone, surrounded us, high enough for privacy, not so high as to be imposing. There was no real lawn, but instead small white pebbles were laid out underfoot. Terracotta pots sat at intervals around the upper garden in which fleshy succulents and herbs grew: Spoon Jade, Red Flames and Aeonium, oregano, basil and thyme. A sagely fig tree watched us from its corner.

In the days to come, I would set a blue wicker chair under its flowering branches, out of the blazing sun, and sit for a while, reading, writing my thoughts, drinking coffee. It was a lovely place to be when the bells of the church campanile sounded out the hour, and there were many times when I would count the chimes and be taken aback by the lateness of the hour and how long I had been out there.

Our Andalusian maid told me that my shade-giver was the Charybdis fig tree, so called because its branches had saved Odysseus from the whirlpool monster, Charybdis. She regarded it with awe and was delighted that I was so fond of it. However, when I said it was a pity that it was not yet in fruit, she gasped at me in horror and raised her hands, shaking them and exclaiming in rapid Spanish.

'No, es sagrado! Usted no debe tocarlo!'

I nodded at her in surprise, not understanding her completely but only sure that I must not touch the ancient fig tree, let alone pluck its fruit.

Nearer the house, there was a small dining area, with a mosaic-topped table with wrought iron legs and four chairs. It was a place out of the sun, for the wall lent a shade for much of the day. We would have most of our meals there, and there were many times when Sami preferred it to his study. He would sit out with a drink and work on his papers as the ants took away the crumbs that had fallen on the ground. He made some important decisions there, he told me; the peace brought about it its own clarity.

The day after we arrived we set out after breakfast to explore. Anna had suggested that we start off looking at the church whose bells we could hear from Casa Azul. The morning was pleasant, with a gentle breeze blowing from the east, and the streets smelled clean and fresh.

We passed few people as we made our way through the back streets, away from the main road that had brought us to Casa Azul the previous day. The people that we met stared at us, the older ones stopping to watch us walk past. Sami would always smile at them, saying in his outsider's accent, '*Hola, buenos días*' and sometimes, '*¿Cómo está usted?*' And they would reply with a smile, nodding and saying, '*Muy bien, muy bien.*'

I was glad to have Sami with me, cheerful and quite happy to be seen by strangers. He made me bolder, too, as I walked by his side, admiring this little town, quite taken with it.

Once, we met a car making its way tenuously along the narrow lane and we waited in a doorway to let it past, crawling as it was to avoid the houses that were packed in close around it. The man who drove looked nervous, a frown on his face, he barely glanced at us as he passed.

The Inglesia de Santa Maria stood as a magnificent edifice and we had to shade our eyes from the sun as we looked up at the top of it, where the campanile was housed. We climbed the pale, stone steps up and walked around it and into its interior. It was the first church that I had been in. It was so very different from the mosques that I had known: all the imagery, which was illuminated by the sunlight that came in through the stained glass window. There were rows of pews lined up, orderly and severe, with hard wooden seats, all facing the altar with its red, velvet coverings. A young woman sat with her head bowed at the front, running a black stone rosary through her quick fingers. She wore a black scarf over her hair, much like the covering that Muslim women wore on their heads for prayer.

'It is very peculiar,' I whispered to Sami. 'It is so quiet. I feel that I should be quiet here, also; to respect the quiet of others. I do not know why.'

'Yes, it feels a very solemn place, does it not?' he whispered back.

The woman rose from her seat, bowed to the altar and walked quickly to it to light a solitary candle.

'What is the meaning of that?' I asked.

Sami shrugged. 'Maybe it is for the prayer that she has said, much the same as some Indian women tie a piece of cloth around the rails of a saint's grave.'

From the church we took the path that led under the archway, eastwards up the cobbled steps and along a narrow wall that curved like a crescent moon. Around the corner, an avenue of trees led to a row of houses that were painted like a citrus fruit bowl, with balconies of earthenware pots in which bright red begonias bloomed. Beside this avenue ran a path which opened out into a small courtyard, with a fountain at its centre. A church, smaller than the Inglesia de Santa Maria, stood out in the open with a stout round tower and pale stone walls.

We followed the path round to the back of this quaint church and found ourselves staring out into the mouth of a vast, imposing gorge that twisted its way far into the distance, like a slithering serpent. We were silent for a while, gazing down into the bottom of this abyss where the water ran, a trickle under the blaze of the summer sun; just gazing across the huge stretches of its time-chiselled walls.

I made to walk further down the path, to the crude steps leading at an acute angle to the gorge below, but Sami called out to me.

'Tomorrow we will go and explore the gorge.'

I turned my head and looked quizzically at him. 'Tomorrow?'

Sami was staring out at the lower reaches of the gorge, at the ledges where a handful of wild olive trees grew.

'Tomorrow morning will be a better time for the walk. We will set out very early. There is a hotel, El Ventoro, not too far from here. We can walk there. I am hoping to meet Elias there and I would like you to meet him, too. He is most pleasant.'

'All right,' I said. 'I suppose it will be a better walk if we go earlier, before the sun becomes too hot.'

'Good. I will call him later this afternoon. He lives not too far away from Alhama, but I cannot remember the name of the town.'

I had bought a camera before we left England. I had promised Abbaji that I would send him photographs of Granada, the Alhambra and the grand mosque of Córdoba. I used it now, taking some photographs for me, memories for when we would no longer gaze upon this sight.

As I was choosing my frame with care, an old lady came past dressed in a simple black skirt and blouse with a white cotton scarf around her head. She had a basket in the crook of her arm and she walked with the gnarled steps of infirmity. How I wanted to take a photograph of her, to capture her in a timeless frame against the pale stone of the church, just as the sun was coming up behind, so that the light from the rays would illuminate her features.

As I put my camera to my eye, she looked at me and I froze with the directness of her stare, the certain disdain that seemed to come at me. I tried to smile at her, but she turned and walked away from me, muttering to herself in terse Spanish. I looked to see whether Sami had seen this, but he was still standing by the little wall, gazing down at the drop that led to the rivulet far below. I put my camera back into my bag. We continued on our way.

We bought coffee at one of the cafés that overlooked the square and sat outside. The coffee was strong and sweet. The square was busy now, with parents playing in the playground with their noisy children. Little, dark creatures, with supple limbs and excited laughter. The elderly men were still there, hanging by their benches, more chatty this morning with their eyes quite lively and eating pastries that they had bought from the bakery. Occasionally, one of them would break off a piece of pastry and throw it to one of the stray dogs that hung around.

'You must take care of the dogs here,' Sami told me. 'There is rabies here in Andalusia. It is almost as bad as in India.'

I nodded in agreement. Growing up in Sikimpur, I had a natural wariness of dogs for many of them were rabid. Despite the government's efforts to rid the country of the disease, the dogs bred at a feverish pace, and the chaos that reigned over India's human population meant that they had little chance of succeeding in their promise. The dogs of Alhama looked much like those that wandered aimlessly through Sikimpur's streets. Mangy, their eyes full of a hunger that was always ripe; they were scared of people and yet hung around them in the hope of some food scraps. They tolerated many kicks and much abuse for those few morsels.

From my bag I pulled out Mr Hariman's copy of *Tales of the Alhambra*. It was in immaculate condition, the spine barely creased and the pages still brilliant with their words and pictures. Mr Hariman had obviously read it with great consideration; in the margins were written notes in his tiny neat handwriting. Mr Hariman revered his books. They were, in his words, 'My eyes and ears into other worlds; into lives that no longer exist, but that I can imagine as real as my hand appears before my face.' I felt privileged that he would entrust me with his treasured possessions and was in awe of his quietly spoken knowledge and wisdom.

Sami was slowly sipping his coffee, his attention very much on the square, very much, I realised, on the children that were playing there and their parents who joined in. I felt a terrible shiver run through me. It struck all my nerves at once and my body quivered ever so slightly.

Sami caught my look and said by way of explanation, 'There is something about children that is quite arresting. Whether they are asleep or playing, they make you stop whatever it is you're doing and just think. Baba would say that. The joy of the angels, he called them. He used to say, whenever there was a child in the room, the devil took his leave of it, for all the backbiting and wicked talk would be forgotten.'

I looked out at the children on the slides and the swings, kicking their legs out, backwards and forwards they went, high into the air, calling out to go higher, to slide down faster. A couple of older boys were playing football with their father, chasing after the brown leather ball. They led such carefree lives; such happiness was reflected in their faces without a trace of malice.

'You are very lucky that you have your nieces and nephew, Sahira, especially Isa,' Sami continued. 'You were very close to him, I think. It must have been hard for you to leave him.'

I thought of the little boy with ruddy cheeks and an ever ready smile.

'Yes, it was hard to say goodbye to him, very hard. I think I miss him the most, actually. I looked after him a lot when Laila was expecting Noor, and afterwards too. He would stay the night with us quite often and sleep in my bed. He became very grown up because he was a big brother now. In the mornings, he would dress himself and then go out to the kitchen to help Mina with breakfast. He even offered to accompany Maha to the *sabziwallah* so that he did not try to cheat her.'

'That is very grown up indeed.' Sami became very quiet all of a sudden. His voice dipped to a whisper, a hopeful, timid whisper. 'Maybe, one day, you will have your own little Isa.' His eyes were not on me; they were not yet on the children. They were buried somewhere far out across the square to where the brilliant white houses stood with their colourful balconies and dark brown tiles on their roofs.

I smiled a little too widely.

'Of course,' I said brightly. 'One day.'

Sami left me with half a cup of coffee still. He wanted to speak with Elias before it was siesta time.

'Are you sure that you will be all right?' he asked. 'I can wait, if you would rather; if you are unsure of the way back.' He looked down at my cup that was not near empty. His face was reluctant, and his tone also.

But he was lucky, for today, at this moment I did not want him to wait. I would rather be lost a hundred times than have Sami's company, than have Sami talking further of children and such.

'No.' I shook my head with truth. 'I don't want to rush. I'm enjoying sitting here. I feel quite safe here, and I am sure that I can find my way back. It will be good for me to do so, to get to know my way around.'

Sami nodded with a smile. 'It is not hard. You can return the way that we came or try a new route.' He patted my shoulder and pointed to the little road that led behind the square. 'You just need to follow that road and it will lead you straight back to the street where we have parked the car. You will see it there and know that you are almost home. It is only a few minutes' walk from here.'

'I am sure that I shall be fine. I will finish my coffee and come. It is almost time for lunch and I don't want to make Anna wait.'

Sami stood up straight. 'Then I shall see you soon.'

I watched him walking away briskly, happy with his thoughts, leaving me despondent with mine.

I drank my coffee as slowly as I dared, even though it was quite cold by the time I finished. It was almost one o'clock and the sun was fierce in its cloudless sky. I felt a thirst that more coffee would not quench, and so I made my way back to Casa Azul for lunch, going through the town rather than back past the gorge and the Inglesia de Santa Maria.

Anna was busy in the kitchen when I arrived, laying out plates of olives and bread, and goat's cheese. She refused any offer of help from me and ordered me outside to sit at the table. In a little while, Sami joined me.

'I have spoken to Elias,' he said. 'He will meet us by the swimming pool tomorrow. He takes his son to swim there in the mornings. I am looking forward to meeting him again.'

We ate under the shade of the large umbrella, waving off the flies that were attracted by the smells of our Andalusian meal. Anna had bought a melon from the market that morning. It was a beautiful, ripe yellow and, when we bit into our slices, the juice ran in sticky rivulets down our arms all the way to our elbows. We were quite greedy, like children. It was our first taste of melon since we had left Sikimpur.

Chapter Nineteen

Early the next morning we set out for the gorge. The bells of the campanile rang out the hour of eight and the sun was not yet strong enough to make us sweat. The path down to the gorge was some way behind the little church, past an upright house that was guarded by a couple of lively dogs, who leapt at us from behind the safety of their iron gates and made us jump. We smiled nervously as we edged past them.

Small, loose stones slid beneath our careful tread, throwing up wisps of dust about our feet. Far above us, ragged trees and shrubs grew from rocky outcrops and, hidden amongst the gorge's lower reaches, were caves, dark and dank, unwelcoming places that were to be found well away from the warmth of the sun.

'I wonder if those caves provided shelter for the fleeing Moors,' I said. 'I can well imagine them hiding there during their retreat from the armies of the Castilian King and Queen.'

Sami climbed up the rocks to look inside one. He stood astride the uneven platform and peered in, sniffing at the air.

'It seems that the animals have found them out since then. The floor is littered with goat droppings.' He bent down and his voice became muffled in the cocoon of the cave. 'But I don't think they have come here recently. The droppings do not look fresh.'

'Maybe they use it in the winter months only, when the snows and the rains come down. I have read that the winter time is very harsh in Andalusia, maybe even more so than in Yorkshire. I am glad that we have come in the summer. It seems odd to think of the cold and wet here when it is so hot at the moment.'

We left the caves and continued on our way until the path forked. We stopped here and looked to where the left path led, back towards the town of Alhama. It looked so precarious, sitting as it did on the edge of the gorge, with its whiteness rising skyward from it. The tower of our campanile loomed high, splendid and angular against the azure blue sky.

We followed the right fork that took us up, along a crumbling path, and soon came in sight of a cottage below, a wizened and unkempt structure. At the back of it, however, was a grand oasis of canes with creepers crawling up them; beside them, vines spread over trellises. The garden was beautifully hoed, such neat earth rising and falling in waves and troughs. I stopped to take a photograph of this vegetable garden against the backdrop of the gorge, my camera clicks echoing off the walls of this vast canyon.

There were two pools at Pato Loco. The main, larger one was filled mostly with young people; teenagers, who wanted to be cool and hung around the tiled edge and chatted, and youngsters, who bobbed in the water and splashed each other with playful glee. The mothers of these younger children sat on towels and old, rickety deckchairs talking to each other, watching closely the fat little toddlers that ran about.

In the small pool were young mothers and fathers with their babies, holding them close to their bodies, smiling down at them, encouraging them to enjoy the water. The few men who were there had bellies that were round and chests that were hairy.

One of these was Elias, although he had only the start of a full paunch, being still quite young. He recognised us and waved; we were the foreigners who stood out. Our features were different and Sami was lighter-skinned than many of the native Andalusians, who were quite brown. But they did not seem to mind being so brown.

All around there were teenage girls clad in bikinis lying out on their towels under the full exposure of the sun. Ammaji would have been most astonished by this, this disregard for the delicacy of one's skin. And embarrassed. She would have shaken her head and averted her eyes, saying, '*Tauba*, why do these people want to be so *nanga*? Have they no *shurum*?'

Elias waved to us and Sami waved back. We made our way over to him and shook hands.

'*Hola*. It is good to meet with you again, Sami.' Elias spoke with an accent made thick by the heavy moustache that he sported. A small boy, who had been playing with a yellow plastic ball, came to Elias's side. He clasped his father's legs with his small fingers and hid behind his knees, poking his head out so that his eyes, so big and dark, could see us. Elias laughed.

'This is my son. Come Jax, come and say hello to our new friends.' But Jax would not and finally, Elias let him be.

'Please sit down,' he said. 'You must be tired after your walk across the gorge.'

'Oh, it was not too bad,' Sami replied.

'No,' I agreed. 'We set out early so we did not catch the full heat of the sun. It was quite pleasant this morning. And the gorge is quite a sight to see.'

'Yes, it is impressive. Although, I must admit that I have not been that way for a very long time now. I must take Jax there, as my father took me when I was a young boy. We shall see, maybe next year he will be ready for it. Eh, Jax, what do you think? Would you like to walk through the gorge?'

Jax nodded. 'Gorge!' he repeated with glee. Then he laughed and pulled away from his father, running back to his ball. Elias watched him, proud and indulgent.

'He is a good boy. Our house pool has not yet been filled with water and so I must bring him here to swim. It is good for his mother also, so she can have some rest. She has been unwell, but she is now getting better.'

Sami nodded. 'I am glad. It must be difficult for you. Especially as you also have the farm to take care of.'

'Oh, but that is not so hard.' Elias shook his head. 'It is, how do you say, the farm of the family; so I have my brothers to look after the working of it and I am free to pursue what is my real interest.'

A waiter came to our table, attracted by Elias's beckoning finger. He ordered a pitcher of beer and one of water. When they came, he poured some water into my glass and some beer into his own and Sami's. Sami did not stop him. Instead, he looked at me and I raised my eyebrows. He shrugged back. What did it matter if there was beer not water in his glass? What did one glass matter?

I watched Sami raise the glass to his mouth and drink. I did not say anything, but turned my gaze away from him and onto the hills that surrounded us and the olive trees that grew on them. It was a grand scene and I was altogether taken with the beauty of it.

'I hope you will not be bored with our talk.' Elias smiled apologetically at me.

'No, no,' I assured him hastily. 'Do not worry about me. I have brought my book. I shall enjoy reading it in this beautiful setting.'

Elias nodded in approval. 'Yes, this is a very lovely part of the world. Andalusia is famous for its mountains and wild forests. This is a very fertile area of Spain.'

'What is it that you farm?' I asked; the daughter of a farmer, after all.

Elias waved at the hills around us. 'As is usual here, we have many acres of olive trees and also of grapes. *Vineyards*, as you say. These products we sell in different parts of Spain: Madrid, Barcelona and Seville. Maybe soon, we will introduce them to Britain. That will be a very big step for us. Ah, but the regime of Franco is reluctant to join this new Common Market of Europe, so maybe that idea is for the future, the free future.' Elias shrugged and stroked his moustache. 'For the local peoples we grow vegetables: peppers, courgettes, tomatoes. My brother's wife is very involved with this; she too grew up on a farm, and so it is in her blood to make this produce and to sell it at the markets.' He glanced at my hands and then looked solidly into my eyes. 'I do not think that you have done much selling at markets.'

I sat up straight in my chair. 'No, I have not. But that is because our food production is large and we do not sell at the local markets. It is not a common thing to do in India if you have large amounts of land.'

'Ah, so that is the reason, and not because you are - how do you say, a *princess*?'

I looked at Elias with curiosity. I could not tell whether he was teasing me or he was being serious. I did not know how to answer him. Instead, it was Sami who answered for me.

'Sahira may look like a princess, but some of her roots lie deep within India's more modest populace.'

Sami's words were meaningless, I thought, and bland.

'My mother comes from a poor village,' I said crossly. 'Actually, in India, all villages are poor. So, far from being a princess, I am actually a peasant.'

Elias laughed and clapped his hands. 'No, no, you are far from being a peasant, Sahira, and closer to being a princess, I think.'

I blushed, for I felt a little foolish with my show of temper. 'Maybe you are a little right,' I conceded. 'Maybe just a little.'

Chapter Twenty

Lake Bermejales lay some ten kilometres to the north of Alhama, just outside the village of Arenas del Rey. The bus that I was on lumbered through its narrow streets, throwing up a dust cloud from the back of its tyres. Arenas del Rey was the sleepiest of sleepy villages. Not a soul was to be seen; it seemed in the middle of a hundred-year siesta.

I watched it go past from my window, exhilarated by this prospect of being in the open country: an adventure in itself. Sami had seen me off at the bus stop in Alhama, ensuring that I knew exactly where to get off. Anna, who accompanied me, shooed him away, gesturing at him to stop fussing, for I was in safe hands. A young couple, who were waiting to climb on, had been kind and reassured him that they, too, would make sure I was all right. I knew that I would be fine but, for his ease of mind, I let myself be taken care of.

Sami had set aside today to do some work and, although he was reluctant for me to go out beyond Alhama without him, I was determined to go. I had seen enough of Alhama and had heard from Anna about the lake.

Her son, Enrique, would bring us back, she told Sami. He worked at the hospital nearby and could pick us up on his way back. He was not a doctor, she said, but he knew very many medical things and had helped her out with her bunions and mouth ulcers. Yes, he was a good boy. He would wait for us at the campsite opposite the lake at four o'clock and he would drive me back home. Thus, was Sami somewhat appeased.

I sat on my hard seat, listening to all the chattering Spaniards, animated voices that rose above the rumble of our antiquated transport. Anna, joining in at first, soon fell asleep, her head resting on the metal frame of the seat. I held onto my bag tightly. Although it contained no more than a small towel, my lunch, camera and book, still it was the only thing familiar to me.

The young couple had taken the seats across the aisle from us, but they ignored us mostly; talking to each other, the man occasionally feeding his girl a grape from the bunch that he kept in his handkerchief. He had offered me one at the start of our journey, but I had declined and he did not seem pleased with that response. He had muttered something to his girl, who had sniggered and bent down to take it up from his hand with her mouth. I turned my head away to look out of the window.

Even with our slow and careful speed, the journey through Arenas del Rey took no more than ten minutes. Soon, we left behind the whitewashed houses and the empty pavements, and came into the open again, with woods on either side of us and a track that stretched out long into the hills. It was like a well-sung song that scene, an undulating tune of browns and greens.

We rolled on. Dipping down to the level of the lake, the path ahead was seemingly endless and I closed my eyes, letting the rhythm of the bus gently rock me until I was shaken by the shoulder. It was the young man. He was smiling now, his girl too. She was pointing out of her window in excitement.

The bus had stopped and everyone was waiting for us to get off. I woke Anna hastily and gathered myself together. We walked down the aisle, with the other passengers saying goodbye to me, sounding bemused.

'*Adios.*'
'*Véale más adelante.*'
'*Tenga un buen día.*'

I recognised some of what they said, and so I nodded, replying, '*Adios.*' '*Gracie.*' '*Adios.*' It was almost all that I knew of Spanish, a few words that I had picked up from the people that I had passed in the streets of Alhama, and from Anna.

The bus left us in a flurry of dust, everyone waving as we stood by the entrance of the campsite. I could see no other people around, only tents put up randomly, pegged down into the dry, hard soil. Ahead, on the other side of the track, was a thin layer of trees and, between their branches and trunks, coming in sharp, brilliant bursts, was the light that bounced off the cobalt blue surface of Lake Bermejalis.

Anna took hold of my hand and led me across the road, making our way through the trees onto the pebble beach that surrounded the lake. Scattered here and there were the bleached skeletons of desiccated water creatures. They were like pieces of frayed lace, and fragile, as though woven by a dedicated spider.

'*Es hermoso. ¿No es así?*' Anna spoke with a wide smile.

I nodded. I had heard the word *hermoso* many times when Anna spoke of things Spanish.

'It is very beautiful.' I agreed.

I gazed out at the placid lake, so dazzling in the sunlight, so blue. *Azul*, was a word I knew; *lago azul*. It was mesmeric, watching the water sparkle, casting a spell over me. On the sandy bank to the left of me, a turquoise bee-eater had built its nest, and soaring above were a pair of magnificent eagles; *águilas imperiales*, Anna told me, Spanish imperial eagles, a rare sight.

Of course, I did not possess a swimming costume, but the day was hot and the waters so inviting and, apart from Anna, there was nobody around to witness whatever it was I wished to do. I left Anna to lay the blanket on the beach and took myself to the water's edge. I let my bag slip out of my grasp, onto a piece of driftwood just beyond its lapping tongue, and folded the bottoms of my forest-green trousers up, right up to my knees. Then, unhurriedly, I waded in.

The water that licked my feet, my shins, my calves was cool. I lifted my hair away from the nape of my neck and the breeze passed over it, refreshing it with that contact. I allowed the water's coolness to swallow me further.

Soon, I was waist-deep, my shirt sticking to my skin as they both became soaked, and still I would not stop. The water came up over my shoulders, my chin, my mouth, my nose, my eyes, my forehead. I held my breath for as long as I could, and then I began to flail. My arms and legs thrashed the waters around me as I strove to push them under and to pull myself up and out.

It lasted a few seconds, probably no longer, but I gasped for air when I reached the surface and began to gulp it down. My flailing limbs began to relax as oxygen reached them and they were no longer drowning in acid. Slowly then, I drew myself out, back into the warm air, lifting my body out of the water, half walking, half swimming back to the shore. Through my water-clogged ears, I could hear Anna shouting at me, scolding me for my lunacy.

'*Estás loco! ¿Cuál sería el Señor Sami decir si regresaba con usted ahogado? Muchacha loca!*'

'*Lo siento,*' I said to her in Spanish, and then quietly, 'but actually, I am not sorry. I feel so alive for having done it.'

She dried me down with a brief towel rub, tutting as she did so. It was rough against my skin, causing it to go red. When she had finished, she tied the towel around my body and indicated to me to pull off my wet clothes from underneath it. She took them from me and laid them out, my trousers and shirt, onto the sun-baked pebbles to dry. I sat down on the blanket and began to lay out lunch. Anna came to join me, chatting away happily, not caring that I did not really understand; she may have been talking to herself.

She had packed us a fine meal. My hunger was sharp after my time in the water and I ate most of it there and then. Fresh bread from the bakery, juicy, plump tomatoes and a hard cheese that smelled ripe. I drank down the water from my bottle and wiped the remnants from my mouth and chin. I felt somehow primal in the simplicity of my existence; temporal as it was, I was there, with barely a stitch on me and such primitive fare.

On the far side of the lake the mountains rose, a soft blend of purple and misty blue, their peaks smudged under the haze of the post midday sun. I spotted something out on the horizon, too far away to clearly make it out, but I thought it was a small boat, maybe some of the campers out for a lazy boat day or some of the local youths fishing. So, we were not alone with our own private beach and lake. But no matter, they were a distance away and did not disturb my tranquillity.

I pointed it out to Anna, who smiled. '*Ah, un barco. Cuando yo era joven, pasé muchas horas en este lago, con mi padre y mi hermana. Él nos enseñe a pescar. Tuvimos un montón de diversión...*Veree lovelee.'

I pulled my camera out of my bag and looked through the lens. I zoomed in on the bobbing little speck and thought I could make out a solitary figure lying casually across the bow of a battered old boat. I could not tell if the figure - a man, I guessed - was sleeping or taken ill, until he lifted up an arm and waved it aimlessly in the air, much like he was shaking off a persistent insect, a stonefly maybe, for I had noticed quite a few around me.

I put the camera down and turned to Anna, but she was now engrossed in her magazine. The sun and my swim and my lunch began to have their gentle effect on me and I felt tired.

There was a log to the right of us, under the shade of the tall trees. It had been there a while, for its bark was flaking off and its core no longer solid. I took myself over to it and sat down; it was warm against my back. I had meant to read out the rest of my time at Bermejalis, but I could not have managed more than a few pages when the drone of the dragonflies and the weight of the hot air around me took their toll. Anna was dozing now, having packed away lunch and lain her rotund body out on the rug. Her dress flapped gently in the breeze and she had placed her magazine over her face. It seemed too much effort to read; my book fell neatly into my lap and I let myself be led by nature's soporific way.

I awoke with Anna gently prodding me. The late afternoon sun was shining and I felt the daze that unfamiliar surroundings bring. Anna was pointing in the direction of the campsite.

'I visit,' she said loudly, holding her fingers together and putting them to her mouth. '*Me voy a comprar algunas verduras de allí.*'

I recognised the word for vegetables, but the rest was unknown. I shook my head and shrugged. '*No entiendo.*'

Anna sighed and pulled out some coins that Sami had given her that morning. She pointed vigorously to the campsite and said loudly, 'I buy.'

I nodded with enthusiasm, to show her that I finally understood. 'Yes, all right.'

Anna pointed at the watch on her wrist. 'Come, four.'

Nodding again, I watched her trudge over the soft sand, thankful to be alone.

I looked at my watch. It was not too close to four, when Anna's son would be waiting to pick us up. Just enough time for a final wade in the lake, I thought, to bring me round. But, I did not want to get my clothes wet again, and I could not go into the water with my towel on. There was only one thing to do. I looked around me, staring into the trees and along the beach. There was nothing stirring other than my constant companions of the afternoon, the insects, the breeze and the kites that flew high above us.

I walked cautiously to the water's edge, not quite certain until I got there that I was really going to do it. I looked around again, here and there, but all was still, quiet, such a piece of isolation like a bird soaring into a cloudless sky. I began to remove my towel when a noise echoed through the air, a crack of a twig or a sharp tread on a pebble.

I whipped around to where the distraction had come from and it was then that I noticed the boat, the one that I had seen as a blur through my camera lens. It was tied up down the beach from me, quite some metres away, and it was empty. I pulled my towel tight across my chest and looked towards the clump of trees that laced that part of the lake, that part where the promontory rose and then disappeared behind the wood.

A man emerged, hunched down and messy. His hair was matted tight and raised from his scalp as though the wind had suddenly caught it. He had a beard, a mass of dark, wild hair and his clothes were no less unkempt. And, although he was the deep brown of a summer nut, I was sure that he was not a local man. He had the appearance of an outsider, an appearance that startled me and caused me some consternation. He had not seen me, for his gaze was concentrated on the ground as though he was searching for something.

I took my chance to save myself. Gathering my belongings, I dived behind my log. There, I dressed as fast as I could, ignoring the sand that layered my legs and arms. Then I rose, tentatively, peering above the log. It was thus that I was spotted. The man waved to me, smiling and friendly, but I did not feel so sure of him and so I turned away, without a reply, walking fast, running and stumbling across the pebbles and into the trees. I stopped when I reached the road.

There, across the road was a red truck and inside was Anna with her son, Enrique, waiting for me, with his window down and the smell of his cheap strong cigarette drifting over to me. I inhaled it with a great relief.

Along the road home, Enrique did much of the talking in broken English, about his job, about his girlfriend. He showed me a picture of her, holding the steering wheel with one hand while his other felt around in his shirt pocket and pulled out a crumpled black and white photo. So creased was it that the pouting girl could have been anyone. But I smiled and said she was very pretty. Enrique smiled back. Anna clicked her tongue and looked proudly at her son. Then she said something to him and he laughed.

Turning to me, he said, 'She tell me you try swim with the fishes.'

I blushed and said nothing. I hoped that Anna would not tell Sami about his *muchacha loca*.

Arenas del Rey was awake now. The shops were busy and the people were walking along the pavements, the young girls in their summer dresses and the boys in shorts. Back in Alhama,

Enrique dropped me off at the bottom of the road and said he would take his mother back home. I nodded and thanked him.

'No problem,' he said. 'Next time, I bring my Gabriela for meeting with you.'

Inside Casa Azul, Sami was playing a game of solitaire. He stopped when I came in and was pleased that I had returned to him safely. I told him about the lake that was *muy hermoso*. He smiled and looked a little left out.

'Tell me about it, so that I can form a picture in my mind,' he said

I did not tell him about the strange man at the lake. If he knew of my encounter, he might be unwilling to let me to wander at will. Still, he sensed that something was wrong.

'Tell me, Sahira, was your trip to Lake Bermejalis completely *muy hermoso*? You did enjoy it, did you not? Did something happen?'

'No, not exactly.' I shook my head slowly. 'No, it was nothing. Lake Bermejalis is absolutely beautiful. It is idyllic, so picturesque. You must visit it.'

I became quiet as I thought of the stranger who had frightened me so. It was silly, for I had no reason to believe he would have done me any harm, but there was something about him, his odd appearance that I found disconcerting, that I translated into danger.

Sami was looking at me with interest. His eyebrows were raised and his mouth set with expectancy. I realised that I would have to tell him. I sighed and, with some caution when describing the man's strangeness, I told him of my visit. I tried to make light of just how startled I had been, and did not mention that I had fled at the sight of the stranger, being now embarrassed by this sudden flight. I looked up when I had finished, expecting Sami's face to show some signs of concern. Instead, I found him with a smile on his face. He sat back in his chair and flicked the ash from his cigarette.

'So he has returned,' he said casually.

'Who has? You know this strange man?'

Sami shook his head. 'No, I do not know him exactly. I have heard of him only. He is a journalist, and knows Elias.' Then he cocked his head. 'At least, I think he is the person that you almost met.'

'Then, he is harmless?' I said with some relief.

Sami nodded. 'And also you will know him when I tell you—'

His sentence was cut short; the shrill bell of the telephone rang out, startling us both. It was Sami who leapt up to answer it.

I heard his voice, saying a bright *'Hola'* - expecting Elias, most probably, to answer him back. Then there was silence, and then a surprised *'Asalaam-alaikum'*, and he began to talk in Urdu, quietly. His voice became muffled and I realised that he had shut his study door.

I frowned. Anxiety brought a sweat to the palms of my hands. I did not move, but sat rooted to my chair, my heart beating fast. I heard the telephone click, but Sami did not come out for a while. When he did, he stood before me and I was shocked to see his face that was pale and his eyes that were moist. His hands were shaking. He did not sit down.

'What is it?' I asked, my voice shaking with an uncertain fear. 'Tell me. Please. It is something bad.'

He did not speak immediately, and when he did his voice was uneven. 'There has been an earthquake. In Sikimpur. Six days ago. It was a strong one and there has been much damage. And...'

'And? Who has been hurt?' I asked sharply. 'Has anyone...' I could not say more than that. I dreaded to hear an answer to that unfinished question.

'No, no. No-one has been... I mean no-one in the family. There have been a number of deaths, of course, across the city, and beyond it. But no-one within the family. Ammi is fine, Gulabi Ghar has only minor damage, Shamshad Bagh a little more. It is Laila who has been hurt. Hurt quite badly.'

'How badly? Will she be all right? I must go to her.' I stood up too quickly and my head began to spin. I put my hand up to my forehead to steady it a little. 'I must go and see her. Ammaji will be very worried. Please help me to go back.'

Suddenly, I did not know how to breathe any longer. I was holding my breath until this dream was torn out from my mind and from my heart.

Sami shook his head. 'No. You will not do any good going back.'

'What do you mean? I must go! How can I possibly stay away when Laila is so badly hurt, when there is such turmoil? Ammaji will not know what to do. She needs my support, and you should also go back. To see Ammi. She must be very scared, too.'

'But your Abbaji does not want you to return. That is not why he telephoned. I don't think they would have let us know about the situation until Laila was out of danger but there is something else that they need from you. From us.'

'Yes?'

'It is your nephew, Isa, you see. He is upset, very upset. He was sleeping in his bedroom, alone, when the earthquake struck. He ran out into the garden and hid under the car so that nobody could find him. He would not answer when they called for him, and when they found him he would not come out. He has been asking for his mother and wondering why he cannot see her. He has not been able to sleep since then, especially with the aftershocks that have been occurring.'

'Poor little one,' I said quietly. 'He must have been very scared.'

Sami nodded and, at last, sat down. The day was growing dimmer now and his pale features stood out starkly against the relinquishing light. He did not notice the fireflies that danced about him, small flecks of light that skipped as if on a burning flame.

'Yes,' he said. 'That is why they do not want you to return. That is why they would like Isa to come to you, to us. To stay for some time, until Laila is better.'

Sami paused and reached out for my hand and, although I wanted to pull away, I let his hand stay there, covering mine, which was bereft of all feeling.

Then he continued. 'Laila's baby, you see, was also hurt. Not so badly, but her arm is broken, and so the whole family is most preoccupied with them both. Isa, of course, does not understand this.'

Noor! I thought of Noor, Laila's baby, just a tiny thing when I had left. She was a year old now, walking with unsteady feet, and looking more like me, so Laila had written in her last letter. Poor Laila. Poor Nasir. What strain they must be under. It would break Nasir's heart to send his son away from him, but his heart must be very heavy with the worry of his wife and daughter weighing upon it.

'Of course Isa must come to us,' I said. 'We will look after him. But how will he come here?'

'Hana will bring him,' said Sami, 'She has agreed to accompany him on the plane.'

I nodded thankfully, automatically, for I was still dazed. 'It will be a long journey for them both. Hana is very good to have agreed to come with him.'

Later, when it was dark, I lay in the bath and washed the sand off my body. The lake water had evaporated away, leaving me speckled with innumerable tiny grains. I thought of Isa, the happy little boy who was now so very unhappy. I could not imagine him without a smile, without some innocent mischief on his mind.

Sami was in the garden, walking up and down. Streaks of cigarette smoke came through the open window. I inhaled them deeply. I had never smoked, not so much as placed a cigarette in my mouth, but I had always liked the smell of it. There was something heady about it, something that I could feel stream through the synapses of my brain. Maybe this was the reason why Sami smoked; it settled the rough edges of one's nerves and laid them flat with calm.

A tear ran down my face and plopped into the murky water that I sat in. It was followed by another, and then another, until there came a relentless flow that joined with the waters that I sat in, until my heart had wrung itself dry. Then, I stopped and took my body down into the water until my head was covered and I had to hold my breath.

Chapter Twenty-One

Isa came to us three days later, early one morning. I knew him as soon as he stepped from the plane - a small and defiant thing in dark blue trousers and a white, short-sleeved shirt, looking so like his mother that I let out an involuntary cry. Beside him stood Hana, looking about her, frowning, her right hand shading her eyes from the bright morning sun and the other holding on tightly to Isa's tiny hand. They both looked lost.

Eventually, Hana saw us and waved wildly. Then she kneeled down and pointed us out to Isa. The little boy looked shyly at where she was pointing and crept closer to her, till he was almost hidden behind her. Such a vulnerable little figure he was.

It was Sami who went to greet them. He greeted Hana first before kneeling down till his eyes were level with Isa's. I watched as Sami spoke to him before holding out his hand. Isa looked at it, hesitated, and then flung himself upon Sami, clasping his hands around his uncle's neck. He whispered something into Sami's ear, which made him return Isa's hug with feeling. I walked across to them, with quick steps and a smile that I had practised over and over again.

All that day, Isa stayed close to Hana. He sat with her in the back of the car on the way to Alhama, holding her hand at the beginning of the journey and then, eventually, moving to the window and gazing out. All without speaking. Yet, I remembered his voice so clearly, a babbling brook it had been.

By the time we reached Casa Azul, Isa was fast asleep. Sami carried him in and laid him in his new bed, where he stirred and muttered for his mother, while I stroked his hair and hushed him till he was quiet again. His head rested on a patterned pillowcase, his dark curls softened by sweat, framing his innocent face. I dare not kiss him for fear of wakening him, though I longed to do so very much. I left him there, covering him with a light sheet and leaving the door ajar, in case he should wake up and call out for someone, for Hana.

Downstairs, Hana was sitting at the kitchen table drinking the tea that Sami had made for her. Her feet were resting on the wooden support of the table. She was telling Sami about the earthquake, holding her cup tightly in her hands as she used to in Newton Kyme.

'It was as though Yajuj and Majuj were stamping through the earth. We had no electricity, no lights and so we were all in darkness. It was very frightening.'

Hana trembled and her voice faltered. I placed my hand on her shoulder. I could not imagine what that darkness must have been like. I remembered how it was in Sikimpur, when the power failed during the night and we had to use candles; but to be left in darkness when the earth was heaving and in tumult? I shivered. For Laila and for Suha, worried for their children, it must have been terrifying.

'When I left,' continued Hana, 'your sister, Laila Bibi, was at least out of danger. And her baby, too, was much better. Her arm is healing very well. Your mother says that it is because she is so young and her bones are still soft and able to mend more readily. It is what the doctor has told her.'

'Does Laila know that Isa is here?' I asked.

Hana nodded and looked surprised. 'But yes, of course. Do you not know that it was she who wanted him to come to you? Even when she remembered that you were here, in... I cannot remember the name of this country, but that you were not to be in England. Both she and her husband were determined that Isa should not remain in Sikimpur, where the family was still so worried.'

Hana rubbed her eyes, which were reddening, and yawned. 'I am sorry,' she said. 'I have not slept very well since that day. I do not think many people in Sikimpur have. We are still experiencing aftershocks. It is hard to sleep when you have that kind of fear inside your head. Your body cannot relax. It is always ready to run outside. Indeed, many people are sleeping outside, even though there is still the threat of the monsoon rain.'

'You must rest now, then.' Sami took Hana's empty cup from her and set it down on the table.

'Your bed is ready for you,' I told Hana. 'I made it myself, especially for you. I think that you are ready for it, also. Come on, I will show you where your room is.'

Hana pulled her feet off the wooden support and pushed her chair from the table.

'Yes, I am very ready. I did not sleep very well on the aeroplane. I was too anxious, and Isa was not so settled. I think he was glad to see the ground far below us. He was glad to be far from it in case there was another quake.'

As I showed Hana to her room, we heard Isa stir in his bed. We stopped, Hana by the door and me by her bed, and waited to hear more, but Isa slept on, little snores escaping through the gap between his door and doorway. I closed the window, which Anna had opened that morning. The room had been shut up for some time and the air in it had been stuffy. Now, it smelled quite fresh with the breeze that had blown through and the bright flowers that Anna had arranged on the pale pine dressing table.

I watched Hana remove her shoes, dusty still from the Sikimpur earth that the quake had so violently stirred. She climbed in, graceful and beautiful still through her weary limbs and drawn face. It was so strange to see her here, in Alhama, under the roof of Casa Azul, beneath a Spanish sky. She was dressed in a yellow shalwar shirt, which did not suit her pale skin, for it was the yellow of a narcissus petal rather than a daffodil.

I hung around the iron rail at the foot of her bed,

'I know that you are very tired, Hana, and I am sorry, but I must know how things really are back in Sikimpur. I am sure that Ammaji is fretting about Laila and Noor. Of course, she is always concerned about one thing or another, but this is real worry, real fear. Even when Laila was in hospital having Noor, there was no real fear in her, just the ordinary anxiousness. But now...' I sighed. 'And what about Abbaji and Suha? How are they? And your father? And Sami's mother?'

Hana sat up and put her hand on mine to stop my blurting words.

'Please sit down, Sahira Bibi. It must be very hard to be here and not to know, but only to imagine. Yes, your Ammaji is naturally very worried, but she does not show it. She is very calm, in fact. She does not speak so much about your sister and your niece; I think she keeps it for her prayers. She is making herself busy, helping with the shelters that the local government have set up for those who have been left homeless. It is good for her. Certainly, she seems very serene. It has surprised everyone, for your Ammaji is usually...'

'Very vocal.' I helped her finish her sentence.

'Yes,' Hana smiled back. 'She likes to say what she is thinking.'

'And she thinks far too much,' I mused. 'But, at least, she does not dwell on it.'

'They are all fine, Sahira Bibi.' Hana yawned and brought her hand up to her pink lips, touching them, but the yawn remained, and so I rose from her side telling her to sleep now.

I shut the door tightly but she called out to me. 'Leave it open, Sahira Bibi. I shall not be able to hear Isa if he calls for me.'

So, I opened the door, leaving it quite wide open. I felt a tinge of jealously that my nephew, who had shared my bed when he was a baby, and whom I had taught to swim, would call out to Hana, who had, after all, only accompanied him on an aeroplane journey to me.

The afternoon was a solid sheen of heat, and so I went to my own room and lay down on my bed, but the sheets were too warming and my mind too restless. I lay awake, waiting for Isa to call out, eager to go to him if he cried out in fear.

In the end, I could not wait for Isa to call out. I crept into his room when the bells of the campanile struck three and stood looking down at him, a little figure huddled under a crumpled, cream sheet with only his head to be seen. Eyes tightly shut and a mouth slightly open, hair wet with sleep. Every now and then he shuddered, and I longed to pick him up, but he was asleep and not to be disturbed.

I kneeled at the side of his bed, on the rug that lay over the stone floor. With my chin resting on the backs of my hands, I watched him, quite still, until the bells tolled the half hour. Then Isa began to stir - small movements at first, twitches really, that then stretched out through his limbs into wakefulness. His eyes blinked and, slowly, he unfolded his little body and slipped from under his sheet so that his legs slid either side of me. He fell into my arms, warm, childishly warm, and we held onto each other for a long time.

Hana stayed with us for a week and then she told us that she wanted to go back to Newton Kyme.

'Back to James?' I asked. 'You must have missed him very much.'

She was out in the garden, bending low to smell the purple lavender. My question made her stop and think, before shaking her head slowly.

'Actually, I have not missed him. Not so very much. Does that surprise you? Yes, I can see that it does. But I had not thought of it. I have only just now realised it when you asked.'

I was not sure she truly meant what she said. It was the shock of the earthquake, I told her, that was making her talk this way, but she shook her head resolutely.

'No. It is the garden that I have missed. It is the garden that I shall return to. Not James.'

Chapter Twenty-Two

Each morning that I awoke, I would look over to the pillow beside mine at the sleepy head that rested there, and smile. The afternoon that Hana left us, Sami had moved his belongings into the room that Isa had slept in and Isa's suitcase into our bedroom.

Our room faced due east so that it was the first to greet the sun. In these early hours, I would listen to Isa's breathing, my eyes searching his face in the stillness of the new light; the rounded upturn of his nose, the slight openness of his mouth and his flawless skin, with its flushed cheeks. Such a brave face, I thought, for all that he had gone through.

Eventually, he would stir and stretch, and I would wait for him to awaken fully, slowly, reaching out for me, my hand, my shoulder, my familiar form. I pretended to be asleep, for the sheer pleasure of feeling him draw close to me. Soon I, too, would wake, opening first one eye and then the other, and I would grin into his grin.

In all of this, Sami showed great kindness and tolerance towards Isa. He allowed him to monopolise my attention and, when demanded, he gave his own freely. There were times when Isa, so used to being spoilt and adored by all who knew him, called on Sami to leave whatever it was he was doing and play with him. He would stamp his little foot and command, '*Aw. Meray satt kaylo!*'

At these times, I would begin to remonstrate with him to be more polite, but Sami would hush me with a smile and a raised hand.

He would take Isa by the hand and take him out into the sunshine, onto the gravel of the upper garden, and there they would throw and catch a small yellow plastic ball over and over again. I would watch them for a while from the hall window as Sami talked quietly to Isa in simple English, teaching him as he went along.

'Well caught' 'Now throw to me.' 'Hold the ball up, higher. Yes, like that.'

It was Sami who put Isa to bed at night, stayed with him, talking to him. As Isa drifted off, Sami would stroke his hair until his breath became even and he became still. Occasionally, I would watch from the doorway, marvelling at how easily Sami took to this. He had the knack of it, I thought to myself, something that I could never do. I did not have that slow patience that children sense and are assured by.

So, this was Sami with a child, I thought ruefully. What a good father he would make, although I had never doubted that. He had all the patience, all the yearning, all the desire to teach through steady perseverance. And the love of it, too.

In this way, we made a core family; a man, a woman, a child.

Soon, Elias's new swimming pool was completed and, to celebrate, he invited us for lunch with his family at their farm, one Sunday afternoon.

'Come early,' he told Sami. 'Before the sun is too hot, so that the children can play and we can talk.'

It took thirty minutes to drive out to Elias's farm, along the Carretera de Granada that led out of Alhama, following the Rio Alhama north for almost twenty of those thirty minutes. The road passed by the old Arab bathhouse and over the little bridge and through a mountain pass, craggy slopes on either side with clumps of olive trees growing here and there, sprouting at nature's behest.

Elias met us at the crossroads of an outlying village - a 'pueblo', he had called it. The road from here to the farm was difficult to follow, he said, and it would be better if he were there to guide us. He was waiting in his car, which was covered in the dust of this road, and he waved to us as we drove up to him.

We followed close behind him. The road that he took was indeed convoluted; sometimes it was not even a road but a track made only usable because of the traffic that traversed it. It was a bumpy ride that threw up small stones, which hit the sides of the car and rattled us in our seats. Isa was delighted with this. He held onto his wooden toy car tightly and shouted with excitement.

Soon, we turned off this minor track onto one that was smothered in loose, dried mud and we saw ahead of us a set of large, iron gates. As we neared them, Elias tooted his horn and a man in a khaki uniform appeared from a little wooden hut behind them and pulled them open, saluting to Elias as he drove by. As we followed Elias in, the man stared at us through our open window, his salute wilting slightly with his inquisitive gaze. He was old, this man in khaki; a spritely thing, with a face burnt brown from the sun.

Elias stopped his car in front of a large, white villa, rising high into the sky. A garden surrounded the villa; the grass was not cut and daisies grew in cheerful clumps throughout. At one end of this vast lawn stood a small forest of fir trees and, from two of the lower branches, there hung rope swings.

Beyond the villa, the olive groves took over the landscape to the right and, to the left, there crept the tendrils of numerous grape vines. We had to shield our eyes to see all this, for the sky, as ever, was swept clean by a brilliant blue brightness. And, as if there were not enough beauty in this scene alone, there stood far, far into the distance, so majestic and proud, the Sierra de Loja mountains.

'This is beautiful,' I said. 'You are very lucky to be met with such a view every day, Elias.'

'It is true.' Elias nodded. 'Yet sometimes, I hurry so much with other things that I forget to stop and look about me.'

Elias's wife, Patrine, came out to greet us. With her small frame and pale green eyes, she appeared delicate beside her husband. A babbling baby swung gaily on her hip and, when she talked, she spoke a beautiful English that was accented like a welcoming smile.

'*Buenos días*, it is so lovely to meet you at last.' She held out her hand to Sami and hugged me closely, while the baby in her arms wriggled impatiently between us. Then she turned her attention to Isa. She did not touch him, but stooped down and said gently, 'Isa, I think. I am very pleased to meet you.'

Isa hid his face in the blue denim of my jeans, refusing to be seen by anyone until he heard another voice, a child's voice, Jax's voice. The little boy came bursting through the front door of the villa, shouting in Spanish, '*Mamá, mamá, ¿qué está pasando?*' and then stopping abruptly at the sight of us, becoming suddenly shy.

Elias called out to his son. 'Come now, Jax. Greet your guests properly. You must say *Hola*, Hello.' He turned to Sami and me. 'He has been very excited about having a new playmate. Talking about him all the time. But now...' He spread his hands out in feigned resignation. 'You see how he is.'

'Oh, do not be so harsh. He is but four years old.' Patrine shook her head. 'He is a very hard father to Jax. Because he is the eldest, he expects too much.' She jiggled the baby on her hip. 'But with this one, he is more relaxed, more loving, more fun. It is like two different fathers.'

Elias wagged his finger at his wife and smiled. 'Now, you are being harsh on me. You know I love them equally. But it is true. I expect from Jax maybe something more than his years.' He sniffed in acknowledgement and let the boy alone. He turned to me. 'So, how is the situation now in India? Are your family well? I have heard that your sister-'

'Yes, yes, she is doing much better,' I interrupted him, not wanting Isa to hear about his mother. He might or might not understand what it was we were talking about, but I did not want to find that out.

Elias understood and lowered his voice. '*Bueno, bueno*. It must be a big worry, but it is not something to talk about now when the day is so lovely and the children are here. Even if they stay hidden away.'

Jax and Isa did not stay hidden for long. They were coaxed out soon enough; then, the two shy little boys, who could not understand each other, became friends, playing, chasing each other across the grass where the daisies grew, and climbing the lower branches of smaller trees.

Elias and Sami wandered off to the olive groves, talking of matters mechanical, and of nature too, leaving Patrine and I to watch the children from under the shade of a fir tree. We were seated on wrought iron chairs that were ornate and painted green. They were old and felt rooted to the soil, with a dusty layer of lichen growing round their legs. Patrine sat her baby down on a blanket, pushing a rattle into her chubby hands and tickling her lightly under her chin.

'It is good to see how children make friends so easily,' she observed. 'They do not seem to think of how to do it. It comes so naturally to them. I think it would be good for the adults to learn something of this.'

I nodded. 'Yes, even when they cannot speak each other's language, it does not stop them from making friends.'

'Maybe, then, it is they who should be governing our countries. Maybe, the world would make more sense?' Patrine laughed and apologised. 'I am sorry. I have the influence of a political father. He was, you see, an English man who came to Spain to fight the Republican cause. He did not approve of the Kingdom of Spain that Franco declared. He died when I was but ten years old. He died fighting for his cause. Of that, I am very proud. It is something to be proud of in Andalusia: to die fighting for the Republican cause. In fact, I think it is why Elias married me. His father, too, was very outspoken, but Franco let him live, for he was a very important man in this region. He was allowed to die a peaceful death.'

Patrine fell quiet, and then she said with some hope, 'Still, I have heard that the General is ill, and if there is something in that, then–' She stopped and laughed again. 'And now, I must say sorry once more. Let us talk about other things. Elias does not like it when I get caught up in the memory of my father. He says that I am determined to make everyone feel the misfortune of our country.'

'Your father sounds like a very brave man, and I can see that you miss him terribly.'

'Yes, that is so. Even though it has been some seventeen years since he died, I miss him still. I hope one day to go to England and see some of my relations there. I read books and listen to the BBC World Service, so that I can feel his presence still.' Patrine fanned herself with a child's paperback book. 'Ooh, the sun is beginning to climb high now. Soon, it will be too hot for the children. I will fetch some lunch for them and then they must go in for their siesta.'

We found Isa and Jax sitting down by a circle of broken daisies. In their plump little fists were clutches of the white and yellow flowers.

'For you!' called Isa, holding out his hand. I took the flowers from him and smelled their light fragrance.

'They are lovely,' I said, pulling one of the daisies out from its bunch and threading its stalk through my hair.

'Now you are even more lovely.' Patrine put her hands on her hips and grinned.

The morning's exercise had sharpened the boys' appetites. They ate with a greedy hunger so their cheeks filled out and their plates emptied fast. They sat back in their chairs afterwards, their eyelids heavy and their stomachs quite round. It was easy, then, to persuade them to go to bed. They both settled into Jax's large bed and did not notice when Patrine and I left them.

'We have done well there,' Patrine said quietly. 'It is not easy always to leave Jax in his bed. Usually, I must sit with him until he grows tired.'

Lunch for the adults was being laid out on a vast oak table at the back of the house, under a covered area by the side of the new pool. It looked perfect: fine white tiles and still blue water. Isa would enjoy swimming here, I thought. I told Elias so, and he nodded with a serious smile.

'He is happy, your little one. I am sorry that I was very stupid before. I was not thinking.'

'It is better news from Sikimpur,' I told him. 'We received a telegraph only yesterday from my father. My sister has been brought home and her baby also. And I don't think that there have been any more tremors. The earth has settled itself once more.'

'That is good news, indeed. You must be much relieved.'

I nodded. 'It is wonderful news, indeed. Although, Isa does not seem to want to go home yet. He has not asked to. I think he is still in fear of the earthquake returning.'

'At least he feels safe here. With us,' Sami said. 'Besides, he is truly enjoying himself. It has been good for him to come here; playing with Jax has allowed him to be a child again.'

Sami had been quite taken by the romance of Elias's farm, by the part that he had seen, the sacred olive groves.

'You must come when it is harvest time,' Elias said. 'Then you will see the fruit of the groves. but unfortunately, you cannot yet eat them. They are too bitter when they are taken from their branches. I will send for you some from last year's harvest that have had their sour taste removed. You will enjoy them, I am sure. They are the queen of the olives in this region, much superior to the others for they have a little sharpness to their flavour.' Elias smiled. 'It is as with the chess pieces. The queen has the greater power.'

'I look forward to trying them,' said Sami. 'I must admit that I have not tasted olives before. Not before I came to Spain, that is. It is not a produce that is grown in India. I am not sure why that is, for we have the climate for it.'

'Maybe, it is because we have less need for it,' I suggested. 'Anna uses olive oil for the meals that she cooks. I do not think it would complement the flavour of the food that we are used to eating.'

'Ah, now that is a dish that I have no experience of.' Elias spoke with a mouth full of bread. 'Curry. I have heard that it is something quite unlike anything we have here in Spain. It can be very hot, for you use all variety of chillies, which we do not use here, although we make fine use of our own hot peppers. Jalapeños. They have a wonderful flavour to them.'

'But curry is not one dish, nor yet one flavour,' I objected. 'And India is a very large country. What is eaten as curry in Kashmir will be quite different from that eaten in Madras. Besides, it is not necessarily the chillies that make a dish hot, for Indians use many spices to produce flavour: garlic, ginger, black pepper. These are spices that you have here, I believe.'

'That is so. It was our Moorish invaders that brought these to us,' Patrine said with irony, 'and the one part of that heritage that we are happy to hold to.'

'And, also the grapes that they brought with them,' Elias spoke with a smile. 'We still enjoy very much the food and drink of our foreign invaders.' He swept his hand out to where the vines grew in the fields. 'My ancestors made good use of those grapes that were introduced to our province of Granada. We had a magnificent winery here for many hundreds of years. Until my father stopped its production.' There was a pause as a shadow of emotion passed through Elias's eyes. 'We were made to pay a tribute to Franco every year. The first crate of wine that was produced had to be given to him by way of respect-'

'By way of payment!' Patrine interrupted her husband with some emotion.

Elias shrugged. '*Si*, payment is the more accurate word. It is why my father destroyed the winery of his forefathers.'

'That is sad,' said Sami, 'to lose something of your heritage. But you still produce the grapes; you still have many vineyards, and they appear to be bearing much fruit.'

Elias nodded in pride. 'My father could not bear to destroy his precious vineyard. But we no longer produce the wine. We harvest the grapes and they are sent elsewhere. But, who knows? One day, when we are free, we will yet again produce our beautiful wine.'

A couple, a man and a pregnant woman came into view, walking carefully through the grass and towards us. Elias waved and the man waved back.

'Ah, here is my brother, Antonio, and his wife, Luisa. Their house is to the other side of where the olive trees grow. Antonio is the true farmer, the one who keeps the weeds down and the harvest coming in.'

In appearance, the two brothers were very different. Antonio was slender, with a scholar's face. On his head he wore a tatty straw hat and when he took it off, his hair was cut close to his head. Both husband and wife looked very young. Luisa, pale-skinned and tired, looked little more than an adolescent. Her baby was due sometime soon.

'A harvest baby, we hope.' Luisa sat down gratefully.

She kicked off her espadrilles. Her light cotton dress barely covered her knees and sat loosely over her egg-domed belly. The sun and its heat exhausted her, for she had grown up with the cool, fresh air of the hills, and found the hot summer months of the Andalusian plain too much. Thankfully, this particular lunch time was more pleasant; for, when the breeze picked up, it brought the cool of the pool's waters to us, and also a little colour into Luisa's cheeks.

Antonio did not sit down. He smiled nervously at us and then spoke to Elias in Spanish, pointing and nodding his head towards the front of the villa.

Elias nodded back and rose quickly from his chair.

'Excuse me,' he said. 'There is a man who I must speak to. I am sorry to leave you. I was not expecting him to come at this time but he is passing this way and has come anyway.' He turned to Sami with a twinkle in his eye. 'Maybe you would like to join us. It is a matter of business. This man is an old family friend and I would like to introduce you both together.'

I saw Patrine roll her eyes as Elias raised his eyebrows.

'Go,' she said, 'Be with your friend but please remember we have guests.'

'Of course.' Elias grinned cheerfully and slapped the back of his chair. 'I will make sure that Sami is well looked after.'

Sami, who stood beside me, smiled down and said, 'I will be back soon.'

I nodded with an uncertainty and watched as the three men walked away; three different figures, Elias broad and brown, Sami paler and light-footed, Antonio holding himself very erect.

When they left, Patrine set up some resting chairs. 'Come,' she said, 'we will be more comfortable here.'

I helped Luisa from her place while Patrine pulled down the bright yellow awning at the side of the house. Luisa spoke English much better than her husband, who could understand only a little.

'There was an Englishman who came to stay in my village some years ago,' she told me. 'He helped Papa with his goats for one year and then he moved away. He left our village and I followed him.'

Luisa shaded her eyes to look out beyond the boundaries of the farm, up into the peaks of the mountains. 'Do you think that it is all Englishmen who are so cruel with their love? Are they all cold in their emotions? For James Bond is the same, is he not? He does not truly love; instead, he uses the women that he meets freely, and then he leaves them.'

'I... I cannot answer that.' I was taken aback by Luisa's blunt questioning; her openness to a stranger. 'I do not know many Englishmen. After all, we have just recently moved to England. Besides, I am married.'

'It does not matter.' smiled Luisa. 'I only ask for the fun of it. In truth, I am thankful to this man for, although he broke my heart, I came here and found Antonio, who has mended it. So now, I am completely happy.'

Luisa did not look completely happy. Maybe it was the burden of the baby, maybe she missed the hills and her goats, but her brow was creased and her mouth a little tight.

'Yes,' she continued, 'Spanish men are more alive to their emotions. They know how to show their women their passion.' She soothed her belly with her free hand and whispered to it in Spanish.

Patrine went to Luisa's side. She placed her hand on her sister-in-law's shoulder.

'Come, let me take you inside,' she muttered with a gentle firmness. 'The sun is becoming too much for you. You must lie down also.'

Luisa put her cheek on Patrine's hand. 'She is being my mama when my own is so far away,' she said tenderly. 'Very well, I will go.'

Left alone, I closed my eyes and thought how good it felt to sit quietly that afternoon as the world carried on around me. In the distance churned the noise of farm machinery and I could well imagine that I was back in Shamshad Bagh once more: in the lull after lunch, when everyone had slipped indoors, and I went to my bedroom or into the quiet of Abbaji's drawing room to read.

When Patrine returned, we sat and ate some fruit and talked quietly. There was a peaceful silence all around us for a while. It was the quiet of an hour or so until siesta time was over and the children woke up. We could hear them up above us, small voices at first, and then their laughter came flooding out from the open window.

Patrine brought them out, both boys with tousled hair and flushed cheeks.

Isa ran over to me and jumped into my lap. He put his head into the crook of my arm, where the elbow bends and where he could stay hidden for a while, until the sleep was drawn out of him. Then he wriggled away from me and watched Jax, who was playing with a ball around the corner of the steps.

'Play!' shouted Jax. 'Play!'

Isa laughed and jumped away from me to join his young friend.

Soon, Luisa too emerged from her rest. The sleep had left her looking fresh again, with a bright smile and cheeks sweetly blushed. She sat beside me and talked to me about the beauty of the Andalusian hills.

'I miss them very much. The spring is my favourite time, when the land is recovering from the winter snow and the animals are being put back onto the pasture. They sense the new season, I think, for they have a new energy to them. Do you not miss your home, Sahira? You have travelled much farther from your homeland than I. And England is far different from India.'

I did not answer her immediately, thinking carefully before replying, 'I've enjoyed the change. Even when the weather was so cold, we still had much fun; everyone being hidden under all their clothes and the shivering of one's body. It is something else to experience.'

'Ah, I prefer the warmth of our Andalusian summer,' smiled Patrine. 'The sun is bright and everything shines with it. I love it very much.'

'You are as mad as the children, then!' Luisa announced. 'Look at them!' She shook her head. 'They care nothing for the heat and only want to play.'

I looked out at the two boys. They were running quite freely, chasing each other and tumbling in the long grass. They became hidden there, amongst the stalks of slender green and only their voices could be heard, loud and shrill. Where we sat, we could have been in the garden at Shamshad Bagh. If it were not for the clear blue water of the swimming pool, we could have been back home.

Soon, Patrine called out to Jax and the little boy came running to her, falling just before he reached her. She went to pick him up, kissing his upturned face and rubbing his grazed knee. She spoke to him in gentle Spanish and, slowly, through his tears, he grinned and nodded, and she put him down. He ran to Isa and said something to him, pointing to the swimming pool.

'Do you think, perhaps, Isa would like to swim?' Patrine asked me. 'It is the perfect time of the day for it. The sun will have warmed the water nicely now.'

It was a while before the men returned, Elias and Antonio whistling and Sami with his hands in his pockets; they were cheerful in their stride. Sami was talking as they walked, his eyes to the ground and his face with an earnest expression on it. The children were splashing in the pool. Elias's nephews had joined them. Tall, young boys, they were the sons of Elias's elder brother. They took care of their young cousin and Isa very well.

Sami came to sit with me. When he drew quite near, but not so very near, I could smell his breath - the sweet, heady smell that I had smelled off many people since I had arrived in the West. When I looked at him closely, I saw that his cheeks were flushed and his eyes a little bright. He was smiling without any real intent.

'You have been away for so long, Elias,' Patrine scolded her husband jovially. 'Who was it who came to see you?' She shook her head and laughed. 'No, do not tell me. I think I know.'

'I am sorry, Patrine. You are, of course, correct. It was Serge. I had to introduce Sami to him properly. He is, after all, very important to our business here.' Elias turned to me. 'Serge is our accountant-'

'Oh, but he is much more than that!' Patrine cut in. 'He is, how do you say it in English? Somebody to share a drink with. To share *many* drinks with.'

I rose from my chair in a manner that I knew was haughty. 'That is all right. But it is time that we were going. We have been here for so very long and have taken up too much of your hospitality. It is getting late and will soon be Isa's bedtime.'

I called out to Isa, but he would not listen to me. His ears were full of water and there was so much fun to be had. I called again, more sharply this time, and then I began to go to him. Patrine called me back.

'Oh, but it will be such a shame to leave now. It is not so late, the afternoon is barely gone. And, they are having such a good time. Jax rarely is able to play with a boy of his own age. During the holidays, at least.'

I stood where I was and looked around at Sami who stared back at me and said quietly, 'Surely, we can stay a little longer. After all, there is nothing that we need to hurry back for, is there?'

I smiled feebly and sat back down, allowing the party to continue. There was much laughter and, although I laughed too, it was a cautious, wary laugh, for I did not feel that I was a part of this wine-doused camaraderie.

From time to time, Sami put his hand over mine and squeezed it, smiling in a stupid manner. I tried to smile back at him, but my mouth would not relax and my hand tightened under the clammy, warm weight of his. Sometimes, I saw Luisa watch our tense exchange with interest, placing her own hand on Antonio's knee.

Under the light of the purple sunset, we ate paella and listened as one of the farm workers played the Spanish guitar. It was a beautiful, plaintive sound, full of fading hope. Isa and Jax fell asleep on a heavy blanket that Patrine had laid out on the soft grass and the stars came out. I watched as the deep red liquid in the carafe grew less and less, and was replaced time and again.

It was late when we left, driven home by one of Elias's employees, for Sami was not too sure of himself. I was relieved to be leaving for I had not enjoyed the last period of our visit. Only Luisa and I did not drink, I for my principles, and Luisa because the taste of wine made her feel sick in her pregnancy.

'I will bring your car to you tomorrow.' Elias reassured me.

I did not argue with him. The smell of the night was upon us and I was very tired. Sami sat in the front of the car with the driver while I sat in the back with Isa asleep beside me. His head was on my lap and his body sprawled across the faux leather seat, one hand under his resting cheek, while the other clasped his toy car. I looked down at him, his dark eye lashes and his soft curls that were wet with sleepy sweat.

Back at Casa Azul, I laid Isa on my bed and went in search of Sami. I wanted to talk to him while my mind was still fresh with the things that I wanted to say to him. I found him in the garden; I followed the smell of his newly-lit cigarette and the sound of tuneless humming. He was lying in a languorous pose, across the sky blue wicker chair. His legs were flung over one arm of the chair and his head rested upon the other. His eyes were closed.

'What a lovely day today was.' He had heard my tread across the gravel path. His voice sounded hazy, satisfied. 'Such a wonderful family - families, in fact. Elias and Patrine and Jax, Antonio and the pregnant Luisa, and then there was you and me and our lovely Isa. Such lovely families, all.'

I stood by him, looking down at his face. He opened his eyes and stared into mine. 'Ah, Sahira, the lady of the moon. *Chand ki tookra.*'

'Please stop that,' I said stiffly. 'You are talking such nonsense. You are not yourself. That is the trouble with drinking this *sharaab*. You cannot keep a hold of your senses.'

'Mmm, but sometimes that is a good thing, Sahira.' Sami took a long draw of his cigarette and blew out the smoke in a long trail. 'Sometimes, one's senses do not serve any good and they are better numbed.'

'I do not understand what is wrong with you tonight.'

'What is wrong with me tonight is that which has been wrong with me for a long time now.'

I was exasperated by his rambling. 'I had come out to talk to you but I see that I cannot. Not when you are talking like a mad man-'

'Mad? Mad!' suddenly Sami laughed, but not the carefree laughter of that early evening. Instead, it was a low, deep-seated laughter that rose from the back of his throat and was flung from it. 'I am mad, so I love. I love, so I am mad.'

I closed my eyes with the rage that he caused. It seemed to me that he was still filled with the memory of his lost love: the girl whom he had loved so long ago and then left. But why had he let her leave? Why had he not married her? And where did this lost love leave me? I wanted to ask Sami these questions. I clenched my fists tight and pursed my lips. I wanted to lay an assault on him, but I stopped myself. His senses were not with him tonight, and my questions would be fruitless.

Slowly, holding my breath, I put my anger to rest and kneeled down on the patch of grass beside him. It was damp with the night's coolness.

'What a strange relationship we have.' I placed my hands on the arm of the wicker chair, close to where Sami had laid his head. I almost reached out and touched his hair with my fingertips but did not. Instead, I rambled, talking as the words came to me, not caring how they sounded. There was some magic about that indigo night, the stillness and the stars that loosened my tongue.

'I do not know how to describe it. Affectionate? Respectful? They seem such lonely words tonight. So formal, like us. But, I cannot get that girl out of my mind. The one at the Executioner's Spot. *Your lover*. After all, what does she mean? It *was* a long time ago yet you seem to remember it so well. Is that why you drank so much wine today? Ah, I don't know. I do not love you, you do not love me-'

'I do not love you!' Sami suddenly jerked his head up, lurching out of his stupor. He was frowning and his eyes blinked several times, as though he were trying to focus. Then, he repeated the phrase, as though to emphasise the truth of it. '*I do not love you*?' A short burst of laughter came up from his throat, startling me with the silence that we were in.

Then, very slowly and very awkwardly, he moved his legs off the armchair, one after the other, and placed both his feet on the ground. He put his hand on my sloping shoulder and whispered, 'There are many ways of loving, Sahira, and many ways of not loving.'

His breath was a powerful mix of alcohol and cigarette smoke, and I turned my head away with a grimace. When I turned back, Sami was making his way back to the house.

Chapter Twenty-Three

The next day, I took Isa to Lake Bermejales. I had spent the early part of the morning avoiding Sami; although I was determined that I would not be prejudiced by his odd behaviour of the night before, I felt uncomfortable in his company.

Sami, on the other hand, appeared to feel none of this. He rose early, just after the campanile bell tolled the hour of seven. Through the crude, wooden floorboards of my bedroom, I heard him about the kitchen, moving quite slowly, the clinking of the coffee mugs and the kettle whistling as it boiled. Then, he moved outside into the garden and I crept softly out of my bed and went to the window. I pulled the thin net curtain to one side and saw Sami seated at the garden table reading the newspaper, his legs crossed and his back to the crude stone wall. Behind him, the pale morning sun was up. He was shaved and dressed.

I went down an hour or so later, with Isa following behind me, dancing and skipping down the stairs. From the kitchen I could hear voices, Sami and Anna talking, joking. I let Isa go in first; he was fond of Anna, and soon his was the only voice that could be heard - an excited child ordering about those who would listen. When I entered, I concentrated my gaze on Anna and evaded Sami's smiling face.

'Isa has found you, Anna. You spoil him too much.'

Anna had seated Isa on a tall stool and was preparing a small feast for him; bread with butter and jam, slices of banana and a drink of orange juice that she had just squeezed.

'Oh, he my baby,' she said, wiping the juice that was trickling down his chin.

Sami lifted Isa down. 'Please take him into the garden to eat, Anna. It is nice out there.'

Anna nodded, looking at Sami and then at me. 'We go.' She picked up Isa's plate and glass, and led him out into the vast sunshine.

Left alone with Sami, I wanted to leave also, but he stood by the door. He took his hands out of his pockets before speaking to me.

'I am sorry for what happened yesterday. I do not remember exactly all of it but I think that I did not conduct myself as I should have done.'

'It is no matter.' I waved my hand to dismiss the matter, but still I could not look at him. Instead, I wiped a streak of jam that Anna had left on the table surface.

'Please look at me,' said Sami. I did so, as a brief, involuntary reflex before looking down at the stone floor. 'Ah, I can see in your eyes that it is of some matter, but of course, you do not wish to open up to me.' Sami sighed in resignation. 'It is how it is. Maybe it is something that I deserve. I will let you alone, then. But, may I ask what you will do today?'

'I thought of taking Isa to the lake. We can catch the bus again. He will enjoy that, and I can ask Anna to have Enrique bring us back home.'

To my surprise Sami did not baulk at my going alone. Instead, he nodded and said softly, 'Fine. I have work that I must do, unfortunately, for I too would have liked to visit the lake.' He looked at me closely, before observing. 'But perhaps today it is best for you to go alone.'

I smiled weakly. 'Besides, Elias has said he will bring the car back to us sometime today.'

'The car? Oh, yes I see.' Sami blushed, embarrassed by a recollection that was faint within a still blurred mind. He went out through the doorway that he had been blocking and I heard the door of his study shut, ever so quietly, with ever such humility.

After I had breakfasted, I gathered together some items for our venture to the lake - a ball for Isa to play with, *Tales of the Alhambra* for me, towels and lunch. Anna dressed Isa and brushed his hair, blending it with a few drops of olive oil to protect it from the rays of the sun and the salt of the lake water.

Sami came out of his study to say goodbye, looking tired. He must have been asleep at his desk, I thought, for his hair was out of place and his eyelids still raw, but he waved us a cheery farewell and kissed Isa before we left. Isa was sad as we walked out of Casa Azul; he had tugged at Sami's shirt sleeve and pleaded with him to join us. But Sami, not looking at me, had declined over and over again in a voice that was beleaguered.

'I must wait for Uncle Elias to visit. He will be very disappointed if he comes and does not find anyone to talk to.'

'Anna here!' Isa pointed to the sturdy figure who was arranging some flowers in a vase.

'No, Anna must go home.' Sami told him. 'To her own house.'

Then suddenly, Isa cried out. 'Uncle El, car!'

Sami's face fell and, seeing this, I felt a little sorry for him. I took Isa's hand.

'Come, Isa. We shall miss the bus if we do not go now.'

I pulled him towards the heavy front door, barely giving him time to say goodbye to Anna as we went.

From behind us, I heard Sami say softly, 'Yes, I must wait for Elias to bring back the car.'

The sun was striking Lake Bermejales from the east. It shone as beautiful as before. I roused a sleepy Isa when we reached the lakeside bus stop. This time, I had stayed awake during the ride, ignoring the leering grin of the man who sat in the aisle opposite me, and turning to look out of the window; at the storks who had built their nests in the trees and the swathes of vegetation that we passed: green, gold, red and yellow, dainty stalks with their brilliant flower heads.

I thought a lot about Sami, not knowing quite how to feel about him. From the day before, from that moment when I had seen him walking back with Elias, I had felt a change in my feelings towards him. They seemed clogged now by some unknown material. To talk to him that morning had been a labour, whereas before it had been easy, free and friendly. But now, more so than our first night as a married couple, he was a stranger to me.

I rested my head on the window pane and let it be jogged along with the rough rhythm of the bus on its track. I felt despondent for I could not think how our relationship would now continue. I was not used to this very adult dilemma; I was used to my honey jar existence. How I longed for it now.

It was Isa who brought me out of my self-pity. He ran with joy to the lake's shore. I followed as fast as I could, through the line of the trees and over the smooth pebbles. When I caught up with him, we raced together, laughing aloud, until we reached the lapping water's edge and stopped. We breathed in the spray off the lake and the pine-scent of the trees; breathing heavily with our exertion, doubling over, but still laughing.

Isa peered into the water that was stirring beneath him, pointing excitedly down at the fairy shrimps and *Daphnia* that chased each other here and there, unaware they were being watched. I came to kneel by his side and put my hand around his rotund waist.

'Shall we go in?' I began to roll my trousers up.

Isa hung back. He was not sure. A look of curiosity came into his deep-set eyes and I knew that he was tempted. But he would not move. He stood very still, his eyes staring at the transparent creatures, darting about, his legs unmoving.

I picked him up and he held on tightly, clutching the loose cloth of my shirt sleeves. I strode out into the lake, feeling the cool wetness grip at my ankles and moving slowly up until it reached my calves.

It was then that Isa loosened his hold and looked down in wonderment, letting his head hover above the tiny monsters below. He kicked his legs out and squealed with excitement. I let him have his way until my arms grew tired of his swinging weight and I waded back to the sandy bank. I eased Isa down, feeling his body slide slowly down until his feet touched the sand.

'*Ander jana*!' Isa jumped up and down, smothering his footprints with each jump.

I nodded. 'Yes, we will go in, but you must stay close to me.'

From my bag I pulled out a small fishing net that Anna had bought for Isa some days ago and, firmly taking hold of Isa's hand, we made our way in until he was calf-deep in the water. I dipped the net into the clear water, underneath the bellies of the flitting animals and drew them out slowly, watching as they began to flap and thrash in the open air. At once, Isa was fascinated, staring at them and finally prodding them with his index finger.

'No.' I pulled the net away from him. 'That is not a nice thing to do. You will hurt them.'

Isa made a face, but he did as he was told. I let the creatures free again into the water and we watched them swim away. I took Isa back to the dry land. We began to crunch our way over the pebbles, wetting them, darkening them with the water that dripped down our legs and between the gaps of our toes, but Isa did not like the feel of the hard stones underneath his delicate soles and put up his hands to be picked up. So, resignedly, I carried him onto softer ground, onto the speckled grains of sand. There, he clambered down and ran away to where a broken piece of driftwood lay. He brought it to me, sitting down by my side, and began to trace circles and swirls in the sand. Then, he laid out the shells that we found, some in bits, some whole.

We invented stories about them, about the fort and the prince, and the dragon that came to visit him, and the prince's tiger who saved his life. In this way, we let the lazy day take us.

'*Yeh he kila*,' I told Isa. 'The dragon is coming. And the tiger is going to eat him.'

'Ha, ha!' shouted Isa, leaping high into the air and throwing a handful of sand up to the heavens. He made to grab some more, his small fists closing tightly, but then he stopped and, with great enthusiasm, waved with his right hand to something out across the lake.

I looked out to see what it was that had attracted his attention, shielding my eyes from the glare of the bright sun. And I saw, out in the distance, just below the horizon a figure - a man it looked like - in a rowing boat, silhouetted against the purple mountains behind him and waving back. A tall, thin man, erect like a pencil drawing, who sat back down into his boat and began rowing with smooth, practised strokes towards us.

It should have been my instinct to leave: with a stranger making his way in our direction, I should have gathered Isa and our belongings and left this isolated spot. But I did not. Instead, I waited with Isa. I gave him an apple to eat and brought one out for myself. Quite calmly, we waited, watching the figure getting nearer and nearer until he was transformed from a pencil sketch into flesh. My heart beat faster all that while.

When he had almost reached the shore, the man stopped rowing and leapt out of his boat, leaving it swaying from side to side. He was still waist-deep in the water. He lifted a piece of grey rope from inside the boat and began to pull on it, leading it, while his boat followed him in a straight line, going where he went.

Isa finished his apple and was ready to move towards this unknown man. I put out my hand and covered his, tightening my grip when I felt it wriggle.

'Hello there,' the man called out to us.

'Hel-lo!' Isa returned the greeting emphatically.

'I see you've decided to visit the lake again.' The man pulled the boat onto the sand and secured it there.

'Again?' I frowned. 'I am sorry, but I do not...oh!' And then I understood. This was my stranger of before, but with the beard gone and the hair untangled, though the eyes were still as fierce, still as brilliant blue as the sky.

He held out his hand, leaning slightly over me. 'I'm Michael. Michael Calvert.'

I shook his hand, saying. 'And I am-'

'Sahira Altair. Yes I know.' Michael Calvert turned his attention to Isa. 'But I don't know this young man.'

'You know my name?' Again, I frowned.

'Yes. We have some mutual friends, Elias and also-'

'Ah, yes,' I said. 'Elias and his family.'

Michael Calvert let go of my hand and looked hard at me. 'You're not as beautiful as I thought you would be.'

I stared at this man standing so boldly before me, finally saying, 'Well, I do not see how that can be of any importance. I mean, surely Elias-'

'Elias?' Michael Calvert laughed, a hardy, fulsome laugh. 'Oh no, it wasn't Elias who talked of you like that! Certainly not Elias. But, as a foreign couple in a small place, you cause many tongues to wag.'

This Michael Calvert, who stood before me, looked so different today from the man that I had run from on my previous visit. I wanted him to remain where he was, really: hovering just above me, looking at me, and I at him. There was something alluring about him, a sense that I could stay listening to his voice. I could close my eyes and still hear that very voice - a low, slow pace, like a pocket watch counting time.

'You are much changed from when I saw you last,' I said.

Michael touched his face. 'Yes, I suppose I am. I must have given you quite a scare that day. You ran away pretty quickly.'

I blushed, for I did not realise my flight had been witnessed.

Michael sat down on the other side of Isa, who was busy building his forts and palaces.

'I hadn't shaved for quite some time. Nor bathed, either,' he mused. 'I've been away in the States for a couple of months. My publishers are there and they wanted to know what I've been doing to earn all the money that they lavish upon me.'

'You are a writer, then?'

Michael shook his head and grinned. 'Good Lord, no. I can't write. At least, not novels.' He looked out at the blue lake and the purple-topped mountains. 'I was a journalist for a while, until I discovered the art of photography. It's why I'm in Andalusia. There's so much beauty to be photographed here; much that the world has not yet seen.'

In that quiet afternoon we talked some more. He spoke of America as a wonderland, full of the ambitions of its people, and also their grievances.

'I went to quite a few rallies while I was there: against the Vietnam War, against discrimination of the blacks. The protestors kept my camera busy. It's one of the most exciting places to be at the moment. Still...' he laid himself out on the sand, tucking his hands underneath his head and bending his knees, 'I'm glad to be out of there. Even with Franco running this country, I prefer its simplicity to the crass sophistication of the New World.'

As he talked, I laid out a towel and the food that Anna had packed for Isa and me. Michael did not hesitate in joining us. From within his boat, he brought out a cloth parcel and a flask. He kneeled down at the side of our picnic and offered up his lunch: some coarse pieces of bread and cheese.

'Not quite up to the standard you're used to, but you're most welcome to share in some of my modest fare.' From the flask he took a rather large gulp and wiped his mouth with the back of his hand. Then he held it out for me. 'And a share of this, too, if you wish.'

The flask was silver and well-used, and I thought I knew what it was that it contained. I declined his offer.

'No, of course not,' he said, putting the cap back on. 'It's not really your style, is it, Princess? Drinking out of a dirty flask, I mean.'

I glared at him, at the smile that he had on his face and the twinkle in his eye. But he appeared oblivious to my ire and carried on.

'Very well, but you're missing out on some of Andalusia's finest. My fare might be meagre, but it's only the best of the vine for me.'

He put the flask away and settled his blue eyes on me. He seemed to be so very happy with life. Not just satisfied, like

Sami, like Elias even, but happy like a child, like Isa. And it was then that a little bit of his carefree spirit crept into me, making its way across the grains of sand and into my veins. I was happy to spend most of the afternoon with this spirit within me.

After lunch, Isa insisted that Michael play with him and, very soon, they were building the tallest of towers and the deepest of moats. Michael took Isa out into the lake, swinging him round and then putting him down with a gentle splash. I looked on, sometimes reading, sometimes watching a pair of white-winged butterflies flitting around the blue lavender that grew close by.

In the late of the afternoon, Isa grew tired. Michael brought him back onto the beach in his arms and put him down on the towel. Isa yawned and turned over, curling himself into a loose ball, his eyes tight shut and his mouth slightly open so that a trickle of saliva ran out of it, making a stain down the side of his lips.

Michael and I sat on a fallen tree trunk, some two feet apart. It was then that I felt the danger of my situation. Isa was no longer there, between us, and I was alone with a man who was not my husband. I knew I should not be there, but I was rooted in my place, for Michael Calvert had transfixed me. I was glad to be there and there was nowhere else in the world that I would rather run to. He asked me how I had come to the lake for, looking around, he could see no sign of a car. I told him about the bus that had brought us from Alhama de Granada.

'But we will not be taking the bus back there. Our cook's son, Enrique, will be coming soon to pick us up.' I glanced at my watch. 'I cannot believe how fast the time has gone.'

'That is the way of Lake Bermejales. I've spent whole days out on it and felt as though it were only a few hours. That is the way of life here. It's why I love it so.'

Michael stretched his legs out ahead of him, crossing his ankles, one over the other, and resting his palms on the top of the broken trunk. He closed his eyes and took a deep breath and, silently, I moved a little closer to him, keeping my eyes on his profile. He smelled of the fresh lake and grains of sand.

Instinctively, because he resembled a beautiful hero, I placed my fingers very gently on his cheek. If I were bolder I would have leant over and kissed him. He did not open his eyes; instead, he reached out for my hand and removed it from his face. With this motion I held my breath. This was not what I was expecting. Although, what I was expecting was not too clear in my mind. He opened his clear blue eyes and sat gazing up at the cloudless sky.

'I would not have thought you to be so obvious,' he said, quite casually.

At these words, I got up quickly, wordlessly, shrinking inside myself as the blood coursed to the surface of my skin. I moved to arouse Isa, but as I did so, I felt a hand on my shoulder, gripping it hard. I turned to face Michael. There was a smile on his face as though he were my friend.

'You should calm yourself,' he said. 'Enrique has just arrived. I can see his truck through the line of trees. He can see us, too.'

Enrique sounded his horn. Looking up, I saw him leaning out of his window grinning and waving.

'*Hola*!' he shouted. 'I arrive for you.'

Michael walked past me and picked up the sleeping Isa, ever so gently, so that he did little more than stir. He laid his head on Michael's shoulder and was carried to Enrique's truck. I followed behind, trudging along with my sandals full of sand and my bag clutched to my chest.

Michael greeted Enrique, speaking to him in fluent Spanish. Enrique nodded, saying, '*Si, si.*' He jumped down from his truck and opened up the back, before helping Michael inside, still holding Isa.

'Enrique's kindly offered to drop me off at my house,' Michael told me, without an apology but as a matter of fact. 'I hope that's all right with you? It's not too much out of your way, and I think that I've had too much of the sun today.'

'What about your boat?' I asked in dismay. I did not want to have this man close to me again, sitting behind me, his breath making its way to the nape of my neck, to my lips, to my mouth, where I would breath it in.

'Oh, it's perfectly safe where it is. I'll come back for it tomorrow, or maybe the day after that. Tomorrow, I think I'll go trekking up on the hills. I have very few photographs of the flora that grows there. What do you think, Enrique?'

Enrique turned round and smiled. '*Si*. Good idea, Señor Michael. It very beautiful on the hills now.'

The two of them carried on talking, mostly in Spanish, with sociable voices. I, meanwhile, looked glumly out of the window at the swaying countryside, at the fields of red poppies, and the large windmill with its sails hanging motionless in the still air.

Enrique dropped Michael in an area of Alhama that I did not recognise. It was the old Arab quarter, practically on the other side of Alhama from Casa Azul, a quiet area with a few tumbledown houses alongside and the odd touch of a garden. Isa awoke just as we stopped and Michael handed him over to me.

'Goodbye, and thank you for allowing me to share your afternoon. I had a very good time.' His hand briefly touched mine and, to my shame, I blushed and became disconcerted.

'You are welcome,' I said stiffly.

'Goodbye, Isa. I hope we shall build some more towers together soon.'

'I do not think so,' I told him. 'We are going to Granada very soon and Isa will most certainly be leaving us shortly after that. I do not think there will be any opportunity for visiting the lake again.'

'I am sorry, then,' said Michael. He looked directly into my eyes. 'Goodbye, Princess.'

'Goodbye, Mr Calvert.' I reached out and pulled the truck door to. It closed with a great noise. Isa waved sadly to Michael and we set off on our way back home.

Chapter Twenty-Four

'We shall go to Granada tomorrow.'

Sami had before him his diary. In it he had days and dates of early August that were filled with his neat handwriting. Tomorrow, however, was a blank. I nodded my head in agreement; since my discreditable encounter with Michael Calvert, I was ready to agree with much of what Sami suggested.

'Good,' I said. 'I have no plans for tomorrow and shall be glad to be away from Alhama for a while.'

Sami looked up at me in surprise. 'Oh? Have you tired already of Alhama, then?'

'No, but there is more to be seen in Andalusia, and Granada, has a great Islamic history. We have been in Alhama too long; it is time to continue our adventures, I think.'

Sami looked thoughtfully at me. 'You have changed again. You are back to the Sahira of before. I was afraid that our visit to Elias's farm had damaged our relationship too much, and I was very unsure of whether we could ever regain it. I am thankful to you for not harbouring ill feelings towards me. I shall be very careful not to have such a lapse again.'

His open humility embarrassed me. I had reasons for my mildness, and they were not known to Sami. Therefore, he believed that I was a forgiving angel rather than a damnable soul.

Our journey to Granada was almost without event. We talked about the Alhambra and listened to the radio. Sami had found a station that played music from the British hit parade and we enjoyed that very much. Isa, sitting in the back of the car, sang in the most tuneless and joyful manner.

The only event of any note occurred quite early on in our journey, when we passed an unusual scene. To the side of the road, under the shelter of some brush trees, was parked a pale yellow car. A couple were standing behind it talking in an animated manner while, in front of the car, quite within obvious view was a young woman, with thick, dyed hair and very thin arms. She was hunkering down with her knees bent and skirt up about her bottom. She was completely without a care for passers-by, ignoring everything and concentrating only on her own business.

The sight of this caught Sami and I off guard, and we turned to each other with shocked expressions, unable to put our thoughts into words. Then suddenly, spontaneously, we laughed, loudly. We laughed so that the tears ran down our cheeks and our sides ached, and Isa, who was shouting at the back, could not be heard. It was a good moment.

We arrived in Granada just after ten in the morning, and stood for some time gazing about us, not speaking, barely breathing, in deep awe at the magnificence, the grandeur, and the grace of the Alhambra and the snow-capped peaks of the Sierra Nevada.

We parked the car on the Sabika, just outside the entrance of the Generalife, the gardens built by Granada's Nasrid rulers. There was a fresh breeze blowing and we let Isa run wild along the avenues lined with orange trees; we could smell the fruit ripening on its branch and the jasmine and oleander that grew in the gardens. Here, the ladies of the Alhambra Palace would have taken their walks. Here, amongst the juniper bushes and the seven hundred year old cypress tree, it was said that the Sultana Zoraya met with her unfortunate lover, Hamet, chief of the Abencerraj clan.

'This could be the Paradise that is described in the Quran,' said Sami. 'We will be very fortunate indeed, if we reach it.'

On the way to the Summer Palace, in the Patio de la Acequia, we met with a small crowd. The people there had stopped to listen to a troupe of gypsy musicians. We joined them.

'They sing the songs of El Romancero Gitano,' a girl told me.

'I am sorry, but I do not know him,' I said. 'Is he very famous here in Granada?'

The girl laughed at me. 'Not he. El Romancero Gitano is the collections of our great poet, Federico Garcia Lorca. And yes, he is very famous in Granada.'

'Oh, yes. I have heard of him.' I tried to make up for my blunder. 'It is very sad how he died. He was indeed Andalusia's greatest poet.'

I knew of Lorca from Patrine. She had told me about him in great detail, about his brilliant life, and his flight from Franco's thugs, who had pursued him because of his sexuality, eventually catching and killing him. She had recited the lines of his Despedida and translated them for me. They were very moving:

If I die, leave the balcony open.
The child eats oranges. (From my balcony I see him).
The reaper mowing wheat. (From my balcony I hear him).
If I die, leave the balcony open!

From the Generalife, we climbed the staircase down which the waters of the Rio Darro flowed, and walked through the Torre del Cabo de la Carrera and Torre del Agua into the grounds of the Alhambra itself. This edifice, standing for centuries, was the magnificent legacy of the Nasrid princes, each adding their own piece of architectural design to the already existing Alcazba.

There were many other visitors besides us there, taking pictures, comparing their guide books with what stood before them. Isa, no longer running, soon became tired of walking and Sami lifted him up into the crook of his arm and carried him along.

The path that led to the Palacio de Carlos V was littered with stalls overflowing with a multitude of cheap souvenirs: ceramic tiles with mosaic designs, grey and white sketches and pretty scarves of Arab prints. We paused here to peruse these wonders, for Sami was interested in finding something with fine Islamic calligraphy that was so prevalent there. He thought of buying a piece that was inscribed with the simple words '*I am the Heart of the Palace*', but it was a heavy thing and he was not so sure of carrying it with him for the rest of the day.

'No problem,' said the stall owner. 'I keep for the Señor, and he collect when back.'

So Sami agreed and paid the man half of what he asked for, promising the other half later. Sami did not argue the price - three times what it was worth, no doubt - for these people worked hard for the pennies that they earned.

'What is the point of bartering with the poor man,' he always asked, 'for the price of a loaf of bread that he will feed his family with?'

The Palacio de Carlos V stood solidly within a square courtyard. Inside, it lay open, like a hollow shell, round and rigid in its symmetry. Still unfinished, it was a little disappointing for all its grand intentions. *A piece of it is missing*, I thought, *some major part of it, some vein that once ran alongside its major artery*. Maybe it was because it was the aborted ambition of a Christian conqueror, or because it was Occidental rather than Oriental, with its figures of horsemen and mythological creatures, I did not know. I could not explain it, but I felt that the Alhambra wore it ill.

Sami, however, took the contrary view.

'It is still a building of some distinction,' he said, gazing at the winged beasts. 'This is a very fine example of Renaissance art, you know. I am surprised that you feel so strongly against it.'

I shrugged. 'Maybe in an Italian city I would feel differently, but we are in Spain, and in Moorish Spain at that, so all of this seems too much like the conqueror's stamp. Also, Carlos V did not even make this palace his residence after all, but left it in a fragmented form.'

A man standing close by overheard my remarks and turned to us. In his appearance he was a descendant of the Moors, with dark skin and thick black hair that curled tightly. He had the broad features that complemented these and spoke with a clear, strong voice.

'You are right in what you say, Señora. Only recently, has the grand Palacio been given a roof. Before this time, the large pillars have been stood as naked in the open sky.' He looked about him in disgust. 'It is will be the everlasting shame of our religion that our forebears strove this far, gained such glory, and then lost it through misadventure and avarice.' He looked from me to Sami. 'I am right in thinking that you are Muslims, yes?'

'Yes,' Sami nodded. 'We are from India, but live in England.'

The man stretched out his hand. '*Asalaam-alaikum*, my brother. It is good to meet with you.' He put his face close into Sami's and looked over at me. 'I hope you do not mind that I addressed your wife. It is said in the Quran that a man should avert his gaze when he meets with another man's wife. And I did not.' He looked at me critically. 'But, it is not only my fault. I hope you will forgive me, but you should persuade your wife to cover herself, to wear the hijab. You will find many men here who will not avert their eyes.'

I heard every word that the man spoke, but I could not reply to his assertion. I was turned at once rigid with anger at his outspoken manner; but also, I felt a sudden surge of embarrassment and a quick desire to hide away my hair.

Sami let go of the Moor's hand and stared into the man's face. His open smile faded quickly and his lips closed tightly as he frowned.

'I seem to recall the Hadith also say that the decision to wear the hijab is my wife's, and it is between her conscience and the Almighty that the matter rests.'

With that, Sami picked up Isa once again and said firmly, 'Come Sahira. There is still much for us to see.'

The man bowed to us. I could not tell if it were a mocking gesture, for he was still smiling in that very genuine and pleasant manner of his. I passed by him and, with great difficulty, did not smile back. When we were well away from the palace, I stopped Sami's great stride with a gentle touch on his arm.

'Thank you,' I said shyly to him. 'It was good of you to speak up for me.'

Sami brushed away my gratitude with a dry smile and shake of his head. He put Isa down.

'It is I who should be thankful to you. I believe in what I said to that Moor. The hijab is a very personal matter. And...' He looked down at the cobbled street on which we stood. 'I am not one who can judge you, not when I have committed far worse sins than you.' He looked down at me, his face set with a deep sincerity and whispered, 'I have shared an intimacy with another woman, *and* I have indulged myself... well, you know all too well of *that*.'

I did not answer him. I did not know how to. Isa stood too closely between us, giggling at an old man who was pulling faces at him. In my mind's eye, I saw a face with brilliant blue eyes and a cheek that was marked with the prints of my fingers.

'Some things should stay in the past,' I managed to finally say. 'That is their place. We should not allow them too much time in our minds.' I took up Isa's loose hand. 'Come, let us move on.'

And so we passed from King Carlos's palace to one that was very different in both its size and the sheer spectacle of it. For me, from the time of my first sight of it, the Palacios Nazaries stood as the jewel of the Alhambra with its mosaic stone inlays, its fountains, the intricacies of its carvings.

We spent some two hours there, slowly wandering through the many rooms and hallways, through the council chamber of the

Mexuar and into the Serallo where the sultans had once resided, where now the opulence was faded but not gone. Then onward, into the Harem, where the women of the palace occupied themselves. It was impossible to have my fill of this place, for there was a great beauty here; it was a great place of illumination, with its many Arabic inscriptions proclaiming, '*Wa-la ghaliba illa-Llah*', 'The greatest Conqueror of all is God!'

Even Isa, boisterous, laughing Isa, fell silent here. He stared up, wide-eyed at the high ornate ceilings and sucked his thumb, walking slowly and thoughtfully, looking about him at the bright tiles that lined the walls and the alcoves. When he spoke, he did so in whispers and in Urdu, as though he were afraid of being overheard. He held my hand and, together, we wandered through the Sala de los Reyes, into the heart of the harem, and into the Patio de los Leonas, where the circle of twelve stone lions stood, with water pouring from their mouths and a fountain supported on their broad backs.

Sami ran his hand around the rim of the fountain's basin, tracing the ode that was written there, while I muttered under my breath the words of Irving Washington, 'The abode of beauty was indeed here as if it had been inhabited but yesterday'.

This was where Isa found his voice, rising in an excited pitch. '*Deko*, Khalajaan. *Shere*! *Meybe eke shere hoon.*'

Sami laughed at him. 'You are indeed a lion,' he said. 'A very brave lion.'

A girl, with pink and blue and green ribbons in her fair hair, joined Isa and, bending down a little so that her face was level with his, spoke to him in a language that I did not recognise as Spanish.

'It is German,' Sami told me. 'At least, I think so, for it has the very hard, guttural sound of that language.'

We watched as the little girl suddenly darted away, and then Isa gave chase, past the lions and into the cloistered area, where the two of them scampered amongst the pillars of the triple arches there, laughing and giggling. They caught each other, grabbing with small hands at each other's sleeves and then letting go and starting again, having much fun.

Soon, the girl's mother, who stood alone a few metres away from us, wearing a beautiful pea-green shirt, called out to her daughter.

'Heidi, *zurückgekommen. Wir müssen gehen.*'

Heidi stopped her play, and ran back to her mother, waving to Isa and shouting. '*Auf Wiedersehen, mein kleiner Freund.*'

Isa stood where he was and watched, quite happily, as Heidi left. He waved to her and we went to him, waving with him at the girl and her mother.

'Goodbye!' the mother called out to us.

Sami lifted Isa high onto his shoulders. We left the lions to their vigil and made our way to the north side, into the Sala de las Dos Hermanas, with its marble flagstones and stalactite ceilings. It was quiet here in the cool of the many pale arches, each carved at its apex with the mark of the genius craftsmen. How many hours had been spent on these works of art? How many men grew out of their youth and into maturity? I kneeled with Isa by the Mirador de Daraxa and looked out over the symmetry of the courtyard.

'This is where the Sultana used to sit,' I told him. 'From here, she could see the fountains and the peacocks down below.

The drifting sun was lingering on our backs when we left the walls of Alhambra, and made our way along cobbled paths towards the Alhambra Palace Hotel. The hotel rested quite happily on the edge of a cliff, so that looking out was almost like flying high above the city.

We sat out on the high terrace, sipping mint tea and gazing out over the grandeur of Granada; brilliant white in the bulbous sun, and dotted with the odd, architecturally magnificent church, mosque, civil structure.

It quite took our breath away, and Granada, though my hapless mind quite often came to rest upon thoughts of Michael Calvert, did at least try its best to remove them from me.

Up there, high as we were, a breeze came to air us and we stayed peacefully until well past four o'clock, when we reluctantly left the lovely hotel and made our slow way back to the car. Our route was slow; Isa was exhausted, his liveliness over chocolate ice-cream quite drowned now by the still persistent heat and the length of the day. Sami carried him for the most part. Isa's small hands clasped the sweat-beaded neck and his head rested serenely upon Sami's broad shoulders. We looked for all the world like a perfect family, worn out and together.

The path to the car park was fairly empty; we met a handful of fellow tourists, all with the same faded look upon their faces. In amongst these, I also noticed one or two strange-looking characters, women they must have been, but haggard, worn down and incredibly ugly, not in features but in their expressions. Their clothes were ill-fitting, hanging around them in a way that indicated slovenliness and disregard for appearance.

The sight of them shocked me, made me wince in the way one does at finding something distasteful, but also at the depth of a human being's fall. Even I knew that they were prostitutes, so desperately did they leer at the men who were passing by. I hurried past them, averting my eyes as best I could, for I was curious enough to want to stare hard at these unfortunate creatures.

The car was a welcome sight, not just from the still strong heat but from the scene that we had just witnessed. Sami fastened Isa into his seat, gently, so as not to waken him, and we climbed wearily in, too. We downed our water as though it were nectar and felt ourselves fit to set off back home.

Chapter Twenty-Five

On our return to Alhama, Sami became immersed once more in his work.

'Elias has given me a book on theoretical material chemistry, which I need to read. I hope to find the answer to a problem I have; to do with the new polymer that I am working on,' he told me. 'Once I have a better understanding of the chemistry involved, then I shall be able to relax a little.'

It was a day when Sami and I were sitting out in the garden, drinking a late morning coffee and eating freshly-baked pastries from the local bakery. Isa sat out of the sun, under the shade of the Charybdis, working on a jigsaw puzzle that Jax had lent him.

'It would be good to visit Córdoba soon,' I said.

Since our return from Granada, I had become engrossed in James Michener's account of Iberia. There, in those pages, I read of a Córdoba that was so very different from Granada. I longed to see for myself the architectural fairy-tale, the four hundred red and cream-striped marble columns, and the mihrab that was the finest that Michener had ever seen. Also, I wanted to be away from Alhama de Granada. It pained me to feel this way, for I had become so very fond of the little town, of gazing out across the gorge, of sitting out in a café, of walking along its cobbled streets. And, more than this, I missed Lake Bermejalis, its blueness, its trees and the chance to see, once again, Michael Calvert.

'Of course, there is still more of Granada to explore, there is the Albacin, which is quite something, I believe...' Sami continued speaking his earnest thoughts but I was only half listening to him.

My attention was caught by a stirring on the gravel - a beetle that was small and red, tripping and fumbling over the grey and white speckled pebbles. It carried on its way determinedly, disappearing eventually into a tiny crevice in the rough stone wall. Such a simple life it had, I thought, going its clumsy way amongst the stones to get somewhere else, just somewhere else, drawn by some primitive sense towards... what? Food? A mate? That was all the consciousness that it required. Whereas we, with our superior and complex brains made the more trouble for ourselves, for our happiness, our satisfaction. We, I thought, made such a folly of our lives.

The sound of voices from within the house brought me out of my reverie. I found that both Sami and Isa had gone from the garden, and theirs were amongst the voices that I could hear. There were two others besides, both of whom I recognised, one of which blew a chill over the membranes of my heart.

'I spoke to my parents on the telephone today,' it said. 'They're both keeping well. Mother, it seems, has found a new lease of life down in Cornwall. They send you their best wishes.'

Then, Isa's voice came through the warm air, an incoherent, excited chatter, and there was laughter, male laughter; low, guttural and companionable.

'Ah, Sahira, look who has come to visit us.'

Sami came out first into the sunshine, his step light and easy, followed by Elias, smiling widely in greeting. Finally, came Michael, striding out with his head high.

I paid Elias all my attention. 'So nice to see you, Elias. How is Patrine? And the children too? They have not come with you?' I knew that I was speaking too fast, but I could not abate my tongue.

Elias bent down low to kiss my cheek, with his hat in one hand and the other hand on my shoulder.

'Oh, Jax is with his cousins. You cannot tell him that I am come, or he will be very cross with me for not bringing him. The baby is being most troublesome in the night and not allowing Patrine to have much sleep. It is the coming of the teeth, she tells me. So, while the baby sleeps in the day, Patrine sleeps also.'

Elias looked over his shoulder towards Isa and Michael, who were examining the puzzle that Isa had recently abandoned. Isa was sitting in his usual cross-legged manner, his small hands picking over the pieces of his jigsaw, while Michael kneeled down beside him, quite something in pale brown slacks and a green polo shirt.

'I was visited by Michael,' Elias continued. 'And I thought, what a pity it is that Sami is not with us, and so we come, instead, to you.'

Sami brought a chair over for Elias.

'It has been some time since we saw you.' Sami observed. 'The time has gone very quickly since we returned from Granada.'

Elias sat down in his seat, taking up the cup of coffee that Sami poured for him.

'It is a beautiful city, Granada, the pride of Andalusia. But, you have to be... There is a word that Patrine is fond of... *foolhardy*. That is it. To visit Granada in this summer heat, and that also with a little one?'

'Maybe, but we have come at this time, and so we must endure the heat. But you are right about Isa.' I gazed in the direction of the fig tree. 'He was exhausted at the end of it all and was very irritable the next day.'

'You should have left him with us,' Elias remonstrated with me, shaking his head. 'He would have had more fun. There is plenty of time when he is more grown to enjoy the palaces of the Alhambra.'

He pointed up at the sky.

'Next time, you must come in the spring, when the blossom is out and the air is not so hot. Then, you will enjoy walking up and down the hills of Granada. It is a different beauty that you will see, an awakening after the winter snows.'

The sound of the campanile bell came suddenly so clear through the still air. Twelve o'clock, lunch time. I heard Anna come into the house, her energetic singing breaking out into the garden where we sat. I took the opportunity to leave the men.

'I will tell Anna that we have guests.' I looked around at Elias. 'You shall join us for lunch I hope? Unless, of course, Patrine wishes for you-'

'Oh, no, no.' Elias waved his hands quickly. 'Patrine will be quite happy for the quietness that she has been left with. She will not be expecting me to return so soon.'

'Good, that is settled then,' said Sami happily. 'And you also, Michael, you will have your lunch with us?'

Michael stood up, rubbing off the loose soil from his trousers.

'I think, perhaps, I ought to go. I only came for a quick visit, to see you Sami. I've been meaning to welcome you properly to Alhama ever since I returned from the States. We shall meet up some other time. It would be unfair to impose upon Sahira's, and Anna's, good natures.'

'Oh, there is no imposition, is there Sahira?' Sami insisted.

'No, of course not,' I replied weakly. 'But if Mr Calvert has work that he must do, then maybe we should not keep him.'

'But he does not!' Elias interjected. 'Of course not, for he was ready to be at my farm for the rest of today. Is that not so, Michael?'

Michael nodded his head slowly and acknowledged, 'Yes, that is so.'

'Then, there is no question of your going.' Sami smiled. 'Anna will not mind putting out lunch for us all. She always makes too much for just three people.'

'I will go and tell her.' I left the men alone, walking down the stone, unsteady steps with my head low.

Anna was only too happy to see Elias and Michael, for she knew them both; Elias, through the banter and barter of the Friday market, and Michael, whom she called 'Mikel', because he was known throughout the region as the Englishman with the camera.

'He many photos me,' she said joyfully, '*en la iglesia.*'

I helped Anna in silence in the kitchen, following her instructions automatically. My head was in a different place to that sunlit room, and Anna's chatter was but a dull rhythm in my ear. I moved with a slowness that was in sharp contrast to her quickness, and she must have thought me strange at that moment.

Anna had brought with her some soup that she had made at home, a fresh gazpacho with cucumber and green peppers. She soaked some pieces of bread in water and, as I ladled the gazpacho into bowls, she wrung the water from them with a firm fist and placed them in a circle on a terracotta plate. It was an interesting sight.

Then she shooed me out of the kitchen, gesturing at me to take the tray of glasses and water into the garden, while she followed behind, swaying gently with her tray of soup and sodden bread. She still wore her bright, flowery apron that was pretty in the sun, and she greeted everyone with a loud, '*Buenos días!*'

Elias and Michael smiled widely as they leapt out of their chairs to hug her. I felt a little jealous at their very obvious fondness for this exuberant Spanish matron. Anna placed a bowl of gazpacho on the table in front of each of the seated men, and then she placed herself between Michael and Isa. I was left to sit on the other side of Isa, rubbing shoulders with Sami and quite uncomfortable; but at least I did not have to stare into the eyes of Michael, although I could listen to his voice well enough.

'Yes, I managed to get away from the town for a few days,' I heard him say. 'I found a lovely little *pensione* on the lower slopes of the Sierra Nevada and enjoyed myself thoroughly.'

'Did you remember your camera this time?' Elias asked with a wink. He turned to Sami. 'Sometime before, Michael underwent a journey across to Seville - which he had been planning for many months - to coincide with a festival that is important there. But then, after all this, he forgot to have his camera with him. It was a great tragedy indeed.'

Michael laughed. 'Yes, yes, this time I remembered. But would you believe it? In the end, I took very few photographs. I wasn't in the mood. Instead, I was quite happy just to peruse what was before me.'

Elias threw up his hands. 'Ah, that is even more of a tragedy, my friend. To be without the desire, is not right.'

The others laughed at this, even Anna, who could not have understood.

It was now past midday, and the sun was just past its zenith. We were shaded from its fierce heat by the large, marigold umbrella. Isa, not taken with the sodden bread, was dropping crumbs of it on the ground beneath him and watching, with great awe, the ants that visited us at meal times. Picking up the bits of bread and cheese and fruit, they carried them over the stones and the herbs towards the rough-holed wall, into some hairline crack and out of sight.

All too soon, however, Isa tired of his game and became restive, rocking in his chair and kicking his legs back and forth. He grew tearful when told to stop, and so, I took him from his chair and away to his favourite corner to play a game with him.

Sitting by the sweet-smelling lavender, I was thankful to be there, and I concentrated myself in keeping Isa company, losing the time that went by until I heard footsteps coming across the gravel, nearer and nearer and then a familiar voice.

'I hope you don't mind if I join you?'

I looked up to see Michael, staring down at me, rocking gently from one foot to the other.

I stood up and looked about me.

'Where are the others?' My voice was sure to sound strange, a little hesitant, a little in panic.

Michael nodded towards the house.

'I'm afraid that Sami has taken Elias to his study to go through some new ideas of his, while Anna has been asked to make some tea and coffee for us all.'

'Why could they not talk their business out here?'

Michael shrugged. 'I believe there are some diagrams and formulations to look through.' He sat down on a rock and lit a cigarette.

I watched him do this, his slender fingers holding the cigarette between his lips.

'How do you and Sami know each other?' I asked through my discomfort.

Michael exhaled a long, dry trail of smoke. 'We don't know each other. Not really. We have, in fact, just met today.'

'I do not believe you,' I said sharply. 'He knew it was you when I described you to him the first day that I visited the lake. Even with your beard and unkempt manner, he knew who you were. He knew that you had been away.'

'Ah yes, that's right. He would have known about my trip to the States. And I, of course, knew that you were here, in Alhama.' Michael leant forward and grinned. 'You're right, we did *know* of each other.' He leant back again, the smile still broad and his eyes still bright.

'But how?' I came to stand over him in my impatience.

'I will tell you.' Michael looked up at me with a dangerous glint in his eyes. 'But not here. And not today.'

'What do you mean?'

'Tomorrow. Meet me somewhere and I'll tell you. At the lake.' He looked at my face intently. 'No, not the lake. That's too far. What about the gorge? It's close by; you can walk there quite easily.'

'I shall not meet with you again, Mr Calvert,' I said stiffly. 'I have no desire to meet with you again. I shall ask Sami, instead. He will tell me. He already knows of our meetings at the lake. The second one, also.'

Michael examined my face closely.

'But *you* were not the one to tell him, Sahira. It was Isa who told him. Yes? And if you asked him, he would, of course, tell you. But would you be able to ask him such a question? Could you mention my name to him without betraying any emotion?'

I blushed hard. He was right. Most definitely he was right.

'I do not care how you know each other.' I said petulantly. 'I do not care so much about you that I would-'

I suddenly became aware of Isa playing quietly, not so far from us, and also an open window just above our heads. I lowered my voice to a whisper, 'Meet you surreptitiously.'

'How very discreet you've suddenly become, Sahira. But you know, Isa wasn't so far from us when you...'

I turned away from him, not needing to hear any more of this sort of thing, and made towards the bright blue of the doorway, when Michael spoke again. This time, however, his voice was soft. Even with the urgency in it, it was ever so tender.

'Don't go.'

It made me stop. The lavender was swaying in the gentle breeze. From over the high garden wall where the Virginia creeper grew, came a calming sound; someone in the neighbouring garden was strumming their guitar.

'I'm sorry,' said Michael. 'I haven't behaved very well towards you. I have not been a gentleman.'

I blushed again.

'However,' he continued, 'if you meet me tomorrow, I promise I'll behave. I do know how to behave, you know.'

I hesitated with my response. The yearning was undeniably there, but I had not the means.

'How can I meet with you? You are asking something of me that-'

'No, no, I'm not asking for anything improper.' Michael put out his cigarette on the rock that he was sitting upon. 'You misunderstand me. Surely, it's all right for us to meet as friends? I'm not asking for anything more, just to borrow you. To talk and walk for a while. Surely, there can be no harm in that?'

'I think that Sami might wonder at the type of friendship that requires us to meet at the gorge, alone.'

'Maybe, then, you don't have to tell him,' Michael suggested.

'That I am going to the gorge?'

'That you're meeting me.'

I shook my head. 'No. It would be entirely wrong. For a married woman to be in the company of an unmarried man? It would be most unseemly. Besides, there is Isa to think of.'

'Isa shall be at Elias's farm.'

I bit my lip and shook my head once more.

'I cannot. I cannot do such a devious thing. I cannot deceive Sami in such a manner.'

The sky was still a brilliant blue and the sun was still hot in it. The insects buzzed in their flight and the rosemary bloomed, but the inside of my head was in a tumultuous spin.

From inside the house there came voices again, getting louder and ever nearer as first Sami, and then Elias, emerged into the bright sunshine. I went quickly to where Isa was still playing and joined in the game with him.

'Sorry, we have been away from you for so long,' Elias apologised with his ever present smile. 'And now it is the time that we leave. But first I must give to you these.' He brought out of his trouser pocket a jar of plump green olives and handed it to me. 'They are the fruits from last year's crop.'

I took the jar without looking at it.

'Thank you,' I said.

Elias bent down to shake Isa's hand.

'Tomorrow you come to play with Jax, yes?'

Isa nodded with glee and repeated, 'Play with Jax!'

'Good, good.' Elias stood up and clapped Michael on the shoulder.

'Come, my friend. It is time for you to return home. I see from your face you have been out in the strong sun too long. Ah, even now, you are unused to the tremendous heat of Andalusia.'

Elias and Michael bade us their farewells. I picked Isa up in my arms. He was tired, but would not go for his siesta until he had said his goodbyes also. I took him to the stairs just as Sami was leading his friends out of the front door. At the foot of the stairs, by some instinct, I turned and saw Michael about to leave, his face towards me with an expression that seared its way through the pupil of my eye and into my brain. With difficulty, I pulled myself away from his blue eyes and climbed the stairs upwards. I took Isa to his bed and lay down beside him, confused and sleepless, my eyes wide open, staring at the ceiling, so white above me.

I did not sleep that night, but lay awake counting the hours as the campanile bell rang them out. I dare not close my eyes for Michael was there each time I did so, smiling his deceptively innocent smile. And I knew that, if I were to allow myself to be too long in his presence, I would surely fall from a great height.

I could hear Isa snoring delicately beside me and, in the darkness, each breath of his was amplified and my conscience prodded, so that, by the end of that night, I had quite decided that I would not go to the gorge that day. I would not be alone with him, a man who, although I would deny it staunchly to him, I was so deeply interested in. I would not be so imprudent.

With that decision struck, I hoped that I would sleep soundly, but I found that I still could not. I was still restless; the mattress under me seemed primed with all sorts of lumps and I was afraid that Isa would wake up. And so, as the bell struck the hour of six, I rose quietly and made my way to the kitchen to get myself a drink of water. As I turned the tap and began to fill my glass, I happened to look out of the window and caught sight of the Charybdis and the lavender, ill-defined in the dim light of that early dawn. I thought back to the day before, when Michael was there, talking so earnestly to me, and the music of the guitar was drifting to us over the garden wall.

I rested my head in my hands. That image, the memory of that moment, caused my resolve of two hours to shudder most violently.

Chapter Twenty-Six

I had arrived late at the gorge; late because, several times, I had stopped my faltering steps and headed back to Casa Azul, back to the walls that could shut out the open and dangerous world.

In due course, however, I made my way there and saw Michael crouching by the low wall of the small church. He had his back to me and, in his hands, was a camera, a more sophisticated piece than my simple Halina. He was concentrating it on the light stone of the church steeple and silent fountain.

I stood for a while, some ten metres from him, just gazing upon the line of his body, the quick movements of his finger upon the shutter release. His arms were bare and brown. When he finished his work, he rose to his feet and turned to face me. He waved wildly to me, even though I was only a few metres from him, and I almost ran to him in response. I made my way to his side, the top of my head coming up to his nose. I would have to stand on my toes to reach up and touch his hair. He smiled and I smiled back.

Michael pulled a piece of faded blue cotton out of his trouser pocket and held it out. 'I brought this for you to wear.' He unfolded it and, straightening it out, he placed it on my head. 'It isn't wise to be out in this fierce sun without one.' Michael stood back from me to get a better look at his sun hat. 'There, that's much better.'

I took it off and turned it over in my hands, a strained thing that was quite ugly.

'But it is too big,' I protested. 'I can barely see out from under it.'

Michael took it from me.

'Nonsense!' he said and put it back on my head; setting it straight, pushing it back from the front of my forehead so that it sat more upright with its large rim shading my eyes. 'There. Now you can see, and still have its protection. It's an old one of mine, one that I no longer wear but I remembered it just as I was setting out this morning. I wasn't sure that you had one and we couldn't have today ruined because you were overcome by the heat.'

He patted his bag that hung over his shoulder.

'I've brought plenty of water and sustenance for us both.'

Then all at once, he stepped away from me and, letting his hands fall away to his side, he said softly, 'I'm so very glad that you came. I couldn't tell from your expression yesterday whether you would or not. And then this morning, when I kept looking for you and you didn't come, I began to lose heart...' Michael looked up at me and smiled so that his eyes lit up. 'But you're here now so...'

Suddenly, his eyes glanced away from me. '*Oh look!*' he said excitedly, pointing to a bird that had just come into view, sitting on a small rock.

'A blue rock thrush!' He took hold of his camera once again and pointed as the bird took flight. 'Do you see its indigo body and black wings? That means it's a male. The female is brown; not quite such a beauty.'

When he had finished photographing the thrush, Michael replaced the lens cover of his black Leica. Our eyes met briefly, and then he turned purposefully away from me, heading back towards the little church and the gorge.

So, he does wish only friendship from me, I thought. *Well, that is a good thing, I suppose*. But, somewhere deep within me, I was not happy with this supposition.

A shout from Michael tore me away from my entangled thoughts.

'Come on! Are you coming?'

He was waiting by the wall overlooking the gorge. Obediently, I went to him. The gorge fell away from the church as a huge, gaping cavern. Michael led the way to the broken path that ran quite steeply downwards. He stopped there and swept his hand before the vast panorama before us.

'Can you imagine the strength of force that caused this?' He spoke with awe in his voice. 'What a glacier it must have been to break up the earth so? I catch my breath each time I come here, thinking about it. How many years, I wonder, did it take the glacier to shape this landscape, and how many gallons of water passed this way?' His face was radiant when he spoke this way: like an eager schoolboy on a field trip.

We continued along the uneven path, following the same route that I had taken with Sami all those weeks ago, treading carefully on the loose stones that tumbled away from under our feet. Dotted about the landscape were the balding bushes, their branches dry like kindling.

Michael took a photograph of me by a slice of broken rock, some twenty feet below a natural cave. Once, he said, the caves had been used by fleeing Muslims to hide from the murderous armies of Queen Isabella and King Ferdinand.

I nodded wordlessly as he spoke, for I was remembering a similar conversation that I had had here with Sami, when we had first arrived in this little town, when things were not so much a conflict as they were now. I did not tell Michael this. I did not want to talk of Sami just then.

Soon we came to the jagged bend and, once we had rounded it, the village of Alhama stood majestically in the distance, clinging to the edge of the gorge, a resplendent white instability.

'It is so peaceful here,' I said. 'One can imagine it as a piece of poetry. It stirs your heart in the same sort of way. I wonder if the people of Alhama feel this each time they see their gorge.'

'Maybe, who knows? They say that people who live close to such sights are not so easily overawed by them. They become blasé. It's called the apathy of overuse, I believe. Although, I'm not sure I would be so blasé with a falling precipice at my doorstep; I don't think I would sleep too well at night.'

I looked up at the row of houses that seemed as though they had been carved out of the gorge and then painted white. The windows were glinting in the bright sunshine.

Michael put his hands on his hips and tilted his head to one side.

'I'm glad that you decided to come out with me. You're very different when I'm not provoking you. You're young and carefree. The lines on your forehead are smoothed out and you smile much more. I would like to see so much more of that smile.'

He turned back to the ridge of buildings and pointed to some vague spot there.

'There's a restaurant up there, *La Seguiriya*, it's called. You can see it just there, where that balcony juts out at the very edge of the gorge. The food is fantastic. Ah, I wish I could take you there. I wish...' Michael shook his head in self-reproach. 'I wish, I wish! I wish for a hundred things that will never come true.' He looked at me with a great sincerity. 'But I do wish for that one thing that is so simple - to share a meal with you at *La*

Seguiriya. The owner is a retired flamenco singer, and quite a character.' Michael looked back at the balcony and sighed. 'Come on, let's carry on with today.'

We carried on along the ridge that led down into the belly of the gorge. Soon, we came once more to the fork in the path and followed the one that Sami and I had taken. I saw once again, those same olive trees that dotted the craggy walls of the gorge. And, far down from the ridge along which we walked, sat the same tiny, two-room cottage with an oasis of a garden in its yard. The tilled soil was turned green at intervals, as leaves sprouted from it now and tendrils fell in curls from the cane scaffolding.

Everything here was at peace: the air, the plants, the sky, the cottage. Everything, including my heart. It beat easily here: caught up as it was by the beauty of this rural idyll.

I sat down on a large rock overlooking the cottage and munched on an apple that Michael gave to me, while he took out his camera once more, and also a light meter.

'A Weston 4,' he told me in a most concentrated manner. 'At this time of year, the light is fabulous in this part of the gorge. It comes in at just the right angle, you see, so that each layer of rock is clearly marked and its many curves visible.'

He played with a silver dial at the front of his camera. 'There, I have set the shutter speed at $1/125_{th}$ of a second. That should give me some nice sharp images.'

He stood very still as he took a few photographs and I watched him. When he had finished, he turned to me.

'I came last year and took some photographs with my Rolleiflex, but really it's too cumbersome to be carrying about all day. So, when I was in New York, I treated myself to the latest Leica. It's a real beauty.' He showed it to me proudly, weighing it up in his hand, a small black object that was indeed a neat little package. 'Of course, it comes with its own attachments but still it's so much more practical. Plus, I get a greater accuracy with my close-up work. I used it just the other day on a piece of driftwood that I found by Bermejalis and it turned out pretty well…'

I listened to Michael's very serious voice, but I was only slightly interested in all this information. I had my simple Halina and I wanted to be able to take some good photographs. I was more interested in another matter altogether.

'Tell me,' I said, 'how it is that you and Sami know of each other. I have come to the gorge with you, so now you must keep to your promise.'

Michael stopped what it was he was doing and turned around. 'I hope that's not the only reason you came, Sahira. Surely, I make for some good company too?' He was smiling in his teasing manner. 'Haven't you guessed yet? I was sure that you would.'

'No, I have not guessed. Why would I? How would I?' Then I remembered something. I remembered now, very clearly, what I had heard yesterday, a part of the conversation between Michael and Sami, and I said with some triumph, 'He knows your parents. Your parents sent their best wishes to him.'

'And to you also.'

'To me? But I do not know of anyone...' In my head I unrolled names and faces of the all English people that I had come to know. Then suddenly, it came to me. Staring hard at Michael, another face came into my mind - much older and with the eyes faded, but still the essence of his face was there.

'The Burtons!' I shouted. 'You are very much the son of Frederick Burton. But no, how can that be? You are Michael Calvert, not Michael Burton!'

Michael put away his camera and sat down beside me, not touching me, but maybe just a little more than a hair's breadth from my side. He took the hat off from my head and placed a stray strand of hair behind my ears.

'I took my mother's maiden name. Lottie Burton, née Lottie Calvert. I took her name because I didn't want to be known as Frederick Burton's son.'

I was surprised by the last piece of this information.

'But your father is a good man. Why would you not want to be associated with him?'

'You misunderstand, Sahira. It's *because* he's so very decent, *because* of his good character: I didn't want to be well-thought of because of *his* good character. I have my own personality, my own ambitions. It's one of the reasons why I left England and came out to Spain. No-one knows my parentage here; I'm known only for what I say and do.'

'You sound very much like James Hepworth.' I thought suddenly of Hana's postman. 'He is our postman in Newton Kyme.'

'Yes, I know James. And his uncle, also. He was a good friend of my parents. He knew mother when they were children. In fact, I believe he was a little sweet on her. At least, it's the Newton Kyme rumour that he didn't marry because she broke his heart when she married. Although, I rather think the Honourable Alexander Hepworth is married to his work.'

His words stirred something in me and I wondered how it was that people's paths traversed this world, heading this way and that, getting further and further from one another until, suddenly, they changed course and arrived at the same junction. It was a mystery of the meandering life, the thing that caused people to shake their heads and wonder at the ways of the world, at fate and destiny.

Michael nudged my shoulder playfully. 'What are you thinking, Sahira?'

When I told him, he sighed deeply. 'It is how you and I met: on fate's winged chariot. How you met Sami, and he Elias, and Elias me. Where, I wonder, will fate take us?' Where do *you* think it will take us?'

I stared at him for one brief second, a stare that I could not sustain, and so I looked to the bare rock beneath my feet.

'Back to where we belong, of course,' I said resolutely. 'I will go back to Sami and Isa, and you to your little house and your photographs.'

For a while there was silence; only the few birds above our heads could be heard. I wished, too late, that I had not said those words, but I could not stop it now; for fate with all its twists and turns, did not work in reverse.

Eventually, Michael spoke. 'Back to the familiar, eh? Well, if that's how you see it, then that's how it shall be.'

He got up from his place and pulled me abruptly to my feet. My shoes scraped against the stones of the steep path and I felt my heart drain itself of humour. I stared once again at Michael, for he had spoken with a harsh edge to his voice.

'What are you doing?' I asked in confusion.

He glared at me before looking away.

'I'm sorry. Of course, you're right. You mention Sami and, of course, you're right. Even when we've done so little together, we've still done some wrong.'

I felt uncomfortable now. I could not think of what to say and so, instead, I made to climb back down the gorge, but Michael pulled hard on my arm so that I jerked to a stop.

'I didn't ask you here to seduce you, you know,' he hissed. 'I have too much respect for Sami for that, but there always seems to be a barrier between us. Something unnatural because you are -" he paused, as though to double-check his words. '...*playing the role* of his wife. A good and obedient wife.'

'Playing the role?' What a strange phrase that is to use. I am his wife.'

I said this with feeling, yet I did not pull my arm away from Michael's hold and, although he had released it a little, still I kept it there. Instead, Michael let go and put his face close to mine so that I could smell his breath, which was fresh with the smell of his cigarette. I looked into his eyes that were fierce and slightly mocking.

'You're not in love with him.' He moved away from me with a look of shocked understanding. 'You really don't love him! I didn't realise that until just now. Poor, wretched Sami!'

'Why? Why do you say that?' I was becoming frustrated with him. He spoke his mind too freely, and now was speaking of things that he should not. 'He does not love me, either. We respect each other and we-' I began to walk away, my feet slipping over the loose stones as I muttered loudly to the man behind me. 'Whatever we do, it is not a matter that should concern you!'

From behind me, I heard laughter. It rose high into that silent, blue sky and then I heard Michael's voice.

'Oh, Sahira, maybe it is you who I should pity.'

Chapter Twenty-Seven

The days passed by slowly - one day, two days, three days - since I had visited the gorge with Michael.

We had left each other at the foot of the slope that led upwards to the little chapel. It had been an awkward farewell; neither of us had spoken on the way back from the garden with the lovely trellises. A falseness had come into the day that was not in tune with the cloak of friendship that had earlier covered our excursion. When I turned and walked away from him, my heart had been left in a terrible state of flux.

Since then, I had had no sight of him, even though I wandered over to the Arab side of Alhama every day. Isa grew quite fed up with our excursions and eventually refused to come, wanting only the playgrounds, the lake and to play with Jax.

So, I had to relinquish my walks, but with this I became restless and so, one day when Isa had fallen fast asleep under the siesta sun, I took myself out, telling Sami that I wanted to sit at one of the Alhama cafés alone, to read and drink coffee in peace, without Isa's energetic company.

With Casa Azul behind me, and Isa and Sami also, I headed for the old Arab quarter, walking slowly and looking about me at all that I passed. In this way, I ventured out farther than I had been with Isa and found myself on a road that was vaguely familiar to me.

There was the bus stop just beside an old, grey stone fountain and, opposite from where I stood, was the crumbling remains of a wall, the fragments of broken, red roof tiles scattered here and there. And there, across the road, some hundred yards away, was a white-washed house with tall, black railings, around which a creeper was entwined with small, pink flowers. The balcony doors were flung wide open and there was music tumbling out from its open space, down onto the street and over to my ears. A man's voice was accompanying this music, a rich, deep voice that sounded dark with mystery. It was unlike anything I had ever heard.

The house was, of course, Michael's. There were the gates outside which Enrique had parked his truck and the pavement on which Michael had stood to say goodbye. There was the door that he had walked through to disappear from my sight.

I stood in the open for quite some time, just waiting for him to walk out onto the balcony so that I could wave up to him, but he did not appear. Finally I had to leave, looking back with an absurd constancy, until the house and the garden and the railing and the balcony disappeared from view.

I returned to the bus stop for two days after that, leaving Isa to sleep and Sami to work. On the first day, I stayed out in the open, defiant, pleading really for my presence to be known. I brought a book with me and sat on a low wall by the bus stop, ignoring the stares of passers-by and the buses that pulled in and then went away again. I looked up constantly, waiting for some movement, but the house was still the whole time I was there. That day, I went home as on the day before.

The second day went almost the same way, but, just as I was looking at my watch and knowing I would have to return to Casa Azul, I saw a figure on a bicycle stop by the gates of Michael's house, dismount and unlatch the clasp of the gate.

I realised straight away who I was observing: from the way that he walked, pushing his bicycle across the overgrown path, and the way that he leant it on the brilliant white wall; the way he took a flat parcel, wrapped in brown paper and string, from the pannier rack and carried it under his left arm, and then the way in which he touched the door to open it. I recognised the face, the eyes, the mouth, the shoulders, the arms, the hands, the silly hat on top of his head, so like the one that was still in my possession, lying hidden amongst my clothes.

My heart began to beat fast, and in my joy, I started to move towards the house ahead. I wanted to walk through the gate and the door that had been left unlocked. I was almost there, so near to him, when I heard the sound of a voice, heavily accented, very feminine, a cooing, happy sound, and then a response, male laughter that rang in my ears and made me falter in my step. I saw the door open once again and a woman came out, young, pretty and so very confident with herself. She hugged Michael on the doorstep, clutching close to her the same paper parcel that he had taken into the house.

At once, I slipped back into the shelter of the bus stop, blushing with the feeling of an outsider, the embarrassment and anger of Michael's close association with another woman - a flighty thing with thick, raven hair and small, delicate feet encased in pink sandals. She walked by with her head held high, and smiled with bright red lips at me as she passed. I could smell her perfume, flowery and light, like the dress that she wore, that hugged her shapely figure and was wantonly short. I did not smile back at her, but lowered my eyes, for I could not face her happiness.

I sat for a while as her perfume and her presence lingered on me. Then, slowly, I got up from my seat and put my book back into my bag. I looked one last time at the balcony doors that were now firmly closed, and I went away from that place.

A grey stone of humiliation sat heavily in my stomach and I walked very slowly back with its weight inside of me, back to Casa Azul, where Anna was singing as she chopped some mushrooms in the kitchen, and Sami was lounging, with his late afternoon coffee, out in the garden, a paper in his hand and a half-burnt cigarette resting in the white ceramic ashtray. Isa was sitting at the kitchen table, folding a piece of paper with his small hands into an aeroplane, bent over it in concentration, looking so beautiful, so innocent in that white-walled space. He looked up brightly as I came in.

'*Deko*, Khalajaan. *Mey kya bunaya.*'

I sighed and put my impudent heart back into its inevitable place: amongst the debris of my foolish desires. I lifted Isa up off his seat and sat down in his place, putting him on my knee, hugging his warm body tightly.

'Now, show me what you have been doing,' I said. 'My goodness what a clever boy you are. We shall have to take it outside to see how well it can fly.'

I admired his handiwork in a mechanical way, being the good aunt, holding onto him for the support he gave me without knowing it.

Sami came in, just as Isa jumped off my lap, ready to take his paper toy out for its maiden flight. Sami had his newspaper folded very carefully in one hand and his empty coffee mug in the other.

'Ah, good, you are back,' he spoke with a light smile. 'I thought I heard your voice from the garden. There is something that I must talk to you about. A telegram came just after you had left this afternoon. From Sikimpur.' He put his hand into the breast pocket of his shirt and pulled out a piece of thin, blue paper. He handed it to me. 'Here, you can read it for yourself and see what the news is.'

I read what it was that was contained in the telegram. The news from Sikimpur was that Laila, although not fully recovered, was missing Isa so much that she wanted him to return home. I let the telegram fall onto my lap.

'Oh,' was the only response I could muster.

Of course, this day was inevitable, but somehow it was always going to be some day in the future. But now, the words were very clearly in front of me, though the cheap, black ink was slightly smudged.

I realised suddenly that I was alone in the kitchen. It was strangely quiet. From the garden, I could hear the distant voices of Sami and Isa making fun as they watched the flight of Isa's paper aeroplane, and Anna clapping her fat hands in delight and cheering them with her broad Spanish. I re-read the telegram and its words had not changed. We were to give Isa up to his parents once again; he was to go back to Sikimpur's sunshine.

After Isa had gone to bed that night, Sami and I stayed out late in the garden, discussing Isa's return.

'I think it would be best for you to take him back,' Sami said. 'I know that you want to see Laila, and your parents will be very pleased to see you.'

I nodded. 'Yes, I would very much like to see Laila. I have been worried about her and, although the telegram speaks well of her, I would like to see for myself that this is true. When do we go?'

'Actually, I think it is best for *you* to take Isa back as soon as possible. I will go tomorrow and arrange-'

'You will not be coming with us?'

I realised what Sami was saying. It surprised me because I had not thought of travelling alone with Isa, of arriving in Sikimpur as a married woman without my husband by my side.

'No, I do not think I can come with you,' said Sami. 'I have still work to discuss with Elias here. Perhaps, later in the year, we can go to Sikimpur together, for longer. I did not think of your going for too long - a week, maybe. What do you think?'

'Yes, of course. A week is enough. I shall be able to see Laila and make sure that Isa is settled back there.'

Sami stared hard into the night sky. 'I shall miss him when he is no longer with us. I have grown very fond of him.'

'Yes,' I said simply. 'I shall miss him also.'

The days shall be in monochrome, I thought, without his chatter to fill them. How will my mornings be when I can no longer see his sleepy head on the pillow beside me? I will not smile when I first awake. Instead, I shall wake to find Sami there beside me, and that I will find most unusual. Sleeping in the same bed as my husband again will be most unusual.

Sami spoke up again. 'I would like to spend some time with him alone. Perhaps tomorrow he can come with me? I can take him for his favourite pastries and to the playground. I have not done that for some time now. If you do not mind, of course.'

I nodded sadly. 'Yes, of course.'

I looked at Sami. His face was flush with emotion. He would miss Isa as much as I would. Isa had been his child for a while, a boy to play with and to tuck into his bed at night.

As we sat that night, the two of us alone, the ink blue of the sky was reflected in the lamp that rested on the table, throwing out a stream of stars and the brilliant moon. Through the silence of that midnight air, I could hear the dragonflies as they scattered about us, tiny creatures going about their business, mindless of us, mindless of what we were. This is what we would be left with when Isa went away from us, the silence of adults, thinking their own private thoughts.

With Isa and Sami gone the next morning, I took myself around Casa Azul, wandering through its low-ceilinged rooms: the bedrooms, the study, the drawing room, the kitchen. I sat on each bed and looked at the pale, painted walls and the pictures that hung there; of flowers, of hills and vales, of Alhama and its church. I had grown so used to living here. It had become my home, a different home from the one in Newton Kyme, and also from Shamshad Bagh.

Anna would be coming soon and I did not want to tell her about Isa yet, for I did not want to face her sadness too. She would be very sad, I knew, maybe there would even be tears, and I did not want to deal with them. I did not want to cry just then; my melancholy was not so ripe. It lay low still and was not yet ready to surface.

I went out of Casa Azul and took the path I knew I would, along the cobbled stones that led away from the gorge and the cafés. Then, past the shops that sold children's clothes and plastic jewellery and other fanciful goods. I did not stop to browse at any of these places, but walked ever more quickly in case, in pausing to look, I also began to think. I did not want to think, I just wanted to walk fast and to have my head cleared of those things that were making me sad.

I saw many people on my way - old women with their voluminous skirts and old men with their stout waists, children with their shining faces and young people with a purpose in their stride. I smiled at each of them in turn and said many *'Holas'*, but I did not think about them, or their expressions, or what their business was out there on the street.

I walked. Up the steep paths and over the broken paving stones, past the garage and the old men playing an early round of boules, past the school that was closed for the summer break and the long patch of grass that the young boys played football on.

Yes, most certainly I was going to open myself up to humiliation, I knew, but I could not stop myself, for the gong that was my curiosity was being beaten far harder than the gong of my golden resolve.

It was only when I approached the bus stop once more that I slowed down. As I came alongside of it, I halted, my breath heavy with my exertion and the sweat forming in light beads across my forehead. There was a couple waiting at the bus stop, sitting on the seat that I had occupied so well. They had their arms around each other and were talking into each other's eyes, their faces so close that their noses were almost touching. The man had his hand very high up on the woman's thigh and, every so often, he would tighten his grip a little. This made the woman laugh. A silly, high laugh, laughing to please. And, while I stood there, wondering what I should do next, a voice came from behind me, just over my shoulder: a familiarly candid voice, full like the waters of Lake Bermejalis.

'Surely, you have enough courage now to go beyond the bus stop?'

I swung around and found there, standing tall over me so that I had to look up, Michael Calvert. He was not smiling, but frowning at me. 'Are you here to unsettle me again?'

'I... I did not know that you lived... I was just out for a walk.' I could not answer straight. There were only silly lies upon my tongue, and I was not so good a liar as to be bold with them.

Michael leant gently over and whispered into my ear, 'You have been for many a walk around here, lately. Only, today, you are early. What has happened today to make you so early?'

I bit my tongue. It seemed that I had been found out. Now, Michael smiled, a wry, ironic smile.

'I have watched you every day that you have come,' he told me. 'I have hoped that you would venture further from your shelter, and into my lair.'

I closed my eyes. There was an odd lightness in my head and, suddenly, my hearing became numbed, like a dull thud of echoes filling the cavities of my ears. I put out my hand for something to hold and it was Michael's arm that came to me.

'Come,' he said roughly, 'let's get you out of the sun. You don't look too well.'

The inside of Michael's house was very plain. There was a hall and a reasonably-sized living room, 'For which I have very little use,' he told me. Indeed, the furniture there did not look as though it was much loved. It was large and quite ugly. At the back of the house was a small kitchen with pale blue cupboards and an old, metal stove.

'It's not my taste.' Michael caught sight of me staring into the living room. 'I rent the house, and all that you see is my landlady's work. I live mostly upstairs. My studio's up there, and my bedroom also. Everything I require is up there, really. I only come down to cook, and to entertain guests, which is rare now that it's summer. I prefer the autumn months for conviviality. Summer and spring are for the outdoors, and winter is for hiding away. I go back to England then, to visit my family for Christmas, and friends for the New Year celebrations.'

'The Burtons,' I said, still a little surprised by this piece of information.

Michael nodded and smiled. 'You make them sound so very middle class, which of course, they are. Newton Kyme is the epitome of provincial Englishness.'

He looked into the mirror that hung on one of the bare walls, as though he were seeing something beyond his reflection.

'It shall be strange not to have Christmas in that house again,' he mused. 'Strange not to have the tree standing so tall in the hallway, and Father hanging the mistletoe over the doorway in the hope of catching Ava Beresford under it. I shall have Christmas and the New Year in Cornwall. I have not done that for some time. Not since my brothers and I were young boys, and my parents were still abroad.' Michael turned to me. 'We were brought up by my grandparents in Cornwall, you see - in Portcurno where they lived.' He smiled with a faraway memory. 'It was a wonderful place to be; by that seashore, spending our days collecting shells and swimming in the sea.' He looked back at me. 'How strange are the ways of the world? Now my parents live in Cornwall and you live in my mother's childhood home. How do you like it, by the way?'

'I like it very well. We have not changed much inside it and I think your mother would still find her garden very lovely.'

Michael laughed and shook his head.

'Oh, I'm not so sure. Mother was very particular about her garden. Whatever you've done with it, she would most certainly disapprove.'

'Well, that has been mostly Hana's doing, and she has kept it very well. Better than either Sami or I ever could. Her father is my parents' gardener and he taught Hana well.'

'Ah, yes, Hana. I've heard about her.'

'Oh?'

'Yes, she's supposed to be quite a beauty.'

I looked at Michael with curiosity, and some jealousy. 'She is very beautiful,' I said finally. 'How do you know about her?'

Michael tipped my chin up with his index finger. 'Why, Sahira, in the same way that I knew of your great beauty, of course. I told you that you'd come as foreigners to a small place, and people - especially women - must have their tittle-tattle when such things happen.'

I thought back to when Hana had arrived in Alhama with Isa, almost a month ago now. However, she had not been here that long, and, except for the garden, she had not ventured out of Casa Azul in all that time. I thought for some time before saying to Michael, 'Was it Anna then who-'

'No, I didn't hear of you here in Alhama, you goose. I am talking of *England*, your tiny community back in Yorkshire. You stand out inordinately there. There aren't many Indians in Newton Kyme. Or, indeed, Tadcaster.'

'That is true. We attract much attention when we are walking around the town, even now when we have lived there for many months. But tell me, who is your friend that likes to gossip so much?'

'My friend?' Michael's eyes twinkled. 'It's my aunt, actually. Mother's cousin, Aunt Rose. She still lives in Tadcaster.'

'Oh, yes, of course. I do remember that Mr Burton spoke of her.'

We fell silent for a while, an awkward kind of silent, each of us thinking of what to say. I should have left then, there was a perfect opportunity to go, but my feet stayed solid on that pale, tiled floor, until Michael asked, 'Would you like something to drink?'

I nodded, thankful for an excuse now to remain there.

Michael started towards the wooden staircase.

'Come, then. I keep all my stores up here.'

I followed him with some apprehension, our shoes tapping out our trail upwards, until we reached the landing and I saw that the house was now transformed. No longer drab, it came alive, a thing lived in.

Along the length of the floor ran a beautiful rug, faded in its mosaic pattern of blue and green and red wildlife, flowers and tiny birds that flitted amongst its pattern. On the walls were many, many framed photographs, mostly black and white, and mostly of people, not posing in front of the camera but going about their business: a taxi driver tipping his hat before driving away, a woman dancing in a flamboyant red and black dress, a teacher leading her brood of school children across the road, and the most striking, a baker kneading out his dough through a light cloud of flour.

There was only one door on that landing. It stood wide open and inside, where Michael led me, was a very large room, covering almost the entire area of the upper floor. Bright, brilliant light flooded in through the tall, glass doors that led out onto the balcony, making everything in that room dazzling and colourful.

This room, then, was the bedroom and studio all in one. There was an unmade bed in one corner with only one of its pillows used, I noticed, and a settee festooned with cushions. Sitting in the middle of this vast space was a large table on which lay a couple of empty plates and glasses, some loose pages with a scrawled handwriting on them, and photographs, masses of them sitting in piles, some so high that they were in danger of tipping over. In the centre of this table stood a vase of ceramic green in which there were flowers. Beautiful, yellow flowers that had once been fresh, but were now slightly wilting and in need of water.

Michael left me standing in the doorway and went to an old, battered sideboard. There was a record player there, along with a selection of records in their sleeves, resting very neatly beside it. He examined them one by one until he came upon one.

'It's a good time for Otis, I think,' he muttered, more to himself than to me.

He took the black, shiny record from its sleeve and placed it carefully on the turntable. As it spun round and the needle jogged along its grooves, music came out from the speakers, the same music that I had heard the other day, and a man who sang with a deep voice and great emotion. It was so unlike the music that Sami and I listened to back in Newton Kyme. It was unspeakably wonderful.

As Michael rummaged inside the sideboard, I walked slowly through the room and onto the balcony. I leant on the rail there, surveying Michael's room with a strong jealousy.

'Your girlfriend does not look after you so well,' I said sharply

'My girlfriend?' Michael's voice sounded muffled. He took his head out of the cupboard, putting a bottle of red wine into his trouser pocket and then, reaching back in, he took hold of two glasses. On his face was a puzzled look. 'Which girlfriend would that be?' he asked so smoothly.

I took a deep breath. 'The one to whom you give presents, very fine presents from the big hug that she gave you in return. I saw her only yesterday, coming out of your house. She looked very happy. You seemed to have made her very happy.'

The puzzled look disappeared from Michael's face and was replaced by one of great amusement.

'Oh, you mean Clara? Yes, I did make her happy. How observant of you, Sahira. I had just given her rather a large sum of money as well as a present, so naturally she was in a particularly good mood.'

He joined me on the balcony and placed both the glasses on the small, round table. From his pocket, he drew out the bottle and filled one of the glasses with the red wine from it. In the other, he poured some water from a pitcher that was already there. He handed this glass to me, but I was not in the mood for just water. I brushed his hand aside roughly, so that the water rolled about in the glass and some tipped out onto the leg of his trousers.

I did not apologise, I barely noticed. And while Michael uttered a surprised, 'Oh! Look at what you've done now,' and began to wipe away the water with a cornflower blue handkerchief, I reached for the glass that was filled with wine and took a large gulp of it.

It was slightly bitter on my tongue, the taste of it, not as sweet as I thought it would be. I felt it in my head, too, a good kind of lightness, so that I took another and then another gulp of it, until Michael pulled it away from me.

I glared at him with an anger that was ripened by envy and the wine that I was not used to.

'Money and a present!' My voice was shrill and I could feel the blood rushing to my cheeks. 'She is a very lucky girl, then. All that I have received from you is a dirty, old hat and some very bad behaviour. You seem to-'

Michael came quickly to me and placed his hand over my mouth. His other hand he placed around my waist and held me close to him.

'Hush,' he whispered tenderly in my ear. 'Hush, my darling Sahira. I am sorry. So very sorry for my stupidity. I make you angry with me, when all I really wish to do is to make you happy. Happy in a way that you are not.'

And, because of these words that he whispered spoke of my inner self, and because of the red wine that I was not used to, and because I had wanted to from almost the very first moment that I had seen him, I turned my face up to his, placed my lips very firmly onto his and I kissed him. I kissed him so that I could feel the hard, strong enamel of his teeth and the bones of his jaw.

I heard Michael sigh and then he put his arms around me completely and pushed me into his room. I did not struggle.

At the foot of his bed, he began to unpeel layers off of me, and I, off him. When he moved my hair away from the nape of my neck and kissed the exposed skin below, when he ran his fingers down along my vertebrae, I knew that I was lost. Quickly, we wrapped ourselves in each other's arms and the sheets, which were crumpled and untidy. In that bed, I felt the most free that I had ever been: at times with the wildness of an animal, at times with all the gentleness of a snowflake caught on the tip of my tongue. I felt man's flesh as I had not felt it before, and I gave myself up in a way that I had never known possible. And, throughout all of this, I experienced a pleasure that was so exquisite and so very nearly unbearable.

After our passion had been spent, along with our desire and haunting need, I pulled away from Michael's resting body, breathing heavily and said in a manner that was resigned, 'How will you face your girlfriend now? And how will I return to Sami when we have-?'

Before I could finish, Michael placed both his hands on my cheeks and put his face close to mine, so that when he spoke, I could smell the sweet wine that had once been on my lips.

'Now listen to me very carefully. I will tell you this so that you understand clearly. Carla is not my girlfriend, nor yet my lover, nor any of the other foolish things you can think of. She is my landlady's daughter and had come to pick up my rent. As for the present that I gave her, it was in fact an engagement present: a photograph that I took of her and her fiancé, Rutger, a German chap, about whom she is crazy.'

He smiled and kissed me lightly once again. 'So, you see, my darling, you have nothing to be concerned about. Carla is engaged, and I do not consort in that way with women who are engaged.'

'Only with ones who are married, then?'

Michael blushed at the crude irony of my statement, and pursed his lips. 'Only with you, actually,' he mumbled. 'Only you,' he sighed.

I traced the line of cartilage along his neck to the curve where it met his collarbone, and then I placed my lips there and pressed them lightly on it. It was that part of his body that I loved the best. I could put my face into that curve and be done with the rest of the world forever.

The music had stopped now. The record was spinning wildly and there were crackles where the needle was engaging with it. Michael got out of the bed and walked across the room to change it. I watched his naked form as I had not watched Sami's, for I was not made shy by it.

I watched as he chose another record, removed it from its sleeve and, with his hands holding it very carefully so as not to touch its grooved surface, he placed it on the turntable. Then, he lifted the silver stylus and aligned it perfectly. He began to hum softly to himself, in time with the music that came out - more rich tones of a dark voice, a smooth voice this time, a universe away from anything that I knew. It was the mood for this early afternoon.

There was a large iron-cast clock on the wall. It was almost one o'clock, coming up to lunch time. Sami and Isa would be home with Anna, wondering where I was. I needed to be there soon. Sighing and reluctant, I climbed out of bed and began to clothe myself once more, slowly pulling on each item of clothing in the order they had been removed. I listened to the sound of Michael's music and his gentle singing.

'I haven't heard this type of music before,' I said to him.

'No, you wouldn't have.' Michael broke off from his singing as he came up beside me. His voice was low; there was an edge to it, as if his thoughts were elsewhere. 'It's not the sort of music that would be popular amongst the people of Newton Kyme.'

'No, it is very different from the records of Frank Sinatra that Sami plays.'

Michael kissed the corner of my shoulder. 'That's a safe kind of music. Safe, like...' He had just begun to dress himself when he paused. *He cannot not say Sami's name*, I thought. *He likes Sami too much and now he feels the betrayal of him. But he does not know what I know of Sami.*

'Are you sorry, then, for what we have done?' I asked him.

Michael shook his head slowly. 'No, I can't be sorry for it; I can never wish that it were any different. In those few minutes of possessing you, I possessed life.' He sat down on his bed heavily and buried his face in his hands. 'But I am sorry for Sami.'

'Do you think that I should tell him?'

Michael looked up. There was a brief light in his eyes.

'Only if you mean to leave him,' the light faded. 'But I can see from your face that you won't leave him. Even though you don't love him.'

'I... I cannot. It goes beyond Sami and me. Our marriage, I mean. It would mean shame for my family.' I could see Ammaji's face as though she was standing in front of me. I lowered my eyes. 'But you need not worry about Sami. There is his pride, of course, even with Sami, but he does not love me and so—'

'Does not love you?' Michael looked with incredulity at me. 'You said that once before, but you're wrong, Sahira. Are you so blind? Can't you see that Sami loves you very much?'

I stopped straightening my hair and let it fall down around my face.

'No,' I said in exasperation. 'That is not so. You do not understand. Sami loves someone else. Someone from his past, someone who prevents him from loving me. So, you see, it does not matter what we have done, only in that I am still married...' I stopped what it was I was about to say and looked into Michael's expressionless eyes. 'It matters because I love you, and that is something that I did not expect.'

I sat down heavily on the bed. The mattress, which was thin, sank into the metal bedstead. Large, involuntary tears came fast to my eyes and flowed over the rims to run down my cheeks, and my nose began to warm and my cheeks also. Michael came to sit beside me and hold me once more in his arms. He rocked me gently.

'What is it?' he asked. 'Something else is upsetting you.'

'Yes.' My face was buried in his T-shirt, wetting it with the tears that I was crying.

Michael pulled me away from his body. He looked gravely at me. 'Tell me what is making you so unhappy.'

'It is Isa!' I blurted out. 'He is going back to Sikimpur!'

Michael let go of my arms and pushed the hair back on his forehead.

'Ah, so that's it. I understand now. When is he going?'

I shook my head.

'I do not know. Sami has gone to arrange it all. It will be soon, that is all I know. As soon as possible.'

'You're going with him?'

I nodded. 'Of course, he cannot go alone. Besides, I want to see my family.'

'Of course, you do. Of course...' Michael shook his head and stood up quickly. His body seemed rigid, as though the soft edges had been removed.

He went onto the balcony, leaning his elbows on the rail and looking out at the jumbled rows of houses and tree-lined avenues. I could not see his face, but only the stiff bend of his back. I sat on the bed a little longer, disconsolate and grieving selfishly. Then I wiped the last of my tears away, rose and began to pull the covers back over it; pale yellow sheets, just enough to keep him well on the warm summer nights. I was shaking the second of the pillows when Michael returned and put his hand over mine.

'Stop that,' he said irritably. 'You don't need to do that. I can look after myself.' He looked up at the clock on the wall. 'It's time for you to go now. I'll walk you back downstairs.'

'Is that really what you want? That I should go? Now, and in this way? You are turning me away. Why?'

'Because this is the time that I can let you go. If I wait any longer, then... I can't bear for you to go. And not just back to Casa Azul, but to *India*! What have you done to me?' Michael threw the pillow back onto the bed. It landed on the very edge of it.

'But it is not my doing. I-'

But Michael was already heading towards the door, illuminated by the beam of sunshine that streamed through the room. He did not turn back to see if I was following, but kept on. I heard his bare feet padding hard on the grey stone stairs, going downwards, away from me. I could do nothing else but follow him. I put my sandals on and looked about the room once more, putting the pillow back in its place, smoothing down the bed covers as I went.

The record player, the photographs, the half-drunk bottle of wine, they were all still there, they would remain there for some time. Maybe, Michael would drink the rest of the red wine and think of me, playing the same record as before. Otis Redding, he had called the singer. I would find that record, I decided. I would play it over and over again, and think of this day.

Michael was waiting for me at the foot of the stairs. I put my hand on the rough, dark wood bannister. He watched me come walking down towards him, and I watched him. His face had softened so that he looked like a young boy again. The moon and stars are within my grasp, I thought, but I have not the audacity to take hold of their celestial brilliance.

'How would you like to run away with me?' I was almost at the bottom step when Michael finally spoke. 'I could take you away to the hills of Andalusia, or the moors of Exmoor, or somewhere that's just our own, Italy or France. We could be like Atlanta and Hippomenes, wandering through the woods and living off the berries and nuts that grow there. Would you like to do that, Sahira?'

'I would like that very much,' I said. 'Let's do it. Shall we just do it?'

Michael took my hand and kissed it.

'Thank you,' he said. 'Thank you for pretending with me. If only for a moment.' He held my hand so tightly that it hurt, and although I winced with the pain, I did not pull it away for it was still a contact with him. 'Apparently, there's something very noble about resisting temptation,' he said. 'But, somehow, I don't feel debased for having given in to it. Am I wrong to have enjoyed the fall?'

He let go of my hand and opened the front door for me. The sunlight came flooding into that shoddy hallway, lighting it up so that it looked quite pleasant.

'Now, go, please.' Michael stood with his back to the door, his hands at his back, holding onto the gilt-painted handle.

I stood on his hearth, standing almost a foot smaller than him. Reaching up, I touched his neck, running my finger down to the pit of his shoulder blade.

'I will take this part of you away with me so that I can have it forever. I cannot say goodbye to you, Michael.'

I grimaced as the tears came back and my heart beat too fast, so that I already felt out of breath.

'Take care as you go, Sahira,' Michael said softly, 'and don't turn round. Just keep walking and don't look back.'

With my head hanging down low, I continued out of his gate. My body was shaking and I longed to rush back to him, but I heard the door shut quietly behind me and knew that our farewells were done.

'I will not look back,' I muttered to myself over and over again. 'If I do not look back, then I shall survive this,' I continued, 'and I shall see him again.'

I had reached the bus stop and my strength was still holding, but then, fatally, I stopped by a tree that grew on the avenue and leant against it, resting my forehead upon my arm. I heard, so quietly that I thought it was my imagination, the music that Michael had shared with me. A slow love song, full of the anguished heart, and I could not think of anything but him. I looked back up to his balcony, where the big doors were open, and I saw a shadowed figure with a glass in his hand. I saw him put it to his mouth and drink it, downing it all in one go.

Part IV

The One Wild Song

Chapter Twenty-Eight

As the plane left the tarmac of Malaga, Isa sat with his nose pressed up to the window and waved fervently to an imaginary Sami. I did not tell him that Sami would not be there, that he would now be on his way back to the car and soon on his way back to Alhama.

'I can see him,' Isa shouted gaily. 'He is waving to me.'

I smiled without looking at him and stared steadfastly at the back of the seat in front of me. I could not bear to look out onto that landscape. I did not wish to see it, but to bid it an eternal farewell.

At Sikimpur airport we were met by Abbaji and Ammaji, and also by Nasir, Isa's father. At the sight of them, Isa became suddenly unsure of himself. He had been apprehensive at the thought of returning to Sikimpur, and started to awaken in the night with the fear of the earth tremoring beneath him once again. However, when Nasir lifted him up and hugged him tightly, Isa responded with a beaming smile and a tight hug of his own.

My own parents seemed quite changed since I had seen them last, cautious smiles pasted onto their faces for the occasion. The weeks of concern for Laila's health had taken their toll on them. Their faces were drawn and they seemed so frail, like the fading petals of ageing flowers. Their hair seemed greyer, and Ammaji had not tried to disguise hers with ebony hair dye. She had also lost weight and was thin once more, as she had been when she was young. Somehow, it did not suit her now.

I found myself clinging to them in turn, scared to let go in case they collapsed, as though I was holding them together. Ammaji did not cling to me. She did not tell me how much she had missed me and there were no tears pouring from her eyes. She kissed my cheek and told me how glad she was to see me again. She said this calmly, as though I had been gone but a moment and was returning home from school or some party. But she did hold my hand tightly and touch my cheek with the back of her other hand, and smile at me. She had, as Hana said, changed indeed.

'Thank you for looking after Isa.' Nasir's eyes were bright, with the joy of holding his son once more. 'He seems to have grown, but that cannot be right, for he has been gone for less than a month.'

Isa wriggled away from his father and leapt into the eager arms of Abbaji, who hugged him closely and popped a sweet into his eager mouth.

'Laila is most anxious to see him, as you can imagine,' Nasir continued. 'She wanted to accompany us here, but we managed to persuade her otherwise... at least, your Ammaji managed to dissuade her.'

Nasir smiled nervously. The joy of seeing, being with Isa once more, had made him more talkative than usual. He was normally a quiet, thoughtful person, a wonderful artist who painted with a great vitality. His favoured medium was oils on silk screens, and he had painted for me the sandstone fortress of Sikimpur in sunset's pale light. I had taken it to England with me and had it hung in the hall of our Newton Kyme home.

'Nasir, you should take Isa home.' Abbaji nodded Nasir this instruction. 'We shall wait for the luggage and bring it later, tonight or tomorrow perhaps. After all, we promised Laila that you would bring Isa home as soon as possible.'

Nasir took hold of Isa's little hand. 'Yes, of course. I do not want to keep Laila waiting. She will be getting impatient. Who knows, she may order a taxi and come out to the airport herself.'

I kneeled down by Isa's side and hugged him very tightly. '*Khudahafiz*, Isa, *meray chotay* Isa. We are back home now. You must go and see your mummy.'

As I let go of Isa, I felt that I was also letting go of Alhama. It became a foreign place once again.

As we drove out of the airport gates and on to Shamshad Bagh, the old familiarity of Sikimpur came back to me; the smell of freshly roasted monkey nuts sold at the road side stalls, the blaring of a multitude of car horns piercing through the already noisy air. I stared out at the brilliant saris of the women, the sadhus with their bright orange lunghis and wild beards, and the young men posing in their outrageous bell bottoms.

Towering above us were the oversized billboards showing off the film stars Dharmendra and Waheeda Rehman, painted in bright, gaudy colours. The film was *Baazi*, The Rascal, and certainly Dharmendra, with his wicked smile, looked very much a rascal.

Mingled in with all this familiarity, however, were also signs of the recent destruction: buildings whose walls had tumbled like playing cards, and bits of road that had been torn up as the earth beneath moved with great violence.

All along the road were men dressed in their lunghis and vests, working with crude tools to set the land straight once more. They had very little by way of machinery, but instead worked with their hands and their sinew, whilst all about them life continued. I watched all this passing by, loud and brash, so different from the quiet, easy pace of Alhama's streets. My head hurt slightly and I felt ever so sleepy. I could smell the monsoon rain that must have fallen earlier that hour, and became aware of Ammaji talking beside me.

'...after all, earthquakes are not common in this region. But, even if one was to know in advance, how does one prepare for such a thing? I was thankful that at least one of my daughters was safely away from this disaster. Also, we were very fortunate, all of our family and friends, for we only suffered a minority of what was happening elsewhere. Our houses are still intact and we know of no one who was killed. Of course, it is all in the hands of Allah.'

Ammaji raised her hands to heaven momentarily, and then lowered them, smiling. 'Now, tell me how you have been, *beyti*. It is very wonderful to see you once more. You look tired, which is to be expected. We are a large distance from... that place, *arre, yad nehee arra naam*.'

'It is Spain, Ammaji,' I told her softly. 'Where the Moors ruled for so long, in Andalusia.'

'Yes, yes, of course I know of Granada. It is that *chota se gaun* where you stayed, that is the name I cannot remember.'

'*Alhama de Granada*,' I said it slowly for her.

She repeated it. '*Alhama de Granada*. But that is easy to say. I wonder why I did not think of it as easy. It must have been the way that your Abbaji was saying it.'

'Tell me of your visit to the Alhambra, Sahira.' Abbaji, sitting in the front of the car with the driver, turned to speak to me. 'I have a great desire to go and see it for myself, especially after I received your letter telling me that you had been there.'

'It is a magnificent place, Abbaji. It has been restored well and, although some marks of the Spanish conquest remain, there is still enough of the spirits of the Moors there. You would enjoy it very much.'

Abbaji nodded. 'Reading your letter made my heart very happy, and also very sad at the same time, for it made me think of what the Muslim world had in their hands and stupidly let go. All around one can see the foolishness of Muslim rulers: the Ottomans, the Ummayids, and of course, here in India itself, with the Mughals. We let the stones of our empires turn to sand and then we let those sands slip too easily between our fingers.' Abbaji shook his head.

'There is still a large Muslim population in Granada.' I told my parents about the man in the Palacios de Carlos who had berated me for having my head uncovered.

'What he said was right, Sahira,' Abbaji said. 'For, although it is not mentioned in the Quran, the hadith are very clear about the wearing of the hijab by Muslim women.'

'It is a way to hide away a woman's beauty,' sniffed Ammaji. 'Their *zeenat*, so that they do not appear so alluring; so that men are not tempted: many ill deeds occur when men are tempted.'

Yes, I thought, *I know well of the ill deeds that are committed when men are tempted.* Aloud I said, 'But, surely it is not compulsory?'

'Well,' Abbaji replied, 'the scholars differ greatly in their opinion as to that. Some say that the hadith came from an early period in Islamic history. When there was conflict between those early Muslims and the Unbelievers and, as such, it is not relevant today. Others, however, point out that it is indeed very relevant today, for how else are we to tell a Hindu woman from a Muslim woman?'

'Oh, but that is easy,' Ammaji cut in. 'There is a difference in our looks and also in our manners. And, there is also the *bindi* that the Hindu women wear on their foreheads.'

'Yes, yes, to you this might be true,' Abbaji winked at me, 'but not everyone has your eye for such subtle variations.'

'That is certainly true,' I said, and I told them of Newton Kyme, where I was asked so many times why I did not have a *bindi*, and whether we had a shrine for all our gods in the house. 'When I explained to them that we were Muslims and that we only worship one God, they asked me which god is that, and were surprised when I told them that we also believe in Jesus, and Noah and Abraham and all the other prophets.'

I remembered all the questions that were put to me by my middle-class neighbours. Only Professor Hariman had not asked such questions, had not asked any questions as to our religion or our faith. He seemed to have known instinctively what we were; or maybe it was because of our furnishings that he knew, for he had admired them and spoken to me about Islamic art.

'Anyhow,' Ammaji was still talking, 'not wearing the hijab is not so great a sin. There are far greater sins than a woman leaving her head uncovered, such as thieving, and gambling, and adultery. It is these doings that cause the most harm—'

I looked out of the window again, cursing that I had brought up such a subject that would lead Ammaji to speak of adultery, even briefly. It made me think of Michael, and being so far away from him, to feel the proclamation of guilt being laid upon my head.

Ammaji touched my cheek gently and smiled at me. 'You have been wandering about in the sun too long,' she scolded me mildly. 'Your skin is quite dark again.' Then, she put her hand over mine. 'It is no matter. You are here now and I am thankful for it. The house has seemed quite empty without you. And when Isa went away also...'

The large iron gates of Shamshad Bagh lay open. They showed signs of damage where the earthquake had caused them to twist on their hinges. Hana's father was kneeling at one corner of the garden, folding in the soil around the sturdy trunk of the pink bougainvillea bush that had been uprooted. He stood up when we drove in and waved through the car window at us, the gaps in his teeth showing through his broad smile. There was dirt on his hands and knees and, for a moment, I could see Hana reflected in his eyes.

I talked to him for a while after I got out of the car. He pointed to a large gash in the lawn.

'We are needing to fill this in soon, to make it safe once again. But we are being most fortunate that the house itself remains solid.'

I looked about me, examining the grand old building that stood before me; still intact, remarkably unscathed. From the fields beyond the garden, I could hear the joking and laughter of the men who had finished their working day and were now climbing into the lorry that would take them home. I wondered how well their houses stood. Ramshackle houses, huts with corrugated roofs, no doubt. But they sounded happy and I thought that, of course, they would be, for Abbaji would have made sure that they were well looked after, their homes rebuilt and their families provided for.

I breathed in the air of Shamshad Bagh, the particles of its soil thrown up by the fierce monsoon rain and the smell of cooking that wafted out from the open kitchen window. Shamshad Bagh was made familiar to me once more.

My bedroom was as I had left it; left it first for Gulabi Ghar and then for England. The light of the ageing day still came in at a slant, illuminating the left-hand side of my bed. There were flowers from the garden in a red ceramic vase, pale and fragile. I smiled to myself. It was Hana's father who would have put them there, as he did for each of us three sisters when we came back to Shamshad Bagh after we were married. I touched their petals gently and bent down to smell their fragrance.

I left my luggage as it was, sitting by the side of my writing desk. I was not yet ready to unpack. Instead, I lay down on my bedspread, on my back, so that I looked up at the ceiling fan that was turning slowly. It was hypnotic. I followed its unhurried circuit with my eyes, and soon became tired, so I shut them and waited for sleep to overtake me. I waited a while, counting the seconds as the clock ticked on, and then I got up.

From the kitchen I could hear Ammaji's voice, light and carefree as she chatted to Mina in her quick, high-pitched tone. I looked out of my window at the garden with its brown patches where the ground had been burnt by the strong summer sun. They would soon turn green again now that it was the monsoon season.

It was good, I thought, to be here, in Shamshad Bagh, in my bedroom. It was a source of security that I was greatly in need of. A chance for me to coil away from the recent living that I had been doing and just to breathe in an air that did not include Sami or Michael or my muddled thoughts.

It had been only four days since Michael and I had spent our time together. In those days, whatever I occupied my mind with: Sikimpur, my parents, Laila and Suha, somehow all these paths led me back to Michael. Each aspect of him was placed before me, each word that he had spoken, each gesture. I was thankful not to have seen him after that day; I would have all but melted if I had.

I thought back to when he had come to Casa Azul the day before Isa and I left. I had managed to keep myself away, tucked away in my bedroom with the door closed firmly in the hope that his voice would not penetrate it; so that I could pretend not hear Sami call me down for Michael was here, come and say goodbye to him!

Michael had brought with him a present for Isa: a wooden sailing boat, painted red and yellow, so bright and jolly. I could hear Isa's delight when he received it and the low murmur of Sami and Michael's conversation out in the garden.

Then, I heard footsteps coming back into the house and Sami calling out to me. 'Sahira. Michael is here to say goodbye... Sahira?' And then louder still, 'Sahira!'

I had ignored him and, instead, made my way, quietly, into the bathroom and began to run a bath. I had let the tap run fast and long so that I did not need to hear Michael's voice so clearly. It was only when he was leaving that I put my ear right up to the bathroom door and heard him speak.

'I shall be leaving Spain myself shortly, and heading back to England, to Portcurno. It seems that Mother is missing Yorkshire after all, and finding it hard to settle into the Cornish way of life. I don't know that my presence shall alleviate any of her ailments, but I want to return. I think that, maybe, I'm a little homesick myself.'

'Oh, that is a shame,' I had heard Sami say. 'It shall be too quiet here with Sahira and Isa gone, and I had hoped to get to know you better. Still, I suppose it is better that I work as hard as I can in order to finish up here. And, of course, I shall still have Elias to meet with. Our month here has gone quickly, too quickly, but it is time we also returned home to England. I shall be sorry to leave, for I do not feel that I have seen enough of Andalusia. Maybe, it will be something to look forward to another time.'

'Yes, there is always that.' Michael spoke quietly, softly, so that I had to press my ear hard to the door to hear him.

'Well, I shall wish you a safe journey, and please do not forget to give our very best regards to your parents.'

Then, they had said goodbye, and I suppose shook hands: Sami and Michael, Michael and Isa. I heard the front door shut soundly and Michael was gone once more.

And I, upstairs, listening to all of this, had to lean against the hard wood of the door and breathe deeply to fill my lungs and my head once more with oxygen. To hear his voice thrust me into such a maelstrom, but there were to be no tears that day, my tear ducts remained dry. Instead, I had slipped my clothes off and climbed into the warm water of the bath. I rested my head against the hard enamel and closed my eyes, and I pretended that I was back in the waters of Lake Bermejalis.

Later, when we were in the kitchen, Sami had asked, 'Oh, do you know who came today?'

I had shaken my head, concentrating on making a sandwich for Isa, concentrating on cutting, as evenly as possible, thin slices of bread.

'It was Michael, Michael Calvert. He came to say goodbye to us. He is going away too.' Sami had paused for my response but when I did not, he carried on. 'He is going back to England because his mother is unwell. It seems that she is missing her old home, which is strange for she has travelled around so much in her life... but, maybe now that she is older... maybe when one reaches a certain age, one longs for the familiarity of one's childhood. What do you think, Sahira? Do you think that one day you will want to return to Sikimpur?'

I had shrugged and said a little shakily. 'I do not know. It is hard to say when you are young how life will turn out. There is only the present, really...' I had bitten my lip hard to control my emotions. I did not want to be anywhere at that moment. I wanted merely to cut some bread and some cheese, and to beat down the irregularity of my heart.

'I did call out to you,' Sami went on, 'but you must not have heard me. Were you in the bathroom? I thought I heard the water running in there.'

'Yes, that is right. I wanted to have a last bath before we leave for Sikimpur tomorrow.'

I finished what it was that I had been doing and went to the open door to call Isa in from the garden. When I had returned, Sami was standing by the cooker, leaning against it with his arms crossed and a concerned look on his face.

'Are you all right, Sahira? You do not seem so well. I thought that maybe you would be happy to be going to Sikimpur and seeing your family again.'

'Yes, yes, of course, I am fine. My mind is just elsewhere,' I had mumbled bleakly. 'I am distracted by taking Isa back, and also with the packing. Isa has accumulated many possessions since he came here, and–'

I had been interrupted by Isa, running into the kitchen, waving his new toy, showing it off with such pride to me. '*Deko, Khalajaan. Deko, kya mila mer-ko.*'

I smiled at him.

'It is a present from Michael,' Sami told me, still serious, still watching me.

'Oh, that is nice.' I had spoken with an unevenness in my voice. 'Now, let us have some lunch.'

I had taken Isa to wash his hands, passing by Sami, who smiled briefly with his mouth, but whose eyes did not. They had seemed uncertain, troubled. That is how they had seemed to me, but then again, perhaps it was really I who was these things.

Suddenly, I was brought back to the present by Ammaji. She came into my bedroom with a cup of tea. I heard its rattle on the saucer as she set it down on the little table beside my bed.

'Good, you are not yet asleep,' she said cheerfully. 'You can drink this while it is still warm. It will ease away some of your tiredness.'

She came over to the window beside me. The crickets were starting up their chirping in the early evening, and the light was beginning to fade.

Ammaji stroked my hair. 'It is strange for me to be welcoming you back here as an adult. It does not seem so long ago since you were this small,' she placed her palm, pointing downwards, to just above her knee, 'and your Abbaji decided we should have a pool for you girls. How excited you were. Always you were jumping, like a small, wriggling monkey, so wild and so free. You would run out onto the hot earth in your bare feet and climb up the trees to get the ripe mangoes. And now–' She shook her head sadly. 'Time is never as you would have it. As a child it is too slow, and then, as you get old, it passes by too quickly.'

Through the open window a light breeze rose up, cold after the heat of that August day. Ammaji shut the window, turning its clasp tightly and the room became warm again.

'One day you will understand my words,' she told me. 'One day, when you are yourself a mother, then you will understand.'

'*When you become a mother*.' That was what Ammaji was always saying. It was a favourite phrase of hers, and it always made me smile, or roll my eyes. However, today, suddenly, it made me think of Michael and his child. Michael's and mine... but no, surely not? Sami and I had been married for nearly one year and there had been no child. Surely one day spent with Michael would not result in–

From somewhere within the house, a child's happy cry cut suddenly through my oblique thoughts. It took me a while to realise that Suha had arrived, and the child whose voice disturbed me so was that of her daughter, Mariam. A little over a year old when I had left for England, she was now, I counted the months that had passed, eight they totalled; now she was almost two!

'Nani! Nani!'

Mariam came toddling into my bedroom, fat-cheeked and a broad smile. She threw herself into the open arms of Ammaji, who enveloped her, swinging her gently to and fro, and laughing with the force of her embrace.

'*Ooph, bohat burrey horey tum*! *Arre*, you will squeeze the life out of me one day.' Ammaji laughed in delight.

Suha followed Mariam in, her arm linked with Abbaji's. She let go of him to hug me.

'Here you are. Hiding away from us all as usual,' she teased me gently.

Mariam let go of Ammaji to stare at me. She was silent, watching me and biting her lip. I recognised the purple dress that she was wearing; it was one that I had sent over from England for her. I smiled at her and said to Suha, 'She looks so very like Uthman. There is very little of the baby in her now and she does not remember me at all, does she?'

'Of course not, how would she? You have been away a long time for her, enough to wipe your memory from her mind. But she will get used to you quickly.' Suha reassured me. 'Soon, she will be following you around everywhere.'

'*Chalo*,' said Ammaji. 'let us go to the drawing room. Has Uthman come also, Suha?'

Suha shook her head. 'No, he has just dropped me here, but he will come later. He has gone to pick up my clothes from the tailor's. It is my outfit for Faisal's wedding. It is in three weeks' time, but the tailors will start to get busy now because of the Holi celebrations next month.'

Ammaji nodded. 'Yes, you are right to do that. I must get my blouse properly fitted soon. I have already bought the sari, but the *oolu* tailor has sewn my blouse too tightly,' Ammaji tutted. 'They are getting more and more stupid, these tailors, and they also are charging too much now. If our tailor sticks his nose too high in the air, I shall have to threaten to go elsewhere. Who is your tailor, Suha? Is he any good?'

'We use the old Christian tailor, Samuels. Uthman's mother has used him all her life. He is getting slow now, but he is dedicated to the family and always does an especially good job for them. I can ask if he will take in some work from you.'

Ammaji shook her head. 'No, no, if it is their family tailor, then I do not want to interfere with them. I do not want to have to ask your *susraal* for a favour. It is not seemly.'

Suha shrugged and turned to me. 'I do not suppose that you miss all of this *hangama* and wedding talk, Sahira.'

I shook my head. 'Most certainly not. I miss many things in Sikimpur, but its society functions are not one of them. I am quite happy with our quiet life in England, in Newton Kyme.'

'Neew-ton Ky-me,' Suha repeated the words slowly. 'What a strange name that is.'

'There are many strange names around Yorkshire,' I told her, and I rhymed them off, 'Keighley, Roundhay, Spoforth.'

Suha and Ammaji laughed, and tried to repeat the town names after me.

'Oh, I cannot say them!' Ammaji exclaimed, certain that I had made them up.

'Ah, but we find them peculiar only because we are not used to their language,' Abbaji put in. 'It is the same all across the world. After all, the *feringhi* visitors that come to India find that the names of our cities distort their tongues so.'

'*Arre*,' Ammaji sniffed loudly. 'They are too lazy to try.' She turned to me and explained. 'It is all the hippies that come here; thinking that they can find their *dharma* just by going around chanting "*Ram, Ram*" all day. These people are crazy, I tell you, dancing in our streets with their saffron-dyed lunghis and their bare, pale bellies. What is so wrong with their own society that they must come over here again and again? First, they came to loot our wealth and now they come to enrich their souls. They stop the *bael* in the street to drink its urine, because they think it is so holy!'

'Ammaji!' Suha looked shocked at Ammaji's frankness.

'What?' Ammaji's eyes were wide with her innocence. 'I am not saying anything to shock you. It is true. If any of them asks me for help with their karma, I shall tell them to stop being such *oolu*, and that it is washing in the Ganges that is giving them all the diarrhoea that they complain of, not our Indian food.'

'But, they will not be asking you, Ammaji,' Suha said amused. 'You are a Muslim and I do not think that they are looking for the kind of spirituality that Islam offers.'

'Huh!' Ammaji sniffed. 'Of course they are not. There is too much abstinence in Islam for them. Anyway, do you think they care that I am an upright Muslim woman? Hindu, Muslim, Sikh, it is all one thing to them. All they see is dark skin, brown eyes and black hair.'

Suha winked at me, her wicked, gleeful wink, and said, 'But Ammaji, no *feringhi* will have the opportunity to ask you about anything. After all, you do not walk on the streets for them to approach you. You have a driver to take you everywhere in the car.'

Ammaji moved to the edge of her seat, ready, I thought, to give Suha a severe telling off, but then, suddenly, her frown changed to a smile and she pushed her body far back onto the settee.

'Yes, you are right.' She admitted. 'I do not walk so much these days, but when I was much younger I had to do much walking. That too, in my bare feet.'

Abbaji, sitting quietly in his armchair with its lovely upholstery, spoke up. 'Sahira, tell us some more about Spain, and especially Granada. That is what we all want to hear about. Is that not so, Ammaji?'

Ammaji nodded. '*Haun*, Sahira *beyti*, tell us more about Granada.'

Mariam climbed up onto her mother's lap. She sucked her thumb and closed her eyes to sleep. Suha rocked her gently, stroking her hair while I talked of our visit to Granada. I described it as best I could, remembering all the places that we had seen, trying hard to recreate the atmosphere and feeling of awe that the Alhambra inspired.

Abbaji listened intently; he was the most interested, the one taking it all in, the one who wished he, too, could visit it.

'Ah, you are fortunate indeed, to have seen these wonderful sights. I understand that Sami was also busy with some business there?'

'Yes,' I replied. 'Elias, his colleague, lives in Andalusia.'

'Yes, yes, I understand that fully.' Abbaji paused and then said regretfully, 'But, how unfortunate that you missed the Test series. It was the Indian tour of England, you know, and you are quite near to Headingley and so it would be natural, one would think... I know, of course, that Sami is not a great fan of cricket but still, I thought, that even he would want to see-' Abbaji sighed. 'Although, I suppose that he is a genius, so who can tell about the workings of his mind?'

At the end of this, Abbaji rose and came to my side. He touched my shoulder gently and spoke without looking at me. 'It is good to see you again, *beyti*. This house has missed your presence.'

Then he left us, the sound of his evening paper being delivered took him away into his drawing room.

That night, with Suha and her little family gone home, I lay wide awake on my bed, looking up at the fan on the ceiling that was immobile, and thinking of nothing in particular. I felt at peace, a lull that I had not felt for some time now. I wondered how Isa had been when he had seen his mother again, and I felt my heart swell up for the little boy.

My thoughts were interrupted by Ammaji, who came with a glass of warm milk. She had done this often when I had been small, and I felt small once again, a child without any cares. I sat up and took the warm tumbler from her. Ammaji stroked my head and kissed me tenderly, her soft lips gentle upon my forehead. Oh, how I had missed them.

'You must be tired,' she said lovingly. 'Why did you not sleep when you came home?' Shaking her head, she said with a soft scold in her voice, 'You young people, you are not sensible.'

I sipped my warm milk. Ammaji had stirred a little honey in with it. I felt it flow down the funnel of my throat and across the threshold of my belly. Such delight.

Ammaji gazed at me indulgently. 'You seem to be suddenly grown up. Did you miss your Sikimpur home when you were there, I wonder?'

'Of course, I thought of you all often, of this house, also. You are all very dear to me.'

'To think of us, however often, is not to miss us.' Ammaji smiled wisely.

'I missed you very much when I heard of the earthquake. I wanted so much to be here then.'

'Yes, that must have been hard for you. To be so far away and not to know how your family is doing. Nevertheless, it was more important that you were able to look after Isa. We were so worried because of the effect that the earthquake had on him. He was like a stolen child. You and Sami have looked after him well. He has regained his laughter.' Ammaji looked at me with bright eyes. 'We are very proud of you, your Abbaji and I. It was not an easy thing that you did. To care for another person's child, even when that other person is your own sister, is not an easy task. We are very proud of you indeed.'

I wished that she had not said that, for her kind words cut through me. *You are proud of me because you do not know me*, I thought to myself. *What would happen to your pride, Ammaji, if you knew of my dreadful truth*?

Ammaji was still looking at me, and still smiling. I tried very hard to smile back. My effort made her say, 'Ah, I must stop my talking. You are very tired, and tomorrow is a busy day.'

I finished my sweet milk and handed my empty glass back to Ammaji. She placed it on the little mahogany table by my bed, and then she moved closer up my bed. She looked at me with great love.

'Sit forward, Sahira, let me brush your hair. I have missed brushing your hair.' Ammaji took a large handful of my hair and held it out in the air, and then let it fall, bit by bit, like a curtain back onto my shoulder blade. 'It is much shorter now, but not as short as Hana's,' she said. 'I found it hard to recognise her when I saw her again. I am quite sure that her father was not so happy, either. It does not suit her, I think. Or perhaps, I am too used to a Hana with long and beautiful hair.'

'It was best to have our hair short in England, especially in the winter, when it took so long to dry. Hana was very upset when she saw herself without her thick, black hair.'

Ammaji began to comb my hair slowly, holding each parting of hair just below the running comb. It soothed me so and I closed my eyes. We neither of us spoke until she had finished and let my head rest back against the pillow.

'There,' she said. 'Now you must sleep.'

Obediently, I pulled the *rezai* up to my chin and closed my eyes. The night was not cold and I would probably pull it back down later, but for now it was a comfort to be wrapped up in its warmth.

Ammaji bent down and kissed my forehead. '*Shubakhair, meri beyti*. I must be going to bed also. I am feeling my age these days.' She rubbed her neck. 'The cold of the monsoons makes my body ache a little more than before.'

She left me in silence again. I closed my eyes and made my limbs, my stomach, my head lie completely still and sink down slowly, slowly into the mattress beneath me. The rain was starting up outside. Soon, it would be heavy and pattering loudly against my windows. I listened for it and made out in its rhythm, a gentle lullaby.

Chapter Twenty-Nine

The next day I went to see Laila. During the short drive to her house, I felt oddly apprehensive. I had spoken to her on the telephone that morning and she had sounded different, her voice almost unrecognisable. Talking to her, I realised that my sister, who had always been strong and bold, was now a little fragile.

I was met at the door by Suha, smiling and anxious. She hugged me tightly and led me into the house.

'Now, I must tell you this before you see Laila,' she whispered to me. 'She is not yet completely recovered, and still has some pain in her legs so that she cannot walk.' She watched for the response on my face, and then muttered, 'Ammaji has not told you of this.'

I shook my head. 'No. When I asked Ammaji about Laila, she was vague, which is unusual for her. Ordinarily, she gives more information than the question requires. Abbaji, too, was reluctant to say much about her condition.'

Suha nodded and led me into the dining room. There, at the table, so that the late morning light fell fully on her, sat Laila, in a wide chair that was laden with cushions, underneath her and also supporting her back. Her feet were raised on a small footstool. She smiled when she saw me and held out her hands for a hug. I bent down low and kissed her ashen cheeks. Her skin was rough from the scratches and the stitches that were still prominent. She had lost much weight and I could feel the outline of her ribs under her clothes.

Laila pulled away from me, but still held onto my arms.

'Now, Sahira,' she said sternly, 'do not look at me with such sorrow. I am not altogether all right, but I am most definitely better than I was a month ago. Look.'

She pursed her lips tight and, with great concentration, she lifted her right leg off its footstool and let it hang for a second. Then, with even greater concentration on her still pretty face, she raised it back up, this time without the aid of her hand. She breathed heavily and fast, and said with a faint smile, 'There you see, there is some strength there. I will need to practise more, but I will soon be walking, you will see.'

There was such determination on her face that I nodded, saying, 'Yes, Laila, *Inshallah*, you will.'

'Now, let us eat.' Laila pushed me gently away, pointing at the seat beside her. 'Sit down here. Now where is Suha?' She looked about her. 'Ah, she has gone to get the food. I have sent the entire household away. Even the servants, for they fuss about me and it makes me feel a greater invalid, as though I am a cripple and have no hope. Even Nasir has brought in a nurse - Susie, she is called - to watch over me all day, and all night also. I am very cross with him.'

'She is not watching over you now,' I observed.

'No, I sent her away, also. She has gone to see a movie, one with Dilip Kumar... I cannot remember its name. She is quite crazy about films and is always talking about them. She has all the up-to-date knowledge about them. I think it is her sincere ambition to become a film star herself. When she thinks I am asleep, she practises all sorts of gestures and facial expressions in front of the mirror. It is most amusing. And, she wears some interesting clothes; she is very modern, very Western in her outfits.'

Suha, who had come back in with lunch, nodded and whistled. 'Oh, Susie is very daring. Such a low-cut neckline on her *kurta*. All the men that she meets today will enjoy themselves very much. She is not clever to go to the cinema dressed like that.'

'Oh, she is the sort of girl who enjoys that kind of attention.' Laila wriggled on her cushions and manoeuvred an orange one a more comfortable position.

'She is most definitely that!' Suha suddenly swung her hips, pouted her lips and stuck out her chest, and we laughed uncontrollably.

Three sisters laughing under the darkening monsoon sky. Soon the rains would come down. I sighed; it was good to laugh again with my sisters.

'We will go and see a film together while you are here, Sahira, all of us. It will be a grand family gathering. It will be good for us all, and Ammaji will enjoy it.' Suha began to put out some *chana daal* onto my plate. 'It will do her some good. Have you noticed anything about her, Sahira? Does she seem changed since you left us?' Suha became suddenly very serious.

'Yes,' I replied to her question after some thought. Ammaji *had* changed. She seemed somehow more frail and yet more strong than I had ever known her to be. It was the strangest kind of contradiction. 'Yes, I have seen a change in her. She is slower in taking offence, but full of deliberation, as though her heart has been re-shaped. I was surprised that she did not want to come with me today. That is quite unlike her.'

'It is.' Laila spoke with her eyes cast down and a slight tremble in her voice. 'She is still very anxious about me, and she does not talk about it much. It hurts her to see me, even though I am recovering. Most unusually, she does not fuss, just sits by my side and talks very quietly to me, and brushes my hair and brings me warm milk.'

I thought of the night before, when Ammaji had done the same for me. Yes, I realised, that was her way of bringing comfort, both to us and to herself.

'And how do you find Isa?' I asked Laila.

My sister's face lit up. 'Oh, Sahira,' she said happily, 'he has made me smile again. Noor is being most troublesome.' She frowned. 'She is but a year old and does not understand what has happened. Now, that I am back home, she wishes to be by my side always. Of course, I love her truly, but I am finding her very exhausting. She no longer goes to Nasir or her grandparents, and even refuses her beloved *aya*. Only Abbaji can console her. She has always been his favourite. But how often can Abbaji take her away or come here to distract her?' Laila sighed. 'At least Isa has adjusted back to us. I am thankful to you both for taking good care of him.'

Laila swallowed the piece of *paratha* that she had been chewing on before saying, 'Isa talks a lot about Sami. And always with a smile on his face. I am sure that Nasir is jealous of Isa's fondness for his Sami Khalujaan-' suddenly, she winced in pain and put her hand down to her left thigh. 'It is all right,' she said, rubbing her leg. 'It happens sometimes. I will take my tablets shortly.'

'I will get them for you.' Suha rose and went to a bureau by the window, saying as she went, 'You know, Sahira, Sami would be good as a father. I have always thought that. He will be a father that involves himself with his children, and does not think that raising them is the mother's duty. It is an important conviction, one that comes from deep within. He is not like the many Indian men who are busy with their own needs and fulfilments. He is not the selfish type. Am I right?'

Suha came back to the dining table, bringing with her Laila's tablets and a glass of water.

I nodded and said quietly, 'Yes, of course you are.'

Suha looked at me intently. 'Why have you become shy all of a sudden, Sahira? Is the talk of having your own children so embarrassing? Surely not.'

I smiled weakly and stayed quite silent. I hoped that Laila might speak up on some other matter, but Laila, of course, my shrewd Laila, did not.

'I don't believe that Sahira is shy about the prospect of motherhood. I think something entirely different is making her so uncomfortable that she wriggles in her seat, and finds the *aloo begun* hard to swallow suddenly.'

'I don't know what you are talking about, Laila,' I said with feeling. 'You or Suha. I am not shy, or uncomfortable about this topic. I am merely, merely...' I struggled to find the words. 'It is simply that I have not thought about the matter of children just yet.'

'Oh, that cannot be true!' Suha exclaimed. 'Do you expect us to believe that you have been married for almost one year, and not considered the matter of children yet?' She shook her finger at me, chewing as she spoke, her elbows resting on the beige table cloth.

'No, you are right, Suha.' Laila nodded her head with enthusiasm. 'And that also when Ammaji has written to you on this specific subject. You may not have written back, Sahira, but you cannot have been completely oblivious-'

'No,' I interjected, 'but maybe I am just tired of having to think about it. Maybe I do not want to. Maybe, in fact, I am quite happy without children.'

'Or,' Laila said with a frivolous smile, 'perhaps it is that you do not want to have children with *Sami*?' Laila's eyes widened as she realised that she had hit a nerve. 'Oh, I see. I was only teasing, but I see now that that is how it is!'

I let out a sigh. I was defeated. My sisters would not let this go. They had unpeeled some part of a secret and would now have it all.

'Yes,' I answered, defenceless. 'That is how it is.'

'But why?' Suha had stopped eating. She leant forward, concerned.

I shook my head.

'I do not know why. It is a feeling that I get when I think of having a child. There comes up an obstruction that will not move. I have it here, in the pit of my stomach, as though it is something that would be wrong.'

'Wrong? But, *pugli*, that is silly. Where has such a feeling come from? It cannot have been there when you said yes to his *rishtaa*, when you made that decision on your own, without the advice of anyone else.'

'I did not know then... I did not think of that. I thought that I would grow to love him. That is how it should be, is it not?'

'It is how it should be. It is how it usually is.' Laila tilted her head to one side in a way that I remembered so well, and spoke in that hushed, thoughtful manner of hers. 'But for you, I think, it would have always been different. For you, no matter whose *rishtaa* you were to accept, your married life would have been something else.'

'I have tried...' I fell silent. Had I tried? With all the strength and will within me? That was not an easy question to answer. Sami was a most wonderful husband, but still my heart had been unrelenting.

'Do you feel nothing for him, then?' Suha frowned.

I shrugged. 'I have an affection for him.'

Suha made a face and stuck out her tongue. 'An affection? What is that? A sentiment that one has for their *budi* great-aunt whose mind has long gone?' She sighed and sat back in her chair. 'Still, I suppose it is something. I am glad that you are not completely made out of stone.'

I sat up straight and glared at her. I was hurt by these words but inside I knew them to be true. A stone was what I was; most cruel and undeserving.

Laila was shaking her head and then, suddenly, as though she had caught some fragment of my closed thoughts, she asked, 'And who is this Michael? Isa has spoken of him many times.'

'What?' my voice came out as a high pitch, not quite a shriek but certainly something startled. I was not prepared for the mentioning of his name, and I felt a panic rise within me and my heart beat faster. A heat rose through my stiffened body and I could not answer immediately.

I was lucky, for Suha had started to talk of the meal that we were eating, saying to Laila, 'This is a most tasty *palak*. Your *bawrchi* is really quite special.'

Laila nodded. 'Mmm, she has been in the family for so many years and is quite old now. I do not know how we shall manage when she leave us…'

'Michael is someone that we met while staying in Alhama,' I said at last, when my thoughts had steadied and then, anxious to speak of something more neutral, I added, 'We made some other good friends there, I am sure Isa has mentioned them, as well.'

Laila nodded. 'Yes, indeed. He talks about a farm and a swimming pool, and a little boy, Jax, and also his father, whose name is… ah, I cannot remember; this injury has made my memory very poor.'

'Elias,' I told her gladly. 'His name is Elias. They are Spanish. Jax and Isa became very good friends. I think Jax will miss Isa very much.'

I thought about those weeks spent in Andalusia, such pleasurable, heady days that seemed so far in the past now, that they could have been a figment of my imagination. I smiled to myself.

'Yes, he enjoyed himself very much.'

I told my sisters about Elias's family farm, their acres of vineyards and their olive groves, of the purple-topped mountains of the Sierra de Loja range, of the afternoon that we spent there when the sun beat down and the water in the swimming pool sparkled a brilliant blue, and we ate paella and drank the rich grape juice. I remembered it as a fine day, a day that glittered in my mind. Faded was the memory of my displeasure when I discovered that Sami had been drinking too much wine and speaking in a mindless manner.

'But this Michael is not Spanish,' Laila said when I had finished. 'Of course, Isa is young and so he talks of things that are sometimes confused, but he said something about this Michael person that made him sound like an *Angrezi*, a *gora*. I cannot remember what it was exactly, but it was something nonetheless.'

I sighed, for I was forced to think and talk about Michael once again, when I was trying so very hard, if not to forget him, at least to bury him for a while.

'Yes, he was an *Angrezi*. He had come to Spain for a holiday, and then he stayed to photograph it.'

I said this tiny piece about him and hoped that it would be enough, but Laila was intrigued. 'So, how did you meet him? I understand that El-i-ass is a business acquaintance but this Michael... how did you meet him?'

I shrugged and said in as an indifferent manner as I could, 'He lived in Alhama, and was a friend of Elias. That is how we came to know him.'

'But you met him at some lake when you were with Isa.' Laila persisted in her questions.

I nodded impatiently. 'Yes, yes, that is correct. He happened to be at Lake Bermejalis when I took Isa there one day. I spoke to him and found out that he lived in Alhama and knew Elias. He helped Isa to build a fort with the sand, and then we offered him a lift back to Alhama with us.'

'He has also given Isa a toy, a sailing boat that is most wonderful. Such a present surely shows that he knew you well and was very fond of Isa.'

'Yes, I suppose it does.' I looked up at Laila and managed to say brightly, 'Of course, he was very fond of Isa. He is a wonderful boy.'

Laila looked pleased. 'I think it is his smile that makes him so. It is a beautiful smile, is it not?'

I nodded. 'I shall miss it very much when I leave here.'

'Oh, do not talk of going, Sahira,' Suha said sharply. 'You have only just arrived...' She stopped suddenly and laughed. 'There, I have become a proper mother, for I sound just like Ammaji.'

'You do.' Laila shook her head in mischief. 'I will tell her that. She will be most pleased about it.'

Suha winked at Laila. 'She will certainly feel gratified that one of her daughters, at last, understands how she feels.' She turned to me with a more serious face. 'When do you go, Sahira? I know that you are not staying for long.'

'I will be here for only one week, *haftey ke din jary-oun.*'

'Saturday? Oh, that is a shame. You shall miss the *mehndi* of Sarwat Kabir. She is a nice girl. Ammaji is particularly fond of her. Perhaps because she is so demure,' Laila said. 'My *sas* is very disappointed that Sarwat is not marrying her own sister's son.'

'Oh yes, very many mothers with *ladli* bachelor sons are disappointed with this marriage,' Suha said with glee. 'Sarwat was quite a favourite amongst them, and now they shall have to look elsewhere. It is most amusing the expressions on the faces of disappointed doting mothers.'

Laila slowly pushed her plate to one side and rested her arms on the table. 'Although, now of course, my *sas* will be pestering me to find a suitable girl for her darling *bhanja*. I would not mind, really, but her sister is very choosy. There is always something wrong with any poor girl who is suggested to her - this one's nose is too long, that one's hair is too frizzy and all the children will have frizzy hair also. Goodness knows how she managed to find a daughter-in-law for her eldest son.'

'Mothers of sons are always choosy,' Suha observed. 'They become such horrible snobs, you know, because the poor mothers of daughters are so eager to please them. It is most unfair.'

'Mmm.' Laila looked tired now. I noticed that her eyes were pink and her skin had become quite pale.

Suha leant across and rubbed Laila's shoulder. 'You should go to bed now. We must take care not to tire you out; otherwise we shall not be allowed to visit you again. Come, Sahira and I shall put you to bed.'

Laila shook her head and pleaded, 'No, please do not do that. I spend so much time being made to rest, made to lie down. I have enjoyed this time with you both. I feel much better for it. It is true that I am tired, but you have helped my mental state enormously. Just help me to the settee, and then sit with me until Susie returns.'

Suha stood up. 'All right, then. I suppose everyone will be back soon. And, of course, Sahira must stay to say her salaams to your in-laws.'

It was not easy to move Laila from the dining room into the drawing room. She had a wheelchair to transport her from one room to the other, but getting her into and out of that was still a manual job. Suha had done it before and so was more confident than I, but even so, we were both awkward and clumsy, and Laila, although she must have been in some pain with the twists and turns of our rather inept hands, only let out a cry of pain twice. Such stifled, brave cries they were that I was reminded of Isa when he had come to us just after the earthquake, and I felt immensely proud of Laila then.

Finally, we delivered Laila to her settee, set her feet upon it and let her alone, breathing heavily with beads of sweat forming on her brow. I wiped these away and fetched a drink of water, which she took gratefully and drank down fast.

We stayed by her side for the rest of the afternoon. It was a pleasant spot where the settee had been placed, beside a large window that looked out onto the garden. It was bright out there, all the colours of nature resplendent in the sunshine. The light that came through the window lit up Laila's face, giving it a little colour once more.

She moved her legs slightly. 'I must ask Susie to help me with my exercises tonight. I need to get more strength into them.' Closing her eyes, she muttered, 'Talk to me please, Sahira. Do not be quiet, even though you are sad for me. I will not have you here for very long and I do not want all that time to be spent in a sorry silence.'

'I... I...' I shifted uncomfortably in my chair. The things that were on my mind were not the things that I wished Laila to hear. I did not want her to know that my heart ached for her, that I had felt slightly ill when moving her and supporting the flat and insubstantial frame of her body that once had been clothed in generous flesh.

'Come, Sahira.' Laila was sounding oh so tired and also impatient. 'You have not seen me for almost one year; surely there must be something to talk about?'

Suha, who had been placing a cushion under Laila's calves, sat down by her feet and raised them up onto her lap. Her eyes were twinkling and she was smiling.

'Well, I know of something that Sahira will be interested in. I am sure that even she will have something to say about it.'

Laila opened her eyes and said with a little effort, 'Sahira must know already. Sami will have told her.'

Both my sisters were smiling playfully; even Laila's eyes gleamed. *There was something of intrigue there*, I thought. *Some piece of gossip that delights their minds*. However, although I thought very hard, I could not think of anything of intrigue that Sami had told me recently.

I raised my eyebrows. 'Sami has told me nothing that would make you two smile so. What is it? What is your piece of news?'

Suha bit her lip and looked at Laila contritely.

'Do you think it is our place to tell Sahira this news? Should it not be up to her *sas* to tell her? After all, if Sami has not mentioned it then-'

'Oh, tell her the news.' Laila laid her head back on her pillow. 'You have already started. All of Sikimpur knows. Why should she not? Besides, maybe Sami has not yet been told.'

'Very well then, I shall tell her.' Suha looked quite serious now. 'All of Sikimpur is talking about your *sas*, Sahira. I am surprised that you have not heard, but I suppose you have not seen anyone other than Ammaji and Abbaji. Although, it is strange that Ammaji has not said something about it. She is an amazing woman you know, your *sas*. You are lucky to be her daughter-in-law.'

'What has she done?' I asked impatiently. I had spoken with Ammi just that morning and she had seemed much the same as when we had left Sikimpur, calm and full of sense.

Suha leant forward and whispered, 'There is talk that your *sas* and Professor Goldberg are soon to be married.'

'Married!' This news was such a shock to me that I almost laughed at the improbability of it. 'Ammi and Professor Goldberg? I cannot believe it. Surely, that is just the tongues of Sikimpur's women wagging? It is true they are good friends, but that is because of the friendship between Professor Goldberg and Sami's father. If it was true, Sami would know of it, and if he knew of it, he would certainly have told me. No, no, I cannot believe such a thing.'

Suha shrugged and made a face.

'Those are the rumours, my dear *behen*, that your *sas* and your former tutor have developed a relationship that is far closer than mere friendship.'

I was still inclined to disbelief but Suha seemed so sure. She took Ammi very seriously and would not spread a type of gossip that was both untrue and salacious.

'Well, I shall be seeing her tomorrow,' I said. 'I am sure that she will tell me then. She is not one to be coy and evasive. She believes in being open. And I am quite sure that Sami does not yet know. He would have told me. He has the same openness as his Ammi.'

'Yes,' agreed Suha, 'both the mother and the son are very honest people. Upright and honest. You married well there, Sahira. Uthman is always saying so.'

'Yes,' I said quietly. 'I know.'

Those words of Uthman's came back to me, the advice that he had given me when I had announced, so confidently, my decision to marry Sami: '*Make sure that you can stand by it always, for I do not think he is someone who would know what to do if he were hurt.*'

With my infidelity, I had done enough to hurt Sami, and my excuse that he did not truly love me was a muddled defence. My heart was broken and low, and yet I knew that I would not have my indefensible moment taken away from me.

I would not, I could not.

Chapter Thirty

I arrived at Gulabi Ghar in a state of curiosity.

The lawns around the house were in full bloom and the ground sodden from last night's rain. The air was full of the smell of the soil, the heavy, red earth. On the gravel path that ran alongside the garden, Ammi was doing her daily round of the grounds. She had already waved to us at the sound of the gates being opened and then walked round to where the car had come to a halt. Her face was lively, a silver thread of hair falling delicately upon her soft cheek.

Ammaji, who had come with me, leant over and whispered, 'She seems very happy to see you.'

And she was right. Ammi hugged me tightly and I could smell the sweet perfume of talcum powder upon her neck. There was a vitality about her and I wondered at the veracity of what Suha had told me.

'Sahira *beyti*. Goodness, can it be that you are even more lovely than when you left us? Perhaps it is your hair?' She stroked it gently. 'This new style makes you appear less serious.' She turned to Ammaji. '*Asalaam-alaikum*, Razia Begum. It is good to see you again. We have not seen each other for almost two weeks now. You must tell me about what has been happening at Shamshad Bagh. We shall have a good, lengthy chat.'

Ammaji, however, would only stay for a cup of afternoon tea. The rain had started up again and the window panes were thick with the monsoon's flow.

'I will go once the rain has stopped,' she said. 'I want to see Laila on the way home. I have not seen her for a few days now and I have some *gajar ka halwa* for her. It is her favourite sweet. It helped her greatly when she was in labour with Noor.'

When she was gone, Ammi pulled a blanket around herself. She drew her right leg out and rubbed her knee tenderly.

'My arthritis is particularly bad at this time of the year. If my mother were alive she would tell me that it is because I used to walk about in the rain too much. She would tell me that it was all her scolding, which I had ignored, coming back to haunt me.'

I drew a footstool alongside her and began to massage her knee with my hands. Slow, intense movements, almost like dough that was being kneaded. Ammi moved her own hand away and sat back.

'How simple my mother was. When we first brought a television into the house, she would not sit in the same room as it because she was scared that the men on the screen could also see her. She died only a few months before you and Sami were married. I think she was glad to pass away, for she disapproved of the India that was produced when the British left.'

Ammi smiled wistfully at the thought of her halcyon days. 'She certainly did not approve of my participation in the Independence movement, but she did not stop me. My father understood, although he was wary of women going out in public and being with men of unknown character. Even when Nehru came to our house and shook his hand, he remained sceptical. He did not see that we women were discovering our own voices, striving for *our* independence. That was a most historical time, but then—' Ammi sighed and shook her head.

I began to massage her other knee. 'What then?'

'Then, Pakistan was born,' Ammi continued, 'with much bloodshed and sacrifice. All those horrors endured by people crossing the border made us wonder if Jinnah's persistence in setting up a Muslim state was altogether a wise one. Even today, there is still such unrest along our borders.'

I was not a true politician like Ammi, but I had an opinion on what I knew. Everybody in India had an opinion on this topic, from the *paliwallah* in the street to the tailors in their shops. Since the war of 1965, India's recent conflicts with Pakistan had been much in the news; our newspapers and radio were full of them.

'It is hard to see how we may reach a peace with Pakistan when both countries cannot agree about Kashmir,' I said.

Ammi nodded. 'Yes, you are right. For any kind of peace there must be dialogue that is open-minded.' She took my hand from her knee. 'That is enough, *beyti*. It is feeling much better now. Thank you.' She placed the blanket back over her knee. 'I simply cannot see how Kashmir will prosper under the Pakistani flag. The whole of Pakistan is just a collection of regions, each of which is full of its own tribal laws and traditions. It will take a very strong and charismatic leader to realise Jinnah's dream.'

I put my own feet up on the footstool. The rain had started again and it was almost dark outside.

'Sami does not agree with you about Pakistan,' I said. 'He has much hope for the new state.'

Ammi sniffed. 'Yes, he is young and has all the optimism of youth. However, he has not lived through the struggle, only seen the legacy of it. Even the British gave up their hope of controlling the northern tribes; they left them alone in the end.'

'No.' I drew my legs up onto the settee and hugged my knees. 'Even the British could not control their natures or gain an advantage over their mountainous lands. But then, they had enough of the rest of India to satisfy them.' I paused a little before saying, 'I do hope that Pakistan will succeed. It is young, very young...'

'In that, I fear, is the reason that it will fail,' Ammi reflected. 'The tribes have been there for centuries. They will not change their ways. Why should they? A new Islamic union does not give them a strong enough incentive.'

'Still, I hope that it will succeed and that Pakistan will fulfil its promise. Now that it has come about, surely we must all hope for this; that the regions will recognise their responsibility to their people.'

Ammi rose slowly from her chair and began to fold her blanket. 'That is because you are an idealist. You and Sami, and most of your generation. That is good. We, too, were idealists in our youth, and we rooted out British rule. Who knows what sort of revolution your generation will bring?'

She pulled the curtains closed and flicked on the light switch. The single bulb above us lit up and then began to flicker, threatening to go, but instead decided to stay on. I wondered how long the electricity would last tonight. Until we went to bed? More likely we would be saying goodnight to each other by candlelight.

'Maybe,' Ammi said wryly, 'you will bring about some reliable electricity to our free India. That would be a revolution indeed.'

I stayed with Ammi for three days in total and enjoyed myself very much there. She led a very simple life, mostly in her own home, busy with her hands and her mind. Friends would come to visit her regularly, especially at lunchtimes. On the second day of my stay, three of her female friends called on her.

After lunch, Ammi brought out her silver filigree *paan* box and took out several betel leaves from one of its compartments. She placed them on a white cloth and, using a small silver spoon, she spread slaked lime and *chum chum* on each of them. Then she began to line each leaf with an assortment of flavours. For the sweet *paan* she used gulkand and fennel seeds, for the savoury *paan* she scattered crushed areca nut and katha paste to freshen the breath of her guests. Then, with great dexterity, she rolled the leaves up tight and passed them round. I was not a great lover of *paan* for I found the flavour of the leaf altogether unpleasant. I was the only one of the party to refuse one.

Popping a sweet *paan* into her mouth, Mrs Gulshan Kamran, a musical woman who spoke with an asthmatic wheeze, made her way to the gramophone that stood on a fine rosewood cabinet. In her hand she held a shiny black gramophone record.

'A good meal always makes me want to listen to music,' she said. 'I have brought this particular recording for us to listen to. I would like to hear what you all think of it.'

She placed the record on the turntable and set the needle in a groove. There was a brief crackling, and then music and a voice, a man's lilting voice, rose up in a song.

'Ah,' nodded Dr Charu Dammani in approval. 'The sweet tones of Mohammed Rafi.' She cocked her head closer to the funnel of the gramophone. 'One can almost see the musical notes as he sings them. His voice is so clear that it seems to hang in the air.'

Miss Jamilia Sheikh, whose hair was a brilliant bouffant, agreed. 'Yes, he is fortunate in that he is both a good singer and has a good voice, for one does not have to have one in order to have the other. There are many who have beautiful voices but their interpretation of songs lets them down. It is why Ms Bhosle cannot be considered to be as accomplished - or, perhaps, it is more correct to say, as delightful to listen to - as her sister, the excellent Ms Mangeshkar.'

'Oh, no, no!' Dr Dammani was shocked and shook her finger at Miss Sheikh. 'Surely it is not possible for you to be saying such a thing? Ms Asha's voice is very exactly right for the type of songs that she is to be singing. Her style is not being so serious or as sentimental as Ms Lata's. She is an altogether more playful songstress.'

'But my dear Charu,' Miss Sheikh said soothingly, 'that is exactly what I am saying. I am not denigrating your Ms Bhosle. I am merely stating the very genuine fact that she is simply not carrying the same gravitas as Ms Lata.'.

'Enough, enough!' Ammi spat her *paan* juice into a silver pot and held her hand up to stop them. 'You two are always turning your discussions into a conflict. Let us listen to this lovely music in some peace. Let us enjoy it. After all, Gulshan has brought her record for us to listen to and enjoy.'

'Peace and enjoyment! You are sounding like those hippies that one is finding everywhere around Sikimpur these days,' laughed Mrs Kamran lightly.

Dr Dammani giggled like a naughty school girl. 'Oh yes, they are certainly enjoying themselves all over Sikimpur. In our public parks, at the back of the bus stations, everywhere one looks they are there. Although, they are most definitely not being at all peaceful in their pursuit of enjoyment.'

Miss Sheikh grimaced in disgust, her bouffant hair shining like a halo as it caught the afternoon sun. 'Indeed, they are most vulgar, so very vulgar! They are having too much freedom and too little respect for the morals of the Indian peoples whose country this is.'

'Oh, but they are not exhibiting their disrespect on purpose,' said Dr Dammani. 'It is the state of their minds that allows them to behave so freely with one another. They are always taking that... what is it? Oh, I do not know the real word for it, but it is that *kachra* material that gives them *nasha*. It helps them in their quest, I believe, for spiritual perfection.'

Ammi, who had been carefully putting her silver *paan* box back into its drawer, turned to face her friends.

'It is an altogether different type of spiritualism that they seek. They do not want to follow a particular religion or God, but an idea, a philosophy, one that will give them some guidance in their lives.'

'In that they are very right to do so.' Miss Sheikh, who was a staunch member of the Communist Party, spoke up with some passion. 'It is as Marx says, that religion is the opiate of the people. And, undeniably, India is drowning in religion. Our government should rigorously enforce India's status as a secular nation.'

Ammi laughed aloud. 'Oh, we both know that term is used for convenience, and that those who rule us seek the advice of holy men in rags. In fact, the more tattered their rags and the more ascetic their appearance, the more holy and wise they are thought to be. No, India cannot be governed without religion. It is rooted in its soil and flows freely in its rivers.'

Miss Sheikh shook her finger at her three friends. 'And what about all the holidays that are given because of these religions? Such a quantity of labour that is lost! There is altogether too much religion in this country.'

Mrs Kamran nodded vigorously. 'Religions, cultures, traditions. India is overflowing with all these things. I wonder how she shall survive as one nation. The thread that is holding her together is artificial. After all, what do the law makers of Delhi have in common with the Dravidians of Tamil Nadu?'

'I suppose as much as they have with the people who live in Delhi's slums.' I spoke up for the first time during that conversation, blushing as I did so.

Mrs Kamran peered at me through her broad-rimmed spectacles. 'Ah, my dear I had quite forgotten that you were sitting here with us. I am very glad that you have spoken, for you represent the opinions of the next generation of rulers, so to speak. I hope you do not mind if I ask of your age? No more than twenty-three, twenty-four I think?'

'Twenty-two,' I told her.

Mrs Kamran placed her teacup on the mahogany table beside her and moved a little nearer to me. She nodded her head with joy. 'Born at the birth of Independence! You were not there at the struggle for Independence, but you are the first of the generations that are gaining from it.'

'Now Gulshan,' Dr Dammani cut in with a bemused expression. 'You are a most hearty romantic, and I do not like to be the one to cause you disappointment, but what you have been saying is not strictly being true. Not now that Sami and Sahira have removed themselves from all the benefits that independent India is having to offer, and are currently living in *Welayat*.'

Mrs Kamran peered at me once again, this time with a less friendly expression on her radiant face. '*Arre haun*. I had quite forgotten about your relocating to Eng-land. Tell me, my dear, how are you finding your residency there?'

'It is fine,' I said. 'Now that we are settled there we are quite enjoying ourselves.'

'You are settled? Already? In just a few months after leaving your motherland?' Mrs Kamran looked at me quizzically. 'Well, I suppose that is the fortune of youth; being able to adjust to the situations that life thrusts upon you. It is a good thing,' she added with an air of begrudging grace.

Feeling like a clown in the spotlight, I smiled nervously, but the eyes that were upon me did not look away. I cleared my throat and stood up from my seat.

'I think that I will take a walk in the garden, before the rain begins again. The sky is looking quite dark.'

'Oh!' Mrs Kamran was surprised that I should want to leave in the middle of such a discussion. 'I do hope that it is not I who has made you to leave us.' She sniffed and reached out her hand to take her teacup once again.

'Do not take notice of her, Sahira, *beyti*.' Miss Sheikh smiled politely. 'We have all learnt to ignore the nature of her tongue. She has a streak that is wicked and likes to make people uncomfortable.'

'Of course I do not!' Mrs Kamran became at once defensive. 'I am simply interested in...'

I shook my head quickly. 'No, no, of course not. I really would like to walk around the garden for a bit. It has been very good to see you all again.'

As I walked with a stark self-consciousness out of the room, I caught Ammi's eye. She was looking at me with a curious smile and her eyebrows raised.

When I had left the room and was some way down the corridor, I heard Miss Sheikh's amused voice. 'You must watch your daughter-in-law, Amina. She has only just gone to England and already she has learnt the *Angrezi* way of diplomacy, of slipping out of a tricky situation.'

There was an almost imperceptible pause, and then I heard Dr Dammani. 'Oh, but surely Amina will be knowing all about her daughter-in-law from her good friend, Professor Goldberg.'

I stopped when I heard this and held my breath to hear Ammi's reply, but I could not for she spoke with too low a voice. I sighed and left them to their own discussions.

Out in the sunshine, I took a while to adjust to the brightness. The cane table and chairs had been put away under the lean-to by the side of the house. The back lawn was in need of some attention. Ammi and her gardener, Rizwan, had neglected it in favour of the shrubbery at the front, which had been carefully tended to after the mess that the earthquake had left.

Today, Rizwan had turned his attention to this back lawn. He was cropping the grass that had begun to grow quite wild. He worked with a slow rhythm, swinging his scythe back and forth, the muscles of his arms tightening and slacking in turn.

From somewhere beyond where Rizwan and I were, I could hear the sound of children's laughter. I shouted a *Salaam* to Rizwan, who broke from his labour to wave back and smile broadly.

'*Asalaam-alaikum*, Sahira Bibi. How are you? It is good that you have come. Ruqaya has been asking about you.'

I nodded and wandered onward towards the high, back wall of the garden. I soon caught sight of the children playing to one side of a small, lop-sided building, their home that Rizwan had built himself many years ago when he had married and brought home his new bride. In the years that had passed, and as each of his three children had been born, he had expanded it with two more rooms made of crude stone and mud to accommodate them. The roof that had once been made from corrugated iron was now made from intertwining grasses, so thick that even the heavy rains of the monsoon could not violate it.

Rizwan's children were grubby little things. The two older ones – a seven-year old boy and his five-year old sister - had a ball with which they played, throwing it to each other, dropping it and laughing with the effort. The baby lay on a rough grass mat fast asleep, while his mother, Ruqaya, sat some way off. She smiled when she saw me and rose hurriedly, pulling the *pallo* of her sari around her dark and slender waist and tucking it into the waistband of her *lehenga*. She had been little more than a child herself when I had left here, her body so small and delicate compared to the large, round belly that had held her third child.

'*Asalaam-alaikum*, Sahira Bibi, *keyse hein ap*?' She spoke slowly with an accent that was strongly Maharashtrian. She obviously remembered the trouble that I had had understanding her.

'*Wasalaam-alaikum*, Ruqaya. I am well.' I looked at the children. 'They are much grown since I last saw them. They must be going to school now?'

She nodded her head proudly. 'Both are at St George's. Yahya is in class 2 and Lubna in kindergarten. Yahya is very good at learning; he came top of his class last term.'

'That is good,' I said. And it was. Coming top of the class at St George's was an achievement. It was a good school, very middle-class, and I knew that it was Ammi who was paying for the children's education.

'We hope they will go to the college,' continued Ruqaya proudly. 'Even Lubna.'

I nodded. 'Good.'

'Yes. It is important for girls to know reading and writing. Then they can work as a man does, and also to teach their own children. It is important for their futures.'

I could hear in her conviction the voice of Ammi. Ruqaya had come to Gulabi Ghar uneducated, but Ammi had taught her to read and write Urdu and would, I was sure, encourage her to learn some English, too. Her children would be learning English at their middle-class school. I wondered what Rizwan thought of this, the rest of his family learning while he worked away with his hands.

'Our people educate their sons but have no thought for their girls. I do not want that for my girls.' Ruqaya spoke with such pride that her cheeks reddened.

'No,' I agreed. 'Every girl deserves more.'

From behind us there came the noise of the baby awakening, a gurgling, sucking sound followed by a small cry, crying for a mother, a demand for attention rather than any real distress. The little boy moved restlessly on his back and began to kick his legs. Tiny feet with tiny toes. On his ankle was a black thread and his eyes were lined with black kohl, both there to ward off the evil eye. He was completely naked save for that black thread. Ruqaya picked him up and kissed him as she held him in her arms. I gave him a finger to play with and he clasped it tightly like a rescuing vine, and giggled.

Laughing, Ruqaya called over her other two and handed them the baby. The children stared at me, muttering their '*Salaam, Sahira Bibi*' in quiet, well-rehearsed voices, before taking their brother away to play with the ball.

Ruqaya turned to the crude outdoor stove on which a fat, bubbling pot sat.

'I was just making some *chai*,' she said. 'Come and have some. I made extra for Rizwan, but he is busy today and I do not think he will come. You come and join me instead.'

Already I was shaking my head, but Ruqaya, oblivious to it, called Yahya over and told him to bring me out a chair. Then, looking up, she called out for two chairs for she had seen that Ammi had come out to see us. Smiling and waving, Ammi made her way to where the baby sat. She kneeled down and rolled a ball to him, smiling with indulgence.

'*Shukria* Ruqaya. Yes, I will take a cup of *chai*. It is turning chilly now.' Ammi turned to me and said, 'You are safe now. My friends have left for their own homes.' She turned her attention back to the baby and tickled his round belly.

'I hope that I did not seem rude,' I said to her. 'I did not mean to be rude by leaving. I was, in fact, coming in soon to say *Khudahafiz* to them.'

Ammi waved my apology away. '*Kohi baat nahin*. They are my friends and not yours, and they were not talking about the things that interest you. Anyway, it is good that you have come out to see Ruqaya. She often asks about you and how you are doing in London.'

I smiled at this. For the simple people of India, there was only one place they knew in England and that was London. Anybody who left India for England lived in London, regardless of where they actually lived.

I helped Yahya with the chairs that he had brought out. I could see that they were rarely used, for they still had their shiny metal frames and pristine cushions. The family preferred to sit on the ground and the chairs were only brought out when the Burra Memsahib came to see them. I sat down on one of them and took the teacup that Ruqaya handed to me. The *chai* in it was sweet and milky. I had not tasted such *chai* for a very long time and I found it comforting, something of my past and of my homeland that was good.

Ruqaya came to sit beside me, resting her bottom on a low, wooden stool. She asked me many questions about London, and shivered and giggled when I told her about snow and would not believe me when I told her that the English made their *chai* with teabags and no milk.

'But how can they drink it with such a *kurwa* taste!' she exclaimed. 'The leaves must boil with the milk and sugar to bring out their full flavour!'

The children came to stand by her side when I spoke of rainbows; they were fascinated to learn that an arc of colours filled the sky when the rain and the sun came out together.

'Can we go to England, Mama! I want to see the ra-in-boes,' they shouted in delight.

'Maybe, if you are good at your lessons you can go to study in England,' Ammi told the children.

Ruqaya rose and began to collect the teacups together. '*Arre*, Burra Memsahib, that is a good dream, but I do not think it is one for us. We are the poor people and it takes much money to send one person to England. Also, I do not want my children to be so far from me. I hope that when Lubna marries she will find a home close to us, and a husband who will allow her to visit her father's house.'

She went into her little house and we could hear the clang of pans being taken down from their wooden pegs and being set upon the two ring stove. She reappeared in the doorway, carrying with her a large wicker pannier in which she had put a knife, three muddied potatoes, an onion, two aubergines with shiny purple skins and two red apples. She sat a few metres away from us and began to work away with the knife. She sang to herself as she worked, her voice thin and reedy. Occasionally, she would call the children over and hand them a piece of apple to munch on.

I watched her for a bit before turning to Ammi and asking, 'And how about you, Ammi? I know that you have many things to occupy you here, but while we are in England maybe you would like to visit?'

Ammi looked at me closely and then smiled. 'Jamilia was right. I see you have indeed picked up something of the *Angrezi's* diplomacy. You have been listening to the rumours that go around this place regarding me. You are right, I have many things here that require my attention, but I do not have the one thing that you are thinking of.'

I raised my eyebrows with a feigned innocence. 'I am only thinking that it would be a shame for you to miss the opportunity-'

Ammi pulled the *pallo* of her sari tightly around her shoulders. 'Sahira *beyti*, there is no need to be so polite with me. I know that I am the object of Sikimpur gossip these days and, although I know that your family are not amongst those who spread such rumours, I cannot believe that one of them has not mentioned to you–'

'Yes, you are right,' I cut in abruptly and bit my lip. 'Ammaji did not say anything to me about your engagement to Professor Goldberg.'

'No, I did not think so, for your mother is very loyal.' Ammi nodded in satisfaction.

'It was Suha who told me,' I said quickly, 'but only to tell me, not to speculate, or to spread salacious gossip. Even then, she was not sure whether to say anything or to let you be the one to tell me.'

Ammi pursed her lips and looked quite cross. 'Yet, still she told you.' She looked at me with resolve. 'And now you would like me to tell you. Very well, I will tell you something. I will tell you that there is absolutely no truth to these rumours. The Professor is a friend, a very good friend, who has been a great support to me, but there is only one man to whom I have ever been engaged, and only one man that I shall ever be married to.'

'Oh!'

'I see that is a surprise to you. Well, it was a surprise to me when I heard that I was engaged. That particular rumour began some two weeks ago, but the tongues of Sikimpur society had begun to wag quite freely soon after Sami and you left for England. After all, I was a widow who was visited in her home by a man, so what else could our relationship be?

She smiled at me and touched my knee. 'But these things are really nothing to me. Since when have I cared about the opinions of the Sikimpur women? Maybe I was at fault for not quashing them, but I had a little laugh each time I heard them and thought that I would have some fun also. Besides, who would listen if I tried to set them straight?'

'I am glad that they do not hurt you,' I replied, a little shamefacedly. 'And I am sorry that Suha–'

'Do not worry. I know that your sisters do not speak with the same idleness as others. However, I think they should learn the lessons of your parents rather than their circle of friends.'

'She meant no harm by telling me,' I said tentatively, 'and there was no speculation there.'

'I understand.' Ammi looked up at the ever darkening sky. 'You are right to see the best in Suha, she is a good girl. Now, I think that we have spoken on this topic for long enough. It is time to go back indoors. The skies are becoming thick with clouds and we shall feel the monsoon rain upon us soon.'

She got up off her chair and went to Ruqaya, helping her to bring her assortment of cookware back into the house. I picked up the baby and called out to the children. They came with an obedient skip to me. Lubna took my hand and I led them indoors to their mother.

Ruqaya had lit her stove and the room was beginning to fill with a plume of smoke that soon made its way out through the open door. This room was a kitchen and a living room also. They were separated only by a long, rush mat on the ground.

At one end of the living room a large, square cushion lay on the ground and, beside it, on a crude wooden table, was a battered old wireless. By the cushion lay some school books: reading books with pictures of white children playing on a beach and two hard-backed notebooks with lined paper.

On the ceiling there ran three wires, criss-crossing each other. One led from a light switch to a single, naked light bulb, another to a rickety old ceiling fan, and the third led out of the room.

The kitchen part of the room was low-ceilinged and its rough, brown walls were covered with metal and wooden hooks on which hung a variety of cooking utensils: pans, ladles, knives. One of the walls had been cut into to make a series of shelves. The top shelf held plates, bowls and mugs, while on the lower shelves stood plastic and glass jars filled with whole spices that Ruqaya would grind up to flavour the meals that she made. A wire basket hung from the ceiling and, in this, was an assortment of vegetables: carrots, onions and gnarled green beans.

Ruqaya took the baby from me and shooed the children out to wash their hands. Ammi and I said *Khudahafiz* to them all and left them to themselves, chattering and happy. Above us, the tiny sparrows were flying high, setting off back to their roost. The grey clouds had begun to thicken and there was a smell of moisture in the air. We were due for another deluge. There was a faint rumble of thunder from somewhere to the west of us and then a brief flash of lightning.

I looked at Ammi as the lightning flashed and her beauty at that instance took my breath away. There was such a simplicity to her features; she wore no make-up and the skin on her cheeks was soft. Around her eyes there were tiny lines that were slightly creased by her smile. And, in that moment, I saw in her - reflected quite starkly, quite dramatically – a picture of Sami.

Suddenly she turned to me, as though she could feel my eyes upon her.

'I think, maybe, I have not been as truthful with you as I should,' she said quietly. 'Or, at least, there is perhaps more to the rumours than I have made clear.' She cleared her throat and looked very serious. 'You see, Professor Goldberg did indeed ask me to marry him, some weeks after you went away, in fact. I said no to him then, and he has not asked me again.'

She reached up above her head and pulled at a green leaf from the young neem tree that we were passing under. She broke a piece off and put it into her mouth and began to chew it deliberately. 'I cannot think of a husband for me who is not Sami's father. Besides,' she said slowly, as if to herself, 'to marry a *feringhi* is no simple matter.'

Chapter Thirty-One

All too soon my time in Sikimpur came to an end. It had been a week in which I had been brought back to my past, taking my life with an astonishing ease. It was the best season to return to my homeland, when the rains were on, when the sun did not burn the ground and the grass could grow green once more.

I was not ready to leave it. I was not looking forward to finishing with this innocuous week. This time, when I left Sikimpur, it would not be to an unknown place that gave me a tingle of excitement. Instead, it would be to a Sami whom I had been disloyal to, and with a heart that would forever remember another man. My only consolation was that I was going straight to England; an aeroplane flight to London, followed by a train journey onwards to Leeds, and then Newton Kyme.

Thankfully, I was not returning to Alhama. I could not bear to return there, to live again in Casa Azul, to speak to Elias and Patrine, to be near Lake Bermejalis and the gorge.

Sami had telephoned while I was still at Gulabi Ghar to let me know that he was going back home the next day. He was ready to return to England.

'I will stay in London until you come and then we will go together to Leeds. I hope that is all right with you? I know that you had wanted to visit Córdoba...'

'No, no,' I had reassured him quickly. 'I am very happy about that. I am happy to return to England and not to Spain.'

'Good, good.' Sami had sounded relieved. 'I am glad to hear you say that.'

And so, I was brought to this night, my last one in Sikimpur, and I was once again preparing to leave. Slowly, I folded my clothes and packed them into my solitary suitcase. I did this with a heavy heart, a labyrinth of emotions pressing down on my chest. Ammaji was helping me quietly. We were both listening to the sound that came from Abbaji's drawing room, the sound of laughter and talking, of Abbaji and his friends playing a game of cards: rummy maybe, or coatpees.

'At least, this time you will be going when the weather is still warm,' Ammaji said as she handed two bars of sandalwood soap to me.

I tucked them into the folds of my clothes and nodded. 'It is September now and shall be quite pleasant. I am glad that Aida is coming with me. I shall be glad to have her company on the aeroplane.'

'Mmm, I am glad also. It is a long journey for one to take alone, firstly to Delhi and then on to London. And, although your Abbaji would like very much to come to England one day, the thought of undertaking such a journey just to get from one place to another is altogether most prohibiting.'

'Yes, it takes many hours to reach *Welayat*, but can you imagine those days before the aeroplane, Ammaji? When the people would journey on ship? Those journeys were many days long.'

'Yes, it is true, but I think those were also more romantic journeys, for there were many things for a passenger to see and to do. When we were very young, my Abba would regale the stories that his *Angrezi* officers told of life on board a ship; of the games that they played and the walks along the promenade breathing in the fresh sea air. It sounded most exciting to us as children. However, to sit for many hours in one seat...' Ammaji shuddered. 'It is fortunate that you are young and are able to tolerate such discomfort, and that you will have Aida as company. It was a surprise to us that she decided to stay back in her village for so long. But I am glad that she and her brother have been reconciled somewhat. It will be good for her to know her family once again.'

'I do hope that she will be here tomorrow.'

'Oh, I am sure she will be. Her train is due to arrive here in the morning and your aeroplane leaves at... what time?'

'It is in the afternoon, at four o'clock.'

The voices of Abbaji's friends became louder, being out in the open air now and saying *Khudahafiz* to each other. Soon, they faded altogether and Abbaji came to join us.

'Ah good, you are almost finished with all your packing, I see,' he observed. 'I have brought some *mithai* for you both. They are a gift from Akbar Sahib, for his son has passed his accountancy exams and is soon to be going to America. He was in particularly high spirits this evening.'

He opened the brightly coloured cardboard box that he was carrying and peeled back the lightly greased paper. From inside, he picked out a pale brown *gulab jamun* and broke it in half. He gave one half to me and the other half to Ammaji. Ammaji took her share with one hand, putting it carefully into her mouth, whilst holding her other hand under her chin to catch the crumbs that fell.

'Ah, yes he is a very clever boy,' she mumbled through her full mouth. 'Yunis Akbar. He will do very well in America. Although, being his mother's only son, she must be finding it most difficult to send him away.'

I ate my *gulab jamun* in one go; it was my favourite *mithai*. 'I shall miss these when I am back in England,' I said. 'Even Aida has not managed to make them quite so well.'

'I will send some to you,' Ammaji said with enthusiasm. 'They should be arriving fine at your end. I am sure that Nasreen Begum sends her son and daughter-in-law such items, and they are living in America, which is even farther from Sikimpur than England.' She took another *jamun*, this one a dark brown, and popped it into my mouth whole. 'There, you must have all the *gulab jamun* that are in this box.'

Abbaji and I laughed at her earnest face, and I was sure that, at the corner of her eye there was a single shiny tear, which she wiped away with the end of her sari *pallo*.

When my parents had gone, back to their own beds, I stood awhile by my open window. The scent of the garden with its jasmine, bougainvillea, and roses was brought to me on the soft breeze that was blowing out there. The crickets were chirping and, in the distance, I could hear the blasts of car horns that were still out on the road. The air was warm that night and the sky so clear that it did not look like a monsoon sky. And all of a sudden, I found that I did not want to sleep inside the house that night. I could not bear to leave Sikimpur without having spent some of that night up on the roof.

The door of Abbaji's drawing room creaked as I drew it open, ever so slowly. I stopped still and listened, but I could hear no other stirrings from within the house and so I carried on my way, across the veranda to the side of the house where the stone steps were. I put my hand out to touch the cool, white wall and used it to guide my way up to the flat roof.

When the monsoon rains were again over and the nights became sultry and hot once more, Ammaji would have a large, coarse carpet thrown over the floor of the roof, on top of which would be placed a couple of charpoys so that Abbaji could sleep out there sometimes, where the air was not so stifling and one could smell the heady fragrance of the garden's full blooms. He would take his transistor radio with him and, in the hours of the early morning, would listen to the BBC World Service, while he stretched his body and walked around the boundaries of the rooftop breathing in the evaporating dew.

Tonight, the roof was quite empty, quite dark, with only the fallen leaves of the nearby peepal tree for company. I had brought an old blanket and a winter *rezai* up to the roof with me. I laid them down on the ground. The *rezai* was a bulky thing, heavy with its stuffing and thick cotton; a favourite of Abbaji's, who would wrap it around his shoulders on winter nights when he sat in his drawing room to read.

I took myself to the roof's edge, just by the low wall with its simple pillars, and looked out at the world beyond me. At the far side of the drive stood the old gatehouse with its gloomy windows, now used as a shed by Hana's father to store his tools: muddied spades and ripped sackcloth bags of soil, splintered bits of wood, rusted metal and frayed pieces of twine.

A taxi rolled quietly by the gates of Shamshad Bagh and disappeared down the street. A breeze blew gently through that early night, rustling the leaves of the peepal trees, and there was a bright crescent moon out. A dark silhouette of a bird rose up from amongst the branches of the mango trees, startling me. I took a sharp intake of breath, and in that breath I tasted the thick aroma of roasting peanuts that hung warm in the air. I watched the bird's flight across the ink-spot sky and past the tall advertising boards that were visible from this, my high up position.

Painted on those boards were images of plump, rosy-cheeked babies being fed Marie biscuits and women with beautiful skin because they had used Lux soap. Walking along the streets was the lazy, ambling youth of Sikimpur; thin-hipped men in wide bell-bottom trousers, slick moustaches and their arms around each other's shoulders, joking and chatting gaily. Occasionally, they would stop at a peanut vendors stall; their features lit by the glow of the charcoal, and buy a paper cone of roasted peanuts before continuing on their indolent way.

The better-off youth cruised through Sikimpur night-life in their cars - shiny Fiat 1100s and classy Ambassadors, some leaning out of the windows, idly smoking a cheroot while the transistors on their back seats beat out the tunes and songs of a capricious, untameable love. All of these young men, rich and poor, were adorned in various tight-fitting nylon trousers and brilliant patterned shirts with long and pointed collars.

I felt a loneliness witnessing this lively scene. The breeze was playing with the stray strands of my hair and I felt an unexpected lethargy overtake me. I put both palms of my hands onto the hard, stone surface of the roof wall and looked down to what was below me.

It so happened that I was directly above the spot where my parents had stood on the night of my wedding, waving goodbye to me; Abbaji with his protective, comforting arm around Ammaji, and I remembered their closeness, their love for one another. In the solitude of that rooftop memory, my knees buckled and I came to kneel upon the ground, with my forehead resting on the back of my hands, and I broke down and cried. I sobbed for all the wretched anguish that was behind me and for the unknown that was ahead of me.

I stayed there for some time, in that miserable position, until my sobbing had subsided and I could hold myself once more. Slowly, I stood up, my legs bearing my weight again, and wiped all the wetness off my face. Lying down on the *rezai*, I drew my blanket over me. I had not brought a pillow with me, so I rolled up one end of the *rezai* so that it served as a crude rest for my head. I laid my head down on my makeshift pillow and closed my eyes.

All about me I could hear Sikimpur sounds, but deep within my senses I found myself back in Alhama, with Michael looking down on me with a smile on his face, his eyes a deep indigo under the moon's dim light. Oh, how I wished that he were here with me. I would show him the lights of Sikimpur, have him breathe in the fragrance of jasmine and mangoes, and sit by my side on this roof of Shamshad Bagh.

I wondered what he would make of it all. What would he photograph in this large, alien land of mine? I would never know; that was the sadness of it. I could never know what he thought of anything again. How I hated the goodbye that we had had to say. There was such a striking falsity to it, because he would always be with me. His smile and his eyes and his voice would be in every part of me that would ever live. And, although my heart had done with breaking, I wondered would it ever truly heal? Would I ever want it to? There was a certain sweetness in that pain.

I opened my eyes to see the stars once more and felt the air about me cool a little. There were fresh clouds about now, pulling across the crescent of the moon and casting out the brilliance of starlight. I shivered underneath the blanket and drew it tighter about me, but there was too much chill within me to settle properly. The hardness of the stone roof penetrated through the *rezai* beneath me and I became increasingly uncomfortable.

I fidgeted with a restless spirit and my determination to remain in the open monsoon air began to wane. I could feel it ebbing from the veins and nerves of my body, and soon it overcame my will altogether. I rose slightly unsteadily, holding onto the blanket, clasping it around me with one hand still, and from under it I took out my other hand and picked up the *rezai*. It was somehow heavier now and the blanket fell off my shoulders as I held my arms up high to shake it and then to fold it as best I could.

The gaining breeze had scattered a flush of wet leaves along the path that led me down from the roof and onto the veranda. The air had become still, as though a thunderstorm was about to break, and the sounds from the street outside had grown faint as the threat of the monsoon rain had chased everyone indoors.

It was as I was shutting the doors of Abbaji's drawing room that the rumbling, tumbling sound of thunder came through the lattice doors, and, when the lightning flashed, the bosom of that room was lit up for a brief second. I saw the playing cards that were put neatly away and the hookah standing empty, with its pipe wound around its pewter body. I could feel Abbaji here, a secure, loving presence.

I left the *rezai* and the blanket where the laundry was kept, knowing that I would have to explain them somehow to Ammaji tomorrow. Then I took myself off to bed, with the rain coming down in heavy drops, hitting the window hard. I changed out of my clothes, for they had taken in some of the chill from the outside air. I shivered slightly although it was warm in my bedroom. Lying down quickly in my bed, I pulled my own *rezai* over me, hugging it close to my trembling body. I began to warm up just as the rain outside was abating; at least, its sound grew fainter, but perhaps it was I who was passing out of the conscious world.

As I was falling asleep, someone bent down over me to kiss me goodnight. It was not Ammaji, but Michael, of course. Slowly, I took my hand out from under the *rezai* and traced the outline of his jaw, felt the bone that lay under his skin until I reached the point of his chin. Then, I raised myself up and kissed him there. He took my lips and placed his own upon them in a hard and brutal fashion. I did not struggle, but felt my heart beating faster and faster, feeling the unfairness of the cleft that was tearing into it. I fell into the dream of it, like drowning, giving up a fight and just going under.

When I awoke, there was a pale light filtering in through the flower pattern of the closed curtains, shining pink and orange across the walls of my room. I could hear the voices of the servants going about their morning duties. Soon, Ammaji would come in, telling me gently that it was time to get up. She would tell me that Aida would be arriving soon, and we would have to leave Shamshad Bagh early if we wanted to see Laila on the way to the airport. She would pass me the green cardigan that was hanging on the back of my chair and then draw back the curtains.

She would stare out across the horizon at the new day in Sikimpur that was already up and, most certainly, there would be tears in her eyes that morning, for it was the day of my return to England.

Part V

Moonlight and Sunlight Both

Chapter Thirty-Two

Sami met Aida and me at Heathrow airport. He was waiting at the other side of the immigration desk, smiling broadly, and when I saw him I felt a little nervous but also glad. We hugged in a perfunctory sort of manner, for all around us people were hugging and kissing one another.

'It is good to see you both,' he said brightly.

I nodded wordlessly as Aida replied, 'Oh yes, it is good to be being back down on this earth for the skies are for the birds and not for us people.'

Sami smiled at this piece of wisdom from Aida.

'Well, you are safe now, Aida. Let's pick up your luggage from the carousel. I have a taxi waiting to take us to our hotel. We are set to go to Leeds tomorrow. I have booked a carriage for us on the morning train.'

I nodded again. 'Good, I shall enjoy sleeping in a proper bed tonight.'

That night, we ate and slept in the Metropole Hotel, the same one that Sami and I had stayed in last December. The large, glass doors of the hotel entrance were opened for us by the same concierge as before and, although I smiled at him warmly and said a bright hello, he showed no sign of recognition. Instead, he returned my smile with one that he surely used for all the patrons that he welcomed. I tried to resist the feeling of disappointment that rose within me, because it was only natural that he should fail to recognise me; he must have opened many doors to many people since he had seen me all those months ago.

We took our dinner in the ornate setting of the hotel's dining room, eating a simple meal, for Aida and I were tired after our lengthy journey over the seas and continents.

'I will be glad to be back in our home once more,' I said.

Sami looked pleased.

'Yes. I must confess that I was quite relieved to be leaving Alhama. There was something missing when you left with Isa. I did not feel that I wanted to remain there for longer than I needed to. It is a strange thing to have happened, don't you think, that the place where I felt so comfortable and happy was suddenly changed into a place where I felt an alien?'

'I, too, am happy that you decided on that, Sami Sahib,' Aida said bluntly. 'I was feeling ready to be out of Sikimpur, and to be returning to *Inge-land*. I could no longer be with my family. They were much trouble before, and now with a wedding to be planned, they are even more quarrelsome. *Arre*, I had to hold my temper many times when speaking to them.' She sniffed. 'I had to show much patience while I was with them.'

We had returned to an England that was still warm. The early September sun of this island did not burn so fiercely as the late August sun of Andalusia. Still, it warmed the seats of our carriage nicely and made our journey back to Leeds a very pleasant one.

The view from the carriage window was the same as when we had travelled in the sharp chill of last December, but it was also completely different. Gone were the fields that lay dormant under dazzling white snow, and in their place were the fields of early harvest, the golden wheat and barley being mown down by enormous combine harvesters. And this time, there were three of us, chatting freely and ordering tea and sandwiches from the buffet car. We were being taken to Leeds with an effortless rhythm, a Sunday morning amble. We were alone in our carriage and so we were carefree in our manner and our joking and conversation.

The three or so hours of our journey passed quickly, with the country slipping past our window and the majestic sun reaching its zenith as we talked.

We found Newton Kyme as we had left it. The garden was ablaze in colours, and the house smelled of the freshly-cut flowers that Hana had filled the hall with. She was at the door to greet us as we drove up in the taxi, shining from head to foot with a radiant smile on her beautiful face. She hugged Aida and me tightly.

'I am glad that you have come at last. I have been looking for your taxi all this afternoon.'

We left our suitcases at the foot of the stairs as Hana ushered us into the drawing room.

'I shall make you all some tea for that is the English way, is it not? Mrs Beresford has told me that, when it is four o'clock, then everything must stop for tea.'

When we were inside, sitting with cups of tea held in our cupped hands, Hana turned to Aida with a teasing smile.

'Why did you stay in Sikimpur for so long? I have been most lonely being in this big house by myself. And also, I have had to learn to do some cooking so that I did not die of hunger. It is not so easy, I have found, and some of the food that I have cooked has been almost black.'

This last remark caused Aida to throw her hands up in horror.

'*Aaiee*, my poor kitchen!'

Hana shook her head and grinned.

'No, no, you may be assured that your beautiful kitchen is the same as you had left it, for I have been most conscientious in my cleaning.'

'But surely, you have not been too much alone?' I asked in surprise. 'Surely, James has been most keen to see you once more?'

Hana looked at once embarrassed and her cheeks reddened.

'I have not seen James for some weeks now. He is at the military college that his uncle was most anxious for him to join.'

Sami, who was seated at the bureau looking through some of the letters that had come while we were away, looked up in interest.

'Oh, I am most surprised by that news. He seemed to be very much against such a commission. Do you know what was it that made him change his mind so drastically?'

'I...I do not know for certain,' replied Hana.

Sami nodded. 'Mmm, it is a decision that must have made his uncle very happy; I do not think it suited him to have a postman for his nephew. But military college? I thought he would choose medicine rather than becoming a military man. Still, he shall make a fine officer, I am sure.'

He rose and gathered his letters all together, layering them into a neat pile. 'I shall take these into my study. There is some work that requires my attention. Could you bring some more tea for me there, please Aida?'

He put up his hand as Aida, ever willing to please Sami, put her own cup on the table beside her and prepared to rise also.

'But only when you have finished your own,' he said. 'There is no hurry. You must take things easy today for there will still be some tiredness from your long journey.'

Sami left the room and Hana turned to Aida. 'I will take Sami Sahib his cup of tea, Aida. He is right; you must be tired after your journey from Sikimpur. It is a long way to travel. Even more further than my travelling from Sikimpur to Spain. I was most tired then, I remember.'

Aida shook her head stubbornly.

'No, no, I am most anxious to see my kitchen once more. You have made this cup of tea, but now I will continue with the cooking. I have missed all my lovely, shining pans and my stove. I am quite rested enough. And you know that I find it most relaxing when I am busy in my place.'

'Very well then.' Hana sat back down and crossed her legs.

When Aida had left us, I leant a little forward in my seat and looked straight into Hana's eyes.

'I remember you said something in Alhama about James that was most strange. I thought at the time it was because you had been in Sikimpur, and you would change your mind when you saw him once more. But now, I see that your mind was truly made up. Why, Hana, did you turn James away? You were both so happy. I think, perhaps, the decision he made was because of something you told him. Am I right?'

Hana looked back at me, her mouth tight and her eyes betraying the thinking that was going on behind them.

'I was happy, yes,' she said at last. 'But the happiness I felt was not enough to keep a marriage. I had a long time to think when I was in Sikimpur. I have been worried since even before I left England that James and I had too many differences. Or, at least, there is one difference between us that I do not think can be ever reconciled. Although we are still to be friends, we are not the same friends of before.

'Is it because he is an *Angrezi*?' I said in surprise. I remembered Ammi's words, that marrying an *Angrezi* would be too complicated. I thought it odd how Hana and Ammi could come to the same conclusion.

Hana shook her head.

'No, that is not a problem for me. How can it, when I have the blood of the *feringhi* in my veins? No, it is something that is altogether more important and more difficult to overcome. It is the matter of religion, you see. For James there is no God, and to die is to be erased from life and death forever. And this he feels as strongly as I feel the other way. So, whatever it is that I feel for him, it will never be strong enough... you must see that our marriage would most certainly be impossible.'

Her conviction made her so beautiful, I thought. How James' heart must have ached when she had said these things to him with such an earnest look upon her face, like a deserting angel.

When I thought about Michael, I did not care for such matters. I was not as highly principled as Hana. I did not know what it was that Michael believed in. I remembered seeing a crucifix, large and wooden, on a wall of the house that he lived in. However, that house was not his and, therefore, the crucifix may not have been his. His parents were church-goers, that I knew, for Reverend Bramley had spoken of the flowers that Lottie Burton would bring from her garden for the church altar, and also that Dr Burton had been occasionally called upon to play the church organ.

I could admire Hana and her convictions, but I felt such an anger with her just then. The obstacles that she spoke of were ones that she had built herself. They were surely not so insurmountable, not a reason to turn away, so unalterably, the man who would have loved her for always.

And whose love she had once returned.

Chapter Thirty-Three

Two weeks after we returned I began to feel anxious. I had counted my dates carefully and then recounted them, and each time I could only fear the worst. There was a dull sickness in the pit of my stomach, and I felt that all my energy had left me and was replaced by an inexhaustible worry.

I told no-one of what I felt in those first few days and kept my suspicions to myself, but soon my fretting was noticed. Hana, especially, was concerned and would insist on my staying in bed - for which I was thankful - while Sami bought me all forms of remedies for headaches and colds, and Aida made me foods that at any other time I would have certainly relished.

Eventually, I made an appointment to see my doctor and my pregnancy was confirmed. Four weeks going by my dates, she told me, smiling while holding onto the stethoscope around her throat. Was it my first? Well, she was sure that I would be fine, even if I was some thousand miles from home. My husband was bound to be delighted. Had he come with me? No? Oh well, that was not so unusual; fathers were still in the background when it came to childbearing.

Dr Trimble opened her drawer and leafed through some papers with her ageing hands. Finally, she found what she was looking for and brought out two leaflets.

'Read these, my dear. They will be useful to you, all about diet and morning sickness, and also a few exercises that will help you with your posture and backache in the later months. Now, you can phone me if you need anything. I will post you out another appointment time and organise a midwife for you. In the meantime, just read those leaflets and take it easy. I see that you live in Newton Kyme, so that should not be too hard. It is a lovely place to live.'

I did not tell Sami straight away. Being four weeks pregnant meant that he was not the father; three weeks would have been better for him. I would have to tell him three weeks, I decided, for he would have to regard the baby as his own. It was a cold decision to have to come to and, sitting in the garden that afternoon, I felt the isolation that this resolution brought.

The air was still around me and I could hear the Beresford children in their garden, returned from school and having their tea out in the sunshine. They were talking in their high excited voices, their words mumbled as their mouths filled with food. They talked over each other and their mother scolded them half-heartedly, then gave up and laughed with them. They were happy, a genuine happiness that came from being a family. Soon, Dr Beresford would be home. He would come out to join them; calling to them with his booming voice, and the children would push back their chairs roughly and run to throw themselves upon him.

As I listened to these happy sounds, my thoughts still on my dilemma, I realised there was something I needed to do before I told Sami about the baby. A thing that was hard, as hard as turning away from Michael and resolving never to see him again.

I took myself into my large, empty house and climbed the carpeted stairs into my bedroom. There, I opened the bottom-most drawer of my wardrobe and pushed my hand deep into the pile of clothes that lay folded inside. From within the depths of cotton and linen, I pulled out the crumpled hat that Michael had given to me to shade my eyes from the fierce rays of the Alhama sun.

I had kept it with me since that day, taken it out occasionally to hold and remember our day at the gorge. Now I closed my eyes, put it to my lips and my nose, and breathed in its old, faded smell. Then I made my way back downstairs, into the garden and round to where the bin was. I lifted its lid and held the blue hat over that dark, open mouth for a few seconds, teetering on my heels before closing my eyes once again and letting the crumpled thing go.

I replaced the lid without opening my eyes, hearing it clang into place, and then I opened my eyes again and I walked away. With that gesture, I had done my best to put the sin of my past truly behind me. With a baby on the way, I had no choice but to look to that point in the future, when Sami would welcome it as his own and we would become the family that he had wanted so much.

The next day I visited the library. Hana came with me for she wanted to visit the wool shop; she was learning to knit and wanted to make us all jumpers in time for the coming of winter.

'I will need to get some patterns,' she said. 'I shall start by knitting a jumper for myself and then, when I have made it perfect, I shall make some for you and Aida and Sami Sahib. What colour do you think I should make the one that is to be for me?'

'Blue,' I replied absent-mindedly. 'It shall go nicely with your grey eyes.'

'Yes,' Hana nodded eagerly, 'and blue is also one of my favourite colours. But shall blue be a good colour for the winter time?'

'If you choose the correct shade, then I am sure that it will look very pretty. A warm shade of blue, I think. It will contrast nicely with the grey sky.'

We said goodbye outside the library, where I climbed the stone steps to the large, double doors and Hana continued on down the road to the wool shop.

There was little information that I could find on pregnancy: a Dr Spock's book concerned with the bringing up of children, and a memoir of a woman's pregnancy.

The librarian strolled past me several times. She was young and plump, a few years older than me and very pale, as though a mist had descended upon her. Her blue eyes were brilliant though: cornflowers in a traditional English rose. Eventually, she stopped by my side, smiling and friendly. She seemed hesitant, unwilling to impose on my private browsing, but wishing as well to speak with me.

I smiled affably back at her. 'Hello.'

'Eh, hello.' She looked down at the book that I was holding - the memoirs. 'I'm sorry. I don't want to intrude on you, but I couldn't help but notice that you're interested in that book. We don't get a lot of interest in that particular book. In fact, I don't reckon as it's been taken out more than a half a dozen times.' She spoke as one who had grown up in the Yorkshire Dales.

I opened the book at the front cover and looked at the dates that had been stamped there. 'Four times,' I counted.

The girl nodded. 'Yes, that sounds about right, and always by women with a bun in the oven.' She giggled suddenly and bit her lip.

I did not understand her at all and smiled apologetically.

'I am sorry, but that is not a phrase with which I am familiar. A bun in the oven?'

The girl looked blank for a second and then giggled again.

'Oh, that's all right. I should have realised, what with you looking so, you know.' She glanced at my foreign face, and then continued. 'A bun in the oven,' she put her hand deliberately on her stomach, 'is what I have in here!'

It was then that I realised what she meant. An odd expression, I thought, to describe a pregnancy thus.

'I'm so excited, you see.' She looked down and pushed out her stomach. It was beautifully round, perfectly shaped. She looked at me curiously. 'I take it you're also...?' She patted her belly once more.

'Yes, eh... yes.' Her forthright question confused me, for it was the first time that I had admitted it to anyone, and that a stranger.

'How far are you gone?'

It was another phrase with which I was unfamiliar. I repeated it slowly. 'How far am I gone? Oh, I see...' I became at once embarrassed. 'Erm, almost a month, I suppose. Not really pregnant at all. I have no proper sickness yet.'

'Lucky you.' The girl rolled her eyes. 'I've been sick right from the start. Mostly in the morning, but sometimes, when I'm really tired, then I just can't keep anything down.'

'That must be hard for you.' I tried to sound sympathetic.

She ran her hand over her belly in a slow, round manner. 'It's all right. I mean, it's worth it. We've been trying for long enough.'

She took the book from my hand and opened the front cover. She pointed to the last date that was stamped on it, 3rd June 1968.

'That one's mine.' She closed the book again and handed it back to me. 'It's not bad, a little too wishy-washy for me, too flowery. It's more like a piece of literature than real life. But it did help in some ways, I suppose.' She shrugged and said cryptically, 'It tells you about everything. Not just the sickness and the backache but also,' she lowered her voice and came closer to me, 'the intimate stuff, you know, between a man and a woman. I mean, when you're pregnant.'

Her words repulsed me, but she did not notice my revulsion and said, rather shyly, 'I found that stuff really useful. Nobody wants to talk about it but it's important.'

'Yes. I suppose it is. I had not thought about it,' I said slowly and tried not to think about it again. I held out the book to her. 'I do not think that I shall take it, after all.'

She looked puzzled, but did not take the book from me.

'Are you sure? I haven't frightened you, have I? There's nothing to worry about, you know. It's all perfectly natural.'

Her concern made her accent stronger. She lost the genteel edge that she had earlier put on and I saw, at last, her simplicity, her homeliness. I wondered, too, whether she dyed her hair.

I shook my head. 'I just do not think that I need it.' I could not think of a better excuse. 'I do not want it.' I said feebly.

At last, she took the book with its rainbow cover. *The Sunshine and The Rain* was its subtitle. Even that seemed optimistic.

'Good luck anyway, dear.' The librarian spoke to me as though I was the novice and she the master of what awaited us both. 'I probably won't see you again any time soon. I'm off from next month on pregnancy leave. It's early, but my ankles are playing up something awful, I can tell you. And there's still so much to do. Who'd have thought that such a tiny thing would need so much? I'm lucky my mum lives just round the corner from us, in Ilkely. Jim's mum's in Garforth and she's a dear, but there's nothing like your own mum to look after you, is there?'

I shook my head. 'No,' I murmured, 'it must be nice to have your own mother to help.'

I walked out of the library slowly, thinking about the excited young librarian with the sunny disposition. Although I did not know her and would most probably never see her again, I hoped that she would always remain uncomplicated and simple. It was a good formula for happiness, I thought.

As I walked along the High Street, I became aware of other women who were either expecting or pushing a pram. Unsettled by them, I hurried on my way: these women looked unafraid, capable. By contrast, and a very miserable contrast, I felt that I was not capable. I was unsure of this child that I had conceived - I had not even told Sami. I had known now for a day and I had told only a librarian. What did that make me? What sort of creature was I that I was prepared to let Sami hold, love, nurture a child that was not his?

I could see Hana walking towards me. I took a deep breath and sunk my disquiet far below the surface.

'Did you find some wool that you liked?' I tried to sound light, without care and without conflict. 'What colour did you get?'

Hana smiled and held up the bag that she was carrying. 'Blue, just as you suggested. Sky blue; that is the name that the lady in the shop gave to it.'

'Good,' I said. 'I hope that I was not too long for you. I was in the library much longer than I had thought to be. I had some trouble in finding the book that I was looking for, and the librarian was new, I think. She did not know the library system and took a long time in helping me.' I stuttered with my lie.

Hana looked with interest at the book that I had finally taken out from the library. She read the name and title slowly. 'Er-nest Hem-ming-way. Fi-es-ta. What is Fi-es-ta?'

'A big party, a celebration, I think.' I was not entirely sure. 'It is a story about Spain and I thought it would be nice to remember our holiday there.' I felt perturbed as I said this. It was the wrong book to get. I wished I had not taken it out now.

Hana looked at the picture of the bull tossing its hoary head, and the red and gold sand of the bull ring.

'I would like to go back to Spain one day,' she announced. 'I did not have the desire to stay for long then, but I hope that I shall have the opportunity to visit it properly someday. It seemed a very pretty country. Very much alive, I think.'

I took the book back from her and put it away in my bag.

'Yes,' I said quietly. 'It is both those things and much more.'

As we walked home, Hana said, 'There is something that I would like to ask you. Something that I have been thinking of for some time, from when I returned to Newton Kyme. When I was alone in the house and I could think on many things.'

She sounded so serious that I looked at her closely.

'What is it, Hana? What is this thing that you would like to talk to me about?'

'I have been thinking that maybe I would like to study, to go to a college and learn properly about plants. Oh, there is a name for it: hor-ti-culture. That is it. I would like to study *hor-ti-culture*. In Sikimpur, I did not think that such things were for the daughter of a gardener, and to go to college was not a thing on my horizon. But now... there is a different opportunity for me here and I would like to use it.' Hana spoke quickly with her shyness and her enthusiasm.

Daylight was now beginning to fade and there were more people on the street with us: leaving their offices, school children walking home.

'I would like to be as the students who came home from college, and talk about what they have learnt, the things that have interested them. The proper names of plants and the types of soils and how to work with the seasons of this country.' Hana looked squarely at me, with her mouth set in a determined way. 'I would like to do that much more than to be cleaning a house all day.' And then, quickly, she added with a plea. 'Naturally, I shall still make sure that the house is looked after but I would like to do more than just that.'

I nodded my head. 'Absolutely. You have a talent with the garden, and it should not be wasted cleaning and tidying. I will talk to Sami. You are right. There are great opportunities for you here.'

Especially now, when you have turned James away, I thought privately to myself. *You must have something else to occupy you.*

Hana looked very much relieved. She smiled and thanked me, for which I felt a little embarrassed; to think that Hana should be grateful to me for agreeing that she should realise her ambitions. That was a strange power to hold.

I told Sami my news the next day. It was Saturday, late morning. He was at home, sitting in the light of the full sun as it came through the large French windows. Laid out on his lap was the newspaper. This time was precious to Sami; it was his time to relax and think about the world outside his work. It was his time to loosen his mind.

I watched for a few minutes from the doorway. The door had been left ajar. I was careful not to make a noise, for I did not want to disturb him just yet. Instead, I saw him, almost sideways to me, peering down at the writing on his lap, his face unwound, a bright pink patch on his cheek where the sun was warming it.

Then I went in, shutting the door behind me. The gentle click of the door startled him. I had brought him a cup of tea and a plateful of samosas that I had asked Aida to make. He looked puzzled; but then seeing the tray, smiled broadly, folded his newspaper and set it down by his side.

'Samosas and tea. Marvellous.'

He moved a small table nearer to the settee and took the tray from me. I pulled the armchair a little closer and sat down. We talked about the news in his paper; he told me that the football season was starting up and that he had been looking for a team to support. Leeds United was the obvious favourite, but he was unsure because of their reputation for fierce play, which had earned them the nickname of Dirty Leeds.

'Of course, I am also influenced by David Walker, who is a great fan and goes regularly to watch them.'

He set his cup down on his saucer so that they both rattled.

David Walker was Sami's accountant. I had met him once, when he and his wife had invited us for a grand dinner party. There had been very many people there, all brought together by this enigmatic couple. David Walker, himself, had seemed very young and possessed too acerbic an intelligence for me to warm to him completely. His jokes mystified me and made Sami smile wryly. His wife, in contrast, had a placid humour and appeared to float through her guests in a pastel dress that had wide sleeves and a high neck. As I watched her, I remembered the lines from a poem of Tennyson's that I had had to analyse at college: Elaine the fair, Elaine the loveable, Elaine, the lily maid of Astolat.

'Unfortunately, the stadium where they play is far from here and so I am unsure-' Sami stopped talking and tilted his head to one side. There was a quizzical look on his face. 'But, I do not think that you have brought me these delicious, hot samosas only to hear me speak about football.'

'No,' I replied, slightly embarrassed. My heart was beating very fast and, as I spoke, my voice sounded quite peculiar to me. It was my lips that spoke, but with some inner voice that was quite detached from me. 'I have some news for you. I have been to see the doctor because, for some time, I have thought...' I took a deep breath. 'She has told me that I am pregnant.'

When I looked up I was unsure of Sami, for his face was expressionless. He swallowed hard and seemed to hesitate for just one second, and then suddenly his face broke out into a wide, beaming smile. He leapt forward in his seat and clasped my hands across the table and, in an uncharacteristic expression of emotion, he kissed them emphatically.

'This is most wonderful news,' he said with great joy. 'I cannot believe it! I did not think you were ready.' He kissed my hands again. 'Oh! I am so happy. We must celebrate.'

Then he stopped and asked with some apprehension, 'It *is* a celebration, is it not? You are happy?'

'Yes. Yes, I am happy too.' And then, because I was sure that I sounded unconvincing, I added, 'I miss Isa. I miss his antics and listening to his chatter. I miss those extraordinary feelings that arise from a child's presence. He has caused me to change how I feel about having a child. I did not think I would feel that way for a long time.'

Sami left his seat and came to kneel on the carpet in front of me. He looked with such an eager innocence into my eyes.

'You have made me so very happy today. It is a day that I have thought of many times, but I believed that it would be a dream for some time yet.'

Chapter Thirty-Four

I was taken very good care of in those early days of my pregnancy. I had no real signs of sickness, and was quite relieved at this. Sami was attentive to my every need, as I knew he would be. I allowed him this indulgence. The guilt that I felt was easily overridden by the desire not to destroy his harmony. Or rather the feeling that, in telling Sami the truth, I would not bring about anything other than misery and distress - for Sami, for my parents, and for his mother. What, I reasoned, would be the point in shattering hearts in order to clear my conscience?

So I let Sami bring me breakfast in bed, said nothing when he plumped up my pillows, and thanked him as he brought me magazines and a blanket when I sat out, listening to Reverend Bramley rehearsing his sermon for evensong.

Sami wired Ammi to send my favourite tealeaf over - Lhasa Lamsa - a blended tea that hinted of chocolate. Ammi had to order it from Hyderabad where it was drank widely. When it arrived, Sami took to making my morning tea himself, brewing it just so, in an almost scientific manner: not too milky, not too sweet, and timing it carefully so that the flavour was maximally imparted without the tea turning bitter.

'I do not need pampering,' I would say to him. 'I am not sick.'

And he would nod in agreement. 'True, you are not sick. Still, you must enjoy waking up to the smell of Lhasa Lamsa? Besides, your mother would scold me harshly if she felt that I was denying these little luxuries to you.'

'She might even come over to look after me properly.' I returned his teasing with a mischievous grin.

Most certainly I enjoyed these times greatly; when the morning sun was just risen and it seemed altogether too early to awaken completely, when I lay waiting for the gentle rattle of the tea tray and Sami's soft tread across the carpet.

September was turning cool now; the last rays of summer were fading and the autumn chill would set in soon. The birds no longer sang with the vitality that they had shown from late spring, and they were most probably preparing to migrate to warmer climes.

At this time of the year in Sikimpur, Ammaji would have treated us to early morning chai; the monsoons would be receding and our exams would soon be in full swing. We would have been up till late in the night, studying by the light of flickering gaslight, until our eyes were sore from the straining and our brains numbed with information, and we would finally fall asleep, sometimes with our books still half open on our laps.

Then, just as we were in deep slumber we would be woken again by Ammaji, rousing us with a cup of steaming hot Lhasa Lamsa, telling us that it was time for *Fajr*, the morning prayer. She would sit by our sides as we sipped our tea and gently encourage us to work hard and pass with *achay numbera*.

With her village background, Ammaji knew the privileges that we took for granted and she made sure we did not waste them. For us to do that would have caused her a great deal of hurt. She had witnessed the struggles of her cousin, working at two jobs so that he could pay for his studies, so he did not have to stay in his father's shadow and become a low-level tailor in a backwater village. He would read under the light of a flickering flame, for there was no electricity in Lalmali at that time.

'His own father used to beat him,' Ammaji would tell us. 'He did not want his only son to study and leave the village, but your Mamujaan was so stubborn. Even when his father refused to let him have any food during Ramadan, he did not falter. He would have a sip of water and then continue with his reading. In the end, his mother begged her husband to give in. "You cannot win against a will such as his," she told him. "He will die before he picks up a needle and thread." And now my cousin is a most eminent barrister and we are all very proud of him, especially his father.'

Chapter Thirty-Five

It started with a drop of blood, so small that I hardly worried about it, but then it continued and the tiny drop grew to the size of a six penny piece. At first I said nothing, but worried in silence and prayed within my heart. However, each time that I checked I found my prayers had gone unanswered. I was lost as to what to do, what to think. I was a leaf that the autumn winds had let fall.

I miscarried towards the end of September; a fresh, autumn day when the winds were blowing fiercely from the north. I knew that it was coming. I had been to see the doctor that morning for I had some notion of what was wrong. There was a tangible feeling inside my belly that something had given way, like a mountaineer letting go of his rope; as though something inside of me had fallen away - so that, all of a sudden, I felt empty there.

Dr Trimble was on holiday and so I was shown in to see Dr Montgomery instead. He had not looked concerned, but taken my blood pressure and weighed me. Then he had signalled to me to lie down on his couch and pressed my belly here and there.

Finally, he said, 'I cannot see why there should be anything untoward, Mrs Altair. Of course, you are quite early on in your pregnancy and the risk of miscarriage is therefore higher than-'

Dr Montgomery was a Scottish gentleman, who had the look of a healer. He spoke with a practical tone and was a very competent doctor. As a consoler, though, he was rather poor.

'Miscarriage? Do you really think that I shall miscarry?' And, although I was almost certain of this outcome, I had been shocked by his directness. 'But I have been most careful. How is it possible for me to miscarry?'

Dr Montgomery had shaken his head quickly. 'Now, now, calm down. I did not say that you were miscarrying. What I simply meant was that you obviously feel anxious, as any young mother would. Your body changes in so many ways with pregnancy and it is not always easy to predict how things are going to go. Some women have morning sickness, some do not; although, that is very rare and can be an indication that all is not right... Erm, then there is back-ache, haemorrhoids. Some women are lucky, some are not.'

I had stared at him in bewilderment and he had sighed. 'Just one minute, please.' He left me alone in the room.

A nurse had come to see me in his stead, one who had smiled and called me 'love'. She had sat down on a chair beside me and asked me some questions; the specific so very skilfully being mingled in with the general.

'It is a very emotional time,' she had said, 'what with your hormones all over the place and then your own concerns. I won't say that there's nothing to worry about but chances are you're right as rain. Now, let me see...' She took the notes from Doctor Montgomery's table and glanced over them. 'Your blood pressure is fine and your weight also.' Then she had turned to me with a serious look. 'I understand that you have no symptoms?'

'That is right. There has been no sickness or tiredness, which is most unusual, I understand. Just a missed...' I ran the back of my hand along my back. 'But now I have pain here and also along the bottom ridge of my stomach.'

I was miserable with these thoughts and had felt a cold wave of sickness pass through me. In the pit of my belly now rested a small, hard stone.

'I do not feel that things will stay as they should...' I paused and then muttered in a very small voice. 'I am afraid...'

'I understand.' The nurse seemed to speak with some reluctance. It must have been difficult for her to deal with me and she chose her words carefully. 'Sometimes, things are not always all right inside, love, and then... It's unfortunate, but your body decides. You understand?'

She had spoken gently; she had spoken like one relaying some dreadful news. Looking back at my notes she had smiled with a forced optimism. 'You are young, only twenty-two. You have many more childbearing years ahead of you.'

I had left the surgery feeling so low: the lowest since saying goodbye to Michael. There was nothing to do but wait. The nurse had tried her best to sound optimistic, but in her eyes I could see that, in truth, she did not hold the same expectations.

I had told Sami when I got home and he had put his arms around me and held me tight. The pain in my abdomen was getting worse and worse. I went to bed early that night, with a pillow held close to me, and no real hope of repose.

It was in the middle of the night, when there was not a cloud in a sky that was at its darkest and the moon was shining brilliantly, that I lost the baby. It slipped out of my body, unformed and unknown. I felt a huge, cryless grief, as though I were swimming in the sea: swimming out, out, further and further out until I reached the horizon and I existed no more.

I did not get out of bed the next day. Hana and Aida came to see me, asking how I was, asking if I wanted anything to eat, to drink, to read? Each time, I would shake my head in silence. The room was in semi-darkness, for the curtains were still closed. It was the gloom of the mood. I barely spoke that day, and did not cry. Sami phoned Ammaji and Ammi, and protected me from their grief.

The next day, he came and sat by the bed. I was staring down at the tray that Aida had brought for me. On it was a bowl of soup and an untouched white roll. The soup was now lukewarm, and would probably go cold in that state. Sami moved the tray off my lap and put it on the table at the side of the bed.

I had heard the telephone ring some minutes ago and I had heard him answer it. I asked him who it had been, not because I really wanted to know but because I did not want to talk about what came naturally to us now. Sami looked ashen-faced and pensive. I doubt that he had slept at all since I had told him.

'Oh, it was nobody,' he said with such hesitation that I looked hard into his face and repeated my question.

'It cannot have been nobody, for that does not make sense.' I said. 'It was somebody. Tell me who it was.'

Sami pursed his lips. I saw in his face that there was some news that he did not want to pass on to me, but I reached out my hand and touched his. 'Tell me, please.'

'It was Elias,' he said at last with a deep sigh.

'Is all well with them? What is the news that he telephoned to tell you?'

'He wanted to tell us that–' Sami stopped again and then, taking a deep breath, he added quickly, 'Luisa has had her baby. A little girl.' His voice faded away and he put his hand to his face and rubbed his cheeks so that they became red.

I did not reply to this news. Inside of me a scream, shrill and high, rose from the very base of my abdomen and into my lungs and, from there, it was thrust into the top of my throat. My mouth, however, stayed shut and so the scream remained unheard, remained within me, rolling round and round in the cavity of my body.

Oh, how I hated Luisa just then. Luisa, with her beautiful new baby, and her husband whom she loved, and the year that she had spent on the hills just being with Michael! Oh yes, I had found out that the Englishman who had tended to Luisa's father's goats and had left her broken-hearted - the one whom she had followed away from her village - had been Michael, the same Englishman to whom I had also given my heart.

It had been Patrine who had told me about Michael and Luisa, on a dry summer's day, the day before Isa and I had left Spain for India. She had told me in an expression of innocence, a mere imparting of information: a throw-away line that had changed my engaged smile into a frown.

'Luisa and Michael,' I had said slowly. 'I would not have thought of it.'

'That is because you are now seeing Luisa with Antonio,' Patrine had replied, 'and the happiness of the two of them. But yes, when Luisa came here it was in pursuit of Michael. She was much unhappy then, and also very angry. Luckily, Antonio fell in love with her and, slowly he won her heart away from Michael.'

Then, Patrine had turned her conversation to some other matter.

'Isa is a very handsome child; he has the colouring of an Andalusian, like you. Sami is more like a Castilian, fairer.' She spoke blithely, but my thoughts were fixed on a young, carefree Luisa in love and the handsome man who made her laugh, and a summer up on the hills with the sun and flowers and beautiful green pastures.

Chapter Thirty-Six

I left my bed soon enough, for the time of lonely mourning was over. Sami was hurting also, and Hana and Aida were conversing in whispers and moving through the house with soft treads.

I found Sami sitting in the drawing room, the doors of the French windows standing open. He was sitting forward on the settee, hunched over a low table in front of him. The table was strewn with papers and maps of green and brown, on which there were pen marks tracing roads along rivers and through mountain passes, and a large circle drawn around a built-up area, Córdoba. A notebook lay open, its lines covered with Sami's meticulous handwriting. Sami looked up as I came near, a concentrated look on his face which turned into an unsure smile.

'Ah, you are out of your bed. How are you feeling? Come, sit down.' He rose quickly and ushered me onto the settee.

I glanced down at the maps.

'I have been trying to plan another trip to Alhama,' Sami explained. 'Not in the immediate future, of course,' he added hastily, 'but perhaps next year, so that we may visit Córdoba as we had wished to do.' He shrugged when he saw my uncertain expression. 'It was really just to occupy my mind. I did not want to think of work and I could not concentrate on any of the books that I tried to read, so I thought-' He looked down and waved his hand over the spread of papers.

'Yes,' I said weakly. 'It is a good way to keep oneself busy.' I sighed and forced myself into a full smile. 'Tell me about it. I would be interested to know what you have been thinking.'

Sami sat down eagerly beside me and pulled a book up from the table, and using his finger, he pointed down on the map.

'See? I have traced a route from Alhama to Córdoba that follows the slopes of the Sierra Nevada mountains and the Gaurdelina river. It shall be most picturesque.'

I pointed to a town along the route that Sami had circled with his pen.

'What is this place that you have already marked out?'

'Ah, now that is a village called Zuheros. The journey to Córdoba will take a good few hours and there are many little villages along the way. I thought that perhaps we could stop to visit some of these little villages. It shall not be easy, for Zuheros is located at the very top of a hill, and I am sure that the path to it shall be steep and narrow, made for donkeys and not for the motor car. We shall have to take great care.'

Sami moved away from the map and lifted up my guide book on Iberia that was lying open.

'I have been reading about the Mezquite, in Córdoba. See, we can enter the courtyard of the great Mosque from any of these gates. There are many, many rows of orange trees growing there, and a fountain in the middle.'

'It shall be just as it was in Granada.'

'And see,' Sami went on, 'there is a tall church bell tower looking over the courtyard.'

I nodded and took the book from Sami, turning the pages until I came to a drawing of the forest of red and white columns that stood inside the Mezquite - endless columns and arches until one came to the Catholic cathedral at the centre of it. As with Granada, Carlos had made his stamp here, also.

Córdoba itself rose up from a nest of buildings and one-way streets; a labyrinth of unfamiliarity, gay bodegas and an old Moorish castle with palms and fabulous mosaic floors.

I read a passage that described a particular delicacy of Córdoba's cuisine, stewed bulls' scrotum. '*For a fuller favour,*' it said, '*the scrotum is best taken from those young bulls that have fought in the bullring, so that the elevated levels of testosterone add greatly to the muscle composition and flavour...*'

I shut the book and placed it back onto the table, for I did not want to read about Córdoba or its Mezquite or its bustling Juderia. I had left my bed for only one purpose. I needed to talk to Sami, to tell him something that was pressing itself hard against my breastbone. To let him rejoice for the birth of a baby that was not his, was a spectrum away from letting him mourn for its loss.

Lost in these thoughts, I did not realise that Sami had been silent for some time. It was only when I looked up and saw his frown that I noticed the quiet of the room. Sami rose and closed the door of the drawing room. He did not return to sit beside me, but instead stood with his back to me, rubbing his temples with his fingers.

Then slowly, without turning round, he spoke. 'But, I do not think that we shall be going back to Alhama de Granada, or maybe even Andalusia. I do not think that I shall ever wish to see that place again.'

I could not understand what Sami was saying, although I heard his every word. Why had he been studying maps and books and making notes about Córdoba if he did not wish to go there again?

He turned to face me finally, with a look of great sadness.

'I find that I cannot think kindly of Andalusia. Not really.'

'But you have been planning...' I waved my hand over the table with its medley of paperwork.

Sami nodded in response. 'Yes, I had thought of it seriously. I thought that perhaps it would make you and me happier; take away some of the pain of the miscarriage, and bring us back some of the happier times that we experienced. But, when you came into this room today...' he paused, selecting his words. 'I do not know why, but there came a thought into my head, one that I cannot remove. A sudden thought that I-' His words ceased.

'What is it?' I urged. 'What is this thought of yours?'

'Do you know,' Sami put his hands on his hips and his mouth became a thin line. 'I do not think that I have ever heard you call me by my name.'

I became even more confused by this announcement.

'You are sounding quite peculiar.'

'Maybe it is because I feel most peculiar. I have become suddenly aware of things that I was not aware of before, and with that I find that I am ever more lost.'

There was a silence. I did not fill it because I had no words that would, but Sami had some more words, and these words were to throw the most profound shock my way. He came forward to me and bent down low, and quietly he whispered, 'I was not the father of your baby, was I? It was Michael Calvert's baby that you carried. *His* baby that you lost. I am right, am I not?'

My heart began to beat so very fast. I looked straight into his eyes with a horror that he could utter such a thing, that he knew. How did he know?

Slowly, Sami stood upright again and his face twisted with the pain of his statement.

'I thought you might deny it. I thought that I might be wrong, but I see that I am not.'

He dug his shaking hand into his pocket and dragged out a packet of cigarettes and lighter.

Still, I could not say anything. I could only think to apologise, but what use would that have been?

'Please, feel free to say something,' Sami said as he lit a cigarette and took a long, slow draw of it. He sounded hard, as though his voice had been set in steel.

'Yes, it was Michael's baby. I wish that it was not...' At that moment, I wished this most ardently. 'I did not mean to hurt you.'

'Then what, *Sahira*? What was it that caused you to do such a thing?'

'I, I do not know. It was not for any reason that has an explanation.'

'Yet, I must ask you for an explanation, Sahira.' Sami's face was cold, his cheeks set rigid, but also there was a plea in his eyes.

I tried to think, think back to the feelings that were so ripe at that point in time. But to speak of those feelings aloud to Sami was not an easy thing. I closed my eyes and replied with an almost whisper.

'I wanted to know about love... once. I wanted to feel what it was that people who loved felt. I did not mean for anything to happen, but it did. Afterwards-'

'Afterwards, you came back to Isa and to me, and you behaved no differently,' said Sami coldly. 'You had no guilt about you. There was no change about you.'

I hung my head and tried to explain as clearly as I could. 'I buried my guilt away. I... I knew that you did not love me and so-'

I was sharply interrupted by Sami, who exclaimed suddenly. 'I did not love you?' He looked at me with incredulity and repeated, in a quieter voice, 'Not love you! Why do you say that? Are you trying to insult me further?'

'No, no!' I shook my head fervently. 'I mean no insult, but I... you loved somebody else.' I was suddenly unsure of what I was trying to explain away. All at once, looking at Sami's face and hearing his voice, I saw that I had been wrong. How was it that I had been so wrong? 'The girl. The one you told me of, after your father died, at the College, the Executioner's Spot...'

'That was not love! I am sure that I did not describe it as love. That was something else, the desire for my grief to be any other emotion for some small time. How could you think of it as anything else? How could you think that I would have married you if I loved another girl?'

I shrugged, ashamed of myself.

'I am sorry. I do not know why I thought it.' I fell silent, thinking, remembering how he had spoken of her: golden, like the sweat of the sun.

I said nothing aloud, because maybe it had been convenient for me to think that way. Perhaps, I wanted to use it to excuse my own brief excursion into love.

'I have loved you since I first met you. Since I chased *patang* with you on my parents' rooftop.' Sami spoke with such a heartbreaking simplicity. 'Of course I loved you. Did you not think of that when you received my *rishtaa*?'

I could not remember now what it was that I thought. Had I thought at all? It seemed so far away, that brilliantly sunny day, that telephone call, that answer that I gave of yes.

Sami continued talking. 'You were wearing a white shalwar and purple *chappals*. And you rolled out the string of my *patang*.'

'Yes, we were up on your roof, when your father had passed away.'

'You were twelve years old,' Sami nodded, 'and I was sixteen. Your parents had come to see Ammi, to pay their respects.'

I remembered it well - a solemn house, a mourning widow, and an awkward son.

'I was so taken with you. You sat still and did not move. I could not forget you. I felt so ashamed of myself. My father had just passed away, but it was you that I thought of, you who I promised myself that I would marry. It was a foolish promise, the promise of a boy, but it stayed with me all those years that passed after it. So finally, I proposed. Of course, I did not expect you to love me at once, but I hoped that would change. I had hoped I could make it change, but it appears that I was wrong. It seems you see me only as something familiar, a constant presence, not someone to miss or to enjoy time with.'

Sami looked away from me to the pale blue pattern on the carpet. 'I tried so very hard to make you love me. Each thing that I did was to lift myself a little higher to you. I tried to ease my pain by drinking and then, when that angered you, I gave it up altogether.'

I looked blankly at him and he laughed mirthlessly.

'You did not even notice,' he said miserably. 'It was my grandest gesture and you did not even notice!' His voice became a little unsteady. 'I have not touched a drop of alcohol since that night at Elias's farm. I felt such shame to have you look upon me as you did, that I began to despise myself, and I vowed that I would not drink again. But to what purpose? Your attention was elsewhere; someplace beyond my perspective.'

Sami cradled his eyes in the palms of his hands and then, looking up, he said with an ironic touch, 'Michael Calvert. I liked him so very much. What was it that made you love him? What did he do to you? What instance was it when you fell in love with him?' He frowned at me and shook his head. 'It does not matter now. I do not want to know. I know too much already. For now, even the word Andalusia is ruined for me.'

He left the room then, putting his cigarette out in the ashtray and walking away without looking at me. He turned the knob to open the door and then closed it quietly behind him. I watched him go, sitting still in my place, my tongue struck dumb, my limbs slack upon their rest.

I was not to move from there for a long time. I fell asleep there, for some time I suppose. It was dark when Aida came into the room, noisily because she did not know that I was there, pulling the curtains closed and then catching her breath when she saw me. I shivered when she called softly to me, for I was being woken from a restless dream. I was awakening into a cooling evening.

'*Arre*, Sahira Bibi, what are you doing here? I did not know you had come out of bed. I would have seen if you were in need of some food. You are not wise to be here, in this cold. I will bring you something to warm you.'

I let Aida fuss over me. She brought a cup of tea for me and a sandwich.

'Where is Sami?' I asked her.

She made a face.

'Sami Sahib has taken himself into his study, and I think that he will stay there for a long time tonight. He has asked for his dinner to be taken there. And...' Aida looked uneasy. He has let it be known that he does not wish to be disturbed. It will be all work for him again. A baby was going to be a good thing and now-'

Aida stopped suddenly. Her words were caught in the hiccough of a sob. 'Oh, I am sorry, Sahira Bibi. I am very sorry for the baby that is lost.'

I put my arm around her until she quietened down. I felt nothing for her emotion, but I wanted to stop her noise and her sorrow.

I went up to bed shortly afterwards, deeply fatigued by all that had been going on. I passed by the study and hesitated, letting my hand hover over the silver handle for a few seconds. I held my breath and listened hard but there was no sound from inside. What was Sami doing, I wondered. Was he really working? I could not imagine that he was. All I could imagine was a sad and humiliated man, sitting at his desk with his head in his hands, wondering at the past and what lay ahead in the future. I moved along quickly for I did not want Aida or Hana to find me there.

Before I got into bed I opened my window, just so a sliver of breeze could enter. I did not sleep for some time but lay with my eyes closed, thinking of those years gone by when I had joined Sami and his cousin up on his roof. When I had held, with great trepidation, the spool with its long piece of string wound around it that was laced with sticky aloe vera and chippings of glass, and then raced with him, delighted at each *patang* that he snagged. I could see Sami then, and his cousin, but I could not see myself clearly. I could not see what girl it was that Sami could have fallen so deeply in love with.

It was a long time, I thought, for him to keep that image in one's heart and to act upon it.

I awoke from my slumber to find myself still alone in my bed. A new day was lighting up and the birds were singing merrily amongst the branches of the orchard. Across the room, slumped in the wide armchair with its William Morris upholstery, slept Sami. Like a child, he was hugging a blanket around him. As I watched, he began to stir and stretch his numbed muscles. He shivered slightly and began to rub his body underneath the blanket to warm it. It was not long before he saw me.

'I did not want to sleep in my study,' Sami sounded sleepy and uncomfortable. 'Aida and Hana would have wondered about it, and I did not want that.'

I nodded and sat awkwardly up in my bed.

'Sami, I am sorry for what I have done. I am sorry for the hurt, and also for what I did not understand about you. I cannot think of what to do now. To make up for what I have done.'

Sami looked at me for a long time before answering. 'So at last you have called me by my name. That, at least, is something good to come out of this business.'

I blushed and felt that he was being unkind, but that I must take some unkindness and not complain about it.

Then Sami asked a question. 'What do you think we should do now?'

'That is for you to decide,' I said after some time. 'I do not think that I am the one who can decide upon it.'

'Very well then, I shall ask you another question.' Sami moved uncomfortably in the armchair. 'What is it that *you* would like to do?'

I took a deep breath. 'I have made a mistake... it is something that is to most people unforgivable... But I cannot see a life that is without you. I truly cannot. I have hurt you tremendously and so our fate, mine and yours, lies in whether you can forgive me.'

'Forgive you?' Sami said these words slowly, as though they were alien words, unfamiliar sounds, and he needed to get used to them. 'I have had no thought to forgive you. I have had no thoughts other than what you have done. Yet, if we are to be together then I suppose there must be forgiveness.

He pulled his blanket closer to himself. 'Forgiveness is such a noble function of man, it elevates him upwards towards heaven, and I do not feel so noble. No, I feel the injustice of your actions, and I feel a fool, and there is nothing heavenly in that.'

'You are not a fool. I am the one who has been foolish,' I rose up out of bed and went towards Sami, prepared to kneel before him but he held up his hand to stop me.

'Do not come near me, please, for you will weaken my resolve.'

'So you have made up your mind what it is that you wish for us, then?'

Sami looked gravely at me and shook his head.

'I do not know that I have made up my mind. I do not feel that my mind is my own. It is fuelled by my heart where you are concerned, and I am indeed made a fool.' He turned his eyes towards the increasing light that was coming in through the window. 'I only know one thing: that I cannot let go of you. I cannot imagine saying a *Khudahafiz* to you that would mean an eternity without you. You see, when I said that I loved you, I really did mean it. It is a love that I cannot erase; a love that even you, with your infidelity, cannot erase.' He closed his eyes tight and his face creased up with the emotions of pain and resignation. 'So... I suppose that, in the end, I will have to forgive you.'

I sighed with a great sense of relief.

'It is right, this marriage,' I said earnestly. 'I have not told you this before, but when I accepted your *rishtaa*, I also had been thinking of that day on the roof when we flew *patang*. That cannot be a coincidence, can it? There has to be some connection.'

Sami looked at me with an ironic expression upon his face. 'A connection between our collective memories. A rooftop many years ago. Who could have foretold back then the consequences of our flying *patang* on my parents' roof?'

Chapter Thirty-Seven

There was a noticeable strain in the days that followed. Sami and I turned into virtual strangers. Not, I think, because we either of us wanted to, but because the current of our relationship had stalled. Hana and Aida did not remark upon it, but they must have noticed. Maybe they thought it was just the way of things after a miscarriage.

When he was not at work, Sami spent much of his time in his study, where I would bring him cups of tea and platefuls of samosas and pakoras, biscuits and buns, each with a smile, an observation on the day outside or a remark about the food. And each time, Sami would answer with a polite thank-you and a smile of his own, not so wide as mine, for he was not the one who needed to make amends. In time, his stiff acknowledgement was accompanied with a few more words. When this happened, the twisted stone that had lain in my stomach these past few weeks began to unravel a little.

In this way, I made myself into an attentive wife. I learnt that it was the little things that were important, and so I took note of the things that Sami liked and those that he did not. I made sure that it was I who opened the door for him when he came home in the darkening evenings. I talked to him of things that I would not have thought to mention before: how Hana and I had found a hedgehog burying itself deep under a pile of fallen leaves and earth, preparing to hibernate, or how I had seen a robin hop across the lawn to a worm that it had spotted in the soil. How I had managed to darn the tear in his woollen socks, with some help from Hana.

With time, I came to realise that the fork in the path that I had chosen all those months ago had, itself, reached a fork. And, as I chose one of the paths and made my way along it, I began to discover a whole new set of feelings for Sami that had been lying in the undergrowth waiting for me. One could call them the instigators of love, I suppose. I certainly thought of them as so. It was a very different love from that which I had felt for Michael. It was a simple and gentle thing, like a rosebud worn in a lapel.

In this way, my heart's form changed. Like a master acrobat, it moved from point A to point B without fully knowing it.

The first few days of October were fiercely cold. The north wind blew through us when we dared to venture out, and there was even a swirl of a snow flurry one day. Soon, the trees in the orchard began shedding their leaves, and Hana and I spent a whole afternoon raking up the fallen leaves into large mounds of russet red, golden yellow and burnt brown. Seen from the house, they made glorious mountains of colour.

Our evenings were spent indoors, for the evening air became quite bitter then. It was the time for Aida to light the fire once again, and I would sit on the settee sometimes, mesmerised, as she cleaned out the fireplace, placed the briquettes upon the grate and then put some crumpled-up newspaper in the middle to light. She would do this every evening when the light from the low sun was beginning to fade, and every morning when the air still hung in a chilled nip. Each morning also, she would get breakfast for us all, making Sami the steaming hot porridge that he so enjoyed, and that Hana and I could not understand; this lumpy, tasteless meal that we turned our noses up at.

In this time, I had a visit from Ava Beresford and also from Professor Hariman. Ava was full of news that the Landens were moving out of Newton Kyme.

'They are going to live in France, would you believe? Lizzy has always been something of a Francophile, of course, and I really think that she is behind the move. She is forever spouting on about their fabulous culture, their cuisine, their style. Although, she had better watch her husband, with all those pencil-thin mademoiselles tapping their heels along the Champs Elysees. I'm not sure how he shall fare with all that French cheese, and no corned beef. I dare say he shall make a good fist of it, anything for a peaceful existence. Poor Arthur, he really didn't know what he was getting himself into when he married Lizzy...'

Professor Hariman, on the other hand, wanted to know what I thought of Spanish culture, and how it was a reflection of Spain's turbulent history. He was also very interested in how the country was faring under the grim rule of Franco.

'I envy greatly those principled men, such as Hemmingway and Orwell, who took it upon themselves to go out there and strike a blow on behalf of democracy and freedom from tyranny. I have always felt something of a coward for not joining the great battle against fascism. True, I did my stint in the RAF, but that was when my own country was in danger of being overrun. To fight for the liberation of others is something truly magnificent, I feel. It is holding aloft the ideal; true heroism, you know.'

I did not tell any of these good people of my miscarriage, smiling civilly with them instead, and serving them tea and biscuits as I had done before. In a very strong way it was good that they did not know, for to re-tell the grief and to then deal with the ensuing distress would have been to relive it all once again.

The process of regaining Sami's trust was slow, I discovered, and required much work from both the trust-breaker and the one betrayed. In time, a genuine smile came back onto Sami's face and his eyes lost their dull, aching look. Then finally, on the eve of our first wedding anniversary, we came together once again, under the still night with the stars watching over us.

As the tension passed from Sami's body and was replaced by relief, I felt that the wrongness I had committed was, in some part, forgiven. I felt that my autumn leaves had curled upon their branches and I would not have to strive so hard to find another spring. Beyond the house, the orchard lay shrouded in its own mist, a pale sort of rising but, around it, the air was clear like an unused ink well.

Chapter Thirty-Eight

In the swoon of late autumn there came a time to be happy again.

It was a Friday and the sun was shining in an almost cloudless sky. I was sitting reading in the drawing room in a house that was peaceful. Across the room from me, Aida had fallen asleep in her armchair with her magazine - a copy of *Shama* that Ammaji has sent for her - lying on the carpet beside her. Her mouth was open and she was snoring gently in her sleep. It was the most peaceful that I had ever seen her, and I felt a sudden melancholy for her. She had a façade that was like tar, unmovable and undissolving, but lying there she appeared like a child with a liquid soul.

I was pregnant again, I was sure of it. I was more than a week late and there was something within me that stirred in a different manner from my normal state. And this time, I felt terribly ill. When I was awake I was aware of a headache that was dull, and there was always a taste of iron when I ate. I had a sickness in the early morning that lasted until at least lunch time. All this made me very happy. As before, I had not yet told Sami. Tomorrow I was going to see the doctor, my own doctor, Dr Trimble, and then I would tell Sami and we would celebrate with great pleasure.

In her armchair, Aida began to stir. I got up from my seat, for I did not want to be there when she awoke; she would not like to have been asleep under someone else's gaze. Opening the French door very carefully, very quietly, I walked out into the still bright day. Sami would be home soon and I wanted a little bit of air before the cool breezes of the evening took over.

It had been a year since Sami and I had married. Soon it would be a year since we had come to England, and then, after that, a year since we had moved to Newton Kyme. We would have seen the garden through all the seasons. The fruit of the orchard had been collected and was long gone, and the tops of the apple trees were now tipped with green buds, the first bulbous growths of mistletoe, whose berries would erupt in a white burst just before Christmas.

My baby would be born in August, when the birds would be singing and the bees foraging deep into the flowers. There would be coriander and fenugreek growing with the other herbs in the herb garden.

I breathed in the autumn air, let it fill my lungs as though it was the breath of life, and then let it out slowly.

Across the way, the Reverend Bramley was out again, singing in his deep, rich tenor voice. It was such a beautiful hymn I heard coming over the wall that I stopped to listen to him.

*'Dear Lord and Father of mankind,
Forgive our foolish ways;
Re-clothe us in our rightful minds,
In purer lives Thy service find,
In deeper reverence praise, in deeper reverence, praise.'*

I said a silent prayer to myself, caught up in the ethereal beauty of that refrain, caught up in the solace of that perfect, late autumn day. Here I was, I thought, and there could be no better place to be; not under my banyan tree, not by the shores of Lake Bermejalis, nor yet in Michael's arms. No, that last thought I had to wipe quickly from my mind, for that last thought was one that I could linger on too long; to think of it at all was to think too long.

I leant upon the branch of a plum tree and listened to the Reverend until he finished and made his way back indoors. When I heard his door shut tight, then I, too, made my way back indoors. It was growing quite cool now and I pulled my shawl tighter around my shoulders.

I found Sami and Aida sitting at the kitchen table. I had not realised that the day was so late now and that Sami had returned home from work while I had been out. I bit my lip in some annoyance, for I would have liked to have been there when he had come home. Aida had made omelettes and *paratha*, and the two, with their cheeks bulging, were talking about the day. Aida had done well from her afternoon slumber. Her face was intensely radiant and she looked like a delicate songbird in her pale blue shalwar.

'Ah, you have returned from your walk in the garden.' Sami looked up from his plate.

'Yes.' I smiled. 'I was just taking in the fresh air while there was still some warmth left in the day. I was thinking that I shall have to do more in the garden when Hana starts her college course. I didn't realise how late it had become.

'Maybe we should employ a gardener,' said Sami. 'The garden is large and takes much time to tend.' He licked his fingers of the oil from his finished *paratha*.

'Well, I should like to tend it myself. It will keep me busy and I am sure I will grow to enjoy it.'

'It will be much hard work. To look after such a large garden will not be easy. You will have to learn as Hana did about how to maintain the flowers and shrubs that are growing in it.'

'Then, I shall be kept busy.'

Aida nodded in approval. 'Yes, it is right to be kept busy with something that is your own, and also to keep your interest.'

Suddenly, Sami jumped up from his seat. It scraped across the floor with a sound that was harsh to the ear.

'*Arre*, I had quite forgotten. I received a parcel from India this morning. It is a recording of Mukesh that I have wanted for some time now. I have been looking forward to listening to it for all of today.'

'Oh,' I said, a little put out. 'I did not know. If you had asked me, I could have very easily brought it back from Sikimpur with me. You had only to ask me.'

'Yes, yes, I would have asked you, but I had forgotten about it until I heard it being played on the World Service a few weeks ago. I telephoned Ammi straight away before I forgot again.'

Sami left Aida and me alone in the kitchen. Aida began to clear away the plates, and asked me whether I wanted something to eat also, for there was one egg left and enough dough mix for one more *paratha*. I told her that I would wait until it was time for dinner, as I was not hungry.

In truth, I was feeling a little nauseous and would have liked something, but not the heavy, oil-rich weight of Aida's omelette or *paratha*. So, when Aida was busy with the plates and the cutlery, I took down the tin in which she kept the biscuits and took out two that were covered in dark chocolate. Then I left the kitchen also, eating as I went, and wandered slowly to the drawing room where Sami was. I watched him from the doorway, munching through my second biscuit.

He was studying the cover of his record, holding it with great delicacy between his finger and thumb, and smiling as he looked down at the black disc with its circular grooves and shining surface. He placed it with great care onto the indolent turntable of his record player and, lifting the stylus over it, set it spinning. As he let it rest on the first groove, music leapt out: the strings of a sitar, the beat of the tabla, and then the famed voice of Mukesh rising through the air, melodious and rich.

Sami sat down on the carpet, leaning against the cushions of the settee with his knees pulled up and his chin resting on them. He closed his eyes and was lost to the world. Quietly, I sat on the carpet near him and he opened his eyes, surprised to see me. He smiled for one small second before closing his eyes once more. The music played on. The night took over the day, and the moon and stars came out. I looked on as Sami swayed slowly, tapping out the rhythm with his fingers, content in that room.

Chapter Thirty-Nine

I walked through the doors of the doctor's surgery with a feeling of apprehension. I had done the very same thing not so long ago - and, indeed, for a very similar purpose. I was thankful that I was to see Dr Trimble again. She welcomed me with a sympathetic smile.

'I see from your notes that you had a miscarriage, my dear. That cannot have been easy for you. I'm sorry that I was away at the time and could not see you. Not that I would have been able to stop it, but perhaps Dr Montgomery was not the best...' She shook her head suddenly and pursed her lips. 'Well, that is of no matter now, for I understand that you believe yourself to be pregnant again? Congratulations. Many women find that they are able to conceive quite easily again after suffering from a miscarriage.'

She took some dates from me and nodded her head while rotating two overlapping cardboard discs, each of which had all the days of the year marked on them.

'So, I make the date for your baby's arrival to be the beginning of August. Good, good. I shall be back from my summer holidays by then. Now, how are you feeling this time? Any sickness? Or is it as it was before?'

I told her about the nausea and the headaches and also the taste of iron, and she nodded her head cautiously.

'Good, good. That is good to hear. Not that it is any guarantee of a safe pregnancy, of course, but it is a sign that your body is producing the hormones to sustain a full-term one. At any rate, you must continue to look after yourself and be careful, especially at this early stage. Do I understand that you have not yet told your husband?'

I shook my head. 'Not yet, but he is to meet me in Tadcaster, later. I shall tell him then. I shall take him to a tea shop and buy him a cream bun, and then tell him when his mouth is full.'

Dr Trimble laughed quietly and opened her drawer. She pulled out a couple of leaflets and handed them to me. 'Will you be in need of these again? They are the same as I gave you before, but if you still have them-'

I took them from her quickly. 'Yes, thank you. I shall need them again. I had thrown the others away after...' I fell silent and bit my lip hard for the relief that this pain brought.

'I understand,' Dr Trimble nodded. 'Well, let us hope that this time they shall be of more use to you.'

She took the urine sample that I had brought for her.

'I will post the results out to you.' As she wrote on the envelope, she smiled to herself. 'You know, in my day, getting the results for one's pregnancy test could take almost a week. It was a nervous time for many of us women. But we were more patient in those days. The war taught us to be patient, I think - waiting for our men folk to come home, waiting for the war to end. And then, when it did finally come to an end, we still had to wait in queues for our rations.'

She talked on for a bit more while she weighed me and took my blood pressure.

'Well, you are much the same as before,' she said with satisfaction.

I stepped out of the doors of the doctor's surgery and breathed in the late November air that smelled of falling autumn leaves and warm bread. I was due to meet Sami in the tearoom that was just a few streets away. Looking at my watch, I realised that I still had some time, an hour almost, before I was to see him and tell him my news.

I wandered through the busy streets of Tadcaster rehearsing what I would say to him, and I grew excited at the thought of his surprised and happy face. I passed by a shop that had, in its front window, a crib made of a beautiful pine wood. Above it, there was a drape of pale yellow, looking so pretty as it hung in the air. Beside the crib, there was a low table on which sat a doll's house, with white-washed walls and a bright red door. I could not help but stop and stare at these things, and beyond them into the shop itself.

I found myself opening the door to this small place. Inside it smelled of polished wood. From the ceiling there hung many toys that were carved out of wood, floating on strings, moving gently on their way: aeroplanes, trains and animals.

There was a row of shelves along the back wall with little clothes folded neatly on them: crocheted cardigans and knitted pullovers, of pink and blue and green. Some of them had tiny flowers sewn on. My hand passed over these and I picked up a light blue pullover that had a boat knitted into it. I imagined this with a pair of dark blue shorts; boy's clothes, I thought to myself. Yes, I saw Sami with a little boy, maybe because I was so used to seeing him with Isa.

The shop owner came to talk to me. She reminded me of Lottie Burton, for she had that quiet dignity about her.

'That is a favourite jumper of mine,' she said, smiling. 'My niece knitted it.'

I folded up the pullover and put it back in its place. 'It is lovely. Your niece is very clever.'

The owner nodded. 'She has three children, all grown now, so she's well-practised at knitting and sewing. It's her hobby, now. I think she's practising for when her own grand-children come along.'

I smiled and said goodbye to her, not wanting to be questioned about what it was that I was doing there, in her shop, browsing through those little clothes.

It was almost midday now, still some time before I met Sami. Unhurried and day-dreaming, I made my way to the tearoom, Maisie's, and found a seat that was close to the window. I wanted to look out onto the avenue, to watch the people as they went along their way, to watch for Sami as he made his way to me.

I ordered a cup of tea and a sultana scone while I was waiting, for the nausea was building up again. The waitress who attended me smiled shyly as she took down my order. Her uniform was beautifully pressed and pristine; the black dress and the little white apron that she wore over it. Her pencil was newly sharpened and her notepad clean. I was her first customer on her first day, she told me nervously. I smiled back at her and she licked the tip of her pencil and carefully wrote down my order.

The park across the street was busying with school children, let out early from school and loud with home-time energy. Through the clear glass of my window, I could hear their laughter and enthusiasm. The older girls wore their skirts very short and walked with such a poise and confidence that I found myself staring at them with a great curiosity. Alongside them hung a bevy of boys in smart blazers and crooked ties. They seemed quite immature by contrast, for they tripped along, smiling with nervous hopelessness, looking on the girls with adoring eyes.

The younger school children played freely in the playground, on the swings, the slides and the merry-go-round. There was maybe only two or three years between the jolly girls of the playground and the girls with their short hemlines, but there was a decade of difference in their manners and behaviour.

I watched them, deep in thought, thinking back on the girls of Sikimpur, who remained like the playground girls, giggling, chasing each other well into their teenage years, and who, for the most part of their lives, were entirely unaware of their sex appeal. I did not know which was a better way to be - sophisticated and worldly, or naïve and without guile.

My mind was thus occupied, lost in the antics of the school children, when I imagined I saw someone, a familiar form, in the park near to the playground. It was a vision that caught me unawares and startled me, so that I frowned and cursed my imagination; but I looked on and saw that it was no trick of my mind. For there was Michael Calvert, striding purposefully through the fallen leaves on the path, dressed in a bottle green jacket that was buttoned up to the neck and flared jeans. I gasped with the improbability of it all and sat transfixed in my chair. He had come out of the park gate now and was crossing the street, whistling to himself in that fresh autumn air and with his hands in his pockets.

Soon, he was passing by the tearoom and, because I could not move, he could not fail to see me. He stood very still, peering at me, slowly recognising me and then smiling broadly. I did not smile back. Sami was to arrive soon.

And then, without my realising it, Michael was standing in front of me, his thigh level with my table with its brilliant white tablecloth, saying a shy hello. I looked up at him and muttered an uncertain hello in reply. Without invitation, he sat down opposite me, with his elbows resting on the table and those earnest, blue eyes looking over me.

He leant forward. 'Hello,' he repeated very softly. 'It is so very lovely to see you again. I did not think I ever would.'

'No. I did not think that we would meet again. We were not supposed to.'

The girl arrived with my tea and scone, and Michael ordered one too, looking apologetically at me as he did so.

'If you don't mind. I do hope that you don't mind. I have been out all afternoon and am absolutely parched.'

And, although I did mind, I shook my head anyway, for I found that I could not resist him still. But I knew that I needed to stand firm, for I had left Michael behind on the shores of Lake Bermejalis, at the edge of Alhama's gorge, on the balcony of his house. For the salvation of my soul and my marriage also, I had to believe that he was a continent and an ocean away from me.

I pushed my chair away from the table. It scraped along the wooden floor.

'I have got to go, anyway. I do not have time for my tea. You must have it, and my scone, also. I expect that you are hungry as well as thirsty.'

I struggled to take some money out of my purse. The coins were caught in its lining and in the end, exasperated, I spilled them out onto the table. They rattled noisily on the table surface, spinning around and around, eventually coming to a rest. There were too many there, I knew, but I did not look down or count them.

Instead, I said deliberately, 'Goodbye, Michael.'

He was staring at me in surprise at my abrupt behaviour and, as I was about to leave, he grabbed my hand and pulled on it hard. People stopped what they were doing and looked at us with curiosity. I sat back down, for Michael would not let go of me until I did so.

'What is it that you want?' I whispered angrily. 'Why are you here? You have no right to be here!'

In reply, Michael looked solidly at me for a second and then, with pursed lips he said, 'Actually, I have every right to be here.' He leant back in his chair and said with incredulity, 'My God, I do believe you think I followed you here?' He let out a sudden guffaw. 'But, even if that were true, I would hardly have sprung myself upon you in a tearoom on Tadcaster High Street.'

'Then *why* are you here?' I asked again. 'It is too much of a coincidence.'

He leant forward again and smiled in amusement. 'Well, would you believe me if I told you that I am visiting my Aunt Rose? She is my godmother, so I feel duty bound to look after her. Have you forgotten about her? I did tell you. She asked me to run an errand; there was a parcel waiting for her at the post office. You see?'

Michael held up a small package, wrapped up in brown paper and tied with string that I somehow had not noticed before. The name on it read: Mrs Rose Sitwell, Stonebury Cottage, Engleton Lane, Tadcaster, ENGLAND.

I felt foolish in thinking that he had come all this way just to see me again. I apologised in a low, flat manner, and Michael waved my apology away.

'Still, it is good to see you again. I have longed to know how you are keeping, longed to be sitting by your side and talking to you.'

'It is not possible for us to do that,' I said despondently. 'Each goodbye that I have had to say to you has been harder than the last, and I do not know how many more I can bear.'

My head was dull with an ache that came from the conflict of my heart, and the nausea was building up once again. I let my shoulders sag and my head hang low, and closed my eyes.

'Are you all right?' Michael sounded concerned. He put his hand over mine and pressed it hard. Ah, that touch. At once familiar, but also missing for so long.

I shook my head.

'No, I am not all right. My head is aching and the pit of my stomach is churning.' I looked up and gazed into his eyes. 'And, along with all of this, I am pregnant with Sami's baby.'

Michael lifted his hand away from mine quickly and I heard him take a sharp intake of breath. He said nothing for a while and then smiled bleakly.

'Then I should say congratulations to you. Sami must be very happy.'

'He does not know yet. He is meeting me here and I will tell him then.'

Michael rose up from the table and stepped away from me. The shadows were shortening all around us. Soon, the street lights would be lit and it would be the end of another day.

'Goodbye it is then.'

Michael's eyes were frozen upon me for a brief moment, and then he turned away. I watched him go, out of the shop and down its steps. He walked at a furious pace, getting smaller, while I sat, stunned and numb, feeling only the beating of my heart. I let my head fall into my hands, pressing on my forehead, pressing out of it the feelings that had gathered there once again.

Then, I took a deep breath. *Enough with this*, I thought. *Enough with these feelings*. I would not let my morning's optimism flounder. I would not return to a wasteland.

I gripped the handle of the fine china teapot, and with my hand shaking, I poured my tea into the matching teacup. I did not notice its taste, or that of the scone into which I bit.

The waitress arrived with Michael's tea and placed it opposite me. I did not tell her that it was no longer needed. As I sipped my tea, I stared, once again, out of the window, across at the park. The school children had left by now, but my attention was caught by the sight of a young father sitting on a park bench, under the ancient oak whose leaves had been shed. On his lap was a little girl, with blonde hair tucked loosely into her woollen hat. He appeared to be telling her a story, his face animated with each scene that he described, and his daughter was listening, her eyes shining with the tale.

With the sentiment that was coursing through me now, I thought of Abbaji, who used to sit with us and tell us tales with an equal enthusiasm. I thought also of Idris Mehboob, our hapless ancestor, thrown into battle without any purpose or will. And suddenly, by a strange juxtaposition, I felt much the same as he had; bound by duty and quite lost within each circumstance that my destiny thrust upon me.

Chapter Forty

It seemed an age before I saw Sami arrive. I was still gazing out of the window; the father had gone by now, taking his little girl's hand and disappearing down the path that led towards the red-brick terraced houses.

Sami parked his car on the other side of the street, some fifty metres down it, near the pharmacy. And now he was walking towards the tearoom, whistling, and then waving when he saw me looking out at him. Anxiously, I glanced in the other direction but there was no sign of Michael, and so I was able to smile quite brightly when Sami came in and sat down opposite me.

He unwound the scarf from his neck and, seeing my empty plate, remarked, 'Ah, I see that you could not wait for me. You must have been hungry.' Then he looked down and noticed Michael's untouched, cream teapot and teacup at his side. 'And, you have also ordered something for me, I see. How very thoughtful.'

I could not bring myself to lie with an outright 'yes,' but instead limited myself to a stilted smile. All would have been well, then. We came close to it being good and well but the new waitress, seeing Sami, came eagerly to take this new customer's order.

She looked puzzled when she saw that Sami was helping himself to some of Michael's tea.

'Oh, has the other young gentleman changed his mind about staying for his cuppa then, Miss?'

I did not answer her but nodded without smiling. Out of the corner of my eye, I saw Sami, no longer smiling but looking quizzically at me.

'Oh, was there someone else here?' he asked.

The waitress seemed reluctant to leave us; maybe she wished to hear my explanation also. Eventually, however, she did go and it was time for me to speak. I took a deep breath. A thousand words were racing through my mind and I had to think carefully, hurriedly, of which ones to select; which ones would make a tangible sentence, which ones would help.

In the end, I told him the truth. 'It was Michael. Michael Calvert. He saw me through the window and came in to say hello.'

'And to join you for some tea.' Sami put down his cup of half-finished tea and pushed it away from him.

'No, that is, yes, but it was by accident, a coincidence. He had to pick up a parcel for his Aunt Rose at the post office, and saw me through the window...' Suddenly, I felt constrained in that busy tearoom.

'Yes, you have said that already.' Sami sat very upright in his seat.

'It is the truth.' I reached out my hand to take his but his sad, pale eyes made me afraid to do so.

'I know it is,' said Sami softly, unhappily. 'Nevertheless, that does not make it easier to hear that you and he...'

'I did not ask him to stay. In fact, I asked him to leave.' My voice was unsolid; the desperation in it was so obvious. I did not want to talk of this. I wanted, instead, to tell Sami of my morning, my visit to the doctor, how I had imagined him with a little boy. But Sami, not knowing of these things, was focused on the news that had hit him with a mighty force.

He stood up and looked about him, at the ordinary people around us, talking of ordinary things, drinking their teas and eating their cakes.

'I must go. Just for some air. I need to breathe.' He stopped suddenly and dug his hand deep into his pocket, looking at me in bewilderment.

I stared at him, pleading silently as he pulled out his cigarettes. Clumsily, he put one in his mouth, almost biting into the end of it. I could not bring myself to say anything, for the words that I had planned were lying, dry and sterile, somewhere in the deep capillaries of my mind. Then, with a brief look back, Sami walked away, towards the door with its shining brass handle and bright blue paint.

It was that look back that made me leap from my chair. He had already shut the door after himself and was trudging down the steps of the tearoom, when I made to rush after him, to reassure him fully, in a way that I had not done; in a way that would make him understand, make him turn to me with a smile again, to tell him about the baby.

Sami's pace was a slow one, and I should have been able to catch up with him, but an elderly couple were standing on that top step of the tearoom. They looked in surprise as the door was flung open to them, and smiled in response to my flustered presence.

With an ill-hidden impatience I let them in, all but ignoring their thanks, replying with a lightly flung, 'You are welcome.'

I rushed out into the hurly burly of Tadcaster High Street, where the November chill was causing the pedestrians to hurry on their way. Sami had finished with his cigarette and flicked it out of his hand. He pulled his scarf to loosen it slightly and dug his hands into his pockets. I began to run, shouting at him loudly, wildly so that people stopped to stare.

'Wait, Sami! There is something I must tell you. Please listen to me!'

But he did not stop. I could not make him stop. Even with the loudness of my voice, he could not hear me; he was staring ahead of him, oblivious, of me, until that is, he began to cross the road, and the angle of his body changed so that I came into the periphery of his vision. He frowned upon seeing me, still crossing the road, still making his way towards his beautiful, red Morgan, with his eyes on me, his attention on me, so that he did not see what I could.

I yelled out a warning to him, 'Look out!'

The warning came too late. The workman's shabby truck was going faster than it should have been on that busy high street and, although the man in the truck realised what was about to happen and reacted to avoid the impact, he could not do so, for he was far too close.

All this time I could see what was going to happen. I was running towards Sami, but of course, I was too slow; and so began the exaggerated loudness and slow motion of it all. The horn blaring, the look of terror on Sami's face, the screeching of brakes, and then, the final blow.

The truck driver had been sitting high up in his truck. He lurched forward with the collision and hit his head badly on the windscreen of his truck. There was some blood, a stream of it bursting through a blood vessel and slowly winding down the side of his forehead and then his cheek. He put his hand out and touched it in shock and fear. And then he saw what had happened to Sami and he struggled out of his seat, arriving by him at the same time as I did.

Of course, Sami, the solitary figure, had borne the brunt of the collision. The truck driver kneeled on the pavement by his side and people were gathering around; somebody shouting for an ambulance, a doctor, someone to help. But I knew, as I held onto Sami, that there was no help for him now. I had known the instant that he had hit the pavement with an unbearable crash. His blood was warm and sticky against my body and his breathing was becoming shallow. The tears rolled slowly down my cheeks, for Sami had been but a moment away from being happy.

I spoke to him softly, of anything that came into my mind, tuneless things that meant so little. And then I remembered the news that was meaningful and I told him that. But I think I said this important news too late. I do not think he heard me when I told him I was having his baby. I think that, perhaps, the last breath had left his body by then.

Chapter Forty-One

The day that Sami died has very little place in my memory. I have heard it said that it is a way of preserving oneself, one's sanity, to lay deep those recollections which cannot be faced.

I ended the day at home, brought there by Hana, who had been contacted by someone who had witnessed the accident and recognised me. Aida was the one to show the most emotion. She spent many hours in her room, crying. But we all of us moved slowly through the house, talking quietly so as not to awaken too many thoughts.

'There is a cloud that is hanging over us,' Hana said the next day. 'It is the same as when you lost the baby.'

'The baby?' I was puzzled for a second. 'Oh, yes, you mean the other baby.'

'The other baby?' Hana raised her eyebrows.

'Mmm,' I said dully. 'I am expecting again. I have not told you yet, have I? I have not told anyone, not even Sami. I was going to tell him yesterday, when I met him at the tearoom. But, oh...' suddenly, I remembered. 'Actually, I did tell him, but he did not hear me. He was already...'

Hana put her arms around me and we both began to cry.

Sami's body was flown back to Sikimpur, to be buried alongside that of his father. It was washed and wrapped in its white burial shroud by Ammi and the other women folk of her household. There was much mourning for the young man who was much loved and, now, much missed. The house and its surroundings were soaked in a gloom, right from the early dawn, when a mist rose along with the sun. It was as if the sun was too ashamed to show its brilliance amongst all this sorrow.

Like the other women, I did not go to the funeral, but joined them in reading from the Quran, praying for Sami's soul, which was surely going to *Janaat*, anyway. The floor of the drawing room was covered in a fresh, white sheet, which the ladies sat upon, cross-legged, in their sober-coloured saris. They each chose one of the thirty chapters of the Quran to read, and soon the house reverberated with their low, rhythmic chanting.

When the men returned from the cemetery, a simple meal was laid out for all, with the men and women sitting in different rooms. Abbaji sat beside Sami's uncle, who had led the funeral prayer, both men ashen-faced within their own grief.

When the day was over and Gulabi Ghar was quiet once more, I sat with Ammi in the twilight. We sat in silence for some time, drinking our warm *chai*. A dog was barking somewhere in the distance, sounding harsh in that still air.

Finally, Ammi spoke. 'I am glad that you came to love Sami before he passed away.'

I looked up at her in surprise, not sure of what to say. Ammi nodded her head and carried on, 'My sorrow is making me more outspoken than I would be otherwise, but I must say this, for now you are to have his baby. That is how I know you finally loved him. I am no fool, Sahira. I knew from the beginning that the feelings you held for my son were not the same as the ones he held for you. But, I kept faith that one day you would. I told myself that when that happened, you would, at last, have a baby.' Ammi shook her head. 'Oh, I am talking such nonsense. I am talking all the thoughts that I have been thinking for some time.'

I did not reply immediately, for Ammi's words were too honest. She did not mean to hurt me with them, but I knew that her grieving was loosening her tongue.

In the end, I nodded and said, 'It is true. I did not love Sami in the way a wife should love her husband, but that was, I think, because of my own complicated way of thinking. It was only when things became unravelled that I came to realise how love was something so simple.

'Yes, it is a pity,' said Ammi with a wry smile. 'A great pity how we come to realise these things too late.'

Ammaji enjoyed taking care of another expectant daughter, and was as overprotective and excited as ever. I let her have her way, for I knew that she and Abbaji grieved for Sami as though he was their very own son.

'It is said that Allah takes back those that he loves all too quickly,' Abbaji said with a simple smile. 'We must always be thankful for the relationships that he gives us, and for those times that we share together.' He paused for a moment and swallowed hard. 'We were fortunate to have known Sami, even if it was for a little while only.'

Deep in myself, I felt Sami's loss like a thing that was almost beyond me. There was nothing that I could grab onto or clutch. In a way, I thought that his death was inevitable. It was our story unfolded, completed - from the laughter on the rooftop to the alien land of Newton Kyme, from the orange groves of Granada to the tearoom of Tadcaster.

Only the child was left, given by Sami to me, to nurture, to educate, to love. In that way, I could fulfil the love that I finally felt for him.

I stayed in Sikimpur for all of December and January, too. Then, I knew that I needed to return to the home that Sami had bought for us, the home that he had intended for his family. Aida and Hana had already gone, sometime in the New Year, the very beginning of 1969. Hana was enrolled in her horticultural college, while Aida had no desire to remain in India where, despite her love and patriotism, she felt herself too near her difficult family.

Ammaji did not understand my need to go back to the cold and mist of North Yorkshire.

'What is there for you, now? You have your family here. They will support you in this most testing of times. It is not good for a woman to live alone without a husband, especially with a baby.'

'I shall not be alone, Ammaji, for I shall have Hana and Aida to help me. They need me there, also, for where shall they go otherwise? And,' I said pointedly, 'Sikimpur is not such a friendly place for a widow to be in. I do not want to be talked of again, to be the subject of Sikimpur's socialites. I have had a lifetime of it, Ammaji. Those tongues are still as sharp as they have ever been.'

'Oh, they will always be busy about something, those tongues. As you say, we are both used to their wagging.'

But I was determined and shook my head stubbornly. 'Now, it is different. I do not want to bring a child into this society. I have grown to enjoy my life in England.'

'And what does your *sas* have to say about this?' asked Ammaji. 'I cannot imagine that she welcomes your news. She cannot want you to be so far away in your condition. It will be her first grandchild and with Sami gone...'

'I have not yet told her,' I said quickly. 'I will tell her tonight.'

I was nervous about telling Ammi. Level-headed as she was, her emotions were raw, and it was only natural that she should baulk at my leaving, with her unborn grandchild, to live on an entirely different continent.

I waited until dinner was over to approach Ammi. My words came out in an unrefined manner, but, to my surprise, Ammi took my news very well. She did not try to dissuade me; she did not even question my decision. I could not tell if it was because she was still numb from the loss of her son.

'I was expecting you to feel this way soon,' she admitted. 'I had always thought that Sikimpur was too small for you both - Sami and you, that is. I will not stop you, although, as your sas, it is what I would be expected to do. But,' her eyes suddenly twinkled, 'I am not known to hold with conventional ideals.'

I sighed in great relief. I had been nervous, of course: as much as I could argue and persuade Ammaji, I did not wish such a confrontation with Ammi.

'There is one thing that I ask of you, though, Sahira.' Ammi became serious. Her eyes lost their twinkle and became determined. 'Whatever happens to you, from this time onwards, you must make sure that my grandchild is aware of its father. You must always remember Sami to it.'

'But, of course. There is no question that I would do otherwise.' I was surprised by this request, this application.

'No, do not be hurt by what I say. It is not said with any thoughts that you would do otherwise. It is for my own satisfaction, part of my duty, I suppose. And also...' She turned away from me to look out of the window, at the bougainvillea that had been planted when Sami was born. 'You are young, and lovely, and in England you will not be closeted away as you would be here, in Sikimpur. I will not dictate to you, what you should do with your future, for I know the loneliness of widowhood, and I came to it late in life. You, with your youth... well, it is as I ask. Please do not allow my grandchild to grow up without knowledge of its father.'

She left the room quickly, walking with dignity, her head held high, but clutching the *pallo* of her sari close to her, disguising the tears that were wetting her face so rapidly. I let her go. I had not told her my true reason for not wanting to stay in Sikimpur, for not wanting to stay with her. She did not know, nobody did, why it was that Sami had been so careless in crossing that road; that it was I who had distracted him, that he had been walking away from me in the first place.

I was quiet about it right now, and I would stay quiet about it until I left, but I was afraid that if I did not leave soon, I would tell them this whole truth.

Chapter Forty-Two

I returned to Newton Kyme in the middle of February, the day after St Valentine's Day. It was a mild February that greeted me. I was disappointed with this, for what reason I could not say, but the feeling was there.

The sickness that I had felt at the beginning of my pregnancy was gone, leaving me with an energy that I forgot I had. With this renewed vigour, I tried to give myself to our house in Newton Kyme, but I found that I did not know what to do with it. I felt engulfed by its largeness and also with my own isolation.

Hana was gone most of the day, returning in the evenings, full of college news and the lessons of the day. Aida was still happy with her kitchen. She had also, with great daring, taken up Reverend Bramley's offer of joining the bell-ringing group. We were very proud of her.

I, however, with all my hopefulness, could not be made to think of grasping life again. There was something missing, not just to do with Sami, but an emptiness that lay with my own special susceptibility. Ava Beresford told me that this was only to be expected.

'It is your hormones, darling. They play havoc with our emotions at the best of times, but now, well, you are very vulnerable right now. I was in a terrible state with both my pregnancies. Poor Richard was quite fraught at times, not knowing how to deal with me. I felt ever so sorry for him'

'Yes, I remember with both Laila and Suha how pregnancy affected their moods.'

Ava rose from her seat and kissed me on both cheeks. 'I must go, darling. The children will be home shortly, and I have not started on their dinner. Now, I shall pop over tomorrow to make sure you are all right.' She looked at me with a gravity that I had not seen in her before, and I thought that there were tears in her eyes. 'After all, Sami was a dear friend and, well, you must call on me whenever the need arises.'

She let herself out, insisting that I remained seated. I did as I was told, but when she was gone, taking her light, bright chatter with her, I cried, suddenly and quietly until Aida found me and scolded me for being so foolish.

'You must be strong. It is not good for the baby that you should be this way. Maybe you should ask your Ammaji to come and look after you?'

I took her words seriously, but only for a moment. I shook my head. 'No, I cannot do that. She may come nearer the time but for now I shall be fine. After all, I have you and Hana to look after me. It is, as you say, just a foolishness on my part.'

I sat up straight with that resolve. I had left Sikimpur because I wanted to be away from it, because I had told Ammaji and Abbaji that I was happier here. I could not let them know that I was frail. I had only just returned, it was this time of adaptation that was making me uncertain, that was all.

In late spring, just as May was upon us, I had a visitor. I was walking in the garden, my hand making circles across my belly, soothing the baby that was moving and growing inside. I was lost with the song that I was singing and the beauty of the flowers that were blooming. The sun was high again in a cloudless, blue sky, when I heard a voice that I had not heard for some time, a voice that startled me from behind.

'Hello, again,' it said, bold and clear.

I stopped singing and turned quickly, not quite believing what I had heard. But he was there, standing at the side of the house, with an uncertain smile upon his face. I did not reply, not at once, but took my time, to drink him in, to grow accustomed to seeing him again.

'Hello,' I said at last.

Michael smiled briefly. 'How are you? I heard about Sami, a while ago now, but I did not want to intrude. I was going to write. Actually, I did write, many times, but all my words sounded faintly ridiculous,' he hesitated, 'after how we had left things. But I am sorry, you know. Truly sorry.'

I nodded and made my way towards the house. 'Would you like to come in? For a cup of tea? It is, after all, almost four o'clock.'

'Teatime,' said Michael slowly. 'Everything stops for tea.' He turned quickly. 'I'm sorry, I should not have come…'

But I interrupted his apology. 'No, you should be here. This was, after all, once your home.'

Inside, Michael gazed about him. 'I didn't think I would ever see this house again. I'm glad that you came to live here, Sahira. I think you were meant for it. My mother would not recognise it, but you know, I think she would be quite glad, also, that it was you who moved into it.'

'How is your mother?' I began to reach for the teacups that were placed a little too high for me.

'Let me do that.' Michael pulled me over to a seat and made me sit down. 'I always used to for Mother. She would complain that Father had had those cupboards put in too high for her. I used to make her tea, you know, when I was here. I would make it strong, the way it should be made, she would say; whereas Father, being a southerner, always made it too weak.'

It was so easy to talk to him, I thought, now when there was just the two of us, now when we could just be ourselves. But where would this meeting lead to today? Each of our other meetings had been fraught with a beleaguered optimism. I let this thought go, for I did not want to dwell on it.

'How are you feeling?' Michael glanced at my belly.

'Better,' I said. 'It was hard, at first, without Sami. But now, I have grown used to not seeing him. I loved him, in the end, you know.'

Michael frowned briefly before replying, 'I know. I realised that when I saw you. I realised it was best to leave you as you were.'

'Yes, except that when you left... Sami found out that you had been there. The waitress wondered where you had gone. It was the reason he was not paying attention to the road that he was crossing.'

For a moment, neither of us spoke. I could see my words make their mark on him.

When he finally spoke, Michael's voice trembled. 'I see. But, surely he didn't think that you and I had intended to meet?'

I shook my head. 'No, but knowing that we had met was enough.'

Michael stayed for an hour, longer than he had intended, he said. When he left, he bent down low to kiss my cheek. I felt the familiarity of his lips once again and the smell of the skin about his neck. It was a good feeling, and I knew that, whatever I had come to feel about Sami, however happy our life together might have been, it was Michael, in the end, who made each of my sensibilities real. I said nothing to him about this. I did not need to.

He left and I went back to the kitchen, washed out the tea leaves from the teapot and put the teacups back in their place. Then, I took myself into the drawing room, watched as the light began to fade, and listened out for Hana to come home. I turned on the transistor radio and heard an old tune that Sami used to hum, over and over again, until we would yell at him to stop. I closed my eyes and saw a smiling Sami, happy with his place, content now. I whispered to him, told him that I had seen Michael again. I told him of how I felt, and Sami nodded, an acknowledgment of what he always knew, I think.

Sami's baby was born on the 14th August 1969 at Sikimpur Royal Infirmary, just in time for Ammi to celebrate India's twenty-first Independence Day. This made Ammi very happy, very happy indeed.

The midwife passed the baby to Ammaji, who held her new grandson tightly, and thanked Allah that he was healthy and well. I named him after his father; he had all the colouring of Sami, and I prayed that he would have his temperament also. I stayed until the baby was two months old when; then, satisfied that I could look after him well enough, my family bid me a tearful farewell once again.

Michael came to meet us at Heathrow airport, took us to Leeds on the train, and then onto Newton Kyme by taxi. He had painted the nursery in pale blue, with the crib that I had seen in the shop on Tadcaster High Street, and a carousel that played a pretty lullaby.

And, of course, it was Michael who brought my son up, taught him to play cricket and ride his first bike; and it was Michael who taught him, and his younger sister, to fly *patang*, making them dip and sweep across the blue skies, sending the children running after them, much like another girl and boy had, across a Sikimpur roof all those years ago.

The End

Made in the USA
Charleston, SC
11 August 2015